COURAGE IN THE STORM

Laurel Blount

BERKLEY ROMANCE
New York

Berkley Romance
Published by Berkley
An imprint of Penguin Random House LLC
penguinrandomhouse.com

Copyright © 2023 by Laurel Blount
Penguin Random House supports copyright. Copyright fuels creativity, encourages
diverse voices, promotes free speech, and creates a vibrant culture. Thank you for buying
an authorized edition of this book and for complying with copyright laws by not
reproducing, scanning, or distributing any part of it in any form without permission.
You are supporting writers and allowing Penguin Random House to continue to
publish books for every reader.

BERKLEY is a registered trademark and Berkley Romance with B colophon is a
trademark of Penguin Random House LLC.

ISBN: 9780593200247

First Edition: April 2023

Printed in the United States of America
1   3   5   7   9   10   8   6   4   2

Book design by George Towne

This is a work of fiction. Names, characters, places, and incidents either are the product
of the author's imagination or are used fictitiously, and any resemblance to actual persons,
living or dead, business establishments, events, or locales is entirely coincidental.

If you purchased this book without a cover, you should be aware that this book is stolen
property. It was reported as "unsold and destroyed" to the publisher, and neither the author
nor the publisher has received any payment for this "stripped book."

Praise for *Shelter in the Storm*

"With lovely, evocative writing, Laurel Blount brings to life a tender story of two wounded hearts healing and finding lasting love in the wake of tragedy."

—Marta Perry, national bestselling
author of *A Springtime Heart*

"Laurel Blount's *Shelter in the Storm* is the perfect mixture of sweet romance and family drama. Naomi is a fully fleshed[-out] character who will win your heart with her sincerity and wisdom as she and Joseph face an unthinkable tragedy. Their Amish world is as fascinating as their struggle to remain grounded in their faith. Readers will relate to their unflagging efforts to hold on through a season of storms. As Joseph's father says, 'When our world goes dark, then we must hold hard to the rope of our faith, and trust Gott to lead us out.' This is the kind of hope-filled story that readers are hungry for."

—Dana Mentink, national bestselling
author of *Secrets Resurfaced*

"I couldn't stop reading *Shelter in the Storm*. Laurel Blount mixes comforting, homey Amish romance with exciting suspense and cliff-hanger chapter endings. Her characters are real and appealing, and I was rooting for them from start to finish. I'm so glad there will be more books in the Johns Mill series. It is off to a wonderful start!"

—Lee Tobin McClain, *USA Today* bestselling
author of *Cottage at the Beach*

"Two very different worlds clash in this heartfelt story of faith, family, forgiveness, and love. Endearing characters warm the heart in this hopeful love story."

—Tina Radcliffe, author of *Ready to Trust*

"This is a very good book. Laurel Blount's *Shelter in the Storm* had me hooked from the first line. . . . This sweet, tragic story is touching and honest and beautiful. I highly recommend this book, and I can't wait for the next book in the Johns Mill Amish series by the amazing Laurel Blount."

—Lenora Worth, *New York Times* bestselling
author of *Seeking Refuge*

This book is dedicated to the memory of my dear friend,
"Monday tea sister," and avid Amish romance reader,
Debbie Fordham, whose steadfast loyalty, unquenchable
faith, and mischievous humor blessed all who knew her.
One day we will laugh together again.

CHAPTER ONE

THERE'S A POINT IN EVERY LONG WINTER WHEN IT seems spring will never come.

For Miriam Hochstedler, that moment came on the first Sunday in March—yet another cold, winter-brown day. It was visiting Sunday, which meant her older sister, Emma, and her brother-in-law, Sam, had come to have lunch at the family farm. Their company and the hot beef-vegetable soup and fresh sourdough rolls Miriam and her sister-in-law Naomi had prepared should have brightened the dreary afternoon right up.

Somehow those familiar comforts hadn't done the trick. Not today.

Setting her empty teacup in the sink, Miriam tugged aside the kitchen curtain. She gazed over the bedraggled farmyard, listening absently to the happy voices behind her.

Her brother Joseph and Sam were nowhere in sight. The two men had gone outside half an hour ago, most likely to Joseph's woodshop. They'd not be doing any work, of course, not today, and the shop—a converted dairy barn—would be uncomfortably chilly, but Miriam didn't blame them for slipping away.

She wished she could slip away herself.

As soon as the dishes were washed, Emma and Naomi had settled at the freshly scrubbed table to chat. Since both women were well along in their first pregnancies, it was natural the conversation turned in that direction. They'd been talking babies nonstop for almost an hour, laughing and planning over a pot of peppermint tea.

Miriam was happy for them, she truly was, but every word they spoke pricked her heart like a forgotten pin. The year and a half since her parents' deaths had been hard for them all, but now everyone in the family was looking forward to better days.

Everyone except her.

"Miriam," Emma called from the table. "I meant to tell you. I picked up the material from Yoder's for the baby's quilt. I forgot it today, but I'll bring it next time."

"That's all right," Miriam reassured her. "Plenty of time yet, and crib quilts don't take long. Have you decided what pattern you'd like?"

"I want you to decide," Emma said. "This baby will be nearly as much yours as mine, after all."

"That's a wonderful idea," Naomi agreed quickly. "Miriam, you pick the pattern for mine, too. Whatever you make will be beautiful, and like Emma says, you're going to be a favorite *aent* to these little ones. It'll be special for them to have a quilt you planned out all on your own."

Miriam forced a smile. "All right. I'll do my very best. Naomi's first, and then yours, Emma. They'll be ready before the babies arrive."

The two women smiled at her, then bent their heads back together.

She loved these two sweet women with all her heart. They were going out of their way to include her, and of course, she was delighted at the prospect of having two new little ones to love. Still, all this mother-to-be and "favorite *aent*" talk prickled.

She knew why Emma and Naomi kept telling her how much their children would love her. They figured Miriam would probably never be a *mamm* herself. Since that terrible day when she'd witnessed an *Englischer* shoot *Mamm* and *Daed* at their general store, her anxiety had kept her a prisoner here in the house where she'd grown up. There wasn't much chance of meeting a nice fellow and starting a family when you were too terrified to leave your brother's farm.

Miriam washed her hands and picked up a dish towel. She'd best snap out of this mood. She shouldn't let envy spoil the afternoon, not when she'd been so looking forward to this visit.

She'd missed Emma since her sister's marriage to Sam Christner some months back. Since his buggy accident, Sam didn't see so well, and her sister liked to stay close by her new husband, helping in their general store and around the house. Nowadays Emma couldn't come by her old home more than a few times a month.

That, of course, was as it should be. And if things were different—if Miriam were different—she could have hitched up and driven into town to visit Emma whenever she liked. Johns Mill was only a half-hour buggy ride from the Hochstedler farm.

As things stood, though, it might as well have been on the other side of the world.

"Naomi," Emma was saying now, "I don't want to be a bother about the cradle. Joseph's woodworking business is doing so well that I'm sure he's got orders backed up. The pieces he sends to the store sell like hotcakes. So I thought I'd speak to you first. I want you to tell me plain if he doesn't have the time."

"Don't be silly! He's busy, *ja*, but he'll find time to make a cradle for you," Naomi assured her. "Family comes first for Joseph, always. Just you tell him what you'd like, and he'll see to it."

"I really like the one he made when you two were courting," Emma said. "One like that will do fine. I'm glad—hopefully it'll be in use a good long time as the children come along, and I know Joseph will make it sturdy and beautiful both."

The jealous splinter in Miriam's heart twisted. *Ja*, there would likely be plenty more babies for Emma. For Naomi, too, if *Gott* blessed her. And that, she told herself, was wonderful, a thing to be thankful for, to have many little nephews and nieces around to dote on.

It would be almost as sweet as having a husband and *kinder* of her very own.

Almost.

Her hands crumpled the towel into a wrinkled ball. She should get away from this kitchen before the other women picked up on her gloomy mood. Maybe she'd go outside and see Breeze. She'd not had the time to visit with the horse earlier because there'd been the lunch to get ready. Miriam quietly opened a cupboard door and took a few sugar cubes from their box.

"I'm going out to the barn for a minute."

"Oh, but Miriam—" Emma and Naomi exchanged glances. "I so wanted to spend time with you today. Come sit down with us, and let's talk about the quilts."

"Don't worry. I'll be right back." Miriam tried a half-hearted chuckle. "You know I won't be going very far." She hadn't been off the farm in over a year.

"But—"

Before Emma or Naomi could protest further, Miriam snagged her bonnet and shawl off their pegs and slipped out the door.

She felt a shamed sense of relief at her escape. She didn't know what was wrong with her today. It wasn't the usual panic. Nowadays, as long as she stayed at home and away from *Englischers*, she was able to stave that off.

Mostly.

This was different. She felt . . . fidgety. Restless. She'd been feeling this way a lot lately, as if she were waiting for something important to happen—but it never did.

It was the weather, likely. Winter had overstayed its welcome. Once spring arrived, she'd feel better.

In the meantime, count your blessings, she lectured herself as she headed across the damp, chilly yard. *Not so long ago, you couldn't set foot outside the house without having one of your attacks, but now you can go to the barn and the chicken house most days without a scrap of trouble. And you've a family who loves you in spite of the fact you're more a burden to them than anything. That's something to be thankful for, too.*

That was true, but knowing it wasn't helping much, at least not today. Maybe a visit with Breeze would distract her.

She was about to push open the barn door when she heard her brother's voice.

"He's your horse, Sam, but if you want my opinion, it's not looking too *gut*."

Miriam froze. So that's why Sam and Joseph had slipped away—to talk about Breeze. No wonder Naomi and Emma hadn't wanted her to go outside.

She'd known this was coming. Breeze was as wild and unpredictable as he'd been when the vet unloaded him a few weeks after Sam's buggy accident. Joseph was getting frustrated. He felt it was time for Sam to decide what to do with the animal, and he'd said so a couple mornings ago at breakfast.

But she'd not expected that decision to be made today.

She heard a series of horrible thumps as Breeze reared

and kicked in his stall—making the door shudder under her hand. He did that whenever Joseph came in the barn, even though her brother had never raised a hand to him. He wasn't much calmer when Miriam was alone with him, though she'd been slipping out for weeks to drop a sugar cube or an apple slice into his feed bucket.

The horse trusted nobody, no matter how kind they were. He always backed away to the farthest corner of the stall, positioning himself to kick anybody who approached. Miriam never tried, and after a time, he'd settled down some with her. At least he didn't beat himself bloody against the walls of the stall anymore.

Unless she moved too fast. Or spoke too loud.

"*Nee*," Sam answered slowly. "He's not improved much."

"He's not improved at all that I can see."

It was wrong to eavesdrop. She should make her presence known. Instead she pressed her head against the door, her heart beating hard.

The sound of Sam's sigh came through the wooden planks. Like everything about her burly brother-in-law, the sigh was big-sized.

"It's a shame. Breeze was always stubborn, but before the accident, he was on his way to becoming a *gut* driving horse. Now . . ." Sam's deep voice faded out, and Miriam bit her lip.

"He can't be managed," Joseph finished grimly. "Nothing calms him enough so I can work with him. Of course, I don't have your skill with horses, Sam. I never did. Maybe if you could train him yourself, it would be different."

"I doubt it. I can't see his eyes so good, but I can hear how he moves. Fear's got the best of him. That'll make any horse a challenge, but a horse with Breeze's temperament? He'd likely be beyond my help, even if I could see."

Miriam's heart sank. Any animal beyond Sam's help was hopeless for certain sure. Before his accident, he'd been the best hand with horses in all of Johns Mill.

"If that's true, there's nothing to be done." Her brother spoke her thoughts aloud.

"*Nee*, that's not so. There's folks better than me. I know one fellow in particular, but he costs a lot, and he doesn't like . . ." Sam stopped short as if measuring his words. "He might not be willing to come here. He's no fan of the Amish."

"Which leads us back to where we started. It's time to make a decision, Sam."

For a second or two the only sounds were the wintery caws of some distant crows and the thudding of her pulse in her ears.

Please don't say it, Miriam pleaded silently.

"*Ja*," Sam responded. "I can't ask you to keep him on any longer."

Actually, Sam hadn't asked in the first place. The local vet who'd taken on Breeze's care after the accident had asked Joseph what to do with the animal. Her brother had gladly agreed to board Breeze until Sam recovered.

But Sam's five-year-old niece Janie had been badly injured in the accident, and of course, there'd been the worrisome damage to Sam's eyes. The horse hadn't been at the top of anybody's list during those troubling days. It wasn't Breeze's fault he'd been left to stew in his fears, and it seemed unfair to give up on him now. Where would Miriam be if folks had given up on her?

Sam cleared his throat. "You've been kind, keeping him when he's such a trouble. If you've done your best, there's not much left to talk about."

"I can't think of anything else I can do. It's been months, and he still won't let me near him. With a little one coming soon, it worries me to have such a skittish horse on the property. While Enos Miller was here picking up a table he'd ordered, his boy Jerry ducked into the pasture where Breeze was and went right up to him—or tried to. I almost didn't get to him in time."

Miriam frowned. That had been a scary day. They'd all

been thankful the boy hadn't been hurt. Although she privately thought Jerry would do better to mind what he was
told and not go bothering other people's horses.

"It's a pity," Joseph was saying. "I don't think he's mean-
spirited at heart, but in the state he's in now, he's a danger."

"True. I'd not feel comfortable selling him to anybody
else as he is. With the scars he got in the accident, he's not
pretty enough for most horsemen to take an interest, not
with the amount of work he'd be. That only leaves Adam."

Miram pressed one hand to her mouth and backed away
from the barn door. Adam Stoltzfus was the knacker man,
the one who collected animals for slaughter.

She'd figured Breeze would be sold, and she'd been sad
enough about that. Something about the horse, ornery as he
was, spoke to her heart. Maybe because they both had their
struggles with fear.

She'd never expected this.

"I'll go to the phone shack tomorrow and call to arrange
the pickup." Joseph sounded resigned. "It's a shame, Sam,
but I don't see any other way."

"I can make the call from the store, if you want."

"Best let me do it. I'll need to work out a time when I'm
available to lend a hand. It'll take me and Adam both to
load him, certain sure."

"All right."

The men's voices grew louder, which meant they were
walking toward the barn door. Miriam stepped to the side,
ducking into the old lean-to. She pressed her back against
the door, her arms clenched over the front of her apron,
trying not to cry.

She'd wait here for a few minutes, until the men had
gone into the house. Then she'd slip in and drop the sugar
in Breeze's bucket. She'd best show the poor animal all the
kindness she could because she knew Joseph would call
Adam first thing in the morning. She could hear in his
voice how much he hated the idea of having the horse put

down, but since the decision had been made, he wouldn't procrastinate.

When it came to facing hard things, her brother set his jaw and did whatever it took. Since her parents' deaths, he'd had plenty such tasks on his plate. She wanted to plead with him to spare Breeze, but she'd only be making this decision more painful.

She'd caused Joseph more than enough trouble already, with all her problems.

Bowing her head, she prayed the prayer she'd been offering up for months.

Please, Gott, help me. Heal me, so I don't cause worry and work for my family. And so . . . maybe . . . someday I can have a life of my own.

A firm knock sounded on the door behind her. Her eyes flew open, her heart skittering into the panicked rhythm that always came before one of her attacks.

"Miriam?"

At the deep rumble of her brother-in-law's voice, Miriam's pulse slowed, and she breathed a grateful sigh of relief. Sam had that effect on people. His heart was as big as he was himself, and whenever he was around, troubles seemed to shrink.

She scrubbed at her eyes, squared her shoulders, and opened the door. Sam stood framed in the doorway, his broad face creased in concern.

Miriam made herself smile. Her brother-in-law didn't see well enough to read expressions, but he would hear the smile in her voice, maybe.

"Hi, Sam—I was just—" She fumbled for an explanation. "I was tired of staying in the kitchen so I came out for some fresh air." That was true enough.

"You were listening at the door just then, ain't so?" When she didn't answer, Sam went on. "That's the thing about not being able to see so good. A fellow picks up on other things sharper. I heard you, and it wondered me you didn't come inside. And now you're hiding here in Joseph's old workshop because you're upset."

"I'm all right."

Sam's expression gentled. "Joseph said you'd been slipping out and giving Breeze treats, so I figured you'd be pushing into the barn, taking the horse's side. Emma would have done." He sighed and shook his head. "She'll likely do it yet. That's one reason I've been putting off dealing with this. Emma's going to hate the idea of Breeze going to Adam. I don't like it any too well myself, but truly, Miriam, what Joseph said was sensible."

"*Ja*, I know." She was shamed by how her voice sounded, clogged with tears as if she were a foolish little girl instead of a grown woman who knew better than to cry over something that couldn't be helped.

"Breeze hasn't let you touch him, has he? Or feed him by hand?"

"No," she admitted. "He won't even eat the treats I bring him while I'm in the barn. But," she hurried on, "he doesn't kick so much now when I come in as he did to start. I've not tried to get close to him. Maybe if I did—"

"Not a good idea," Sam interrupted. "Breeze ain't a hurt chipmunk or a kitten. Joseph's right. He's dangerous. I don't like doing this, Miriam. I truly don't. But when I think of what could've happened to Jerry . . ."

"That wasn't Breeze's fault. Joseph warned Jerry to stay clear of the horses."

"*Kinder* don't always do what they're told, 'specially young ones. That's why it's not wise for a man with a growing family to keep a horse that can't be trusted around little folks. Would your own *daed* have done it?"

She knew the answer, much as she disliked admitting it. "No," she whispered. Family came first. *Daed* had believed that as much as Joseph did. "But, Sam, couldn't you sell him to somebody other than Adam?"

Her brother-in-law sighed. "I don't see how. I'd just be passing the danger on to another family. I couldn't live with myself if that horse hurt somebody, and I could have prevented it."

"But surely there's some other fellow, somebody without a family? Somebody who's good with horses who'd be willing to take him on?"

"It'll take more than somebody good with horses. Breeze has changed since the accident, Miriam. Some horses might have weathered such a thing, but Breeze was always more skittish than most. More stubborn, too, and that's never a good combination. His mulish streak won't let him trust anybody enough so they can coax him past his fear. As long as he's like this, he'll be nothing but trouble to those who have the keep of him. I can't ask your brother to do more than he's done. His plate is too full as it is."

Miriam winced. "*Ja*, Joseph already has one fearful creature causing him trouble," she murmured. "Me. And I'm not getting much better, either."

Sam's expression shifted into remorse. "That's not what I was saying. I only meant with the family growing, and all the orders he's been taking at the workshop, Joseph's got his hands full."

No, Sam hadn't meant to hurt her feelings, but the truth had sharp edges. "I'd . . . best be getting back inside. Emma and Naomi will wonder what happened to me."

Sam's good-natured face creased with an agonized sympathy. "You and Breeze aren't the same, Mirry. Just because we don't think he'll get better, that doesn't mean we don't believe you will. One thing has nothing to do with the other."

"I understand that—in my head anyway. My heart will catch up to it. Don't feel bad, Sam. None of this is your fault. You and Joseph have done all you could for Breeze. I know that."

That seemed all there was to say, and they really did need to head back to the house, but he didn't budge. "There's one thing we could try yet, I guess."

Miriam frowned. Sam's expression was a funny mixture of reluctance and guilt. "What?"

He dug the toe of one large boot into the dirt. "There's that fellow I was telling Joseph about."

"The one you said was expensive?"

A smile flickered across Sam's face. "I ain't the only one with good ears. *Ja*. He's pricey these days from what I hear and worth every penny. He's the best hand with horses I've ever seen."

A high compliment coming from Sam. "But the cost . . ." She bit her lip. "I've some quilt money saved up. I'd be glad to give that, if it would help."

Sam shook his head. "Breeze is my horse, Miriam, so he's mine to see to. Anyhow, he'll likely cut me a deal if I ask him to come."

"I thought he didn't like Amish folks."

"He doesn't, which is why I didn't want to ask him. But," Sam went on uncomfortably, "as it happens, he feels like he owes me a debt."

Miriam waited, but her brother-in-law didn't add anything more. There was obviously some story behind this, but Sam didn't seem willing to tell it. She nudged gently. "Who is this man? Somebody I know?"

"*Nee*. He's from Indiana. I met him at a horse auction, and we struck up a friendship. Our paths have crossed a few times since."

"You think he'd come if you asked, this fellow?"

"He'd not be happy about it, but he'd come if I sent word." Sam sounded certain. "Reuben Brenneman's that sort of fellow. He pays his debts and keeps his word. I'll have to talk it over with Joseph first, though. And remember, there's no guarantee Reuben can help. I've never seen him stumped by a horse, but Breeze is a special case. But at least we'd know for sure we'd done all we could. Reuben's no great hand at getting along with folks, but when it comes to horses, I've never seen the beat of him."

"Reuben?" Miriam asked cautiously, confused. "That sounds like a Plain name."

"He was raised Plain, but he jumped the fence a long time ago. He lives among the *Englisch* now. Among them and like them. Has for years, and from all accounts, he bears some kind of grudge against the church." He paused. "That going to bother you?"

Englisch. A tickle of apprehension ran up Miriam's backbone at the word, but she shook it off. Sam believed this Reuben fellow could help Breeze. If he'd been raised Plain, he wouldn't be so scary, maybe, even if he didn't like Amish people anymore. Her own brother Caleb had jumped the fence, too, and she'd never be feared of him.

Anyhow, she could keep well away from the barn while this Reuben was around. She'd not even have to see the man, likely.

"No," she said, lifting her chin. "It won't bother me."

Sam looked doubtful, but he nodded. "Come on, then. We'll see what your brother has to say about the idea."

Miriam smiled. She already knew what Joseph was going to say. He would agree. He was kindhearted, and he never minded going out of his way for others. If Sam wanted to give this Reuben a try, Joseph wouldn't argue.

They were halfway to the house before she remembered the sugar cubes she'd tucked into her pocket. She'd slip out to the barn later, after Emma and Sam had gone, and give them to Breeze. There would be time for more visits and treats—at least for a little while.

Because this fence-jumping friend of Sam's would be Breeze's last chance. Miriam was sure of that.

As they walked up the back steps, Sam shivered. "You'd never know it was March," he said. "Winter's taking her sweet time leaving us this year." He smiled at Miriam. "But spring always comes. If we just hang on, sooner or later, better days will get here."

Miriam shut the back door behind them without answering, casting one last, worried look back at the barn.

She sure hoped Sam was right. She prayed better days were coming, for her and Breeze both.

CHAPTER TWO

✆

A WEEK LATER, REUBEN BRENNEMAN TURNED INTO the driveway the GPS indicated and slowed his truck to a stop. He flipped his wrist to check his battered watch.

He'd made the trip from Louisville in record time. Normally that was a good thing. Not today. For once, he hadn't been in any particular hurry to get to a job.

He scanned the yard, dread settling over him like a smothering blanket. Nobody was in sight, but this had to be the place Sam Christner had told him about—Joseph Hochstedler's farm.

He'd have known this was an Amish farm even without the row of Plain dresses and pants flapping on the clothesline. He felt it the way he sensed when a horse was about to kick, often before the animal knew it himself.

Outsiders were always talking about how peaceful it all was. How pretty. Maybe it was—to them. Reuben had never found Plain life peaceful. His *daed* had seen to that.

He glanced up, meeting his own gaze in the rearview

mirror. There were sun wrinkles around his blue eyes now, and his sandy hair was parted on the side and trimmed in an *Englisch* style, which would have infuriated his father.

The reflection was proof that he wasn't the bruised-up twenty-year-old kid who'd walked away from Ivan Brenneman's farm—and out from under his fists—nearly a decade ago. It was the smartest move he'd ever made, and Sam Christner had helped him make it. That was why Reuben was here when he'd rather have been just about anyplace else.

Nobody but Sam could have convinced him to take a job on a Plain farm. Others had tried. The Amish had plenty of horses, after all, and they needed their animals sound and dependable. Reuben's reputation got around, and sometimes when folks had a troublesome horse situation, they grew conveniently absentminded about his background and called him.

Reuben never forgot, though, and he'd curtly refused—until Sam was the one asking. Then he'd said yes, even before he'd heard the whole request. It hadn't mattered what Sam wanted. Whatever he needed, he'd get, although the thought of being back on an Amish farm made Reuben's skin crawl.

But this is the end of it, he promised himself. He stepped out of the truck, shoving a few apple-flavored horse treats into his jeans pocket. *This marks the last time I'll set foot on Plain property.*

He cut a glance toward the white farmhouse, then turned his back to it and walked toward the barn. There'd be time to talk with Sam's brother-in-law later. First he wanted to see the horse. He needed to know what he was dealing with before any plans could be made.

Sam had explained the situation over the phone, but Reuben put little stock in what people told him about horses, even a fellow like Sam, who knew them well. He preferred to let the horses tell him themselves.

Unlike people, horses always told him the truth.

He'd know once he saw the animal if he could help or not. Usually, he could. Most of the time there was a . . . connection. A sense of both where the horse was now and where he needed to be. Reuben had learned to trust that feeling—when it was there.

If it wasn't, going ahead with this job would be a waste of everybody's time.

The barn door stood ajar, and the wind worked against him, wafting his scent ahead. As he walked inside, he heard a horse blow a warning. His gaze zeroed in on the bay Standardbred in the far left stall.

That would be his horse. Breeze, Sam had called him. The animal tensed, staring at him.

"Hello, boy." Reuben approached, his eye intent on the animal, assessing.

He suppressed the urge to whistle in admiration. It would have been warranted. Sam had always had a good eye for horses, and Breeze was no exception. This was an extraordinary animal by anybody's standards. He had excellent conformation: a flat, long back; a straight neck; and a well-shaped head.

He also had some nasty scars. Bad enough that Reuben could see them from a distance in dim light, but healed up well, best he could tell. Pity because they spoiled the horse's looks, and that was something most people cared a lot about.

Before the accident, this horse would have cut a fine figure, and he'd have been fast, too. That was surprising. This wasn't a typical Amish driving horse. Except for the young men who were looking to impress girls, Plain horsemen went for practicality over style.

It wasn't just this horse's looks, though, that would've made them leave the animal alone. This gelding had spirit. It was there in the way he held his head and tail, in the quick, decisive way he moved. The Amish preferred calm dependability—in their people and their animals.

Not him. Reuben admired gumption. On the other hand,

there was no doubt, a high-strung horse was going to make his job tougher.

As he neared the horse, he frowned.

This horse's temperament wouldn't be his biggest challenge. A more serious problem showed in the flash of white around the dark eyes, and in the way the horse angled himself in the corner, shifting on his feet and blowing.

Reuben had lived his first couple decades in close quarters with fear, and he could smell it as keenly as any animal. His familiarity with terror was what made him excel at his work. Fear, he'd found, was at the root of most horse issues.

People issues, too, not that he cared so much about those.

This barn stank of fear. This horse's scars went deep.

"We've got our work cut out for us," he murmured. Because, of course, it was already *we*. He'd known the minute he'd laid eyes on the animal. It would be Reuben and this scarred-up horse against the world, from now until the job was done. He took another slow step forward, into a dusty shaft of sunlight slanting from a window set high in the right-hand wall.

In that instant, two things happened. A soft gasp came from a corner, and Breeze's eye rolled in that direction.

Then the horse exploded.

He whirled to face Reuben and went berserk, rearing, kicking, and snorting. He slammed his chest against the slats of the stall, trying to break through. The old wood creaked loudly, threatening to give way.

Those sturdy boards had probably seen good use in this barn for fifty years or better, but they were no match for this horse. They'd not hold him long, and once they splintered, Breeze might easily rip himself open pushing past them.

Because once he made any kind of gap, he'd come charging through it, straight at the man he viewed as a threat. Reuben stayed where he was, thinking fast, taking stock.

This horse was a fighter. No big surprise there. The accident, from what he'd heard, had been bad. This animal had not only survived, but he'd hung on to enough of his spirit to keep two experienced Amish horsemen at bay.

The only surprise—and there was one—was why Breeze was fighting so hard right now. A horse only fought like that for his herd. There were no other horses in the barn. And as for people, Sam had told him the horse wouldn't allow anybody to get close, and that they'd pretty much given up on him because of it.

But this horse was protecting somebody. The question was who—and why.

Reuben shifted, peering into the dim corner where the gasp had come from. Sure enough, an Amish woman stood plastered against the dusty wall, both hands clamped over her mouth. She was breathing fast, her eyes wide with panic.

Reuben's eyes narrowed. No wonder fear hung so thick in this barn. Terror rolled off the woman like a wave, feeding into the horse's fear—and his anger—like a stream flowing into a river. Another board cracked ominously. He had no idea why this woman was so scared, but right now that didn't matter.

"You there. Come here to me." He pitched his voice low and calm. "Show him I'm nothing to fear. He's going to hurt himself otherwise."

At the sound of Reuben's voice, the horse redoubled his efforts, kicking, blowing, and ramming at the splintering wood. He'd injure himself any second. Why wasn't the girl moving? She just gaped at him.

He set his jaw. People. They were ten times harder to deal with than horses.

"You're making him worse, acting like you're scared of me." He made his voice firmer. "And it's foolish. I'm no threat to you. Sam Christner sent me. You know Sam, don't you?"

Still, she didn't move, and Reuben heard another threatening crack. The horse would be out of that stall in another minute. Then they'd really have a problem.

Was the girl what the Amish called *special*, maybe? Was she not able to understand what he was saying? He took another step toward her, trying to get a better look. When he moved in her direction, she made a faint, distressed sound and sank down onto the floor.

The bay instantly intensified his assault against the stall, and Reuben realized two things.

First, if he and the girl didn't get out of this barn quick, Breeze was likely to skewer himself on a broken bit of wood. If by some miracle the horse didn't kill himself, he'd do his best to stomp Reuben into the dirt. Neither of those things sounded like a good way to start off this job.

Second, whatever this girl's underlying problem was, her fear had paralyzed her. She wasn't going anywhere unless somebody moved her. Likely the horse would settle down if Reuben backed off, but he couldn't be sure. He didn't know enough about Breeze yet, and Sam—who understood horses better than most—had said the animal was dangerous.

There were too many unknowns to leave this maybe-special girl in a barn alone with the bay. He'd have to take her out with him.

Reuben never faltered once a decision was made. Hesitation, he'd learned, only caused more trouble. He strode toward the girl, who stared up at him mutely, her eyes huge and her breath coming in ragged gasps.

"We've got to leave so he'll calm down. If you can't get up by yourself, I'll have to carry you."

He tried to keep his impatience out of his voice, but it made no difference. This girl was too far gone. She couldn't have stood if her life had depended on it.

Which at the moment, it very well might.

He reached for her, and she made one sharp, desperate sound of protest. Then her eyes rolled back, and she sagged against the rough boards of the barn, unconscious.

As she did, the horse went still, ears forward, focused intently on the girl on the ground. It was only for a split second, but Reuben's instincts pinged.

Yeah, the horse knew this young woman, whoever she was—and what's more, he cared about her.

How Sam had missed that, Reuben didn't know, but it was a good sign. It gave him a handle to work with, and he was going to need it. That much he could tell already.

Breeze wasn't still for long. The girl's limp form had him more enraged than ever. The kicking and rearing redoubled, and Reuben heard another crack as the weakest board began to give way.

Time to move.

Swiftly, he leaned over, scooped up the girl, and carried her out of the barn into the sunlight.

CHAPTER THREE

❧

REUBEN HAD CARRIED GIRLS BEFORE—OUT OF NE-
cessity. He had sisters with short legs, and a father you had
to get far away from when an ill mood took him. But until
now he'd never carried an unconscious girl, nor one who
wasn't related to him.

She was a soft, warm weight in his arms, and her head
kept lolling back in spite of his efforts to keep it in a more
comfortable position. Once safely outside, he glanced down
at her, trying to assess her condition. She was pale, but she
was breathing all right. That was good.

She was pretty.

That fact registered in some small corner of his brain.
Her hair was the color of a chestnut bay. It was curly and
seemed bent on escaping from the *kapp* she wore. She had
a sprinkling of freckles over her nose and a pointed chin
with a smudge of dirt on it.

The last thing surprised him. Not the dirt. The chin. It
didn't fit.

Chins like that usually came with some gumption, but this poor girl didn't seem to have a shred of spunk in her. Which, he reflected, was most likely a good thing. A feisty spirit wasn't much appreciated in Plain circles.

He knew that firsthand.

When he was halfway across the yard, the back door of the farmhouse flew open. A heavily pregnant Amish woman hurried down the steps with surprising agility. A bearded, dark-haired man followed her, pausing to clasp her arm and say something to her in urgent *Deutsch* before leaving her behind and sprinting across the yard.

When he reached Reuben, his face was pale with alarm. "What happened to my sister?" he asked. "Is she hurt?"

"Not that I know of. She passed out in the barn when I spoke to her." Reuben transferred the limp girl to her brother's arms.

"You'll have frightened her. You went out to the barn by yourself? It would have been better if you'd come to the house first. We could have explained some things to you."

The man—Joseph Hochstedler, Reuben was guessing, was polite but curt. Obviously, he wasn't pleased.

"I usually check out the horse before talking to the owner. I didn't know your girl here was in the barn."

He also didn't usually wait for someone else's permission before doing what needed to be done, what he felt was right to do. That kind of behavior was something he'd left in the past.

Joseph didn't answer. He'd turned his attention back to his sister. "Mirry?" The girl's eyes fluttered. Reuben caught a glimpse of brown eyes flecked with green before her brother turned away, shielding his sister from the stranger with his body.

The pregnant woman had made it to them, and she clucked under her tongue. "Poor thing. She's been doing so *gut*. She hasn't had an attack in weeks." She glanced up into her husband's face, her expression softening. "She will be all right, Joseph, don't worry. She just needs some time, like usual."

The man searched his wife's face as if looking for comfort. He must have found it because his tense shoulders relaxed. "*Ja*, she will be all right, Naomi. We will see to that, you and I."

Naomi smiled. "Carry her inside and up to her room, Joseph, *ja?* I'll follow in a minute."

"All right, but take your time, and do not hurry on those steps like you did before. We can't have you falling," her husband admonished.

Reuben shot a sharp, assessing look into the other man's eyes. How Joseph Hochstedler treated his women was none of Reuben's business. But still . . .

Fortunately, the man's face held nothing but kindness and a normal, husbandly worry, so Reuben relaxed. This man was dressed like *Daed*, but hopefully that was where the similarity ended.

Naomi patted her husband's arm. "I will be very careful," she promised.

She watched as Joseph carried her sister-in-law up the steps, levering the door open with his elbow. Once they'd disappeared inside the house, she turned her attention to Reuben.

This woman's eyes were a clear gray-green, and the hair beneath her *kapp* was blond and smoothly parted. There was a gentleness about her, a calm strength which enveloped him like the comforting smell of baking bread.

She might be a good hand with horses, this Naomi. They responded well to the kind of steady peace this woman possessed.

"You are Reuben Brenneman?" she asked now.

"I am." He waited for the usual spate of questions. The name was Plain, but the man was not. Any Amish person would be curious.

And disappointed. He never answered questions. He'd be polite, but his past was his own business.

To his surprise, she only nodded. "Sam speaks well of your ability with horses. We are very thankful you are here. Please, come in to the kitchen, and I'll make you some tea."

She meant to be kind. Hospitality was stressed and expected in her faith. However, the thought of sitting down in an Amish kitchen . . . it didn't set well with him.

"Thanks, but I'm not much of a tea drinker. I can wait out here to talk to your husband. Besides, hadn't you better see about . . . her?" He nodded toward the house.

"Miriam? Oh, *ja*. I will, but I'll get the tea started first. She'll do well with some herself. She always appreciates a cup of tea with some honey after she's had one of her turns. So you come on in. You and Joseph can have your talk more easily at the kitchen table, ain't so?"

They'd made it to the steps, and Reuben fought the urge to steady the woman's arm. He knew better, so he kept his hands to himself, but he made sure he kept pretty close. If she stumbled, he stood a better chance of catching her.

She made it safely to the top and motioned him into the house. "This way."

Reuben hesitated, then shrugged and gave in. He wasn't going to argue with a pregnant woman. He was already here. Going inside the house couldn't make things much worse.

He clenched his jaw, bracing himself as he crossed the threshold onto the small, enclosed porch. The last Amish home Reuben had set foot in had been his parents', and he'd been heading in the other direction, sneaking out the door so his father wouldn't hear.

Naomi led the way into the kitchen. She motioned for him to sit down and then busied herself with the tea.

Reuben glanced around as an unsettling familiarity closed around him like the loop of a rope. He'd never been in this particular kitchen before, but he recognized it just the same.

Like his *mamm*'s, it was spotlessly clean, everything neatly stowed in its appointed spot. The modest refrigerator and stove were run by gas power, and they looked to be in decent condition. That hadn't been the case at home. His father hadn't cared much about his wife's conveniences. The room smelled faintly of breakfast—sausage, unless he was mistaken, and the yeasty odor of good bread like *Mamm* used to make.

His stomach rumbled to life, remembering that bread. It was one of the few things he'd missed. *Englisch* store-bought bread was no match for it—nothing but fluff and air. A man could eat half a loaf and still walk away hungry.

A staircase was set against the back wall, leading up to the family bedrooms, no doubt. He glanced that way, wondering how the young woman with the chestnut-bay hair was doing.

"I've a phone," he said suddenly. "If you need to call the doctor." He dug into his pocket.

Naomi placed a mug in front of him and lifted a chubby brown teapot. "It's kind of you to offer, but there's no need. Miriam's just had a fright, that's all." She poured a stream of steaming tea into his mug, nudged a pot of sugar toward him, and set a spoon on the table.

She didn't seem much worried about her sister-in-law, and if she wasn't, he shouldn't be, either. But somehow, his mind wouldn't settle.

"Does she have these spells often?"

Naomi took a small square tray from a cupboard and arranged another cup and a napkin on it. "Not as often as she did at first. We're thankful for that." She glanced at him. "Sam will have told you, *ja?* About what happened to my husband's parents?" She waited as he looked at her blankly. "The Hochstedlers?"

Realization came flooding in. Of course. The Hochstedler shooting.

A mentally ill boy infatuated with an Amish girl had

walked into her parents' general store and shot the middle-aged couple dead. That had been . . . what? A year ago? No, more than that now. So this was that family.

"I heard about it on the news." At least he'd heard some, likely a lot less than she'd expect, given how much media coverage the tragedy had gotten. He had a policy of turning the channel anytime something about the Amish came on.

That had happened often after the shooting, he recalled. He'd watched very little television there for a while because of it.

Sam hadn't mentioned this connection, likely expecting Reuben already knew. Plain folks rarely needed much explanation about such things. They kept track of family relationships, and they always knew who was related, who'd had an illness, a death, or a birth in the family.

Something like the Hochstedler shootings? Everybody would know exactly what this family had suffered, without being told.

Naomi was still looking at him, waiting. "Miriam was in the store that day, and she saw Trevor Abbott shoot her parents. She's not been . . . herself . . . since."

That was right. The younger daughter had witnessed everything.

He remembered how he'd spoken to her back in the barn, so short and forceful, and how fast he'd moved in her direction. That was no way to approach any frightened creature, especially not one recovering from trauma. No wonder she'd passed out. She must have been terrified, a strange man barging into the barn when she was there all alone.

"It wasn't your fault." Naomi studied him, her expression gentle. "Miriam getting upset, I mean. It's mostly your clothes. She's scared of *Englischers*, especially men. You couldn't have known."

He didn't contradict her. Funny how his old habits reasserted themselves here in this quiet kitchen. It wasn't considered polite to argue when there was no point in it, even if you disagreed with the other person. Besides, in Ivan Brenneman's household, all arguments ended with someone getting hurt.

But this kind-eyed woman was wrong. He'd known—or at least he'd known enough. He'd seen the girl was frightened out of her senses. He should have been gentler, although with the horse doing his best to break the stall to bits, there hadn't been much time for gentleness.

He wasn't so good with that anyway, not with people.

He heard the sounds of boots on steps and glanced up to see Joseph coming down the staircase.

"She's awake now," he told his wife in *Deutsch*. "Still shaky, though."

"I'll go up and take her some tea. She'll soon be all right again."

Joseph nodded, but the worried crease between his eyebrows didn't go away. He glanced at Reuben. "I'm sorry to keep you waiting," he said gruffly, switching to English.

"That's no matter." Reuben looked the other man in the eye. "I'm sorry I upset your sister." He never shirked apologizing—when there was cause. His father had never apologized for anything.

"It wasn't your fault," Naomi repeated, setting a mug of tea in front of Joseph. He sensed she was speaking to her husband as much as to him. "We're real thankful you've come. Sam told us how busy your schedule is. You're an answer to prayer, for certain sure." She lifted the tray she'd prepared and walked toward the stairs.

"Naomi," her husband started, and she made a face at him.

"It's not a bit heavy, Joseph, and *ja*, I'll be careful on the stairs. Don't fuss."

Joseph darted a half-embarrassed look in his guest's direction, but he still watched his wife until she was out of sight. Only then did he turn his full attention to Reuben.

"I guess we'd better settle things up between us, you and

me," he said. "I'm Joseph, if you haven't figured that out already."

"Reuben Brenneman." Reuben offered his hand and tried to focus his thinking. He felt off-kilter, and it was making him irritable.

He generally didn't worry much about the impression he made, but he didn't like knowing he'd scared that girl so badly. It bothered him. His mind kept replaying how she'd looked and felt in his arms—so soft and limp, her pretty hair slipping free from the stiff white *kapp*.

It was distracting, and he needed to pay attention. He was here about the horse, not the girl.

"So I suppose you had a look at our Breeze," Joseph was saying.

"A quick one."

Joseph waited a beat. "And? How bad is it?"

"Bad enough. I couldn't tell much, but I saw enough to know there won't be any quick fix. There's weeks of work ahead, at the least. And that's if everything goes just as it should." Which it rarely did.

"Can the horse be helped, do you think?"

"Depends on what you mean." There was no point sugar-coating this. "Can I settle him? Calm him down some? Pretty likely. How much? Enough to be a safe driving horse for your family? That I can't say. Some of it depends on Breeze himself. He has a mind of his own, that one."

Joseph lifted his eyebrows. "He does. And he's set it against the lot of us."

"For good reason. No," he said when Joseph started to protest. "I'm not suggesting you've mistreated him. But if a kid's been bucked off a horse, he doesn't fear only the one horse, does he? He fears 'em all. Same here. Breeze doesn't trust people. The way he sees it, the only thing cooperating with people ever got him was hurt. With horses, trust breaks easier than glass, and once it's busted, fixing it is long, slow work."

Another beat of silence. Joseph was thinking this over in the deliberate Amish way. "Sam says you know your business well and that if anyone can help this horse, it would be you. He also said your time is hard to come by, so we'll start there. Have you time for this job?"

He didn't, but that didn't matter. "I've already told Sam I'll do it."

"Why?" When Reuben didn't answer, Joseph went on, "I'm not trying to push my way into your private business. But since you'll be living here amongst us, I figure this is partway my business. I'll need to know about how much this is going to cost, too." One corner of the other man's mouth tipped up. "I hear you're pricey."

Reuben didn't smile back. Living here amongst them? What did Joseph mean?

"I owe Sam a favor," he replied shortly. "From way back. So don't worry over the cost. I'll be handling this job for expenses only."

Joseph lifted an eyebrow. "Must have been some favor."

He was giving Reuben an invitation to tell the story—and he was wasting his time. "That's between him and me. All you need to know is that repaying him is important enough that I pushed back two other jobs to come here. I've four weeks cleared, and after seeing the horse, I'm going to clear a couple more. That's the best I can do."

"Six weeks." Joseph whistled. "I'd not expected it to be so long, but we'll do what we can to make you comfortable. With Miriam as she is, having you stay here in the house won't work, so we've had to make other arrangements."

"I never planned on staying here. I figured there was probably some place in town . . . a motel or something."

"There isn't. Not anywhere close by."

Reuben shifted uneasily. "It wouldn't have to be fancy. All I need is a bed, and I don't mind driving some distance. I've got my truck." Remembering that his blue Ford pickup was waiting outside made him feel suddenly better.

He wasn't Amish anymore. That truck served as proof and a quick way off this farm whenever he was ready to go.

Joseph furrowed his brow. "*Ja*, but that brings your costs up, ain't so?" The Amish never spent when they could save. "Gasoline and motel fees. Food, too, likely. But don't worry, we've got it all fixed up. Since you're easy to suit, there's a room out in my workshop that will likely do. We've put a foldaway bed in there and fresh sheets. I added a restroom in the shop last year, for my customers and workers to use. A sink and a toilet only. There's no way to take a bath, but I figure we can work around that somehow."

Reuben tensed, and the sensation annoyed him. "I can't stay here."

There was a puzzled pause. Then, "Why not?"

Reuben fumbled for an answer Joseph would accept— and came up empty.

He should have seen this coming. If he'd been thinking straight, he would have. This was the way things were usually done. The Amish were nothing if not hospitable, and traveling friends and relatives were welcomed into houses on a regular basis.

Joseph and Naomi would do their best to make him feel welcome. He was getting a sense of these Hochstedlers, of who they were and how they'd behave. They were decent folks, and their troubles had only made them kinder. It worked that way sometimes.

Even so, he felt uncomfortable. Not only were this kitchen, these smells, and the sounds of the Pennsylvania *Deutsch* words bringing up a past he'd shoved away years ago, but he felt uneasy around these people. They were part of something he'd left behind, and something about their very Amishness made him feel . . . tangled up inside. Like when a vine looped itself around your boot when you were walking through the underbrush. It couldn't stop you moving on, not if you were bound to. But it tugged at you, slowed you down. And it could trip you if you weren't careful of it.

"Why don't you come see the room?" Joseph pushed back from the table and stood. "Then it'll be easier to decide."

What the room looked like didn't matter. He didn't care about comfort. While working with horses, he'd bedded down in barns, tack rooms, tool sheds, and his truck. When he was dealing with a severely troubled animal, he liked to be close by. He kept a bedroll with him for that purpose. Roughing it had never bothered him.

But he didn't want to live on an Amish farm, not even temporarily. He couldn't . . . breathe here.

Still, he got up. "All right." The walk to Joseph's shop would give him a few minutes to figure out how to edge past the other man's Plain-minded frugality without sharing too much of his own story.

They walked together down a path leading to a large stone building. A sign out in front declared **JOHNS MILL CUSTOM WOODWORKING**, but Reuben knew at a glance this place had started out as something else entirely.

"This was a dairy barn," he observed. A big one.

"*Ja*. My family ran cows for many years."

Reuben grunted. No need to ask why things had shifted. It was an old and familiar story. The traditional businesses, dairying, farming, were being crowded out and replaced by more specialized cottage industries such as this one.

He followed Joseph through the wide door and looked around. It was a nice place. Open, full of light. Clean and organized, with a pleasant tang of new wood in the air. Plenty of elbow room. At least five men could work here easily, but the place was empty on an early Friday afternoon.

"You work here by yourself?" he asked. Sam had said Joseph's business was going well.

"*Nee*. I've two young fellows who work with me, and I hire a delivery driver as needed. Eben and Isaiah Stuber are off to a family funeral in Pennsylvania. They're cousins. They'll be back to work on Tuesday morning."

Joseph pushed open a door. A milking stanchion had been converted into a small bathroom with a toilet and a pedestal sink. He didn't seem to see any reason to explain the obvious, and after Reuben had taken a look, he closed the door and led the way through the workshop to a pair of doors side by side on the left hand wall.

"That one"—Joseph nodded toward the left-hand door—"is an office for doing the paperwork. This one here will be yours while you're with us." He opened the other wooden door.

The room was small with walls of concrete block. A window to the right looked out over a rolling pasture, still gray-brown from winter. A narrow bed covered neatly with a blue-and-green quilt and a simple, ladderback chair were the only furnishings. The place smelled like lemons and laundry detergent, as if it had been freshly scrubbed.

"Miriam got things ready for you," Joseph said. "That's one of her quilts there on the bed. She sells them."

Reuben turned up a corner of the quilt and looked at the tiny, even stitching. Hours of work there. He flipped it back and considered the design.

Pretty, he thought, not that he knew much about quilts. But one thing puzzled him.

"How does she sell them if she's so afraid of *Englischers*? Surely, that's where most of the market is."

"Emma and Sam are running the old family store now, and they sell them for her." Joseph paused. "She's doing better, Miriam is. You shouldn't judge her by what happened earlier."

"I've no reason to judge her at all."

Joseph went on as if Reuben hadn't spoken. "You startled her, I expect, coming into the barn like you did, looking like an *Englischer*. None of us knew you were here. You took her by surprise, and her fear got the better of her."

There was a faint reproach in the other man's voice, but Reuben ignored it. His attention was elsewhere. The store.

That was where it had happened, best he remembered. He felt a tickle of surprise—and respect.

"Miriam takes her quilts there? To the store?"

"No." Another careful pause. "She doesn't leave the farm."

Reuben turned to look at him. "Ever?"

"She used to have trouble leaving her room. Once she got past that, she couldn't set foot outside of the house, not for months. Now she can go anyplace here on the farm. She just doesn't like to leave. But one day, in *Gott*'s good time, I trust she will."

This was none of his business, but Reuben couldn't help himself. "You're saying she hasn't set foot off this property since your parents died?"

"She went to town once. She was working hard and getting better little by little, so my wife and a friend drove her in. It wasn't too long after what happened, and they thought maybe it'd be good for her. They were eating in a café when a man grabbed Miriam and started taking pictures." A spasm of pain twinged the other man's face. "It set her back some."

Reuben clenched his jaw, thinking it over. Yes, something like that would have set her back. He hated to think of that slight-built girl being grabbed by some stranger and frightened out of the progress she'd struggled to make, all for a stupid photograph.

He'd lived among the *Englisch* for a lot of years, but that was one of many things he still didn't understand—their strange obsession with such foolishness. Clients were forever taking his photo while he worked "to post." Sometimes they asked his permission; sometimes they didn't.

He didn't care about such things, so he generally ignored them and let them take their pictures—unless they got in his way.

"She's stayed home since," Joseph was saying.

"She should go back to town," Reuben told him, his mind lingering hotly on what he'd say to a man who'd pester an innocent girl. He'd set such a fellow straight—and fast. "You'll have to work up to it, and you'd better start soon. Fears set in like bloodstains. If you don't work on them quick-like, it's much harder to get rid of them."

There was a short silence. When Joseph spoke, his tone was carefully polite. "I thank you for your thoughts, but you're here to see to the horse, not my sister."

Reuben lifted his eyebrows, but the man had a point. The girl and her troubles were bothering him more than they should. He usually preferred to let folks deal with their own problems. But this time, he reminded himself, he had a reason to care about Miriam's situation.

"From what I saw in the barn, your sister may be the key to helping that horse." When Joseph only looked at him, Reuben explained, "He's bonded with her."

"No." Joseph shook his head. "I don't think—"

"He has." Reuben interrupted. "I saw it. If you want this job done quick and well, I'll need her help."

That was true, and he often worked in tandem with owners, if the situation warranted it. Still, he didn't blame Joseph for looking surprised—and none too happy.

"Help? You?"

"I'd tell her what to do, and I'd do all the heavy lifting. But if she shows Breeze I'm nothing to be feared of, it'll speed things up."

Joseph shook his head. "You'll have to do without the shortcut. She won't want to do it."

"She's a grown woman, isn't she? Ask her and see."

"She couldn't manage it, and asking would only make her feel guilty. I try to respect my sister's fears. I won't push her past where she's able to go." He paused. "I won't have anybody else pushing her, either."

The warning in the other man's voice was gentle—but clear. Reuben met his gaze, but he didn't flinch.

Joseph might respect fear. Reuben didn't. He understood it, but that was different. He hated fear, hated it with a passion that went past every other feeling he had.

Still, Miriam Hochstedler wasn't his concern, and if he had to find another way to reach the horse, so be it. That would take time—more time than he had, likely. Best if he was close by, so he could give this job his best shot. He owed Sam that much.

"Fine," he said shortly. "We'll do it the hard way. This room'll suit. I'll start work tomorrow morning. You've got six weeks. It's all I can spare. Whatever shape the horse is in at that point, I'll have to leave."

When he did, he'd shake the dust of this farm—and this way of life—off his boots for the last time.

Chapter Four

❧

MIRIAM CLOSED THE DOOR OF THE CHICKEN COOP and tightened her grip on the handle of the egg basket, her heart pounding. All sorts of noises were coming from the barn, and they didn't sound promising. The stranger—Reuben—had been out there since the crack of dawn, but judging by those thumps and snorts, his work with Breeze wasn't going well.

She'd been nervous all the morning, waiting for the man to come in for breakfast. She wasn't sure she could handle sitting at table with him, especially not after what had happened yesterday. For all Naomi's soothing words, Miriam knew the truth. She couldn't recall too much of what had happened, but she remembered enough to know she'd embarrassed herself *gut*.

She'd been sneaking a quick visit with Breeze when the truck had pulled up. It had startled her, but she'd figured the stranger would need to go talk to Joseph before doing anything else. She'd been working out a plan for getting back into the house unseen when he'd walked into the barn, an *Englischer*, all by himself, her brother nowhere in sight.

She'd been trapped, and she hadn't known what to do. So she'd hidden in a dark corner, best she could, hoping he wouldn't stay long. But the man had spotted her, and when he'd walked toward her . . . reached for her . . .

It was as if all her nightmares had come true. She couldn't scream—she could barely breathe, until finally everything had gone blessedly dark.

The next thing she knew, she was in his arms, being carried outside. Maybe the cool air on her face had woken her up, she didn't know. She remembered sneaking a look up at him through a fringe of lashes. He had a strong face with an old scar over one eye, and his mouth had been set in an unsmiling line.

Waking up in the arms of this very *Englisch*-looking fellow should have pushed her past all sense, but it hadn't . . . exactly. Maybe it was just the aftereffects of her attack—she was usually like a dishrag afterward—but she'd felt strangely calm.

Her heart hadn't been pounding quite so hard, and the hard strength of his arms underneath her body had felt . . . comforting.

Safe, almost.

It had taken her a while to put that word on it. Safe. Maybe because she hadn't felt safe in a very long time.

It had all been very confusing, and her feelings were still jumbled up. That was why she'd worried about seeing him at the breakfast table. Half of her desperately wanted to get a better look at him, and the other half wanted to hide in her room until he was gone.

All her fretting had been a waste of time because he hadn't come into the house at all. Apparently Joseph had spoken to him when he'd gone out to the workshop after milking. Afterward her brother had asked Naomi to fix a thermos of coffee and pack some breakfast fixings in a lunch box.

"The fellow seems to want to keep to himself," Joseph had said. "He says he's not planning to come into the house to eat. He offered to tend to his own meals, but when I couldn't get him to see reason, I told him I'd bring the food out to him, if that's what he'd rather do. I'm sorry. It'll make more work for you, Naomi, packing it all up when he could just as well sit in the kitchen with the rest of us. But he's giving us such a break on his pricing, I feel we need to see he gets plenty to eat, one way or the other."

Sweet-natured Naomi had smiled and said it was no trouble to pack up the meals. She'd done that plenty of times when she'd lived with her brothers in Kentucky. It took more than a stubborn houseguest to disturb her easygoing sister-in-law, but Miriam was disturbed enough for both of them.

After being *naerfich* about seeing this fellow all morning, Miriam felt strangely let down. Which, she reminded herself, was just silly. This was a good thing, and meant, likely, she'd hardly see this Reuben at all while he was on the farm.

Now she could turn her mind back to her own business. She had plenty of work inside the house to do.

Today was baking day, and she and Naomi would be extra busy. They'd promised to make the cookies for a special lunch being fixed for the scholars over at the school. Naomi would deliver the goodies around lunchtime, while Miriam worked on finishing up a lap quilt—her last project for the store before she started on the two baby quilts. Emma was especially anxious to get this particular piece. One of her best customers had been asking when another of Miriam's quilts might be available.

That news had warmed Miriam's heart. She was happy to think of her quilts going to brighten folks' homes, and it touched her that people admired them so. She'd started praying over them as she stitched, asking *Gott* to bless whoever bought them.

Ja, the fact her quilts sold so easily was a blessing. She was thankful to have useful work to do, and she'd best get to it.

She started toward the house, curving her usual track from the coop to the back door to put as much space as possible between herself and the barn. Even so, she could hear the low rumble of the man's voice between the angry noises Breeze was making.

Halfway across the yard, her curiosity got the better of her. She stopped and tilted her head, trying to listen.

The man's tone was calm and soothing, but from the sound of Breeze's thumping, it wasn't doing much good. She sighed and sent up a prayer.

Please, Gott, help this Reuben with his work. Let Breeze calm down and get better so he won't have to be sent to Adam.

Just when she started walking toward the house again, she caught a word that brought her up short. He was speaking in *Deutsch*.

She took several steps toward the barn, straining to hear, but the man's voice had gone soft again.

She hesitated for a few seconds, then walked quietly toward the barn, careful to keep herself at an angle so she'd not be visible through the doorway.

"*Ja*, I'm still here." The man's deep voice floated out to her, confirming what she'd thought. He was talking to Breeze in *Deutsch*. "I'm not going anyplace, so you'd best get used to me. All I'm doing is putting this treat in your bucket. See?"

His words were followed by angry thumps and a series of snorts. Breeze wasn't pleased with his visitor.

"*Ach*, calm yourself." The familiar words rolled easily off his tongue. How could a fellow who looked so *Englisch* sound so Plain? "You're a smart horse, too smart for this. You've nothing to fear from me, and you're only tiring yourself, acting so. That's foolishness. See? Now I'm backing away. Everything's all right."

He didn't sound frustrated, only calm and patient. Soothing. No wonder horses liked this man—or most of them anyway. His voice was real pleasant to listen to. Miriam hadn't realized how tight her muscles had been until she felt them relaxing.

He didn't sound scary, now that she couldn't see him. Listening through the barn wall, she might have mistaken him for one of her brothers—only neither of them would have had so much patience with a balky horse.

Sam had told her Reuben had grown up Plain, but he sure hadn't looked or acted Plain yesterday. He'd worn jeans and a shirt with lots of colors. A chilly breeze sneaked up to tickle Miriam's neck. Shivering, she pressed herself closer to the barn wall.

"Who's there?"

The question—in English this time—floated out to her ears. He must have heard her.

Miriam turned and fled toward the house. Before she made it to the steps, the barn door creaked open.

"Hey! Wait."

Obedience had been drilled into her, as it was into all Amish young folks. She stopped, but she didn't turn around.

"You're Miriam." When she didn't answer, he went on. "We met yesterday, but you might not remember. You feeling better?"

"*Ja.*" Her cheeks warmed. "Thank you. I'm sorry. I need to get inside." She hated the way her voice sounded—so high and nervous. "There's baking to do."

"I'm Reuben." He spoke in the same calm, unhurried tone he'd used with Breeze. "Your folks have told you why I'm here, right?"

Miriam swallowed. "*Ja,* they've told me." She spoke

over her shoulder without looking at him. "You're here to work with Breeze."

"That's the idea. I don't suppose your brother said anything to you, did he? About you maybe helping me?"

Helping? Her? Alarm sparked in her heart, and she shook her head. "I wouldn't be able to help you. I'm not much good with horses." She fixed her eyes on the back door and started for the steps.

"That's not what Breeze tells me."

Now, that was a funny thing to say. She stopped short and half turned before she thought better of it.

The man hadn't come closer. He was still standing just outside the barn door, leaving plenty of space between them. Her heart gave a painful start, just the same.

This Reuben might sound Plain through a wall, but he sure didn't look it.

He was dressed in jeans again today, and he wore a sky-blue shirt tucked in and a brown leather belt, old and weathered. His light brown hair was cut short and brushed over to the side, just the color of the pecan sandies she and Naomi were planning to bake for the schoolchildren this morning. He sported wide-set shoulders like Sam, but he wasn't so tall as her brother-in-law. Of course, few men were.

Only one thing about him looked familiar—he had the muscles of someone who worked hard for his living. The arms under the rolled-up shirtsleeves were tanned ruddy, too, like most of the Plain men she knew in Johns Mill. Like them, this man must spend a lot of his time outdoors.

"I can explain what I mean, if you'll give me a minute." He waited. "Look, if I walk closer, are you going to fall down in a heap again? If we're going to talk, I'd rather do it without yelling."

Fall down in a heap. This fellow didn't waste much time on politeness. What was it Sam had said? Something about him not being the easiest fellow.

Still, she had fallen in a heap last time she'd seen him, whether she liked to hear it or not. Miriam swallowed, trying to look more confident than she felt. "All right."

She watched him warily. He walked toward her slowly, and to her relief, he stopped when there was still a good distance between them.

"What I'd need from you is pretty simple." He rubbed a hand over his head, ruffling his short hair. "Just introduce me to your horse friend in there. He trusts you, and it'll give me a head start with him."

She was shaking her head before he'd finished speaking. "Breeze doesn't like me any more than he likes the next one. He won't even take a bit of apple or sugar from my hand, not even after all these weeks."

"Maybe not." The man cocked his head and considered her. "But he trusts you, just the same. He may not show it too clear, but he does. Unless I miss my guess, you're the only person left in the world he cares about."

He sounded so certain—but of course, he was wrong. She hesitated, looking for the politest way to tell him so.

"I believe you're mistaken," she said finally.

"I can see that." One corner of his mouth twitched. "I do make mistakes now and again, mostly about people. But I'm not usually wrong about horses or what makes them tick. Anyway." He shrugged. "There's one sure way to find out. Let's give it a try and see."

She shook her head quickly. "I don't think I can."

"You don't think you can." He repeated her words. "Your brother didn't think you could, either. But you don't know, do you? Either of you. Not until you try. Up to you, but it's going to make things a lot tougher on Breeze if this doesn't work. On me, too." A flash of a smile, so quick that it was gone almost before she saw it. "But that's not really your problem."

She frowned. Her mind kept circling around something he'd said. *Your brother didn't think you could, either.*

That stung—although it shouldn't. Joseph had every reason to doubt her. Everybody did. She doubted herself—a lot.

"You think I could help Breeze get better? For real?"

He shrugged. "Maybe. Judging by your chin, probably, if you put your mind to it."

Her chin? She lifted her hand to finger it, puzzled. "What about my chin?"

"Nothing. We'd have to see if you can help me work with Breeze or not. We can't know unless you're willing to give it a try."

She hesitated, her heartbeat speeding up. "What would I have to do?"

"Well." He drew the word out slowly. "To start with, you walk into the barn and put a treat in his bucket."

"I've done that most mornings. It makes no difference."

"And then," he went on, "I want you to back up to the door and wait. See if he'll come take the treat. He hasn't had his breakfast yet, so he's good and hungry."

She shook her head. "He never eats while I'm there. He always waits until I'm gone."

"That's why I want you to wait by the door. I've been trying myself, but I haven't gotten anywhere. He's annoyed with me, so he'll be glad to see you. Stay inside and see if he won't eat the treat with you in the barn."

That would be a first. Miriam felt interested in spite of herself. "And if he does?"

"*When* he does." Reuben put a slight stress on the first word. "It's always important to expect the best from a horse. You're lots likelier to get it. After he eats the treat, go forward, nice and slow, talking to him the whole time. Put another treat in the bucket, and this time back up only half so far. Wait for him to eat it. Keep doing that until he'll eat with you standing right beside him."

Miriam waited, but he didn't add anything else. "That's it?"

"That's it."

"And if . . ." She paused when his eyebrow quirked up. "When," she corrected herself. "When that's done, then what?"

"Then we move on to the next thing. But first things first." He walked to the wash shed and leaned against it. "Treats are in a sack by the door. I'll wait out here. Let me know when you're done."

He wasn't going in the barn with her? Miriam felt her shoulders relax. That would make it easier. She considered.

She honestly didn't believe this was going to work.

Reuben might be the horse expert, but she'd been slipping in to give Breeze treats for months now, and he wouldn't let her near him. If the animal trusted her, he'd done a good job of hiding it.

Still. She nibbled on the inside of her lip and thought fast. Sam had called Reuben because of her—because the thought of Breeze being put down had upset her. And Joseph had agreed, and they were paying the expenses involved, all for her.

If Reuben needed her help, shouldn't she try to find enough courage to make the effort? He'd only asked her to do something simple, after all.

Something her brother didn't think she could manage.

She lifted her chin. Maybe she should try.

She glanced at Reuben. He'd pulled a phone out of his pocket and was studying it, not paying any attention to her at all.

She didn't think it would help, but she'd do it. Just to prove to herself—and to Joseph—she wasn't as helpless as he thought.

She approached the barn, setting the basket of eggs carefully by the door. Reaching into the sack, she grabbed a handful of the treats. They were cookie-like, shaped like chubby half-moons, and they smelled strongly of apples.

She slipped through the barn door. Breeze was in his stall, watching the door, and he tensed and blew as she came in. Once he saw it was her and not Reuben, he settled some.

Only a little, though. He was still uneasy.

"You didn't like having that Reuben here in your barn, did you?" She walked slowly toward the stall. "He's made you *naerfich*. Well," she amended as the horse backed into his favorite corner, "you're usually *naerfich*, ain't so? Like me. But he's made you jumpier. That's all right. He makes me jumpy, too."

She'd arrived at the bucket, and she put the treat in. Then she retreated to the door.

Breeze watched her from his corner. He tossed his head once, his eyes never leaving her face, his nostrils wide, flexing in and out as he breathed.

He showed no interest in the treat. He never did, until she left the barn. Once or twice she'd peeked through a crack and seen him eating whatever she'd left him. But he'd never touch it as long as she was close by.

Of course, thinking about it, she'd never backed very far off. She'd stood near the stall after putting the treat in the bucket.

Surely that couldn't have made much difference.

Miriam glanced over her shoulder, peeking through the crack in the door. Reuben hadn't budged. He was still leaning against the wash shed, intent on his phone.

How long should she wait here before she told him he'd been wrong? She didn't want him to think she hadn't given it a good try. But . . .

Crunch.

She turned her head. Sure enough, Breeze was chewing on the cookie.

Her eyes widened. "Well, look at you," she murmured. "Making a liar out of me, aren't you?"

This Reuben knew more than she'd given him credit for. That shouldn't surprise her. Sam was a good judge of character; everybody said so. Before his accident, he'd been the first man folks would ask about horses, too. If he believed Reuben knew his business, then likely he did.

Slowly, she walked forward. Breeze backed away as she approached, but she didn't think he acted quite as restless as he normally did.

He seemed more watchful than anything. The horse occasionally lifted his head, ears swiveled forward, looking over her shoulder at the barn door as if he was watching for somebody else to come in.

She dropped the treat in the bucket, and backed away again, this time stopping midway between the stall and the door. Not so near, but a good bit closer than last time.

She waited, and Breeze eyed her from his corner. He wasn't rearing or blowing, but he made no move toward the bucket.

"You should know I'm not going to bother you," she said. "I've never hurt you, have I?"

The horse waited another minute then walked slowly forward. A second later, his nose was in the bucket.

This was working! Miriam remained perfectly still. She didn't want to startle him and set everything backward, but she smiled so big, it made her jaw ache.

See there, Joseph. I can do more than you think.

This trick was so simple, it had seemed foolish, but it was working. Reuben was right—the horse did trust her, after all. Only her. Her heart soared, and for once she didn't even try to tamp down the pride she felt.

It felt wonderful *gut*—to be singled out. To be chosen, even by a horse, as a special person. Emma had Sam, who thought she was wonderful, and Joseph had Naomi. Miriam had nobody—and probably never would.

She'd best be thankful for what she could get.

She glanced over her shoulder. Reuben hadn't moved, but the phone had disappeared. Now he was staring off across the yard, his face blank.

For a second, she wished there were some way she could

let him know how things were going. But if she called out, she'd only startle Breeze.

No, first she'd finish the task he'd given her. Then she'd go back outside and tell him.

And she'd ask what he wanted her to do next.

CHAPTER FIVE

❧

REUBEN SHIFTED HIS BACK AGAINST THE WASH SHED
wall and glanced toward the barn. Everything seemed quiet,
and Miriam hadn't reappeared. He took that as a good sign.

Probably.

Either Miriam had passed out in the barn again, or—he
hoped—some progress was being made. That would be welcome news—even if he wasn't the one making it happen.

It's just a sidestep, he told himself. Working with any
animals—but horses particularly—was like planning around
the weather. You never knew what was going to blow your
way, and you had to adapt to whatever did.

His frustrating session this morning had proved one
thing beyond any doubt. Breeze had made up his mind that
Reuben was the enemy. Likely that had happened yesterday
with the episode with Miriam in the barn.

He'd been doing some thinking while he waited out
here, weighing what he'd seen against what Miriam had
told him about the horse not trusting her. Best Reuben

could figure, Miriam's over-the-top negative reaction to him being in the barn had flipped a switch in the horse's fear-addled brain.

Until she was threatened, the horse likely hadn't paid her too much mind. But when she was, the animal's protective instincts had reared up with a vengeance. Miriam—whether he trusted her or not—belonged to him, and Reuben was scaring her. That made Reuben a threat, somebody to be fought with every bit of strength and cunning the horse possessed.

If that was true—and Reuben was pretty sure it was—it was going to make this job a lot more difficult. It didn't help that his own nerves were on edge. Being on this Amish farm was raking up old memories and making him tense. Horses sensed such things.

Frustrating, but it was what it was.

So he'd ignored Joseph's warning and asked Miriam for her help. She was a grown woman, after all, and she seemed capable of making decisions for herself, whatever her brother thought. If she'd point blank refused, he'd have let it go. But that pointed chin had come through, and she'd found the guts to at least try.

Once Miriam had strengthened her own relationship with the horse, he should be able to piggyback onto that and establish himself as trustworthy.

If she'd agree to keep helping him.

He hoped she would. Otherwise, this job would take a whole lot longer, and he didn't know how much more of this he could stand.

He'd been here only a day, and already he felt squirrelly. This morning, he'd woken up to the ordinary noises of an Amish household getting a weekday started. The clink of a metal pail, and the impatient low of a Jersey ready for milking. The smell of sausage floating on the air, and *Deutsch* phrases being tossed casually from wife to husband from the back porch of the house.

Memories of his boyhood had come rushing back. A mix of them, good and horrible, jumbled up together with all kinds of feelings—sorrow, nostalgia, guilt.

Anger, too. And the gut-tightening tension that was a first cousin to fear.

He'd stood by the door in his tiny room, one hand on the knob, for at least two solid minutes, listening to the sounds outside it. His chest had constricted as cold sweat chilled his skin.

This felt like walking back into a prison after being set free, and it had taken all his willpower not to throw his duffel bag in the truck and leave. Finally, though, he'd clenched his jaw and made it out to the barn.

This was temporary, and his memories, as unsettling as they were, had no teeth. Ivan Brenneman wasn't his problem anymore. Reuben had put his past behind him, and that's where it would stay. And when he finished this job, his last outstanding debt would be paid off, and he'd owe no man anything.

That, in Reuben's opinion, was well worth the trouble.

He had to shake this mood off. Breeze already didn't trust him, and the horse was smart and high-strung. The animal sensed Reuben was uptight and stressed out, and that was one reason the session this morning hadn't gone well.

He'd find a way to manage. He already had an idea. When he'd come out of the barn, the sight of his pickup had steadied him. He couldn't work with Breeze nonstop. The horse would need plenty of breaks, and Reuben could slip away to town, go for a drive, do something that reminded him of the man he was now instead of the boy he'd been a long time ago.

He wasn't back to stay, and one thing was for sure. He'd never take another Amish job again. He didn't care who asked.

The barn door creaked, and Miriam stepped outside.

Reuben narrowed his eyes, trying to gauge how well things had gone by her expression.

Well, he realized with a sense of relief. Things must have gone well.

He read the good news in the way she stepped, lighter, surer than she had before. Her shoulders were straighter, and her chin was up. All encouraging signs.

The March sunlight was fitful today. Low, raggedy clouds scudded in front of the sun, and the breeze held a chill. But just as Miriam stepped out of the shadow of the barn, the sun struggled through to brighten the yard. Its warmth fell over her like a spotlight, and Reuben's breath caught in his chest.

She was even prettier than he'd thought.

Her face had lost its pale, pinched look. She seemed almost relaxed, and a smile played around her mouth. A rebellious curl of reddish-brown hair had strayed from her *kapp* to droop over her forehead. For the moment at least, there was no fear in Miriam Hochstedler's face at all, and the beauty of it socked him like a well-placed hoof to the stomach.

"It worked!" she said as soon as she'd come within earshot. "He ate the treats while I was in the barn. I did just as you said, and by the end of it, I was standing right beside him."

She sounded so triumphant that Reuben couldn't help smiling. She reminded him of his sisters. It had never taken much to make them happy.

"Good work!" He pushed off the wash shed and stepped in her direction.

At his sudden move, the light drained from her face. She stumbled backward, apprehension crowding back into her expression.

Reuben felt a flash of frustration. Dumb mistake on his part. Never a good idea to move fast around frightened creatures. You moved slow, giving them plenty of time and space to come to terms with you.

He halted where he was, deliberately relaxing both his stance and his expression and making no move to close the remaining distance between them.

"So? Tell me how it went."

She averted her eyes as she described how things had gone in the barn. Her gaze flitted around the farmyard like an uneasy sparrow, returning to his face only to quickly dart away again.

"Did I do all right?" she asked finally.

His heart softened at the shy hopefulness in her tone. His sisters used to sound the same, starved for approval and fearful of what would happen if they hadn't managed to do what they were asked well enough.

They'd had good reason to worry. At the Brenneman farm, approval was scarcer than money—and there was never enough money to go around.

"You did perfect," he assured her.

Her eyes came back to his face, searching his to see if he meant what he said. He must have passed muster because her lips curved upward again. Just a little, but it was definitely a smile.

"What do we do next?" Her voice already sounded stronger.

Good. She wanted to keep going. Miriam had more gumption than her brother thought.

"The next thing we need to do is start transferring his trust from you over to me. Once I get a toehold, I can really start working with him." He paused. "We can begin right now, if you're up for it."

Her smile faded, and her narrow shoulders stiffened. But after a second, she raised her chin and nodded. "I can try. What do you need me to do?"

"Nothing too hard. This time I'll walk into the barn with

you, just inside the doorway. He won't like it," he warned her. "He's decided I'm somebody to fight, and he doesn't trust me around you. But if he sees you standing calm-like with me, it might change his mind."

He could tell she didn't like the idea much, either. He watched her think it over. For a minute he figured she'd refuse, make some excuse, and run into the house.

Instead, she swallowed and said, "All right."

"Thanks." He walked in her direction, measuring his steps, making his movements loose and easy. She responded the way a nervous filly would, stepping aside, watching him with too much of the whites of her eyes showing.

But she didn't bolt, and all things considered, he counted that a win.

When he came up beside her, she was trembling. She was having a hard time letting him get this close, but she was struggling against the feeling, trying to be brave.

Good for her. If she was a horse—of course, she wasn't. He reminded himself of that as they fell in step together, moving toward the barn. But if she was a horse, he'd consider half his job done already. Some animals surrendered to their fears, ran until they couldn't run anymore, and then gave up.

Others fought back. Those were the hardest to work with, true. But if you could win their trust, it was the fighters who recovered the best. Every single time.

He left plenty of space between them, and he let her set the pace, even though it meant shortening his strides. When they reached the door, she halted, glancing at him. She stood well out of reach, but still, this was closer than she'd come to him since he'd carried her out of the barn in his arms.

She was a sweet-looking girl, he thought. Sometimes living with fear made people harsh and combative, but there was a gentle kindness in Miriam's face. She had nice eyes, too, clear like a forest pool with brown and green leaves layered in its depths. There'd been a pond just like that in the woods behind his house. He'd gone there often, growing up, to find some peace when things took a bad turn at home. Looking in the still water had always quieted him.

"So? What do we do now?" she prompted.

He blinked and came back to himself with a guilty start. He was supposed to be focusing on the horse, not this girl, no matter how pretty her eyes were.

"You go in first," he said. "Stand just inside the door. I'll wait a second or two, and then I'll come in behind you."

A worried furrow carved itself between her brows, but she nodded. "And then?"

"Who knows?" He shrugged. "We'll see what he does."

She pushed open the door and stepped inside. He waited a couple of beats and slipped in behind her.

Reuben saw Breeze's intent focus on Miriam, but only for an instant. Then the horse's attention shifted to him. The horse's nostrils flared, and he blew a warning. Reuben stood still, watching closely, curious to see if his assessment yesterday had been on target.

Yeah, he decided. He'd called it. Breeze hadn't much liked having Reuben in his barn this morning. But now, when he was standing beside Miriam? That agitated the horse much more.

Breeze blew again. When Reuben didn't budge, the horse reared and surged forward to slam his scarred chest against the boards of his stall.

He meant business. *Step away*, the horse was warning him. *Leave her alone. She's scared of you.* He reared again, then—slam. The boards shook, but they held.

Miriam flinched and stepped backward.

"Steady," Reuben murmured under his breath. "It's all right. Your brother was out early this morning, and he reinforced the stall. See the new wood there? There's no danger of him breaking through, not now."

"He's going to hurt himself, though." The horse rammed into the boards again, and Miriam gasped.

"He'll settle." Reuben forced himself to sound more certain than he actually was. A lot of this job was bluff. Pass yourself off as confident, and animals trusted you more. Owners, too. "He's warning me away from you. Talk to him. Tell him it's all right."

Her throat flexed as she swallowed. "It's—it's all right," she quavered. The horse blew derisively, pacing the front of the stall. "He doesn't believe me."

"Oh, he believes you, all right." Reuben spoke easily, hiding his own frustration. It wasn't the girl's fault. She was scared out of her mind and doing her best. "He's reading your tone and your body language. Your voice is shaking, and you're all tense and tightened up. You're telling him you're scared of me, and it worries him, see?"

"I can't help it." Panic edged her voice.

"Try taking a few steps forward. Just a few," he warned as she scurried away from him. "Put a gap between us."

The horse stilled when Miriam moved, his eyes darting from the girl he cared about to the man he distrusted. He blew again, but this time it held less force. Breeze approved of the space between them.

Reuben grinned. This was going to work. A lot of time and sweat lay ahead of them, but this horse could be reached—and the girl was the key to it.

"Talk to him," Reuben urged again quietly. "It doesn't matter what you say. Just talk, and try to forget about me being here."

She threw him an uneasy glance before turning back to the horse. "It's all right," she repeated. "He's not going to hurt you. He's here to help." She took another tiny step toward the stall. "He knows about horses. He'll figure out how to make you better. Won't that be nice?"

Breeze cut another look at Reuben, but his attention quickly refocused on Miriam. The horse stomped a foreleg, but he was settling down.

They were clearing the first hurdle. "Keep it up," he murmured.

She cleared her throat. "Once you're better, you can go out again. You can go on the road, even. You used to like that, Sam said. You must be tired of staying in that little pasture and this stall, *ja?* You'd like to get out and go places again. I would, too." She took another step toward the stall. "It's like being in a cage, ain't so? Having to stay cooped up all the time."

There was no mistaking the sincerity in her voice. Sympathy stirred deep in Reuben's stomach.

He'd never liked to see living things kept in cages. Likely because he'd spent years penned up himself. Cages could be invisible and still be awful tricky to get out of.

"Wouldn't it be nice, though?" She wasn't paying Reuben much attention now; she was focused on Breeze. "To feel the wind against your face, going down the road? Fast, like? Seeing the scenery passing by, not afraid of anything. It'd be just like the old days. Even better, 'cause you'd understand how special it is. It's not something you'd take for granted, not ever again."

Reuben could see only part of Miriam's face, but he knew what her expression would look like. Wistful, hopeful. Sad.

His *mamm* and his sisters had looked like that, too, more often than not. Back home there'd been a lot of wishing— mostly for things that weren't ever going to happen. He'd hated it, but since they'd been unwilling to make any changes, there wasn't much he could do.

People were harder to help than horses. In his experience, horses had better sense.

Breeze nickered, and Reuben snapped to attention. He'd forgotten to watch the horse—he'd been too focused on this girl who was, as her brother had pointed out, none of his business anyhow. He needed to pay attention to his work and stop letting memories bother him like a cloud of mosquitoes just before dusk.

He took in a breath and stepped forward. "You're doing good. Now," he instructed softly. "Talk to me."

She startled, and Breeze did, too. "Wh-what should I say?"

"Doesn't matter. He just needs to see you talking to me, easy like. He needs to understand you're not afraid of me."

She shot him an uncertain look. *But I am.*

She didn't say it out loud, but she might as well have. Maybe she wasn't quite as terrified of him as she'd been at first, but he still made her plenty *naerfich.*

Nervous, he corrected himself irritably, catching the slip into *Deutsch* in his mind. He never thought in *Deutsch* anymore, and he spoke it only when he was working alone with a horse. He'd been on this farm for only a day, and already he was back to thinking in the language of his childhood.

That annoyed him, but he couldn't afford to be irritated right now. He had a job to do.

"Tell me about where you'd like to go," he suggested. "If you could go anyplace, like you were talking about just then. Where would you go?"

She worked her mouth and swallowed. "Th-there's a quilt store. In town."

"A quilt store." Reuben kept his face carefully neutral. All the places in the wide world, and this girl wanted to go to a quilt store ten minutes down the road. Still, it was a distraction, and distractions were good tools. "You want to buy a quilt?"

She shook her head. "They don't sell quilts. They sell the cloth. You know, to make quilts and clothes. I—I like to sew."

He took another step forward. Easy but deliberate. He kept his gaze on Miriam, but he was watching Breeze out of the corner of his eye. The horse wasn't happy, but he hadn't gone berserk yet, and that was progress.

"That's right. Your brother said you made the quilt on my bed."

She nodded jerkily.

"It's pretty." He'd thought so, and he never paid much attention to bedspreads. "I never slept under anything so pretty before. My sisters didn't much like sewing."

"Naomi doesn't, either. Nor Emma. But I do."

She really did. When she spoke about it, her voice sounded stronger. "Why?"

"I don't know." He could see her thinking over his question. For a second, she wasn't thinking about the horse, or about how nervous Reuben made her, coming so close. "I think because a quilt can be anything I want. I pick everything out. The colors, the patterns. And I know how to do it, how to"—she gestured with her hands—"take scraps and put them all together to make something beautiful. Oh!" She turned toward him. "I'm sorry. That sounds proud. I didn't mean it that way."

Her quick move had startled Breeze. He snorted and tensed. Reuben felt the promise of progress slipping away. "There's nothing wrong with being proud of your work," he said shortly.

She stared at him without answering, and he realized— yes—for her, there was plenty wrong with it. Pride ranked up there with rebellion in Amish minds. Humility and obedience were the qualities that were valued.

Which sometimes—when you were dealing with men like Ivan Brenneman—caused a lot of harm to innocent folks. Yet another way the church fell short, in Reuben's opinion.

As if sensing his shift in mood, Breeze snorted again, more forcefully. Miriam turned toward him. "He's getting upset again," she said. "This isn't working. Maybe we should go."

"No." It would be exactly the wrong thing to do, and he couldn't afford another setback. "He just needs a minute.

He's trying to figure out if we're friends, that's all. He hasn't made up his mind about me yet. He's waiting for you to show him I'm all right. That I can be trusted."

She was looking at him now, her eyes wide, her lips half-parted. The little curl had drooped lower on her forehead. Once again, he read her expression as plainly as if she'd spoken her thoughts out loud.

I haven't made up my mind about you yet, either. I don't know if you can be trusted.

He saw her set her jaw—a tiny movement, but the sort of thing he watched for in horses because those little adjustments told him a lot about how the wind was blowing during a session. "How do I do that?"

"Put your hand on my arm."

"What?" Her eyes flew wide.

"Just put your hand on my arm, and talk to me. Let him see you do it. If he thinks you're not scared of me, it'll help."

It might. It might not. Horses could sniff out a lie from twenty paces. That was one of the things he liked best about them, but it sure wasn't going to help him right now.

Still, it was worth a try.

Her throat pulsed nervously, but she lifted her hand and laid it against his upper arm, safely covered by his sleeve. Her hand was shaking, and her fingers felt oddly cool through the thin material. Not a good sign. Her panicked body was pulling all its warmth inward.

"You're okay." He spoke quietly, as he would have to a horse. "I won't hurt you." She glanced at him, and the fear in her eyes went straight to his heart and skewered it. "And while I'm around, nobody else is going to hurt you, either."

Her eyes were fixed on his face. He could see she wanted to believe him. She didn't—not yet. But she was almost to the point of giving him a sliver of a chance.

Almost.

Nine times out of ten, that was all he needed—just one tiny snip of an opening, and he could help. A determined hope rose inside him, but he made himself stay silent and wait it out. You couldn't rush things, especially not at the beginning.

Breeze snorted, and Reuben blinked. Once again he'd been so focused on Miriam that he'd forgotten the horse. Reality rushed in—with embarrassment trotting close behind. This woman's personal struggle with fear was not his business in this barn. He didn't know why he kept forgetting that.

"Let's walk closer," he said. "Just a step or two. Keep your hand on my arm. All right?"

She didn't answer out loud, but she nodded.

"It might help," he said, "if you keep talking to me. Just keep your voice low. It doesn't matter what we talk about."

Breeze had gone still, watching them. The horse was still tense and on high alert, but he wasn't sure what was going on, and his interest was intrigued. He was watching Miriam to see what to think.

Another sliver of opportunity—and this was the one he was supposed to be looking for. Time to push—gently.

Reuben took a step forward, and she went with him, her hand on his arm. "So what do you like besides quilting?" he asked.

"I like chickens."

"Chickens?" Good grief, this woman was Amish through and through. Quilts and chickens. He didn't know whether to laugh or feel sorry for her.

"*Ja.*" It was almost a whisper. "I take care of our laying hens."

"And you enjoy doing that." He couldn't quite keep the skepticism out of his voice.

"I do." She sounded defensive. "They're funny, chickens are. They all have different personalities. Nobody else notices, but I do."

Okay. Good point. "All animals have personalities." He took another step, and again, she walked with him.

Breeze didn't like it. He paced the front of the stall, blowing, and tossing his head.

"It's all right," Reuben said. "Settle down."

This time he used a more authoritative voice. His instincts told him it was time to stand firm, to let the horse know this stranger wouldn't be so easy to scare off.

Unfortunately, Breeze had a point to make, too. He reared and slammed his chest against the boards.

Miriam's fingers flexed against his sleeve. He sensed she was about to step backward, even though probably she hadn't realized it herself yet.

"Don't," he murmured urgently. "Don't move."

For one split second, her fingers clamped on his arm, her short fingernails digging into the skin underneath his shirt-sleeve. Then she sucked in a short, startled breath and staggered backward, releasing him.

His heart fell. He'd messed up.

Sometimes, no matter how careful you were, you stepped wrong. You never knew it was coming until it was too late to go back. He wasn't sure how it had happened, but he'd just taken a very wrong step, and he braced himself for what he knew was coming.

Sure enough, Breeze exploded in his stall, ramming against the wood with a renewed fury. Miriam made one strangled noise. Then she turned and fled.

CHAPTER SIX

❧

AFTER RUNNING OUT OF THE BARN, MIRIAM PACED her bedroom for twenty minutes by the clock ticking on the nightstand, fending off a full-blown panic attack. She prayed as she walked, asking for *Gott*'s help, fighting to fill her mind with His words instead of the ones echoing in her head.

You'll never get better. Never, never, never.

By using every tip and trick she'd learned, she was able to keep the worst feelings at bay, but she couldn't shake a deep sense of disappointment.

Everything had been going so well. She hadn't had much faith she could help Breeze, but she'd been able to do what Reuben had asked. And it had worked. That had felt wonderful *gut*.

Then, when he'd wanted to walk into the barn with her, she'd felt her fear starting to kindle. Standing out in the open with him was one thing—going alone into a building with him made her more nervous.

She knew that didn't make sense. Her mind understood Reuben wasn't a bad man. Sam wouldn't be friends with such a fellow, and he certainly would never have sent a dangerous man here. It was just that, in spite of his Plain name and his ability to speak *Deutsch*, Reuben looked so very *Englisch*.

All *Englischers* weren't dangerous. Her mind understood that, too. Most were fine, friendly folks who treated others kindly. Some were a little too curious sometimes, but they meant no real harm. And even the curiosity that could get irksome at times was a blessing. Many folks in her community depended on the *Englischers*' interest to make enough money to continue living the way they felt called to live.

Her mind knew all that, but her heart wouldn't listen. Deep inside her there was a frightened child, hunched in a corner, her fingers plugged into her ears.

An *Englischer* had shot her parents—and Reuben, Sam's friend or not, lived and looked like an *Englischer*. That was as far as her terrified heart seemed able to go.

She'd tried—she really had. She'd tried to look past the blue jeans he wore and the way his hair was cut short and shaped flat against his head instead of ruffling up along the nape of his neck as her brothers' always did. She'd tried to focus on his eyes.

Reuben had kind eyes. There were wrinkles in the corners of them—laugh wrinkles, *Mamm* had called them.

There was something else, too. For all his unsettling clothing, when he looked at her, she felt . . . well, it was a hard thing to put words to. But somehow, she felt as if he really saw *her*, not only what had happened to her.

Most people looked at her now with a gentle, indulgent pity. Their kindness and compassion had helped her family through many difficult months, and she was grateful. But sometime over the past year or so, it was as if they'd stopped seeing her, herself.

Now Reuben wouldn't look at her the same, either. She'd

ruined all their hard work, running away like that. She just hadn't been able to help it.

After Trevor Abbott had shot her parents, while the gunshots were still echoing in her ears, she'd stood behind the store counter, too shocked to think, her mind unable to grasp what had just happened. Trevor had looked at her with cold eyes, and he'd said exactly what Reuben had said, just then, back in the barn.

Don't move.

When this *Englisch*-looking man had spoken the same words, it had shaken her. The fear she'd been fighting had sloshed up and over her in a wave too powerful to control. She'd needed to escape, to get someplace safe. So she'd run away.

Again.

There was a knock on her door. Naomi cracked it open and peeked inside.

"There you are." She spoke calmly, although she must have noticed Miriam staggering through the house and up the stairs. Her sister-in-law never acted surprised by anything Miriam did or didn't do. She simply accepted whatever came in her peaceful way—something Miriam deeply appreciated. "Are you all right?"

The question was casual—as if Naomi were asking the time of day.

Miriam cleared her throat. "I'm . . . I'm doing better now."

"Good." Naomi's gray-green eyes caught Miriam's, steadying her. "I'm ready to sweep out the bedrooms, but I forgot to bring up the broom. I left it on the front porch, I think. Could you run down and get it while I start with the dusting?"

It was an ordinary request, made by a woman whose pregnancy made going upstairs and down harder than it had been a few weeks ago. But Miriam doubted Naomi's condition had anything to do with this. Naomi was nudging her, encouraging her to get out of her room again as quickly as possible.

She'd have much preferred to stay where she was, but she understood her sister-in-law's concern. For weeks after the accident, Miriam had found it impossible to leave this bedroom, and it had been months before she'd been able to walk across the yard to the chicken coop. Naomi didn't want this fear to settle in again, and neither did Miriam.

"Of course," she said. "I will bring it right up."

"*Denki, schwesdre.*" Naomi smiled. She pulled the door fully open and walked down the hall to the bedroom she shared with Joseph.

Miriam studied the doorway for a few seconds, gathering her courage. Then she squared her shoulders and walked out of her room and toward the steps leading to the kitchen. Her heart beat hard, but she forced herself to keep going.

She was relieved to find the kitchen empty. She headed through the living room and had her hand on the front doorknob when she heard her brother's voice from the porch.

"You shouldn't have asked my sister to help you with the horse. I told you not to push her," Joseph was saying.

"I didn't push. I asked, and she agreed. Isn't she allowed to make decisions for herself?" Reuben didn't sound offended, Miriam thought. Only irritated.

She could imagine her brother's face as he considered the question. Joseph rarely answered quickly—he liked to think things over in his careful, deliberate way. "Of course she is. I would have gone with her, though, if I'd known. It might have steadied her, having me nearby."

"It might have steadied her, but it wouldn't have helped the horse any. You make him as nervous as I do. She's the only one he likes."

"My sister's well-being is more important than any horse.

I saw her run out of the barn just now. She's worked hard to come as far as she has, and I don't want her frightened."

"She was nervous, but she held up pretty well to start with. I'm not sure what set her off, and I'm sorry she got upset. But the bottom line is, I asked her to help, and she agreed. If you're unhappy with that, you should take it up with her."

They were arguing, Miriam realized, even though their voices were calm and unhurried.

"I'm taking it up with you. It's my job to protect my sister. From here on, you must do your work without bothering Miriam."

"Then you might as well put the horse down."

Miriam sucked in a sharp gasp, then pressed her hand against her mouth, hoping the men hadn't heard her.

She shouldn't be listening, but she couldn't budge from this door until she heard what her brother said next.

"*Vass?*" Joseph sounded as confused as she felt. "You came here not expecting any help from Miriam, surely. How is it that now you can't see your way forward without her?"

"I didn't know what the situation was then. Now I do. I've got other jobs lined up and waiting, and I need to get to them. This horse is worse off than I thought, but he can be reached. Working alone with him will take more time than I have to spare. Your sister's the key to turning him around fast."

"She cannot—"

"Yes, she can." Reuben sounded certain. "You didn't see how she handled things before she got spooked. She was doing a champion job, and Breeze made big strides forward. With her working alongside me, I'll have this job finished in a few weeks, and you'll have a usable horse again. If not. . . ." He trailed off into silence, and Miriam imagined him shrugging. "It's up to you, but if you want this job done, she's going to have to help. Otherwise, I might as well pack up and leave now."

There was another pause. "I am not sure what to do," Joseph admitted. "I don't like to see her upset. It could make her worse again, and none of us want that."

"Won't she be more upset if the horse is destroyed? Wasn't that the reason Sam called me in the first place?" There was another pause. "Why don't you ask her? See if she wants to try again?"

"I don't think—" Joseph began.

Before he finished the sentence, Miriam took her courage in both hands and opened the door.

"I want to try again." She glanced into her brother's surprised face. "Naomi sent me to get the broom, and I heard what you said. I don't want Breeze to be put down. It was silly of me to get frightened. It was just—" she started to explain, then stopped short. Reuben's choice of words had been accidental, and bringing it up wouldn't help anything. "He looks very *Englisch*, and that takes some getting used to. I'll try harder."

Joseph studied her, his forehead crinkled. "Are you sure, Mirry?"

"Certain sure. Don't worry, Joseph. I'll manage better next time."

Joseph looked as if he was going to argue, but Reuben spoke first.

"We'll start again first thing in the morning." She shot him a grateful look, and he met her gaze. His expression stayed serious, but his laugh wrinkles deepened, as if he was smiling at her with only his eyes.

A funny flutter started deep in her stomach, and she turned away, fumbling for the broom leaning against the wall. She knocked it over, and Joseph leaned to pick it up.

"Are you all right?" he murmured, his voice low and worried. "Truly?"

"*Ja*, I am fine. I am only in a hurry because Naomi needs this upstairs." She opened the door then hesitated on the threshold. "I'll be ready to help with Breeze as soon as I've finished my morning work," she said. "And I'll try to do better."

Reuben shrugged. "You did fine. Breeze made good progress, and that's what counts."

She nodded and slipped through the door. As she closed it behind her, she heard Reuben speak again.

"Your sister's braver than you thought."

"Mirry is braver than people know. It takes courage to fight such terrible fears, but she's done it—and she keeps doing it every day. I am just trying to make those battles easier, as best I can."

"I'll try not to upset her any more than I have to. Speaking of that. . . ." For the first time, Reuben's voice sounded uncomfortable. "I guess I need to ask you a favor."

Miriam leaned in, wondering what the favor was—and then caught herself. She was eavesdropping again. This was becoming a bad habit, and now she'd no excuse but pure nosiness. Whatever Reuben needed to talk to Joseph about, it was none of her business.

Flushing, she hurried upstairs with the broom. Naomi was waiting for her.

"That took a few minutes. Did you have trouble finding it?"

"No. It was right where you left it." Miriam handed over the broom. "Joseph and Reuben were on the porch talking."

"Oh." Naomi's expression shifted to concern. "I'm sorry. I didn't know."

"I shouldn't have listened to what they were saying, but I did." She hesitated. "Reuben wants me to help him with Breeze again. He says if I don't, Breeze may have to be put down."

"Does he?" Naomi began sweeping out the corners. "Are you willing to help him?"

Miriam bit her lip. "I'm willing, *ja*. I would like to be helpful, if I can."

She truly would. It had felt wonderful good, being able to do something difficult, something that had needed doing but that nobody else could manage.

Even Joseph hadn't been able to get Breeze to cooperate, and Joseph knew horses well. Not so well as Sam, but still, he was good with them. Yet she had been able to make progress with the horse that he hadn't.

Until she'd panicked and ruined everything.

"Whether I'll be able to help . . . I don't know." She waited for Naomi's answer, but her sister-in-law seemed focused on her task. "I'm not sure I can do this. What do you think?"

Naomi straightened, one hand resting on the roundness under her apron. "I think we find out what we can do by trying our best," she said. "And asking for *Gott*'s help to do what's needed. With Him, we can do many things that seem too hard at first. If I were you, I would just try to do the next thing that's needed. And then the next thing after that, and so on."

"You make it sound easy."

"*Nee*." Her sister-in-law smiled. "It's simple, but it's not easy. When I was so sick, growing up, I never knew how far I could walk before my strength gave out. I'd just walk as far as I could, one step at a time. Sometimes I went too far, and someone had to help me, but I usually got where I needed to go, sooner or later. You will, too, I'm guessing." Naomi started sweeping again, the bristles making familiar, brisk noises against the wooden floor. "In your own time, Miriam, and with God's help, you'll find a way to do whatever you're meant to do."

She sounded so positive. "I hope you're right."

"I'm sure of it. Now, you go on to the bathrooms, and I'll

finish up here so I can help you get ahead of your work. We'll want to get as many chores done as we can so you'll be free to help in the barn real early tomorrow. You won't want to keep Reuben waiting."

"*Nee*," Miriam agreed. "I won't."

She hurried down the hall to scrub the bathroom, smiling as she went. Bathroom cleaning was her least favorite chore, but that didn't dampen her spirits. For the first time in a long while, she had something to look forward to, something new and interesting to do.

She just prayed she could keep from falling apart long enough to do it.

CHAPTER SEVEN

❧

THE NEXT MORNING, MIRIAM DID HER REMAINING chores as quickly as she could. Then she covered her dress with her oldest apron and headed outside. Her heart was pounding, but for the first time in a long while it was with excitement instead of fear.

Reuben was waiting beside the barn door. He had his back to her, but he turned when he heard her coming. It took her a minute to figure out what was different. When she did, she stumbled to a stop in the middle of the yard.

He was dressed Plain.

The jeans and *Englisch* shirt were gone, replaced by familiar-looking dark trousers and a burgundy shirt, worn with suspenders.

Those were Joseph's clothes. She'd sewn that shirt for him herself.

They didn't fit Reuben well. He was shorter than her brother, and stronger-built. His muscles strained the shirt-sleeves, and the pants were a scant inch too long, puddling around the tops of his boots.

She glanced at his face and found him watching her. He shifted his shoulders, and she watched the shirt tighten against his muscles.

"So?" he asked. "Does this help?"

He'd changed his outfit for her. He'd borrowed clothes from Joseph, clothes that surely couldn't be comfortable, just so she wouldn't be quite so frightened of him.

And it did help.

His hair was still wrong, and no *mamm* or wife she knew would let a man in her household go about in such poorly fitting clothes. But he looked more familiar now, and the change quieted some of the butterflies in her stomach.

"I think so," she answered cautiously. "*Ja*, I think it does help."

"Good," he answered shortly. He rolled his shoulders again and winced, shooting her a wry look. "I'd forgotten how hot these clothes are. I've gotten spoiled, living *Englisch*. There's things I miss from home. My *mamm*'s good bread. And her cinnamon rolls. She used to frost them with caramel icing, when she had sugar enough. Those things I miss, and I've never had better anyplace else. But I sure never missed the clothes."

"It's kind of you," she murmured, her voice thickening. "To change your clothes because of me. I'm sorry to be such a trouble."

"It's no trouble," he argued gruffly. "It's a shirt and a pair of pants. Easy enough to put on and take off. If these clothes help get this job done, that's reason enough for me to wear them."

"That's kind," she repeated helplessly. "You're a very kind man, Reuben, to do such a thing, and I thank you for it."

He shrugged, looking uncomfortable.

"It's sensible. I've other work waiting, and I'd like to get this job done as fast as I can. The horse takes his cues from you. It's in my own best interest to keep you comfortable.

If changing clothes helps, I'll change. So?" He lifted his eyebrows. "Ready to get started?"

One step at a time. That's what Naomi had said. She straightened and nodded. "I'm ready. Tell me what I should do."

"We've fences to mend from yesterday," Reuben said. "You'll have startled him, running out. So we'll go back to the beginning. You go in alone and work with him with the treats. If we're lucky, it will go quicker this time, and then we'll be ready to move on to the next step. All right?"

"All right."

Reuben, it turned out, was correct. It did go faster this time—much faster. Breeze acted uneasy to start with, but he quickly settled and soon he was crunching the treats as soon as she dropped them into the bucket.

"It's good, *ja?*" she murmured as Breeze angled his nose so he could retrieve the treat. "You like those. You've never had such fancy things before. Cookies made just for horses—what will those *Englischers* think of next?" She held out another one, ready to drop it in, but to her surprise, Breeze leaned forward over the stall, craning his neck toward her hand.

She stood still, her heart pounding as the horse's nostrils flared. He didn't look too sure of himself, but he wanted the cookie. She extended her hand slowly in his direction.

"Take it," she whispered. "It's all right. I won't hurt you."

Breeze hesitated a second longer, then he nipped the cookie from her fingers and crunched it loudly.

Miriam's heart leapt. Another step forward. She couldn't wait to tell Reuben.

Careful not to startle the horse, she backed out of the barn. But once outside, she ran to where Reuben was waiting by the wash shed, bubbling over with excitement as she told him the story.

"I could see he was thinking about taking the cookie

from my hand," she said. "So I gave it a try. I hope that wasn't wrong."

"It wasn't wrong. It was smart. You've got good instincts." His lips stayed straight, but those friendly wrinkles in the corners of his eyes deepened.

"*Denki.*" She'd pleased him. Her heart lifted happily.

"Now, we need to—" His cell phone rang, making her jump. He pulled it from his pocket and glanced at the screen. "Sorry. Just a minute, okay?" He lifted the phone to his ear. "Hello?" His face shifted. "Connie. Yeah, I can talk. Just a second." He glanced at Miriam. "This won't take long."

"Of course." She nodded, stepping back so he could walk around the small building for some privacy.

The phone had startled her, but she wasn't sorry for the interruption. She needed an opportunity to gather her thoughts.

There for a minute, when she'd been so excited about Breeze, she'd forgotten Reuben wasn't just another Plain man. She'd rushed to him as if he'd been Joseph or Sam, eager to share her news. When he'd told her she'd done right, that her instincts were good, a rush of joy had warmed her from the tips of her toes to the top of her head.

Then his phone had shrilled, yanking her back to reality.

Reuben wasn't like Sam or Joseph. He was a stranger, a man who lived out among the *Englisch*, who preferred them to the Plain folks he'd grown up with. A man who knew some woman named Connie well enough that his face gentled when he spoke to her.

The brightness dulled from Miriam's joy, but she clasped her fingers together over the cloth of her apron and gave herself a talking-to. Helping Breeze was what mattered. Reuben wasn't here to be her friend, and his personal life wasn't her business. He'd come to do a job, and she was supposed to help him. That was all this amounted to.

Today had gone real well, and that was something to be thankful for. She'd hang on to that.

Reuben rounded the corner of the wash shed. His expression was grim, and the scar on his forehead seemed to stand out more than before.

"Is everything all right?" Miriam asked.

He shrugged, looking annoyed when the skimpy fabric tightened over his shoulders. "Just some personal business I'll need to see to. All the more reason to keep working today. You've made a good start, but we'd best follow up fast. This time we'll walk in together, and we'll work on making Breeze understand that I'm no threat to him. Given what you've told me, that should go easier this time." He looked at her and lifted an eyebrow. "You ready?"

There were no friendly crinkles around his eyes now. He looked drawn and worried. Whoever this Connie might be, her call had troubled him.

"*Ja*, I'm ready."

"Come on, then." He led the way to the barn and opened the door, motioning for her to go inside.

Breeze looked up expectantly—and he wasn't pleased to see that Miriam wasn't alone. He backed away from the wall of the stall, angling his body the way he'd been doing before. Her heart sank, and she glanced apprehensively up at Reuben.

"What should we do?"

"We'll have to play it by ear. Go on up there, like you did before. I'll stay here, and we'll see what he does."

She walked to the stall. There was no chance now, she knew, of Breeze taking the cookie from her hand, so she dropped it into the bucket, taking care that it made a nice, solid thump. Breeze's ear twitched, but he stayed in his corner, watching Reuben over his shoulder, his hindquarters pointed out, ready to kick.

She could see the tension in the horse's body, rippling over his skin in little waves. Sympathy stirred.

It was so hard to be afraid all the time.

"It's all right," she said. "Look, I'm backing away. You can come get your cookie. Nobody's going to hurt you. We only want to help."

Breeze didn't budge from his corner, and he made no move toward the bucket. Her heart dipped. Looked like they were back to square one.

"Go in."

She glanced over where Reuben stood in the shadows of the barn. "What?"

"Go inside the stall. He won't hurt you, and he'll like having you in there, close to him while I'm around. He wants to protect you every bit as much as he wants to protect himself. It'll make him easier, having you nearby."

Miriam swallowed, remembering how Breeze had exploded into fierce, frantic action the last time Reuben had come close. He was doing better now, but the horse was clearly nervous. How could Reuben—or anybody else for that matter—know for sure what Breeze would or wouldn't do?

She might not know horses so well as Reuben did, but she knew such fear better than most. She'd battled it herself, losing as many times as she won. Maybe Breeze didn't want to hurt her, like Reuben said, but fear could make you act without thinking.

She cleared her throat. "Are you sure?"

"Yes." There was no doubt in his voice. "It's the next step." He waited a beat, then added, "Can you do it? Or are you afraid?" He didn't sound condemning, only like he wanted to know.

She wasn't really scared, she realized suddenly. She was nervous, sure, and worried about getting hurt. But unlike humans, Breeze had no meanness hidden in him. He didn't frighten her nearly as much as people did.

Instead of answering, Miriam moved forward and lifted the latch on the stall gate. She inhaled one deep, steadying breath and slipped inside, closing the gate behind herself.

Breeze was instantly distracted. He whuffed out a breath that sounded to Miriam more like surprise than anything. Then he moved, swiftly positioning his body as a barrier between Miriam and Reuben.

She caught a glimpse of Reuben's face just before Breeze blocked her view. Even in the dim light, she could see him give her a short nod. She'd pleased him again.

"Talk to him. Settle him as much as you can," he murmured. He kept his voice low, but Breeze still didn't like hearing it. The horse shifted his hooves uneasily and blew again.

"It's all right," she murmured. After a second's hesitation, she laid a hand on the horse's glossy shoulder, right above one of the many scars crisscrossing his body. Although the horse's skin rippled under her touch, he didn't move away. But he didn't look at her, either. His attention was focused intently on Reuben.

Waves of suspicion rolled off the horse. He didn't trust this stranger. She understood. She didn't trust strangers, either. Miriam stroked his shoulder.

"It's all right," she whispered again.

"I'm moving closer." Reuben spoke matter-of-factly, as if he were talking about the weather. "I'll take it slow. Just stay calm, and keep talking to him."

At Reuben's voice, Breeze had stiffened.

"He doesn't want you to." Her heart skipped into a rapid beat.

"I'm sure he doesn't. I'll have to do a lot of things he won't like. That comes with the territory, and it's the only way he'll get better." Reuben took another step. "Stay where you are, and keep doing what you're doing, even if he cuts up. Everything's all right."

Breeze blew sharply out of his nose and stomped a foot, making Miriam jump. "Maybe you'd better stop."

"Can't." Reuben stepped forward again, and Breeze

tossed his head. "He's had his own way too long. We're not doing him any favors, giving in. Keep stroking him. No. Firmer. Let him feel you. Run your hands down the length of his body, like."

Miriam tried her best to do as he asked, hoping Reuben wouldn't notice how her hands were trembling.

She didn't know why they were shaking. It was as if the horse's fear about Reuben coming closer was spilling over onto her, too. It made no sense, but then, in her experience, anxiety often didn't.

She tried to breathe deeply and focus. Sometimes that helped.

"He's not going to hurt you," Reuben said. His voice was low, even, and deep. "He's a smart one. You can see it in his eyes. He's getting mad at me, but he knows what he's doing. Keep talking to him."

Miriam had to swallow twice. Her mouth had gone as dry as dust. "It's—it's all right, Breeze," she managed finally.

"You have to sound like you believe it."

There was a tinge of impatience in Reuben's voice now, and Miriam's heartbeat ticked up another notch.

"What if I don't believe it?" The sharp question slipped out.

"Then pretend you do, best you can." Reuben was almost at the gate now. "You're doing all right. See how close I am, and he's not moved? He doesn't like it, but he's not trying to kill me. Not yet anyway. That's progress."

He was right. "It's working." She breathed. She pressed down harder as she ran her hands down the length of the horse's side. "It's all right," she said in a firmer voice. "He won't hurt you. Everything's all right."

"We've got him between a rock and a hard place, see? He doesn't like me and he doesn't trust me an inch." Breeze snorted and shook his head as if he were agreeing. Reuben chuckled. "But he's between you and me now, and that makes him feel easier. Plus, he's very aware of where you're standing, and he doesn't want to hurt you."

"You're not a bad horse, are you?" Miriam asked softly. "Not really."

"No horse is bad." Reuben's answer was quick and certain. "They're not like people. They're not capable of it. Their behavior can be bad, though, and that can make them dangerous." As he spoke, he lifted the latch on the gate. "I'm coming inside. Watch yourself. He's likely to crowd you a bit to keep you away from me."

Sure enough, as Reuben slipped inside the gate, Breeze took a quick step sideways, pushing Miriam backward with his body. She lost her balance and plopped down into the straw.

Her breath whooshed out in a rush, and she made a distressed noise.

Reuben clucked his tongue. "Steady," he said, and the undercurrent of tension in his voice made her insides knot up. "Stay where you are. Let him settle."

Her fall had made Breeze uneasy. He was starting to dance, and more white was showing around his eyes.

She was uneasy, too. She didn't like being on the ground here in the stall, looking up at the horse and at Reuben, especially when both of them were blocking her way out. It made her feel . . . helpless.

She could feel the terror building in her chest, and she swallowed hard.

Please, Gott. Not here. Not right now. Help me.

"I think he's had enough." She started to push off the ground, and Reuben made a quick negative gesture.

"He's just putting on a show. Stay put, I said." He murmured the words without looking at her, his attention on Breeze. As he spoke, he shifted until he stood fully in front of the gate.

She couldn't get out. Miriam's nerves ignited, like dry

kindling touched by a match, and her breath started coming in short, desperate gasps.

"I have to—" She forced the words out.

"Miriam—"

She barely heard him say her name. "—get up," she finished, with difficulty. "Get out. I need to get *out*."

She scrambled to push herself up from the hay. As she did, Breeze snorted and reared, his hooves hitting the wooden stall with a loud *blam*.

Reuben stepped back just in time, narrowly missing being hit. In one smooth movement, he reached around the horse and snagged her by the arm, pulling her out of the stall.

When he did, Breeze exploded, hitting the fresh, strong lumber with sickening thuds.

"Can you get yourself out of the barn?" Reuben asked her, his voice tense and short.

She nodded miserably. She couldn't answer. Her breath was coming in ragged bursts.

"Then go. I'll stay here and see what damage control I can do." He sounded tired and impatient.

"I'm sorry," she whispered. Without waiting for an answer, she stumbled out of the barn and ran toward the house.

CHAPTER EIGHT

LATER THAT AFTERNOON, REUBEN SAT ON THE BED in his cramped room, a piece of notepaper on his knee and a pen in his hand, trying to think what he should write to his sister. He wasn't having much luck, and he needed to get the check she'd asked for in the mail.

He couldn't think of anything to say—at least not anything he hadn't said before. None of it had ever done much good. Connie was the last of his four sisters at home, the only one still unmarried, and the youngest. She'd joined the church a couple of years back, although he'd offered to take her in and help her find a place in the *Englisch* world. She'd chosen to stay in the mess he'd left behind, and nothing he could say now would change that.

He set the notepaper to the side with a feeling of relief and went to work addressing the envelope. Writing letters had never come easy. Besides, even though he was sending the money to a friend's house instead of directly home, there was always a chance his father would get hold of the note somehow.

To be on the safe side, he'd put no return address. He used a post office box when he was at home, one in the next town over. It still felt risky. If his father knew where he was, there'd be trouble. Ivan was never more than a couple of bottles away from an explosion, and according to Connie, his anger at his only son hadn't simmered down much.

Thanks to his bank, Reuben would know when she'd cashed the check. That would have to be good enough. Likely he wouldn't hear from his sister until the family finances grew desperate again.

He figured he'd be getting another phone call in a few weeks. Ivan expected his wife to stretch a penny into a dollar, and he never troubled himself over how food was to get on the table with no money coming into the house. Being able to pay bills and fill the pantry helped *Mamm* and Connie avoid Ivan's temper, and that was what counted to Reuben.

He wished he could send more. This long-awaited chance to pay Sam back had come at the worst possible time, as such things tended to do. He needed to get done with this job and get on to better-paying work.

That was one reason why—fresh on the heels of the conversation with his sister—he'd pushed too hard in the barn earlier. He'd known he was getting close to the edge, not just with Breeze, but with Miriam, too.

He should have backed off. You couldn't rush a scared animal—and scared people weren't so different. You had to take charge, but you also had to watch for cues, letting them set the pace. But Connie's tearful voice had been echoing in his head, and this stupid shirt had cut into him every time he moved. He'd just wanted to get this job over with.

He might get his wish. Reuben wasn't particularly looking forward to his next talk with Miriam's brother. And it sounded like that conversation might be coming sooner than he'd expected.

He paused, listening. Someone was moving softly around the workshop. Likely Joseph—his two employees never worried much about the noise they made. Joseph had been out making deliveries, but he must have come back early.

Reuben finished writing the address Connie had given him. He put in a check, added a stamp, and stood, tucking the envelope into his shirt pocket.

Best to get this over with. Given what had happened, there was a good chance that Joseph wouldn't want him around any longer. No sense in wasting time.

Although he'd been anxious to leave this farm since the moment he'd set foot on it, he felt a jab of regret. He hated leaving this job unfinished, for a lot of reasons. Most important, he didn't want to leave Breeze where he was. The horse was reachable—challenging, but definitely reachable.

There was the business with Sam, too. Reuben didn't like unpaid debts, and he'd wanted to get this one off his ledger.

And then there was Miriam.

She shouldn't have figured into his regrets at all, but somehow she did. He hated leaving things on such a sour note with her. She'd been so pleased with the little progress they'd made. He'd have liked to have seen her face when Breeze was sound and pulling a buggy again. She'd have smiled big, he reckoned.

The smiles she'd given him so far had been small and brief, but even those had made her sparkle. Seeing Miriam happy would have been satisfying, like rubbing oil on a treasured saddle and watching the tooling shine through again, as if it were new. He liked leaving things better than he'd found them. There was too much broken in the world.

He opened the door—and stopped short. Miriam was fussing with a tray covered with a cloth napkin, arranging it on one of her brother's worktables.

At the creak of the door hinges, she looked up, her eyes round. "Oh!"

He stayed where he was, in the doorway, giving her plenty of space. She looked startled like a deer caught in a summer garden with a mouthful of lettuce. As if she wanted to run, but was willing herself not to.

"Hey," he offered gruffly. "You bringing a snack to your brother? He's still out on deliveries, I think."

"No. I mean, *ja*, I know he is not back yet. I made these for you." Miriam flushed.

Reuben drew his brows together. "For me?"

She nodded and folded the napkin over on itself, revealing a small, square pan of perfectly baked rolls, covered with creamy caramel frosting. Even though he stood some distance away, he could smell their rich goodness, and his stomach rolled in hungry appreciation. "You made me sweet rolls?"

Why would she have done such a thing? Especially after what had happened this morning.

She nibbled her bottom lip, watching him warily. "I wanted to apologize for ruining things with Breeze earlier. You said you liked them. That you missed the ones your *mamm* made—these and her bread. Probably mine are not so good as hers, but I thought I would try."

Reuben did some hasty calculations, feeling touched. Yeast breads took hours to make. It had to rise twice, then be baked, then frosted. His *mamm* had made these only now and then. Miriam must have been working on them ever since she'd run out of the barn.

An uncertain warmth stirred in his stomach. She'd gone to a lot of trouble.

"*Denki-shay.*" The old expression of gratitude slipped out so easily that it startled him. Since he'd left home, he spoke in *Deutsch* only with horses—or when it was absolutely necessary, which in his new *Englisch* life was almost never. Still, it seemed only right to thank her in the language she felt most comfortable with.

She waved aside the thanks with a flutter of her hand. "It was the least I could do. Like I said, I'm sorry for what happened in the barn. I messed things up and made things harder for you going forward. I didn't mean to." Her throat flexed, and her eyes wouldn't stay on his, but darted to him and away like summer butterflies.

"No apology's needed. It was more my fault than yours. I pushed too hard." He gestured at her gift, feeling awkward. It had been a long time since someone took such trouble for him. "This was kind of you."

"*You're* the one who's been kind." She spoke with conviction. "Coming here when you couldn't really spare the time, just as a favor to Sam."

"I'm paying back a favor," he pointed out. "That's no credit to me."

"It is, too. Some people don't bother. Then you put on those Plain clothes just to be nice to me, when they don't even fit. They must be uncomfortable, and Naomi said it was likely hard for you to wear them because they'd remind you of—" She broke off short, more pink flaring into her cheeks.

"Old troubles." He finished the sentence. "Yes, they do. There was a time I wouldn't have put them on, but now I'm able to keep the bad memories in my past where they belong. Mostly anyway. That's why I don't mind wearing them. My other clothes reminded you of old troubles, too, and I understand how that feels."

She looked at him then, her eyes lingering on his face longer. He held her gaze, keeping his stance relaxed and open, just as he would have done if he'd been working with a horse.

It seemed to work. Fear, he guessed, was fear.

"You've been kind," she repeated stubbornly. "And I'm . . . sorry I wasn't able to help better with Breeze."

"You helped." He tilted his head. "You can still help more. If you want to."

"I do want to, but—" Shaking her head, she took a step toward the door. "I'd better not. I can't . . . control how I react sometimes. It just comes over me for no reason."

"That's not true."

She studied him. This time he was the one who glanced away. Eye contact was a tool like anything else, he'd found. There was a time and a place to use it.

And there was a time and a place not to—when looking an animal—or a person—in the eye didn't reassure them, but instead made them feel threatened.

He reached for one of the rolls. It came away from the rest of them with the sticky pull he remembered, feeling promisingly soft and yielding in his hands.

He took a bite, and his face spasmed with appreciation. *Ach*, this was good—better than his *mamm*'s, even, and hers had been the best he'd tasted until now.

Miriam must have read his expression. A smile tilted up the corners of her mouth. "I brought you coffee, too." She nodded toward the silver-and-green thermos set beside the tray. "It's only black, but—"

"That's how I like it." He held the roll in his teeth while he unscrewed the top of the thermos and poured himself a steaming cup. Then he took another generous bite. "Almost a shame to wash these down with coffee—or anything else. They're wonderful good. I've not had anything like this since I left home."

He wasn't looking directly at her, but he sensed her relaxing at his praise. "I'm glad," she murmured.

There was a pause while he waited her out. He'd thrown her the ball. She'd either throw it back or she wouldn't. Either way it was up to her.

She cleared her throat. "Wh-what did you mean just then? About there always being a reason?"

He took his time answering. He chewed, swallowed, and took another long drink of the hot coffee. Then he turned toward her.

She was standing in the doorway. Once again, she reminded him of a startled deer, poised to run, ready to dart away at any sudden movement.

"Fear always has its reasons," he said. "It comes down to experience usually. Ever seen a baby wild animal? I mean, a brand-new one, just born?"

She nodded. "Yes."

"They're not afraid of you, are they?"

She shook her head. "I guess not. They don't know to be."

"Because they've no experience with humans. Fear's learned. As wild things grow up, they learn to be afraid of us—either firsthand or from the way they see older animals reacting to people. I don't think people are any different. You've learned to be afraid, Miriam, by what's happened to you, just like Breeze did."

"I don't think it's the same thing." She paused. "Is it?"

He shrugged. "Same in some ways. Different in others. Granted, I know a lot more about horses than people, and what I've learned has been more from doing than from books or classes. I can only go by what I've seen." Moving slowly, easily, predictably, he dragged one of Joseph's wooden stools away from the workbench and sat.

Sitting wasn't threatening. It also sent a message. A person sitting down wasn't going to chase you, but he wasn't planning to go away anytime soon, either.

It was a smart move. She relaxed even more, taking a half step back into the shop.

"The trouble comes when fear sticks around past its expiration date." He'd finished his first roll, and he reached for another one. "When there's no sense in being afraid anymore, I mean. It's not logical. Fear starts in the mind, but it's got roots in other places. Deep ones. It's not always so simple to winnow it out." He shifted gears easily. "These rolls are really good. I appreciate you going to the trouble of making them."

She ignored the compliment. "But you can do it, though? Winnow out the fear?"

"In horses? Yes."

"Always?"

He shrugged. "*Always* is a hard word. Mostly."

She cleared her throat. "Back in the barn . . . you were . . . between me and the way out. And I didn't like being on the ground. It didn't feel safe. I think that's why I—got upset."

"Sounds about right." He should have thought of that. "What about yesterday? Any idea what triggered you then?"

Her face went pale, and she crossed her arms over her chest. "I don't want to talk about that."

"Okay." His senses were on full alert now. Such a quick reaction—horses flinched like that when you tapped the sorest spot on a hoof, the place where all the trouble had started. "You don't have to talk about it if you don't want to."

She nibbled on her lip for a minute before speaking again. "Will you be able to help Breeze even if I can't . . . manage?"

His heart twinged in a mixture of admiration and pity. Admiration because most *Englisch* people with this woman's struggles would be thinking about themselves, but she was only worried about the horse.

Miriam Hochstedler was a *gut* Amish girl. The sort of girl who baked special treats to apologize for causing a trouble she hadn't been able to help, and who'd been taught to put the benefit of others—even a troublesome animal— in front of herself.

That's where the pity came in. His sisters were like that. His *mamm*, too. It hadn't worked out so well for them. Such gentle women were very vulnerable, and in his experience the church didn't always protect them like it should.

Miriam was lucky her brother was good to her. Reuben hoped she found a husband who'd be kind, as well. If she didn't. . . .

The thought turned his stomach, and he set down the rest of his cinnamon roll.

"Reuben?" She was still waiting for his answer.

He stalled by taking another drink of coffee, partly because he was warring within himself about which answer he should give. He should mind his own business—but he didn't seemed able to do that where this girl was concerned.

"You could manage, I think. I could help you maybe."

She worried her bottom lip. "How?"

He tried to think of a good way to say it, but in the end, he just went with the truth. "Half the problem is that deep down you're still scared of me. Breeze senses that, and it's not doing us any favors. Neither is you getting panicked and running off whenever I move wrong. If you were relaxed around me, really relaxed, he'd sense that, too, and things would go smoother."

"I'm sorry."

"Stop apologizing. It's not your fault, and it's nothing to do with me anyhow. I'm a stranger to you, that's all. You wouldn't be so scared of me if you knew me better." He paused. "So that's where we'd start, I think. We spend some time together, and you get to know me."

Alarm flickered in her eyes. She wasn't any too sure of that idea. To tell the truth, he wasn't, either. He was making this up as he went.

"Spend time together doing what?"

"This." He gestured at the rolls. "Talking. Eating. Nothing special. It wouldn't take long. A day or two maybe."

He watched her think it over. "You'd come eat your meals with us, you mean?"

He blinked, feeling as if he'd been trying to jump a fence and had slammed into it instead. No, that wasn't what he'd meant at all, and the thought of sitting down at an Amish table again made him feel sick.

But it made good sense, much as he hated to admit it. She'd feel easier with her family around her, and she'd get used to him that much quicker.

Besides, he couldn't preach to her about getting past her little triggers if he wasn't willing to take aim at his own, could he?

"Yeah. I could do that. And we might go for a walk or something, if your sister-in-law can spare you from your work. Just around here," he added. "You could show me the rest of the farm. It doesn't matter what we do. It's the time that makes the difference. What you're familiar with, you're not so scared of. What do you say?"

She wanted to say no. He saw it in the tremble of her hand on the doorframe, in the desperate way she glanced toward the house, like a rabbit wanting to scurry to its burrow.

But she firmed up her mouth and nodded. "All right. I'll ask Naomi, but I'm sure she can spare me long enough for us to take a walk. A short one," she added hastily.

"I'll meet you in the yard."

He stayed where he was, watching her through the window as she walked back to the house. Like Breeze, she moved with a certain nervous stiffness. But also like the horse, he could see an unusual, fluid grace hidden beneath that tension.

If she ever got past her crippling fear, Miriam Hochstedler, like that horse in the barn, would be a rare one indeed. If the right man came along, someone who saw that mix of spirit and sweetness in her and had the patience and the skill to bring it out, she'd shine, for sure. She'd be one in a thousand, then.

One in a million, even.

But if the wrong fellow came along, he'd crush what was left of her spirit. And that, in Reuben's experience, was far likelier to happen to women like her.

Reuben flipped the napkin back over the rolls on the plate. He'd suddenly lost his appetite.

Chapter Nine

❧

HALF AN HOUR LATER, WHEN MIRIAM CAME OUT-
side, Reuben was waiting by the steps, tapping an envelope
against the palm of his hand as he gazed over the barely
green fields.

Her stomach was skittering at the thought of walking off
alone with him, so she forced herself to focus on his poorly
fitted shirt. Funny how a shirt that looked so well on one
man could look completely wrong on another. She should
have told him he could change back into his *Englisch* clothes.

But she hadn't. Because the truth was, the Plain clothes
did make her feel more comfortable. It was selfish of her,
but she was already *naerfich* enough as it was.

He looked up as she reached the last step. "You ready,
then?"

She swallowed. "Yes."

"Where do you want to walk to?"

She'd given this some thought. "There's a creek at the bottom of the back pasture. It's not much to look at, 'specially not

right now with everything still so brown. But it's kind of nice, if you want to see it."

"Sounds good to me. I've got this letter to mail first if you don't mind taking a detour by the mailbox."

She glanced at the road and suppressed a shudder. "You go ahead. I'll wait here for you."

She'd hoped he'd go on without a comment, but he didn't budge. "The road bothers you?"

"Not so much the road as the people driving on it."

He glanced at the quiet country highway. "Doesn't look to be many folks on it just now. And I'd be walking with you."

She backed up a step and shook her head. "I don't go close to the road."

He shrugged. "All right. I won't be a minute, then."

As she watched him walk away, the door creaked open behind her.

"Everything all right?" Naomi asked.

"He needs to mail a letter, he says." Miriam turned to look at her sister-in-law. "Did you want me to do something before we go for our walk?"

"No." Naomi seemed to be having trouble with whatever it was she wanted to say. "I'm being silly, I expect, but— Reuben's been living *Englisch* for years. Sam says he's never wavered in that choice, not once. He's got hard feelings toward the church, apparently. That's all Sam knows, but he sounded real certain about it."

Miriam nodded, unsure why Naomi was so flustered. "*Ja*, he said something about old troubles. I guess it had to do with his family, but he didn't say anything else."

Naomi hesitated, biting her lip. "You know if there'd been *kinder* here, little ones he might influence away from the faith, we'd likely not have been allowed to have him with us. He's not shunned, of course, but . . ." She trailed off. "It's a ticklish situation when one of our own leaves.

The church frets over it. The new bishop spoke to Joseph about it in town the other day."

"Why?" Miriam darted an alarmed look down the driveway. Reuben had put his letter in the box and was headed back. "Even if the *boppli* comes before Reuben leaves, he could hardly talk a new baby into leaving the church."

"It wasn't the baby the bishop had concerns about. It was you."

"Me?"

"He feels you're in a delicate state, and you've not been able to attend services for so long—they worry over you."

A delicate state. "I'm not simpleminded, Naomi. I can still think for myself."

"I know. Joseph said the same, and it seemed to rest the bishop's mind. But—" Naomi twisted her fingers together. "This walking together business . . . I am probably worrying myself over nothing, but you've been alone out here for such a long time. If things were . . . different . . . you'd be at the age where you'd be meeting fellows, going to singings and such. Reuben's a nice-looking man, and him being unmarried and not far from your age, and you two spending so much time together with the horse and all—"

"Oh!" For a second Miriam didn't know what to say. "Well, you can stop worrying. It's nothing like that. I'm just helping him with Breeze."

"And making him cinnamon rolls," Naomi pointed out softly.

"Those were an apology." And the reason they'd been needed still brought a guilty flush of embarrassment to her cheeks. "Reuben wouldn't be interested in somebody like me anyhow, with all my problems. Nobody would."

"I'm not so sure," her sister-in-law murmured. "I think maybe Reuben's lonelier than he likes people to know, and you're so sweet and so pretty. But he will have to look after his own heart. I'm more concerned about yours. He's a decent man, Sam says, but remember, he's not one of us. He hasn't been for a very long time. I would hate to see you hurt, *schwesdre*."

Reuben walked back within earshot before Miriam had time to reply. So she only nodded.

"We'll be back in a bit. We're walking down to the stream," she said.

Naomi's brow was still puckered, but she nodded and disappeared back into the kitchen.

"So?" Reuben raised an eyebrow. "Ready to show me this creek of yours?"

"*Ja*, sure." She felt even more nervous now. That was Naomi's fault, bringing up such a silly idea. "It's this way."

They walked across the yard to the pasture. He stepped ahead to open the gate and motioned her through.

"It's a good thing we're going now. Aaron will be planting before long," she said.

"Aaron? Is he another brother?"

"No, he's a neighbor. He leases the fields since we don't run dairy cows anymore."

"And he'd be angry about you cutting through?"

"Angry?" Miriam frowned. "No. Aaron is an even-tempered man and a friend. He'd not mind, so long as we were careful. It's just easier walking before the field's ploughed, that's all."

"You do have another brother, though."

She shot him a sideways look. His face was unreadable, and the question seemed innocent enough. Still, she didn't want to talk about Caleb, not with Reuben, a man who'd turned his back on his faith and his family for good. They were all still praying that Caleb would come to see reason.

"I do," she said, then turned the question around quickly. "Do you have any brothers?"

"Only sisters. They're all married now, except for the youngest. Connie—that's the one I wrote the letter to—she's still with my parents."

So Connie was his sister. There was no reason for this news to give her heart a tiny lift, but it did. She felt a sudden sympathy for that last unmarried sister. She knew what it was like to be the only unpicked apple left on the family tree.

She sighed and decided to change the subject.

"How'd you get started working with horses?"

There was a pause before he answered. It ran long enough that she glanced up at his face. A line creased the tanned skin between his brows, and he kept his eyes on the tree line ahead of them.

"I learned from my *daed* mostly. Horses were the family business."

The words were simple, but something lurked underneath them. The way his voice sounded when he spoke of his father didn't sound quite right—as if there was some trouble there.

Whatever it was, she'd not be poking her nose into it. Goodness knows, people had asked her plenty of prying questions over the past year and a half. She didn't like having her wounds picked at, so she wasn't going to pick at anybody else's.

"Sam says you're very good at it."

"He's right."

She glanced up at him, startled. He looked down at her, those wrinkles in the corners of his eyes crinkling deeper.

He chuckled at her expression. "I know, you think it's sinful to say it. But it's the truth. I am good with horses. I always have been. I'm not good at much else, so I might as well take credit where I can."

The church wouldn't agree with him, but his point did seem sensible. People had different gifts. Everybody knew it whether they were allowed to talk about it or not.

"I'm sort of good at quilting," she volunteered. That felt strange to say, and she almost looked behind her to see if anybody else was within hearing distance.

"If the quilt on my bed is any indication, you are really good at it. I don't know much about sewing," he admitted. "But I can tell good stitching when I see it, and the colors are pretty. You sell your quilts, your brother said?"

She nodded. "I do. At the—" She faltered. "At my parents' old store." Her heart beat faster, just saying the words. "Sam and Emma run it now. They sell them for me and bring me the money."

"You should hang some in your brother's workshop," Reuben suggested. "He sells beds and such-like. Folks might want to pick up a quilt at the same time."

"Joseph mostly delivers his work to folks. Not too many people come to the house." A few did and had caused her more than one fright, especially now that Joseph's business was gaining ground.

"I'd wondered why Joseph didn't have his sign out front so folks could see it easier." Reuben sidestepped a patch of soggy ground, greened over with the nubs of barely sprouted grass. "He'd do more business, for sure. But it makes sense. He wouldn't want people popping in unexpected-like and upsetting you."

Miriam stopped and looked at him. "Do you think Joseph's losing customers because of me?"

"Not losing them exactly. Just not going after them as hard as he might otherwise."

Miriam walked on more slowly, her thoughts troubled. She hadn't considered that, but she should have. Of course Joseph would worry about his customers scaring her. The *Englisch* workers who'd refitted the dairy barn for his shop had made her too nervous to come out of her bedroom while they were around. He'd quietly asked Sam to finish up the last of the work, just so she'd not be disturbed.

That was one thing, and trouble enough for her to cause. But to lose business. Miriam's thrifty Amish mind was deeply worried about that.

"That bothers you."

She looked at Reuben. "Of course it does."

"I shouldn't have said anything."

"I'm glad you mentioned it." She didn't know what she could do about it, though. If *Englischers* stopped at the house all the time . . . she might be out in the henhouse or in the barn when they drove up. The very thought made her heart pound.

If she started thinking about such things now, when she was already uneasy, she'd bring on one of her attacks for sure. She needed to change the subject.

"What do you like best about working with horses?"

If he seemed surprised by the abrupt question, he didn't let on. "Animals are honest. They never lie, and it's a rare one that has any real malice in him. And if he does, it's almost always a man's fault for mistreating him. There's goodness to an animal, and I don't like seeing them hurt or fearful. I like to help them, and I'm good at it. There's a satisfaction in that."

"My sister, Emma, would agree with you. In the old days, she was always bringing home a wounded bird or a water-logged squirrel. *Daed* said he never knew what he'd find in the house when he came in for supper."

He shot her a sharp look. "It made him mad, her bringing animals in the house?"

"No." He sure seemed to worry about people getting angry. "Never mad. I mean, he wasn't always happy, like the time she brought in a bat and it got loose in the kitchen. Although I think *Mamm* was the more upset of the two of them. She wasn't afraid of much, my mother, but she ran down into the cellar and stayed there until *Daed* chased the thing outside with the broom." She smiled sadly at the memory. "But they knew it was just the way Emma was. She never could resist a hurt thing, not if she thought she could help it."

She looked up at the man walking beside her. They were inside the tree line now, and the shadows of the bare branches dappled his face. "It sounds like you're that way, too."

"Watch yourself." He put out a hand and caught her arm. She froze, her heart rising up into her throat, and she made a soft, strangled sound.

He released her instantly. "Sorry. You've stepped into some briars." He pointed to a jumble of brown blackberry thorns snagging at her dress.

"Oh! I wasn't looking." She leaned over and began to pull the spiky vines away from her clothing. "Ouch!" She popped a bleeding thumb into her mouth. "Those are sharp."

"Let me." He knelt down and began to pull the briars away.

"Oh, no. I can—"

"My hide's tougher than yours. These little things can't draw blood from my fingers." He glanced up at her with a wink. "Too many callouses and old burns."

She stood there, her thumb in her mouth, watching him nimbly pick away the clinging briars. He was careful, and he seemed not to mind too much about himself. She sucked in a breath when one of the brambles whipped back, scoring a thin red line across his thick forearm, but he paid no attention.

It was strange, having this sturdy man kneeling at her feet, carefully tugging thorns away. It seemed to be doing funny things to her heartbeat. Of course, she was well used to her heart fluttering, but this felt . . . different.

Her thoughts flitted back to what Naomi had said, and her cheeks flushed with a mixture of embarrassment and irritation. Naomi might have chosen a better time for that little talk. It was putting silly ideas in her head.

"There, then." He stood, dusting at his knees and shooting her a rueful look. "I'm not being so kind to your brother's pants."

"Those clothes don't fit you anyhow."

He laughed shortly. "Plain clothes never did, even when they were made for me. Come this way, and you'll be out of the worst of the brambles, I think."

She stepped to the side, her mind lingering on his words. *Plain clothes never did.* She shouldn't pry, but she wondered what had driven this man away from his home and his family.

For Caleb it had been his hot temper—and a thirst for justice that their church wouldn't support. She didn't think it was the same for Reuben—no man who was so patient with animals could be quick-tempered.

On the other hand, there was something hidden there beneath his calm surface. She felt it. It was like watching one of the strong young Percherons, all hitched up and waiting for their chance to pull. Yes, that was the sense she got from Reuben. Power standing by, waiting in harness for a time when strength was called for.

They'd arrived at the creek, and Miriam bit her lip, looking over the burbling water. It didn't look its best now, still brown from the overlong winter and messy with fallen leaves.

"Here it is," she said.

Reuben scanned the scene ahead of them without comment. Of course, there wasn't much to comment on, but she'd always loved this spot.

This creek wandered through the woods, splashing over rocks and fallen branches. She'd always enjoyed the sound of the running water, and on hot days she loved to come here and cool her feet. The overhanging trees were bare now, but in summer they gave lots of shade. Then green moss furred the banks of the creek and crept up a fallen log she liked to sit on. There was a wide spot just here, a pool of sorts. Not deep—it barely lapped over her ankles, but a nice place to wade and splash around.

He glanced over at her. "It's peaceful."

She darted an uncertain glance at him. "It's not much."

She didn't know why she'd thought this was a good idea. Maybe because she'd only been able to come back here a few months ago, and it still seemed like a treat. Joseph had walked her down one day after a snowfall, and she remembered the joy of seeing the creek again, its banks white and sparkling. That was the first time she'd been out of the yard since—

She cut the thought off. "I guess you've been to a lot of fancy places," she said.

Reuben shook his head. "I'm not much for fancy. Places like this suit me better. It reminds me of a pond behind the house I grew up in. I liked going there. It was hidden and quiet. Pretty, too, like it is here."

That made her feel better. "It'll be prettier in the summertime when things are green instead of this ugly brown."

He shrugged. "Brown's a pretty color. So many different shades of it—must be a thousand in horses alone. These browns here"—he leaned, pointing to a spot in the creek bed—"match your eyes just about right."

"Oh!" She couldn't decide if she was pleased that he'd noticed her eyes, or embarrassed that he was comparing them to a muddy creek. She tried a laugh. "Dirt colored, you mean?"

"No." He turned and looked at her, only this time he looked straight into her eyes, examining them. She stared back, feeling like a bird caught in a snare. She couldn't move, couldn't glance away. She could only look back at him.

"They're not dirt colored," he decided. "They're at least four different shades of brown, and there's a sprinkle of green in there, too. It's nice, that. Kind of unexpected. You have real pretty eyes, although I'm sure you've never been told so before." He lifted an eyebrow. "Being as how the church frowns on vanity."

She hadn't been told, and she had to fight the bubble of pleasure his compliment caused.

"Well, eyes are for looking through, not looking at." It was something *Mamm* might have said, and maybe that's why she slipped into *Deutsch*. "It doesn't much matter what color they are as long as they work."

"Eyes are for looking, *ja*." He spoke *Deutsch* easily, naturally. "For seeing the beauty God's put around us." He nodded toward the stream. "Clear, clean water running over smooth pebbles and good, rich dirt." He glanced up. "Bare black branches against a pale blue sky. And a woman's pretty eyes, holding all the best of the browns. It's all beauty, and we do God no service by pretending we don't notice it."

She furrowed her brow. "You're a different sort of a man," she murmured. "Noticing things like that."

"Not so different." He glanced at her and then away. "Plenty of fellows have noticed your eyes, I'm guessing, whether they've the courage to say anything or not."

"I didn't mean that." She felt her cheeks growing hotter. "I meant about the colors and all. I notice them, too. So many different shades, everywhere you look. That's why I love quilting—or it's one of the reasons. I love playing with the colors, mixing them up, putting them side by side to see which ones bring out the best in each other."

He was watching her now. "That's a special gift," he said. "Just like my doings with horses. You should do all you can with it, take it as far as it will go." He looked off into the forest. "Don't let that church of yours teach you any different."

That church of yours. The happiness that had been bubbling inside her went flat. Naomi's words echoed in her memory. *He's not one of us, and he hasn't been for a very long time.*

It made her sad, that—because of what he was missing.

No matter how easy or exciting life might be out in the *Englisch* world, it couldn't possibly compare to the familiar joys of home and family.

She could never do what Caleb and Reuben had done—never. She'd never walk away from her loved ones or, even more important, from her faith. *Gott* had sustained her during this past terrible year. Without Him, there was no way she could have survived her troubles, and yet here was Reuben walking through life alone, without that comfort.

"You talked about God just then, but you don't believe?" When he didn't answer right away, she added, "I'm sorry. I shouldn't ask such nosy questions."

"No," he said. "You're supposed to be getting to know me, and one way you do is by asking questions. It's not your fault there are some I don't much like to answer. There's no way I can look at a horse or these woods and not believe in God. It's the church I don't believe in."

"Why not?"

"For the same reason as most who leave, I reckon. You've a brother who jumped the fence, haven't you? Ask him." When she flinched, he added, "Sorry. I'm not trying to rub salt in a wound. Sam told me something about it."

"Caleb's—we've not seen him for a while."

"He's shunned, you mean."

"He is. He's trying to track down the man who killed my parents."

"Is he, now?" Reuben looked thoughtful. "I can't say I blame him." He shrugged. "Although I'm not surprised the church does. It's long on blame when it suits, but pretty short on it when it doesn't."

She wasn't sure what he meant, but the bitterness in his voice was plain. "You're not shunned, they say."

Reuben stooped to pick up a pebble. He leaned over the creek and threw it downstream. It skipped six times across the water before sinking. "I might as well be. Not that it matters."

"Of course it matters. Caleb's in a terrible fix. His wife, Rhoda, just had twin babies—we had a letter. He doesn't even know about them."

"Would it make a difference if he did?"

"Of course it would! Caleb's let his grief and his temper get the best of him, but these babies will bring him to his senses. He'll come home to Rhoda once he hears. We all believe that."

Reuben kept his eyes on the creek. "It might be better if he didn't. Hot-tempered men don't generally make the best fathers. Come on," he said. "We'd better head back. I'm thinking of making a quick run to town. There are a few things I need to buy."

"All right."

"Want to come along? You could visit that quilt shop maybe."

She'd started up the path, but at his question she stumbled to a stop, surprised. Surely he knew that was out of the question for her. "No. Thank you. I . . . uh . . . don't go to town."

"Yet." He spoke the word firmly as he came up beside her. Together they trekked up the gentle slope back toward the open pasture.

"What?"

"You don't go to town yet. You will someday." He sounded as if there were no doubt about it. "If I'm here when you finally decide you're ready, let me know. I'll be happy to drive you in. We can take my truck or your brother's buggy, whichever suits you best. Standing offer."

"*Denki.*" She wasn't sure exactly how she felt about that.

Her mind played with the idea of going to Yoder's quilt shop with him. She could show him all the colors there, and she had a feeling he'd appreciate them more than anybody else she knew. Even her mother used to get tired of waiting while Miriam dawdled over the bolts of cloth. A man who could see a thousand different browns in horses wasn't so likely to grow impatient while she compared ten different swatches of green fabric to find the exact right one.

But go to town? She couldn't do it. Her heart pounded at the very thought. It was out of the question. She glanced sideways to find him studying her as they walked through the brown grass.

"So? Did our idea work? Are you less feared of me now?"

She blinked, thought about it, and realized something. She'd felt many things on this walk, but not much fear.

No, she'd not felt much fear at all.

"I think it did," she admitted, "at least a little."

"A little is a start."

They reached the barnyard, and he stopped. "I'd best go change," he said, gesturing toward his dirty knees.

"Leave the clothes on the porch," she said. "I'll see to them for you."

"It's not wash day, is it?"

She waved the objection off. "Don't worry yourself. It's no trouble."

"Thanks." He lifted an eyebrow. "Sure you don't want to go with me to town?"

"Not this time."

"You'll let me know, though," he said. "When you're ready."

It was as if he was asking her for some kind of promise. She hesitated a minute, then nodded.

"*Ja*," she said. "I will let you know."

He seemed satisfied with her answer. He gave her a nod and walked toward the old dairy barn.

Miriam watched him go, noting again how the shirt strained over the muscles of his shoulders and his upper arms. Her seamstress mind ticked over the measurements. He needed at least an inch and a half more. Two would be better, and there wouldn't be near that much in the seams, so letting the shirt out wasn't a possibility.

An idea occurred to her. Maybe if she—

"Miriam?" Naomi was on the back steps, one hand resting on her rounded belly, her pretty face puckered with concern. "You coming inside?"

"Oh!" She hurried to the house. "Sorry, Naomi. I was daydreaming."

"*Ja*," Naomi murmured, shooting a worried glance at Reuben as she closed the back door behind them. "That's what I was afraid of."

CHAPTER TEN

❧

YODER'S FABRICS.

Reuben stopped on the sidewalk, peering at the sign on the brick storefront across the street. So that was the place Miriam dreamed of.

It didn't look like much. Curious, he changed direction. Maybe he'd take a look for himself.

He had time. He'd already run his own errands, picking up a few personal items and filling the truck with gas. Nothing important. Mostly this trip's purpose was to get away from the farm, to step back into civilization, into the world he'd chosen.

The world he preferred.

He'd needed the reminder. Since he'd been with the Hochstedlers, old habits had crept back. *Deutsch* expressions slipped out more and more, not only with horses but with people, too. He'd caught himself savoring the smells and the sounds, the quiet rhythms of an Amish day.

And he'd liked how it felt today, walking with a Plain girl. Familiar, like, the way her *kapp* came just to his shoulder, how her face was bare of makeup. And there'd been none of the flirty silliness he'd learned to dodge.

Englisch women confused him. He'd dated a few, but he'd never enjoyed it enough to keep on. They'd made him feel off balance, not a sensation he cared for.

Miriam kept him guessing, but that was different. Being with her felt energizing, like when you were riding a horse and the animal gathered himself for a jump and you weren't sure if he'd clear the fence or you'd take a tumble.

He lingered outside Yoder's for a second, then shrugged and pushed down on the door lever. He'd come this far. Might as well see what was inside.

He hadn't taken three steps inside before he understood why this place was so special to Miriam. The cramped shop was rich with colors and patterns. Bolts of fabrics in all shades slanted against the walls and more stood in the middle of the polished floor.

Yes, Miriam would love this—such colors would draw her like a honeybee to a flower garden.

"Hello." The gray-haired Amish woman stationed behind the counter studied him through round spectacles. "I'm Mary Yoder. May I help you?"

He started to shake his head then glanced around the bright store.

"Do you know Miriam Hochstedler? She buys things here—or her family buys them for her." In most places such a question would have done him little good, but here he figured the Plain folks likely knew one another.

The woman's face brightened with curiosity. "*Ja*, sure. I know Miriam. She's a sweet girl, and a good hand with a needle."

"You know what kind of fabric she'd like?"

The woman tilted her head like an inquisitive bird. "Why would you be asking?"

Reuben frowned. Maybe this place wasn't so different from the community he'd grown up in. All sorts of nosy over things that weren't their business but quick to turn their heads, he'd bet, when folks were having messy troubles and could genuinely use some help.

"I'd like to buy her some, and I want it to be something she can use. But if you don't know . . ." He left the sentence hanging.

As he'd hoped, the shopkeeper's Amish frugality reared its head.

"Oh, I know." Rounding the counter, she made a beeline to a row of green fabrics. "This one here, she'd want." She pulled a pine-colored bolt off its holder. "It's just come in and goes well with other pieces she's bought." Crossing the room, she chose another in a deep, rosy shade. "This one, too. And"—she bustled to the yellows—"this." She glanced over her shoulder. "How much do you want to get?"

"Cut a length of those three. Ever how much she'd usually need."

A gleam of satisfaction lit the shopkeeper's eye. "All right." She carried the bolts to the wide counter and thumped the green one down. She began unrolling it, measuring it against the ruler glued to the edge of the surface. "Miriam making a quilt for you, is she?"

"No. She's helped me with some horse work at her brother's, and I'd like to pay her back." There were those cinnamon rolls, too, but maybe he'd best not mention those.

"Oh, you're that one. The horse fellow. Heard you were coming out." The woman skimmed big scissors along the fabric, cutting a generous swath. She folded it, set it aside, and reached for the rose one. "How's it going with the poor beast?"

"Slow, but that's to be expected, given the shape he's in."

She nodded, squinting through her spectacles as she lined up the fabric's edge with the measuring stick. "Never can tell with horses."

She made quick work of the rosy cloth and followed it with the yellow. "There we are." He waited as she figured out what he owed on a pad. "That's your total," she said. "Tax and all. And . . ." Leaning over the counter, she rummaged in a basket crammed with small rolls of cloth. "I'm sending these scraps along free of charge. Miriam will find good use for them in her quilts. You tell her I miss seeing her here. Of course," she murmured, tucking the fabric into a sack. "I'm glad she's not in town today, given what all's going on."

"What would that be?"

"That movie business! The one they're making about what happened to Elijah and Levonia. They've been blocking the street and causing all sorts of troubles. Sam and Emma closed their store and went home, and I don't blame them."

"They're filming that movie here? Now?"

"Right down the road. Just started today. The *Englischers* running Johns Mill all agreed to it, but there's plenty of us who think it's not so kind, raking such sadness up again. That poor family deserves some peace." She handed him the sack, accepted his money, and counted out change.

He pocketed it absently, his mind sifting through what she'd told him. "*Denki.*"

There was a surprised pause. Then, "*Du bisht welcome.*" Mary Yoder's eyes skimmed his shirt and jeans, her expression remaining carefully neutral.

Uh-oh. He'd slipped up. Reuben moved toward the door.

"You will tell Miriam hello for me, and that I miss her, *ja?*" The woman asked the question in *Deutsch*, testing him.

He almost didn't answer, but she was an older lady, and the politeness his *mamm* had taught him wouldn't stand for it.

"I will tell her," he replied in English. He pushed through the door with a sense of relief.

He peered down the road, focusing on the commotion he'd noticed earlier. The crowd of onlookers had thinned, so maybe things were winding down for the day. Even so, the area was a mess.

Orange cones blocked off the street and the sidewalk, and wooden barricades were set past them with **NO ADMITTANCE** signs posted. Large, unmarked trucks were parked along the side of the road, their cargo areas open and partially unloaded. Small black canopies were scattered here and there, and people gathered beneath each one, intent on various pieces of equipment. He could see a couple of RVs and part of a larger tent farther down, just past the business area. Those seemed to be set up on some *Englischer*'s lawn.

Reuben had no idea what the strange black machinery was—some sort of cameras, he'd imagine—but his eye zeroed in on a trio of horses tethered to one side, their noses in plastic buckets of grain. He walked up the sidewalk, angling to get a better look at them. When he did, he frowned and quickened his pace.

A short man in a striped shirt stood beside the horses, smoking a cigarette. As Reuben came close, he looked up with an annoyed expression.

"You got to stay back," he ordered shortly. "Nobody past the barriers."

"Are you the person responsible for those horses? Because the black mare there needs some attention. She's camped in."

The man shrugged. "Looks all right to me."

"Well, she's not." Reuben set the package with Miriam's material down in a safe spot. Shoving the wooden barrier aside, he walked up to the horse. "See how she's sweating? And how she's standing with her back feet tucked up under her belly?"

"So?"

"She's trying to keep the weight off her front hooves."

"Maybe her feet are sore. She's been working all day,

just like the rest of us." The man shook his head and muttered an expletive. "My feet are killing me, too."

"Yeah, well, the difference is her feet might really kill her if something isn't done about them. Starting with adjusting her diet." Stepping to the front of the horse, he moved the bucket out of reach. His frown deepened as he inspected its contents. Unless he missed his guess, somebody had poured a whole bottle of molasses over the grain.

"Cut it out, mister! Nobody's supposed to mess with the horses' food. Look, you got to get back behind the barriers. They don't let nobody back here unless they work for the film company."

Reuben ignored him. "She shouldn't have any more grain and definitely no more molasses. She's overweight, and that's part of the problem. Give her hay to eat while she's standing around and plenty of water. She's getting too much protein, and she's got laminitis starting."

The man flicked his cigarette ash on the sidewalk and made an exasperated noise. "Like I said, you're not supposed to be back here. These animals ain't none of your business. You can't just barge in here—"

"You don't know anything about horses." Reuben didn't make it a question because it wasn't one. "I do. And I have a feeling these here have been rented or loaned out somehow. Whoever's footing that bill isn't going to want a good horse to go down because you were too foolish to listen to somebody who knows what he's talking about."

"Foolish?" Striped shirt puffed out his chest. "Now, don't start calling names, or—"

Reuben didn't have time for this. "You must answer to somebody. Get him." The man hesitated. "Now."

"I'm going to get security," the man mumbled. "That's who I'm going to get."

"Fine by me." At least that would get this guy out of the way so he could examine the mare in peace.

"We'll see how fine it is." The man stalked off.

Reuben turned his attention to the suffering mare. He ran his hands down her sides, murmuring in *Deutsch* under his breath, getting her used to his touch. Then he pulled a pocketknife out of his jeans and hunched over to take a closer look at the left front hoof.

By the time the handler had returned with a perspiring man in a rent-a-cop uniform, Reuben had scraped through the debris and dung and was pressing on the toe of the foot. The mare flinched.

Yeah. It was tender, all right. Without his hoof knife, he couldn't get down to the bruise itself, but it would be there, purple and angry. He dropped the hoof and straightened.

"Sir," the security guard began sternly. "You're trespassing. You can't—"

"You can save your breath. I already did," Reuben interrupted. "And it's a good thing. Let's quit wasting time. Somebody either owns or leased out these horses. That's who I need to talk to."

"That would be Mr. Sykes, and he's too busy to—"

"Go get him." When the security guard didn't budge, Reuben's patience slipped. "Otherwise, I'll make a call to an animal protection group specializing in horses."

That got his attention. "You're bluffing."

"Try me." He wasn't. He had their number on speed dial. "They'll make a lot more trouble for your Mr. Sykes than I will. He'd rather talk to me."

The uniformed man frowned. "And who are you, exactly?"

"Reuben Brenneman. Here's my card." He dug a business card out of his wallet and held it out.

The guard scanned it. "Go get Sykes," he ordered the shorter man.

Striped shirt looked outraged. "Seriously? Come on. I can't go bothering Mr. Sykes just because some random guy—"

"Do it," the guard interrupted. "Says on the card this fellow's some kind of horse expert, and you know how fussy folks get about animals. It'll be both our hides if something happens to one of these horses and we could've done something to stop it. Go get Sykes and give him this." He handed over Reuben's card. "I'll stay here and keep an eye on things until you get back."

The other man shot Reuben one last irritated look then strode off.

Sykes showed up ten minutes later. He was a middle-aged man with a trim waist and a golfer's tan, wearing a pair of sunglasses that had probably cost as much as Reuben's monthly rent.

"Mr. Brenneman." He offered a handshake. "There's a problem with our horses, you say? Do I need to call a vet?"

"It wouldn't be a bad idea. The mare's the worst off, but they all need better care than they're getting." Quickly Reuben outlined the problems he'd found while Sykes listened with narrowed eyes.

"I don't know much about horses," Sykes admitted. "But I thought Jerry here did."

"Me? I've never looked after a horse in my life," the short man protested. "I was hired to drive a truck, load and unload the equipment, and pitch in wherever I was needed. They said to stand here and watch these three animals until they were needed. So that's what I've been doing."

"I assure you"—Sykes cast his eyes down to Reuben's card to remind himself of the name—"Mr. Brenneman, we want the animals in our care to receive excellent treatment. I appreciate you bringing these issues to our attention. I'll call the local vet and have him come check these horses over. Will that satisfy your concerns?"

"Call him now. I'd like to know he's on his way before I leave."

Sykes nodded toward the guard, who stepped away, pulling his phone out of his shirt pocket. "Done."

"And I'd advise you to find somebody else to look after these horses—somebody who knows something about them. It shouldn't be hard to find someone local, a teenage boy maybe. The Amish folks grow up around horses, and any one of them from age ten up could do a better job than your fellow here."

"Hey—" the short man protested.

"Quiet." Sykes furrowed his brows. "There's a bit of a problem there. Usually when we're shooting on location, we do hire on a good many local folks. We've hired a few here, but no Amish. None of them seem to want much to do with us. I don't mind telling you, it's been very . . ." The man seemed to be choosing his words carefully. "Inconvenient. These horses, for instance. We had to truck them in from two towns over. Normally we'd find a local farmer and rent his horses for a nice little fee. Animal goes right back to his own barn every night, gets picked up as needed for the day's scenes. Everybody's happy. Here it's not working like that."

"I don't suppose it would be, given the subject matter of this particular movie. You're stomping on a lot of feelings, filming this here."

"I'm sorry if people are upset, but me, I'm just here to do a job. But," he added, "I'm certainly not planning to kill any horses if I can help it. What about you, Mr. Brenneman? Would you be willing to hire on with us? Part time, of course. I'm sure you've better things to do than stand around all day waiting until you're needed—and that's what moviemaking amounts to for most of us. But if you could come by every day and check over the horses, maybe advise our people how best to care for them, it would be very helpful."

"No, thanks."

One eyebrow lifted. "You don't even want to hear the terms? I assure you, we pay a very fair wage. For an expert like you, we'd pay extra."

Reuben hesitated, remembering the hefty check he'd just sent up to Indiana. It would be nice to put some cash back in his pocket.

But he shook his head. "Not interested."

His hesitation hadn't gone unnoticed. Reaching into his pocket, Sykes produced his own card. "Take this anyway. Just in case you change your mind."

"Vet's on his way," the guard announced.

"See?" Sykes said. "I'm already benefiting from your advice. You really should let me pay you for it." He wiggled the card.

Taking the thing seemed to be the quickest way to end this conversation, so Reuben did. "Tell the vet the black mare needs a farrier," he instructed as he turned away. "There's probably a local fellow he can call. She'll founder if she's not seen to."

"Says on your card you're a farrier yourself. Think over my offer, Mr. Brenneman," Sykes called.

Reuben didn't answer. He paused to scoop up Miriam's material, thinking he'd toss the card in the trash can by the bench. At the last minute, he tucked it in his pocket, squashing the guilt he felt.

Connie would probably be calling again before long, needing more help. He'd better not burn any bridges. If worst came to worst, Sykes's money would spend as well as anybody else's.

He glanced at the soft package in his hand and thought of Miriam. Her life had been so damaged by the events in this movie that now her biggest dream was to make it a few miles into town so she could visit a small fabric shop.

He'd work for Sykes if he had to, if there was no other way. But he really hoped it wouldn't come to that.

CHAPTER ELEVEN

❧

MIRIAM LIFTED THE LID FROM THE POT OF SIMMER-
ing beans and gave them a stir. Then she leaned over to
check the chicken and noodle casserole bubbling in the
oven.

"Is it done?" Naomi asked as she carried a stack of four
plates to the table.

"Almost," Miriam replied. She saw Naomi glance up at
the clock. "It'll only be a few more minutes, I think," she
added. "Supper should be on time. Or nearly so. I'm sorry.
I shouldn't have tried to squeeze in baking the bread, I
guess."

Her sister-in-law smiled. "Well, the loaf turned out real
pretty, and I know your brother will be happy. Joseph always appreciates a slice of fresh bread at mealtime. It was
kind of you to go to the trouble."

Miriam smiled back but didn't answer. The truth was, it
wasn't Joseph she'd been thinking of. Reuben had mentioned missing his *mamm*'s bread, and she'd thought it

might be nice to offer him some at the first supper they'd share together.

She wasn't about to tell Naomi that, of course. She wasn't in the mood for another well-meant warning. Walking to the creek with Reuben had been pleasant, and she didn't want the memory spoiled.

It felt good to have brand-new, happy memories to think on, even if it was only something so simple as a walk behind the house. Once she'd gotten past her initial nerves, she'd enjoyed having somebody different to trade thoughts with. She was looking forward to seeing Reuben this evening and to treating him to the bread.

Naomi tiptoed to look out the window. "Reuben's driving up, and I see Joseph coming from the barn. We'd best get everything on the table. I'm sure they'll be hungry."

Joseph came in first, and Naomi beamed and slipped into the living room with him for a second of privacy. Miriam busied herself getting the last dishes on the table. She was taking the casserole out of the oven when Reuben walked in the back door, a bag in his hands.

"Hello," she offered cheerfully. "Did you get everything you needed in town?"

"I did." He lingered in the doorway, looking uncomfortable, crinkling the brown paper sack in his hands.

"Supper's ready," Miriam said, "but you've time to run your things out to your room if you'd like to."

"No. I mean, this isn't my stuff. I left all that in the truck for now. This here . . ." Reuben cleared his throat and stepped forward to place the bag on the counter. "I got this for you."

The spoon Miriam was dipping into the steaming casserole clattered clumsily against the dish. "For me?"

"I passed that place you like. Yoder's. I went in, and . . ." He shrugged. "The woman remembered you and said she knew just what fabric you'd want. So I bought you some."

"Oh!" After wiping her hands on a towel, she approached the bag and peeked inside. "My goodness, Reuben. All this is for me?" She glanced at him, astonished. "It's too much."

"It's not all from me. Those little bits, the shopkeeper threw in as a present. The other's are a thank-you for the cinnamon rolls and the help with the horse and all. I hope they suit you."

"They do." The bright colors were beautiful, and she stroked the fabrics with a gentle fingertip. "They suit me real well." She couldn't remember the last time she'd had such a gift, and she didn't quite know what to say. "*Denki-shay*," she whispered.

"You're welcome. You earned it fair and square."

"Good, Reuben, you're here." Naomi came back in, smiling, and Joseph followed a few steps behind his wife. "And just in time. Supper's all ready. That's your seat right there. And look, Joseph! Miriam's baked a nice fresh batch of bread. Nothing would do but she bake it this afternoon."

"Ah." Joseph's eyes lit up as he considered the golden brown loaf on the table. "*Denki*, Miriam. That'll go real good. You'll like this, Reuben. Miriam's bread is a treat. Not," he added hastily, "that Naomi's isn't real tasty, too."

His wife, well used to her husband's way of bumbling his words, only chuckled. Miriam laughed, too, sneaking a look at Reuben as she did.

He was watching her, and the look in his eyes went straight to the pit of her stomach.

"It sure looks good," he said. "I thank you for having me."

"Of course," Naomi said politely. "You're very welcome."

They bowed their heads for the silent grace. When Joseph cleared his throat, Miriam lifted her head, and found Reuben still looking at her. Their eyes met, and she felt her lips tipping upward.

He didn't smile back, but he held her gaze as he reached

for a piece of the bread. As he bit into it, the crinkles in the corners of his eyes deepened, and her heart soared.

He liked it.

"Could you pass the beans, please?" Naomi asked. Miriam blinked and reached for the bowl. When she passed it to her sister-in-law, she saw a worried pucker starting between Naomi's brows.

Naomi's concerned expression lasted all during supper, and it was still there later when she and Miriam were cleaning up the kitchen. Fortunately Joseph and Reuben had already gone out before Naomi noticed the bag of fabric.

"Where did this come from?"

Miriam explained as briefly as she could, watching dismay build on her sister-in-law's sweet face.

"It's nothing," Miriam assured her. "He's only paying me back for making the cinnamon rolls and helping with the horse."

"I see." Naomi tried a little laugh, but her eyes were worried. "Maybe it'd be best if you didn't do him any more favors. You don't want him getting the wrong idea."

Annoyed, Miriam set her jaw. "Well, I'm going to do at least one more. I'm planning to make him a new shirt and hem up a pair of pants so they don't drag the ground."

"I don't know, Mirry." Naomi shook her head. "Are you sure that would be wise?"

"It has to be done. Joseph's shirt is far too small, and you can see how it cuts into him whenever he moves. And hemming the pants only makes sense. He'll ruin them, dragging them around in the dirt and muck of the barn."

"Well, I see what you mean. But maybe I should do it, so there's no . . . misunderstanding."

"That seems silly. You don't sew as fast as I do, and you have plenty of your own work to do. It'd be days before you could get it done. She lifted her chin. "I'll start tonight."

Naomi dipped her head over the dishwater without answering. She looked unhappy, but apparently she didn't plan on arguing further.

That was a good thing. She loved Naomi dearly, and she'd no wish to quarrel, but it felt important to do this for Reuben. After the supper was cleared away, Miriam brought down material and cut out the pieces for the shirt on the kitchen table, ignoring the troubled glances her sister-in-law darted her way.

It had been a long time since she'd felt so determined—or since she'd resisted anything Naomi or Joseph asked of her. She stayed up late into the night, her head bent over her work, and in the morning, she rose early and lit a lamp to sew again.

At breakfast she told Reuben she couldn't help until the afternoon, and after washing the dishes, she ignored Naomi's worried looks and settled down to her work. She'd always been quick with her needle, but she finished Reuben's shirt faster than any she'd done before.

After lunch, she folded it along with the freshly hemmed pants, readying them to take out to Reuben. When she stepped into the hall, the clothes mounded in her arms, she almost bumped into her brother.

"Joseph! I thought you'd be in the workshop."

Her brother cleared his throat. "I thought I'd best have a word with you."

Miriam sighed, exasperated. She was tired, and her neck and fingers ached—and this was silly. "Naomi thought you'd best have a word with me, you mean. About Reuben."

Joseph never dodged the truth, and he didn't attempt it now. "*Ja*, she did. I'm thankful women pick up on such things. I'd not noticed you paying any special attention to him."

"That's because I'm not. At least," she added, "not like Naomi thinks."

Joseph's glance dropped to the clothes in her arms. "Those for him?"

"Yes, they are. He's only wearing these clothes as a

kindness to me. The least I can do is make sure they're comfortable, ain't so?"

"That seems reasonable." Her brother shifted his weight from one boot to the other. "Just be careful to keep things reasonable, Mirry. These last months must have been lonely for you, and you've not had the chances Emma and Caleb and I did as *youngies*, to go out to singings and the like. It's only natural you'd enjoy spending time with a fellow and . . ." He fumbled to a clumsy stop. "But Reuben's not one of us. I'm sorry to speak so plain, but when it comes to this, I'd rather be safe than sorry. I've lost my brother to the *Englisch* already. I've no wish to lose my sister as well."

Miriam's throat closed. "We haven't lost Caleb," she whispered. "Not for good. He'll come back once he hears about the babies."

Joseph's expression hardened. "He'd have heard about them already if he bothered to talk with anybody. Rhoda and her *daed* may not have told him, but the twins are no secret. There's plenty who'd tell Caleb about them given the chance, shunned or not."

Miriam tightened her fingers on the soft material in her hands. She didn't want to talk about Caleb any more. "Well, Reuben's situation is different anyway. He never joined the church, so he's not shunned."

"He never came close to joining, from what I hear. And no, he's not shunned, but he's not seen his *mamm* nor his *daed* since he left home. That's been years, they say. What kind of son does such a thing?"

She didn't answer for a moment. "He talks to his sister. And he sends her letters."

"I'm not sure that's a good thing, not if he's cut the parents out. They may not know of those letters, and such secrets . . ." Joseph scratched at his beard. "They're not *gut*. They can tear families apart, especially if he's tempting her to leave the faith as well. But," he went on, "Reuben's family troubles are his own business. You're the one I'm worried over. Surely you can see he's gone *Englisch* through and through, can't you? No matter what clothes he wears while he's here, his heart left us long ago. When this job's done, he'll be gone again, back to the world he chose."

Reuben gone. Miriam felt a strange pang at the thought, but she lifted her chin. "Then there's nothing for you to worry about, is there? I'm not simpleminded, Joseph."

Her brother's expression softened. "I never said you were."

"You might as well have done, thinking I'm so foolish as to fall for a man outside the church just because he's the first fellow I've spent time with for a while. I've never wavered in my faith, have I? I was the youngest of us all to make the decision to join the church."

"That's so, *ja*," Joseph admitted.

"Besides," she added bitterly, "since I can't even make it as far as town without falling apart, I don't think you have to worry about me jumping the fence."

"I wasn't—I never meant to cast your troubles up to you." Joseph looked miserably uncomfortable. "I don't think of you as simpleminded, and I only ever mean to help and protect you, best I'm able. It just wonders me why you, who was always the meekest of us all, are so determined to befriend a fellow who can't offer you anything but heartache."

He waited, but Miriam said nothing. The truth was, she wasn't sure how to answer that question herself.

Finally, Joseph sighed. "Give me those." He gestured for the clothes. "I'll take them out to the workshop. It'd be best, maybe, if they came from me." He shot her a sharp look. "That's all right, ain't so?"

"Oh." Miriam pushed aside her disappointment. It didn't matter who gave Reuben the clothes, so long as he got them. She handed them over. "If you think that would be best."

"I do. Although . . ." He hesitated, then went on in a

stronger voice. "I don't know that he'll even need them. I'd rather you didn't keep helping with the horse."

"What?" Miriam's ebbing annoyance rushed back. "For pity's sake, Joseph!"

"I know." Her brother looked pained, but doggedly determined. "But it's cutting things mighty close to a line, you two being so *freindlich*. The bishop had questions about this, remember, before Reuben even came."

"But what about Breeze? It might set him back if I stop helping now."

"Probably not. Seems to me things are well started. Reuben should be able to manage from here, if he's as good as everyone says." Joseph paused. "I don't like asking, Mirry, and I can see I'm upsetting you. But I'd appreciate it if you'd go by my wishes on this."

For a long moment, Miriam didn't answer. Joseph truly looked unhappy, though, and her brother had never, in all his life, been anything but kind to her. He'd stood staunchly by her side after their parents' deaths, protecting her and helping her for months. Naomi had, too.

"All right," she agreed sharply. "If nothing else will suit you, I won't help any more. But there's nothing for you or the bishop to worry about. I'm not like Caleb. I could never leave my family and my church."

Joseph winced at her tone, but he answered gently, "*Nee*, you couldn't, Mirry. But this man you're growing so friendly with could—and he did. And after seeing what's happened to Caleb's Rhoda, I can't lie to you, *schwesdre*. That worries me plenty."

With that, her brother clumped down the stairs, the freshly sewn clothes in hand, heading out to get a late start on his afternoon work.

Chapter Twelve

❧

SHE'D SAID SHE'D BE OUT AFTER LUNCH, BUT THERE was no sign of her yet.

Reuben waited in front of the barn, rolling up the sleeves of the new dark green shirt. It fit him perfectly, and it was a relief not to have the other one cutting off his circulation every time he moved.

He'd known, right from the start, that Miriam had made it for him, even though Joseph hadn't told him so. The other man had been oddly abrupt when he'd dropped the clothes off an hour ago.

These are for you. That was all he'd said.

Reuben had put them on right away and gone into the house to thank her. The minute he'd walked inside, as soon as Miriam had glanced his way, he'd known his guess was right. Her eyes skimmed his shoulders, checking the fit, then dropped to the hem of the pants, now hanging neatly above the sole of his boots. She hadn't said anything, but he'd seen a gleam of satisfaction in her eye before she'd turned away.

He'd started to speak, then thought better of it. The atmosphere in the kitchen had seemed strained. It had been so at breakfast as well. So he'd only asked for a glass of water and retreated back outside.

It brought back bad memories, that silent uneasiness. There'd often been tension in the Brenneman house, too, and the safest thing was to keep your mouth shut and get on with your work.

Up until now, it had been different here with these Hochstedlers. He'd dreaded keeping his part of the bargain by eating meals at their table, but it hadn't been unpleasant. In fact, he'd enjoyed it—and not just the food. He'd also appreciated the companionship.

He hadn't fit in anywhere in a long while. His Plain background made him an oddity among the *Englisch*, and they seemed just as strange to him in many ways. Even after living among them for years, there was a lot about them he didn't understand. What he did understand, he didn't always agree with or want to take part in. So he kept to himself mostly. It was a lonesome life, but he'd gotten used to it.

He'd expected his choice to live apart to make him a stranger here, too. But somehow with these Hochstedlers he hadn't felt as awkward as he'd expected.

Well, whatever was troubling these folks, he'd keep his nose out of it. All families had their storms, even good ones, he supposed. He could thank Miriam for the shirt well enough when she came out to work with Breeze.

She opened the door, and he glanced up, expecting her smile. She'd been smiling at him more lately—a big change from when they'd first met. But she seemed to be avoiding his gaze, and his own smile dimmed as he waited for her to come closer.

"You ready? Today we're going inside the stall, remember?"

"I remember, but . . ." She was looking everywhere but at

him, and she seemed tense. Whatever this family squabble
was about, it hadn't blown over yet. It was still troubling her.

And that troubled him.

"But what?"

"I need to talk to you."

"Why don't we talk in the barn? It'll give Breeze a
chance to get used to us before we start work."

She darted a glance at the house. "I think that would be
all right."

That seemed a strange thing to say. After all, they'd
been working in the barn together plenty before now.

As he reached to open the door, he caught her checking
the sleeve of his shirt. He smiled, trying to lighten the
mood. "Don't worry. It fits just right. Although I can't figure how you knew the size to make it."

"I can tell by looking, mostly." She offered a tiny, tight
smile as she ducked into the dim barn. "You're broader
across the chest and bigger in the arms than Joseph, but not
quite so long-waisted. I know his size like the back of my
hand, so it was little trouble to figure out yours."

She must have looked at him awful close, and he'd not
even noticed. That made him feel self-conscious. "Well,
this shirt is a lot more comfortable. I thank you for taking
the trouble."

"You're welcome," she murmured. "It was the least I
could do. You wouldn't be wearing them anyway if I wasn't
so . . . silly."

They'd halted just inside the doorway. Breeze watched
from his stall, his head high and alert, his eyes on Miriam.

"You're not silly. You have your reasons to feel like you
do, just like Breeze there."

"Joseph sure seems to think I'm silly," Miriam muttered.
She darted a look up at him. "Did he say anything? When
he brought the clothes to you?"

Reuben kept his eyes on Breeze, but a wary interest
stirred. Instead of answering, he grunted noncommittally.

Miriam apparently took this as a yes, and she made a distressed noise. "I wish he hadn't! I was going to explain myself why I couldn't help anymore. I've truly not gone as softheaded as he and Naomi think." She blew out a short, frustrated breath.

So the family fuss was over her helping him with the horse? He felt a pang of disappointment. Well, Joseph had never been in favor of the idea in the first place, and apparently something had brought the issue to a head.

Reuben stayed quiet, hoping she'd keep talking.

"It hasn't helped, me being . . . me not being well for so long. Now that *Daed* is gone, Joseph feels it's his place to take care of the family—especially me. And Naomi put this particular idea in his head. It's not really her fault because she's—" Miriam cut herself off short, seeming flustered. "Things worry her just now that normally wouldn't. And there's the new bishop to consider. Everybody walks on eggs for a while when there's a new man in leadership. You don't know yet how he'll react to things."

Reuben studied her. She was agitated, her fingers plucking restlessly at each other in front of her apron.

He still wasn't sure what she was talking about, but she seemed to expect him to say something. Best to avoid the topic of bishops, though. She wouldn't want to hear his opinions about that.

"I have sisters myself," he said finally. "A brother does feel he should look after them, especially if the *daed*'s not . . . able."

"Oh." She looked at him, her hands going still. "Is your father dead, too?"

Dead to me, Reuben almost said, but he shook his head. "No. I'm just saying I can understand Joseph's feelings."

"I'm thankful you do. I wanted so much to keep helping with Breeze, but Joseph . . ." She shook her head. "He's a good person, and he's always been a kind brother to me— even though I've been so much trouble. I don't want to upset him or Naomi by disagreeing with them, and I certain sure don't want to get them in trouble with the church. But it's so frustrating—and pointless. I'm truly not so silly as to—care about you like that."

"What?" The word came out too sharp, and Breeze whuffed a warning.

Care about you. Was that what this was about? Joseph and Naomi thought Miriam had feelings for him?

Miriam flushed a darker shade of pink under his gaze. "I'm not half so *schtupid* as my brother thinks. Oh!" She looked up at him, horrified. "Not that you wouldn't be—or that another girl—an *Englisch* girl wouldn't think you're—" She swallowed, apparently unable to go on.

Breeze had been watching the exchange, and at Miriam's distress the horse blew again sharply.

Thankful for the distraction, Reuben glanced toward the animal. Breeze was growing tense, feeding off Miriam's unease. That wasn't good, and they either needed to calm things down or get out of the barn.

He made those observations automatically, in the back of his mind, while the front of his bewildered brain tried to process what Miriam had told him.

"So your brother's worried we're getting to be—" He cast around his mind to remember what his sisters had called it when a girl and a fellow started taking notice of each other. "Special friends?"

"I told him it wasn't so," Miriam cut him off, embarrassed. "They're just worried because—"

"Because I choose to live outside of the church."

"Yes, but not only that," Miriam hurried to reassure him. "They also seem to think just because I've been kept apart for this past year, I'll fall for any fellow who happens to be handy. But it's not true."

Breeze blew again and paced his stall, pausing every so often to look at Miriam.

Reuben felt like pacing, too. He'd known Joseph was

worried about this arrangement upsetting Miriam, but he'd no idea Joseph was worried about . . . such a thing. And Naomi, too, from what Miriam was saying. He wasn't sure what to say—or feel—about this.

Right now, he only knew one thing. He needed to get off by himself and think things through.

"All this has upset you," he said shortly. "And that's making Breeze nervous. Best to take a break, I think. I'll do no good out here today."

"Oh, no." Miriam bit her lip. "I'm sorry."

He hated the way she apologized all the time—as if everything were her fault. "You've nothing to be sorry for."

"It's a shame to waste the day. Maybe later you could try again."

"I don't think so." He spoke firmly as he led the way back out of the barn. "I've got errands to run in town. Tomorrow morning will be soon enough."

He'd need at least that much time to sort this out—someplace away from this farm where he could think straight.

Miriam stood in the thin sunlight, worrying her bottom lip. Once again, her wavy hair was pulling loose from her bun. It usually did by this time of the morning. She combed it back stern and smooth, but before breakfast was cleared away, the waves had always started to loosen, framing her face softly.

He hadn't even realized he'd noticed such a thing, not until just now. Maybe Miriam hadn't been the only one looking closely.

Good grief. No wonder Joseph thought—

"You'd best get back to the house," he said abruptly. "No sense wasting any more time out here."

"*Ja.*" Miriam blinked. "You're right." She took a step toward the house, then stopped and looked back. "I'll see you at supper?"

"I'll get my supper in town. Let Naomi know, all right?" He waited for her nod, then headed for his pickup. His hand was on the door handle before he realized he'd left his keys in the workshop.

He strode across the yard, his gut churning, keeping his eyes carefully averted from the house. He always had his keys with him.

Always.

The truck had been his first big purchase after he'd left home. Every day since then, it had offered visible proof his old life was over, that he'd never have to go back. He kept his keys in his pocket, handy. When he slept, he left them with his wallet beside the bed, right to hand if he needed them in a hurry.

But when he'd put on these clothes, he'd been distracted. He'd noticed the fine, tight stitching, and he'd imagined Miriam, her head bent over this shirt, sewing it for him. He'd tried to remember the last time somebody had hand-made anything or gone to any such trouble for him—and couldn't.

It had been a long time.

He hadn't even thought of the keys. He'd forgotten them, leaving them carelessly behind, as if they didn't mean anything to him at all.

He snatched the keys from the pocket of his discarded jeans and wheeled around to go back to the truck. He was halfway across the woodshop when Joseph opened the door, coming in to start his day's work.

The two men halted and looked at each other.

Joseph's face was unreadable. He cleared his throat. "You're heading to town, Miriam said?"

"There's no point me trying to work with the horse to-day. Miriam was upset, and that made the horse edgy." He met Joseph's eyes squarely as he spoke.

There was a short silence before Joseph answered. "I've made a muddle out of this. I should have thought things over more careful before I spoke to her. I'm not so good with my words sometimes. Naomi says I hammer tacks with a sledgehammer. It's just that . . ." The other man drew in a long, slow breath. "My sister has suffered a great deal already. I would spare her more pain if I could."

"I'd never have hurt her." Maybe Reuben wasn't sure of much right now, but he was sure of that.

Joseph waited a few long seconds before he spoke gently. "You might not have meant to. But *ja*. I think you would have."

The two men held each other's gazes for a moment longer. Joseph turned away first. He went into the office and shut the door.

Reuben strode out to the truck, gripping his keys so tightly that they cut into his hand. He slid into the pickup and started the engine. As he backed up, he caught a glimpse of Naomi standing at the back door.

She was watching him, a broom in one hand, the other resting lightly on her rounded stomach. Her gentle face looked sad. Her narrow shoulders heaved with a sigh, then she lowered her head and began sweeping the back steps.

As he pulled onto the highway, he expected to feel a sense of relief, but the angry knot in his belly didn't loosen.

He should have seen this coming. The Amish expected people to marry young, and whenever a boy and a girl paid special attention to each other, everybody took notice and started making guesses. The church even nudged folks sometimes, if they stayed single too long.

Marriage was considered both a duty and a blessing, but only when you married somebody within the faith. If the couple was mismatched that way, there was still plenty of nudging—but always in the opposite direction.

And of course, Miriam's brother had jumped the fence, and when that happened, a family—and the church leaders— became extra watchful. A lot of times, once someone left, others followed, one after another, like raindrops dripping off a leaf.

But the idea that somehow he was going to coax Miriam

to leave her family and go back with him to the *Englisch* world—well, that was laughable. Miriam was the most Plain-hearted woman he'd ever met.

She loved quilts and chickens, for crying out loud.

Even so, he liked her. A lot.

He turned that fact over in his mind, approaching it cautiously, like he would an agitated horse.

There was something about her—a shy, modest sweetness that drew him. He'd been around women who shared every detail of their lives freely, but not Miriam. She kept the best parts of her personality—like her sense of humor and her flashes of spunk—hidden, except with those closest to her.

She'd revealed more of herself to him lately. It made a fellow feel special, when such a woman smiled at him or shared a thought. He felt the same when a horse that had been shying away from everybody else stilled for him—a grateful mixture of respect and joy.

Come to think of it, until he met Miriam, he'd never felt that way except with horses.

His eye caught on a familiar black shape in the road ahead. He adjusted his boot on the gas pedal as he carefully skirted the buggy. He'd best mind what he was doing. He'd not been driving much in Amish country lately, and he'd forgotten how quick you could run up on a buggy.

As he passed, he scanned the horse. A fine black Morgan, clopping along at a smart speed, looking well-fed and cared for. Nothing too interesting there. But as he resumed his lane in front of the buggy, he glanced in the rearview mirror, his eyes lingering on the buggy's occupants.

A family—a young one. A man with a sandy-colored beard crouched forward, his eyes fixed on the road. His wife, dark-haired, her bonnet set farther back than would have been allowed in his old community, was holding a baby in her arms and talking to her husband. Whatever she was saying must have been pleasant because the man's lips were curved in a half smile. In the back seat, Reuben glimpsed two small heads, one dark like the woman's, one towheaded like the man's, bobbing along.

A *gut* Amish family heading to town on some errand or other. Nothing special, but Reuben found himself slowing down, his eyes flicking repeatedly from the road ahead to the mirror, focusing on the man's face.

He looks happy, Reuben thought. He shot another look in the mirror just in time to see the man turn toward his wife and say something. Whatever it was, it must have been funny because the woman tipped back her head and laughed.

A blade of jealousy twisted sharply through Reuben's gut. It was unpleasant—and unexpected. He'd never wanted that kind of life, he reminded himself. Never, not for as long as he could remember. He'd seen enough Amish family life at home to sour him on the whole idea. He'd always planned to get out as soon as he could, and he had.

But right now, he had to admit, a part of him would've liked the chance to jog along in a buggy like that, his own young ones safely in the back, the newest *boppli* cradled in the arms of a woman who looked at him with a twinkle in her eye and who laughed at his *dumm* jokes. A woman with brown hair, maybe, and a sassy, pointed chin.

A woman with forest-pool eyes like Miriam Hochstedler's.

"Whoa." He muttered the word out loud as he clenched his fingers around the steering wheel. Where'd that thought come from?

Keeping his eyes rigidly on the road ahead, he pressed on the accelerator. Even after he'd left the buggy and the young family behind, his heart still pounded raggedly. His cheeks stung, too, reddening as if he'd been caught doing something he shouldn't.

Which, truth be told, he had. Joseph and Naomi were

right. He had no business thinking of Miriam that way. And he wouldn't be, he assured himself, if Joseph hadn't put the idea in his head.

He stuck with that excuse for another thirty seconds or so, until he passed the sign announcing the Johns Mill city limits. But in the end he had to give it up.

Because it wasn't true. Joseph hadn't put this idea in his head. It had been there already. He wasn't sure when it had started, but it had been awhile. Maybe even from the minute he'd scooped Miriam up from the straw-littered barn and carried her out into the sunlight.

Not good.

He pulled over and parked in front of a store called Zook's. He needed deodorant and a razor, and this looked like a store that might sell such things. He'd been hoping Sam Christner might be working at Hochstedler's General Store, but a glance in that direction proved otherwise. The movie people were still milling about, and Hochstedler's looked as if it was closed for the day.

He got out of the truck just as a man in Plain clothes passed by on the sidewalk.

"*Guder Mariye*," the man said, his eyes lingering curiously on the stranger. A few other Amish folks were walking nearby, and all of them gave Reuben surprised, quick-and-away glances.

For a second Reuben wondered if they reacted to all newcomers so, but then he froze, looking down at himself. He'd forgotten to change before coming to town. He was still wearing the clothes Miriam had fixed for him.

No wonder the people were staring. Here he was, looking full Amish, stepping out of a pickup truck.

He hadn't just forgotten to change; it hadn't even occurred to him. Something next door to panic quickened his breath. He was losing himself. Wearing Plain clothes, daydreaming over buggies full of children and a wife wearing a bonnet.

He had no serious thought of taking a wife, and given the example he'd been set at home, that was probably just as well. But if he ever did decide to marry, he'd never watch his wife tie a black bonnet on her head. He'd promised himself that years ago.

Reuben stood still for a second as a fierce resolve settled into his chest. When he finally moved, it wasn't toward Zook's. He strode down the street to where the movie folks were congregated.

The black mare was gone, but the two other horses were there. They looked better today, and there was some decent-looking hay and water set out. The man called Jerry jumped to his feet when Reuben walked up.

"Tell Mr. Sykes that Reuben Brenneman wants a word."

Jerry hesitated. "I'm not supposed to leave the horses alone."

"They won't be alone. I'm here. Hurry up."

The man scurried off, zigzagging like a startled squirrel, and Reuben moved to the nearest horse, murmuring softly in *Deutsch* under his breath. The gelding watched him, shifting nervously, picking up on his tension.

Reuben forced himself to breathe deeply and relax his stance. It would be all right, he assured himself. He hadn't slipped far—not yet. This was still fixable.

Sykes walked up, his gaze skimming Reuben's clothing without comment.

"Something else wrong with these horses, Mr. Brenneman?"

"No, and there won't be." Reuben stuck out his hand. "I've decided to take the job."

CHAPTER THIRTEEN

❧

MIRIAM REARRANGED THE REMAINING QUARTS OF green beans neatly on the cellar shelf, wiping the dusty lids and necks of the jars with an old washcloth. As she reached for the pints of cucumber pickles, her fingers faltered.

Pickles had been a sore spot in this house for years. *Mamm* had been a good cook, but she never could make a decent pickle, although she tried almost every summer. It was the only time Miriam remembered her mother's determination failing her. Levonia Hochstedler had never gotten the hang of making pickles, and her attempts had been the brunt of many kindhearted family jokes.

These, though, were good pickles. She and Naomi had put them up last summer. Emma had helped some, too, before she'd gone off to spend the summer nursing Sam's elderly aunt. It had been a bumper year for cucumbers, and they'd stored away a record number of jars.

Miriam picked up a Mason jar, wiped it free of dust, and settled it in a new spot. There were memories bottled right alongside the sliced cucumbers and spices. Some sad ones, because their grief and shock had been barely six months old. Miriam's recollections of that whole summer were stained with sorrow.

Even so, they'd had a right fun time putting up these pickles. Naomi was easy to work with, and she had a knack for making every job pleasant. Doing this familiar summer chore with Naomi had been comforting.

That was the way this world worked, happy and sad, good and bad, all jostled up together. Like right now. She was aggravated with her brother and Naomi for setting themselves against her friendship with Reuben. It was embarrassing, too. As if she weren't old enough—or didn't have sense enough—to know better than to look at him as a potential husband.

That was ridiculous. A fellow like Reuben would never be interested in somebody like her anyhow. He'd had the courage to leave his home and family and make a whole new life for himself among *Englisch* strangers. And here she was, unable to set foot off this farm, not even to visit her own sister a few miles down the road.

Miriam thunked a jar down. It was frustrating to be stuck like this. She was tired of being so fearful. Naomi kept pointing out how far she'd come, but sometimes the progress was hard to see.

She sighed and scooted another freshly cleaned jar into its new spot.

"Miriam?" Naomi's voice echoed down the cellar steps.

Miriam snapped out of her thoughts and began dusting more briskly. "*Ja*, I'm here! Just getting the canned goods organized and making room on the shelves for this year's jars. Canning season will be here before we know it."

"You couldn't tell it by the weather today," her sister-in-law answered. "There's a chilly gray rain that goes right through your clothes. Spring's sure taking its time this year."

Naomi's voice was growing louder. Miriam turned to
see her making her way carefully down the steps.

"Naomi, what are you doing? I could have brought up
anything you wanted, and then you wouldn't have had to
manage those steps."

Naomi laughed shortly and waved a hand. "I can use the
exercise. The truth is, I needed to talk to you for a minute."

"Oh?" Miriam kept her eyes on the jars, glistening in the
dim light of the small windows set high in the cellar walls.
As much as she loved and appreciated her sweet sister-in-
law, Miriam didn't particularly want to talk to her or Joseph. Not today, not until her annoyance had settled a bit
more.

That was why she'd chosen to work on this task this morning. Organizing the cellar was a one-person job, and Naomi
didn't like navigating the steep steps in her condition.

And for good reason. Even though she was going down
and not up, she was breathless when she made it safely to
the bottom.

"That looks real good," she said, nodding at the shelves
Miriam had completed. "Makes it lots easier to see what we
have to use up yet. I hate to interrupt, but Joseph sent me to
get you."

Miriam pushed the last dill pickle jar into its place and
turned to face Naomi. "He did? Why?" And why hadn't
Naomi simply called her up to the kitchen?

Naomi lowered her voice. "Abram is here."

Abram? Miriam's heart halted for a long, painful second. Then it stuttered into a rapid rhythm.

Abram King was their newly chosen bishop, taking the
place of Isaac Lambright, who'd relocated up to Pennsylvania a few months ago to be closer to his daughter and
grandchildren.

An unexpected visit like this was rarely good news. "What
does he want?"

"I'm not sure. I think maybe to talk to us about Reuben." Naomi looked sympathetic, but of course, when a church leader came calling, there was little anybody could do. "He's waiting in the living room."

"You go on up. I'll be right behind you."

For a second, Naomi looked as if she'd like to say something else, but finally she turned and began to make her way slowly up the steps.

Miriam wished she could stay hidden here in the cellar, but of course, she couldn't. After taking a few minutes to breathe deeply and get her nerves as settled as she could, she headed upstairs.

By the time she reached the living room, her heart was lodged in her throat. Abram King was perched on the edge of a chair. Joseph and Naomi were seated on the couch, and there were fresh cups of *kaffe* in front of everyone, and a plate of cookies on the table. Ever thoughtful, Naomi had a cup ready for Miriam, too.

"Miriam." Abram glanced up as she came in, breaking off a serious conversation with Joseph about the unseasonable weather. The bishop was one of the few men in the community who still farmed for his living, so this lingering chill would be a frustration to him. "I am glad you are able to join us."

Miriam shot him an uncertain glance, wondering if that was a gentle reproach for being the last to join the group. She'd known Abram for years, and she'd thought him a nice-enough fellow. When a man became a bishop, though, there was always a nervous time as everyone watched to see how he would handle that responsibility.

There was no reproach in Abram's brown eyes, however, and the chubby man reached for one of the chocolate cookies Naomi was offering with a grateful smile.

"So now that we are all here," Joseph said politely, "what is the matter that brings you to us today?"

Miriam glanced at her brother. She'd heard him telling Naomi this morning that he had a busy day ahead, and he was worried about whether he'd be able to get some pieces finished on time. He wouldn't appreciate being taken away from his work.

She settled in the rocking chair. They waited until the bishop swallowed the bite of cookie in his mouth.

"*Ja*," he said, brushing crumbs off his fingers. "Well, it has to do with this fellow you've got working with your horse."

"Reuben." Joseph supplied the name.

Miriam's heart quickened. Abram had worried about Reuben's influence on her from the beginning, but Joseph had assured him there was no reason to be concerned. Of course, since then Joseph had changed his mind. Had word of that somehow gotten back to the bishop?

She studied her hands clasped in her lap, and waited, wishing her cheeks would stop tingling. She wasn't guilty of anything, but no doubt she looked it. Panic started to build.

"That's him," Abram was saying. "I hear he showed up in town yesterday afternoon wearing Plain clothing. Was that your doing?"

Miriam looked up, but the question seemed to be directed at Joseph. Her brother looked as confused as she felt.

"I guess maybe so," Joseph admitted. "He asked for the loan of some clothes, and we shared what we had. We didn't see the harm in it. He was raised Plain, but he left before he joined the church."

Abram nodded, reaching for a second cookie. "This I know already. It's the clothing that has me confused. He was driving his truck, they said, and talking with the—" The bishop cut a sharp glance at Miriam. "Talking with some *Englischers* in town. But he wasn't wearing *Englisch* clothes. He asked for these, you say?" When Joseph nodded, Abram asked, "And why would he do that?"

There was a short silence before Miriam spoke up. "Because of me."

The other three looked at her in some surprise. Nobody, she realized, expected her to speak up. She rarely did when anybody extra was in the house—anybody she didn't know well. With the bishop sitting across from her—no doubt Joseph and Naomi thought she'd be too nervous to say a word.

She felt surprised herself.

She looked over to find Naomi watching her. Her sister-in-law's mouth stayed straight and serious, but her eyes twinkled at Miriam. *Gut for you*, she seemed to be saying.

The bishop cleared his throat. "And why was that?" he asked in a carefully soft voice.

The extra gentleness annoyed her a little. People had behaved like that around her for almost a year and a half now, treating her with the indulgence usually given to small children and those who'd been born special.

She was neither of those things, and although she knew she should appreciate the kindness, instead she felt irritated.

"He needed me to help with the horse," she explained. "And his *Englisch* clothes flustered me. So he asked Joseph for the loan of some clothes to see if it would help."

The bishop listened, cookie crumbs glistening in his beard. "And was it helpful?"

"Yes."

Abram leaned back in his chair, which squeaked a soft protest. "Why do you think that is?"

Joseph answered before she could. "*Englischers* make Miriam *naerfich*," he explained, although Miriam couldn't imagine why any explanation would be necessary. Abram might be new as a bishop, but he was no stranger to their community. He was well aware of what had happened and how Miriam had reacted to it.

"*Ja*," he was saying now. "This I know. But the man

himself—this Reuben. He is the same, no matter what clothes he has on, ain't so? Why would it make a difference if he dressed as one of us, if he isn't one of us?"

Nobody seemed to know what to say. Finally Naomi murmured, "Fears aren't always sensible."

Abram nodded. "This is so," he agreed. "All right. You have answered my questions. Now, I would like to speak to Miriam herself, if I could."

Joseph and Naomi looked at each other then got slowly to their feet.

"*Ja*, sure," Joseph said, although he didn't look comfortable with the idea. "I'll be out in the workshop, Abram."

The older man nodded. "I'll stop by there before I leave. My wife has been wanting a table for our living room anyhow, and since I'm here anyway—"

"Fine, sure. We'll settle that up," Joseph said. He threw one last concerned look in Miriam's direction, then allowed Naomi to draw him out of the room, shutting the door quietly behind them.

Miriam turned toward Abram, her heart pounding, waiting to hear what he had to say. He considered her kindly.

"I hope this doesn't make you nervous, me wanting to talk to you privately," he said. "I don't wish to upset you."

"I am all right."

She was nervous, but that wasn't surprising. People were uneasy when the bishop—or more often one of the deacons—came calling because it was almost always to talk about something unpleasant. A transgression, usually, something a member of the household had done that crossed church rules in some way.

In their household it had generally been Caleb in trouble. The deacon's buggy had turned in their drive more than once during his growing-up years, and it had never been a happy sight to see.

Here comes that fussbudget buggy again, Caleb would

grumble. The memory brought tears to Miriam's eyes. She missed her funny, hardheaded brother.

Abram cleared his throat. "So," he said. "This Reuben. You say you've been working together?"

"The horse is easier with me," she explained. "So he asked me to help."

Abram nodded. "And in this time you've spent together, has he told you anything about his family?"

"Not much. I know he has a sister because he got a letter from her."

Another nod. "I have some relatives in the area he comes from. My cousin said nobody was surprised when this Reuben decided to leave. Except his parents, of course. That's the way it is oftentimes. The family is the last one to see it coming. I'm sure you know this because of your own brother. When folks are close to us, we don't always see them so clear."

He spoke sadly, and Miriam suddenly remembered that Abram's stepson had jumped the fence years ago. His wife, Ann, had been widowed young, and her oldest son had slipped away one night and never come home again.

"Caleb," she said, "was always strong-minded."

"Our Michael, too," Abram said. "And this Reuben, from what I hear, was the same. He and his father did not get along. Ivan Brenneman is a hot-tempered man, they say, and that and a stubborn son don't mix so well. We can only pray our prodigals will return to us. And of course, we hope that *Gott* puts people in their paths who will nudge them toward home." He smiled. "I'm thinking maybe you could be such a person, Miriam, for Reuben."

Miriam had picked up her coffee, but now she set it down so fast that it sloshed onto the table. "I'm sorry," she said, dabbing at the spill with a napkin. "I . . . I don't understand."

Abram watched her, his head tilted to one side like a friendly dog. "Reuben's had nothing to do with his family since he left. Well," he amended, "his parents have not heard from him, nor has he come back to visit. Not once in all these many years. I didn't know he was writing to a sister."

"He's not shunned," Miriam pointed out. "So there's really nothing wrong in that, is there?"

"No, no. In fact, I think it is a good sign." Abram leaned forward in his chair, clasping his hands together. "As is his willingness to put on Plain clothes again. I believe *Gott* is at work, turning our friend's heart back toward the church."

Remembering the few remarks Reuben had made about the church, Miriam wasn't so certain. "I don't know," she began.

"No, we can't know for sure. But from what I see, we've reason to hope. It may be that *Gott* is even using your own misfortune as a tool in this. And that," he said, "is what I came here to talk to you about."

This conversation had taken a turn she'd never seen coming. Miriam had an unexpected desire to laugh, and she pressed her lips sternly together. "Oh?"

Abram's face was serious as he nodded. "We should always try to bring a lost friend back into the fold when we're provided an opportunity. I would want someone to do that for our Michael. I'm praying somebody is, at this very moment. And of course, you would feel the same about your brother, ain't so?"

She would. "What exactly do you want me to do?"

Abram beamed. "Only to be kind and look for the openings *Gott* gives you to speak. If Reuben has a soft spot for his sister, as seems to be so, then perhaps he might be open to listening more to you than to me. Not that I won't be doing my part as well. I have some ideas of my own."

"And you'd like me to do this while we are working together with the horse?"

"That would seem natural, I think. Encourage him,

perhaps, to come to church. We are meeting next at Aaron Lapp's home, just next door. I am hopeful since it is so close, you might also be able to join us."

Miriam wasn't so sure about that, but one thing did seem certain. If the bishop was asking her to spend time with Reuben, Joseph and Naomi could hardly object. Still, she doubted she could make as much difference as Abram hoped. "I am happy to try, but I'm not sure how much good it will do."

"It may do no good at all. Only *Gott* knows. We will see. However," Abram went on, "you must take care. When we come alongside those who have lost their way, we must be watchful so we do not lose our own footing. From what I have heard of you, I have no doubt that you will guard your heart carefully."

"Of course," Miriam murmured.

The bishop stood. "Good. Since that is all settled, I'll go have a word with your brother about my wife's table." He stooped to snag the last cookie from the plate.

Miriam stood as well. "I'll walk out with you."

In the kitchen Naomi was standing by the stove, her sweet face lined with concern. She seemed surprised to see Miriam and the bishop walk in together.

"I was about to bring in more *kaffe*." Her eyes darted to Miriam's. *Are you all right?* She seemed to be asking.

She was, Miriam realized with a start. She hadn't experienced a single real moment of panic during the entire conversation.

She wasn't sure why. Maybe because she still had trouble thinking of Abram King as a bishop, so he hadn't seemed very intimidating. Whatever the reason, for the first time in over a year, she'd not dissolved into an anxious puddle in a stressful situation, and nobody had needed to rescue her.

She was as surprised by that as Naomi was.

"Thank you." Abram waved away the offer of coffee

with a smile. "But no. I am going out to your husband's workshop, and then I must be on my way home."

"It has been a good visit," Naomi said politely. "You must tell Ann hello from me."

"From me, too." Miriam smiled and lifted her chin. "When you see my brother, please let him know what we've talked about. And tell him I'm going out to the barn to help Reuben with Breeze."

CHAPTER FOURTEEN

"EASY, NOW," REUBEN MUTTERED AS HE WALKED around Breeze in the stall. He held the lead rope in one hand and kept the other on the horse's flank, stroking with a firm pressure. It was time to move close and get him used to being touched—whether Breeze liked it or not.

Breeze didn't like it. He danced sideways, and Reuben looped the lead rope around one of the new planks, tying it off tight so he could use both hands. He moved back to the horse, talking steadily under his breath, never lifting his hands from the horse's side. He kept murmuring, gliding his fingers down the horse's scarred ribs.

As Reuben's hands met the raised marks, Breeze snorted. He shifted, trying to move away, but the rope attached to his halter foiled him.

"It's all right," Reuben muttered. "Nobody's going to hurt you."

Breeze snorted again, plainly unconvinced. The horse was terrified, and that meant going slow and being persistent.

Cautious, too. He'd worked with plenty of frightened animals, but this one was in a class by himself. Reuben had never had a horse kick or bite during this part of the training. Usually they were past that point by now, but he was keeping a close eye on Breeze.

Hopefully, the horse would settle, but Reuben was prepared for things to go in the opposite direction, too. It might not even be such a bad thing. Sometimes you just had to sit back and let the storm break. It would either clear the air or destroy everything in its path. You never knew ahead of time. You had to wait and see.

Breeze tossed his head and tried another sidestep. Reuben moved with him, and the rope gave little play. The horse blew irritably again, looking toward the door.

"*Ja*, I know." Somehow when he was working with horses, the *Deutsch* always slipped out. Maybe because it's what he'd spoken as a *youngie*, when he'd first learned this trade. "You want to know where she is. It's worrying you, her not being here."

He'd reached the horse's rump. He kept the pressure firm as he stepped around the back and started on the other side, trailing up and down the legs. Only as far as the hock for now. His instincts warned him working with the feet was best kept for another day.

Reuben moved back toward Breeze's head. As he'd expected, it was like starting over again. New side, new struggle.

Breeze stepped away, pulling the short rope tight. He snorted, throwing another anxious look at the barn door.

"Sorry. I'd rather her be here, too, but I don't think she's coming." And given his new commitment to keep a careful distance, he certainly wasn't going to ask her to. "We're both just going to have to deal with it."

As if Breeze understood his words, the horse fought the rope with renewed determination. Reuben stayed put, hand on Breeze's flank, gauging how close to the tipping point the animal was.

Close. There came a point with horses when you saw all reason leave them, and Breeze was almost there. Once that happened, the training session would turn into a battle of wills and a waste of time. Reuben needed to end on a positive note, so it might be wise to close out this lesson soon.

That annoyed him. It hadn't been near long enough, and they hadn't made much progress. If Miriam had been here—

But she wasn't, and it did no good to wish things different than they were.

"All right then," Reuben murmured over and over. It didn't matter what you said, just the tone. He ran his hand up the horse's ribs, moving toward the head. "We're nearly done for now, and no doubt she'll slip out here once I'm safely away. Maybe that'll settle you some, and we can try again later."

Suddenly the horse's ears swiveled forward and his eyes brightened. And Reuben knew. He knew even before the door cracked open.

Miriam had come, after all.

She hadn't made it four steps into the barn before he knew something else, too. She was in a very different mood.

Her chin was tilted at a new angle, and there was a new certainty in the way she moved. She came closer without hesitating, and Reuben lifted an eyebrow.

He'd seen this before. When a horse had worked past something and knew it, that's when you saw that little strut, that proud tilt of the head. Those clues meant a milestone had been reached and the next stage of the training could commence.

Sometimes that fresh confidence made the next part even tougher, but it was a success all the same.

Breeze's attention was on Miriam now, his head high and alert and his ears swiveled forward. He whickered softly as she approached.

"How's he doing?" she asked.

"He's been doing his best to give me trouble. Or at least

he was until you showed up." He paused. "I thought you wouldn't be helping anymore."

"That's all changed now. I can help as much as you need." She looked over the horse's nose and met his eyes. "If you still want me to."

The shy hopefulness in her voice made his stomach shift. *If he wanted her to.*

He did. That was the problem.

The part of his brain that still had a grip on logic was sending up warning flares. *Best to keep a safe distance. The old life is putting out feelers, like ivy. Remember how you felt looking into that buggy? If you're not careful, you'll be dragged right back in, and this time you'll never get yourself free.*

"Doesn't matter if I want you or not. This horse wants you," he said. Then he winced at the gruffness in his voice.

Miriam didn't appear to notice. She'd reached out to stroke Breeze. The horse not only allowed it, but he bumped his nose up into her palm.

Reuben cleared his throat awkwardly. "And good for you, by the way," he said. "Standing up to your brother must have taken courage."

She glanced at him again. "I didn't have to. The bishop came by. It was his idea that I should keep on helping you."

The bishop? Reuben's eyes narrowed. He didn't like the sound of that.

"*Ja*," he said dryly. "Nobody has much of a choice when the bishop gets involved. Although why he'd care about horse training, I can't imagine. Seems likely there'd be more important matters needing his attention."

"I thought you'd be glad, but you're angry." Miriam made the observation quietly. "Why?"

He shrugged. "I don't like bishops telling me what I can and can't do."

"Abram isn't telling you anything," Miriam pointed out.

"He was only talking to me. And," she added with a laugh, "to Joseph, whether he knew it or not."

An idea occurred to Reuben. "Did you go over your brother's head and ask the bishop to weigh in on this?"

"No." She didn't add *of course not*, but he heard it in her tone. "I'd not do a thing like that."

"Why not?"

"It would make trouble for Joseph." Her hand stilled, cupped over Breeze's nose as she considered him. "Besides, this is my brother's home now, and he's the head of it."

Reuben flinched. He'd heard that explanation before. He didn't like it now any better than he had when his *mamm* had given it, but he'd learned there was little point in arguing. "I see."

Miriam studied him. "I'm not sure you do."

Breeze shifted his weight and blew softly. He'd calmed some when Miriam came in, but their back-and-forth was making him uneasy again.

"You're too late this morning anyhow. I was just stopping for the day." Reuben gave the horse one last stroke, unclipped the lead, and offered Breeze a cookie from his pocket.

Breeze hesitated only one sulky second before accepting it. Another improvement. He opened the gate to the paddock, and Breeze trotted outside with an air of relief.

Miriam stepped aside as Reuben unlatched the stall door. "Joseph is only trying to look after me."

"So you've said."

"I don't know why you're being so short. I never wanted to stop working with Breeze."

"But that made no difference, did it? Not until the bishop stuck his nose in."

He shouldn't have said that. He had no business arguing with her about this, especially not now, when he was feeling so annoyed.

He shouldn't even be annoyed. But he was, and that irritated him even more. "Like I said, there's nothing more to
do today. You might as well go on back to the house."

"Reuben, wait."

As he passed her, she reached out and put a hand on his
sleeve. He should have brushed on by her, gone on to his
room, and changed clothes so he could get to town—get
away.

Instead he stopped where he was, the gentle pressure of
her fingers through his shirt doing funny things to his
heartbeat.

That light, casual touch was something that would mean
nothing in the *Englisch* world, but here . . . Women didn't
do such things, at least they hadn't in the community where
he'd grown up. His sisters would never have reached out to
touch a man's arm like this, not unless he was a close
relative.

Or a sweetheart.

That thought slammed his heartbeat into its highest
speed. Against his better judgment, he looked into Miriam's eyes.

The light in the barn was dim today. He couldn't even
tell the color of her eyes—not that he needed to be reminded of that. But even in the uncertain light he could see
what he was checking for.

Words came too easy to mean much. Reuben had spent
years looking past them, searching for what was real. And
what was real in Miriam's eyes made him forget to breathe.

There was caring there, but this woman was softhearted
enough to care about a horse that everybody else had given
up on. She'd care about anybody she got to know—as a
sister or a friend.

That wasn't what had made Reuben's breath stall out in
his chest. It was the caring combined with the tremble in her
fingers, as if she were amazed at her own daring. It was the
way her breath was coming too fast, and the little wobble of

her lips that grew more noticeable when his gaze dipped to them.

Truth dawned with a slow, guilty chill.

Naomi and Joseph had good reason to worry about the two of them spending so much time together.

And so did he.

Because whether she knew it herself yet or not, Miriam was starting to see him differently. If he were to lean down and kiss her now, she'd let him. That certainty made his breath come back in a rush, and for a dizzying second he couldn't think straight.

Selfishness rose like a rearing horse, fighting the slim rope connecting him to sanity. His head dipped toward her, just a little, and he saw her eyes flare and then darken. He'd seen Miriam nervous lots of times, but this wasn't panic. It was something sweeter and more hopeful.

She'd probably never been kissed before.

That realization hit him like a bucket of cold well water. He stepped back.

"Reuben." The sound of her whispering his name went down his spine like chilly fingers "Wait."

"I've got to get to town." He wasn't even fully aware of what he was saying. He was locked in a battle of wills—half wanting to run, and half wanting to kiss this woman until she forgot about brothers and horses and bishops.

"Now? Why?"

"I've work to do."

"Work? In Johns Mill?" She frowned. "What work?"

It took him a minute. He didn't want to tell her. But if he was right, if Miriam was starting to feel something for him, he had to. It had been bad enough when he'd only had to worry about his own feelings crossing the lines drawn between them.

But now . . . if he let this go on, Joseph was right. Miriam would end up hurt. Best to put an end to it now, for both their sakes.

Reuben set his jaw and looked her in the eye. "I've taken another job, helping with that movie they're making in town."

Her face went white. She looked as shocked as if he'd slapped her. He'd seen the same expression on his *mamm*'s face more than once after his *daed* had raised a hand to her.

"You . . . did what?" Her fingers tightened on his arm. Then she let go and took a step back. "But you know how we feel about . . ." She swallowed. "Why would you do such a thing?"

Because I needed to put a wall between us. Because being with you makes me want to forget things that I promised myself I'd always remember.

"They pay well, and I need the money."

She stared at him, such bewildered hurt on her face that he couldn't stand to look at her.

"Tell Naomi I'll not be back for supper," he managed. Then he ducked his head and got out of the barn as fast as he could.

CHAPTER FIFTEEN

❧

THE NEXT MORNING, MIRIAM CAREFULLY PACKED A
large tub of church peanut butter spread and several jars of
pickles into a cardboard box. Six foil-wrapped pies waited
on the kitchen table, three Dutch apple, and three chocolate.

"Thank you so much." Neighbor Katie Lapp had driven
over in the buggy this morning to pick up their contribution
to the lunch she'd serve after church. Her daughter Sarah
toddled around the table, looking adorably sweet in a tiny
pink dress.

Naomi kept sneaking glances at the child and smiling.
Miriam knew what she was thinking. Soon there would be
a little one in this house again. They were all looking forward to that.

"Miriam, have you decided if you're coming to church?"
Katie asked. "We talked about it, you remember, and you
thought you might could manage it, since it'll be right next
door."

Miriam kept her eyes on her work. "I don't know."

"Well, it'd be an easy first step for you." Katie gave Miriam's arm a comforting pat. "It's high time you were back. We've missed you."

Miriam managed a smile and fussed over resettling the items, threading an old dish towel through the jars so they wouldn't rattle on the ride home.

Katie was right. She did need to get back in church. Not long ago, it had seemed possible. She'd been feeling so much steadier lately. But when Reuben had told her he was working for the movie people, everything had changed. Her feet had been swept out from under her again.

She'd known the movie was filming in town. Joseph and Naomi didn't talk about it in front of her, but she'd overheard snippets here and there. Katie had even chattered about it this morning until Naomi had shot her a warning look. But mostly Miriam had been able to ignore the whole thing.

Until yesterday. It had felt—harsh, the way Reuben had told her about his job. Almost as if he'd hurt her on purpose. She'd not expected such a thing from him, and the pain had lingered through the night and into the morning.

"I don't think we're doing near enough," Naomi was telling her cousin. "We should be over helping you scrub the house."

Katie waved a hand. "Aaron's cousins are helping me with that. Besides, you need your rest these days."

Naomi laughed, her eyes straying back to Sarah. "So do you," she pointed out.

Katie lay a hand on her own middle, only slightly rounded yet, and smiled. "All the more reason to let the *maidels* do the heavy work. I've got half the unmarried girls in the county helping, so you and I can rest easy. Aaron's hoping for a boy this time, but I wouldn't mind having another girl before the boys start coming. Daughters make such good helpers. You're blessed to have Mirry here. She'll be a wonderful *gut* help to you as your family grows."

Naomi nodded quickly. "I'm thankful for her, of course. Miriam, would you mind going down to the cellar for another jar of sweet pickles? That'll finish us up, I think."

"What's here is fine," Katie protested.

"It's no trouble. I'll be right back." Miriam headed down the steps with a feeling of relief. Naomi—ever sensitive to other people's feelings—had been extra kind today.

She'd probably guessed it was hard for Miriam to hear herself lumped in with the teenage *maidels* who came to help when there was extra work to be done. And it did sting, Katie speaking as if Miriam had little hope of a home and a family of her own.

Because, of course, she didn't.

She scanned the newly organized shelves. Even though she'd rearranged the jars herself, she still looked in the wrong place first. She probably would for weeks, until the changes slowly became familiar.

Changes were like that. Hard at first, but you got used to them. Even the not-so-nice ones.

Like Reuben. Her mind flitted to him, like it did at any opportunity. It had been a big change, having him on the farm. At first, he'd frightened her to death, but she'd grown used to him. She'd liked him, even.

Now she wasn't sure how she felt about him. She probed her feelings cautiously. She was hurt, for certain, and confused.

But not afraid. Her stomach had fallen when she'd caught a glimpse of him out the window earlier, and her heartbeat had rattled, but it wasn't fear she'd felt.

This was more like the wistful sadness she felt when she sent a quilt off with Emma to be sold, something she'd spent weeks working on. Sometimes when a project was done, she'd spread the finished piece out on her own bed just to look at it. Soon, though, it was time to fold it up and send it to the store. Afterward she never saw it again.

That was how she felt about Reuben—as if something special, something she'd worked hard on, was lost to her.

She blinked and chose a jar of sweet pickles. She shouldn't be woolgathering. No matter how many *maidels* were helping her, no doubt Katie had plenty to do at home yet. Jar in hand, Miriam headed back up the steps.

When she was almost to the doorway, she heard Katie say, "That Reuben fellow who's working here, Naomi. How much do you know about him?"

From the quiver of excitement in Katie's voice, she likely had some story to share. Naomi's cousin was a sweet, kindhearted woman, but she did love to carry tales.

Naomi cast a worried look in Miriam's direction as she came into the kitchen. "Not too much. He's Sam's friend, and he's made good progress with the horse."

"*Ja*, that's to be expected. His family's known for horse work, although they say his father has such a short temper, he runs off half his customers."

"People say all sorts of things." Naomi observed lightly. "You know, we can set the pies in the box, too, on top of these jars. It'll make for easier carrying."

"Good idea," Katie agreed.

Miriam began filling the sink with sudsy dishwater to wash the teacups from their visit. Maybe Katie would take a hint and be on her way.

She should have known better. Katie wasn't easily discouraged when she had a juicy tale to tell. "I've heard this Reuben has a temper of his own. I hope you'll be careful of him, both of you."

"Reuben's no danger—not to us, nor to anybody else." Miriam spoke tartly, keeping her eyes on the dishes. She liked Katie, truly she did, and Reuben wasn't high in her good graces at the moment. But after everything that had happened to her family, she'd no fondness for gossip, either.

"Miriam's been helping Reuben with the horse," Naomi murmured.

"Oh." Katie conveyed a world of surprise into the syllable. "I'm sorry, Mirry. I didn't know you two had become . . . friends." She sent a loaded look in Naomi's direction.

"The horse likes Miriam—only her," Naomi explained shortly. "So Reuben asked if she would help him with Breeze's training. The bishop's been consulted, and he feels it's all right."

Katie nodded, the concern fading from her eyes. Anything the bishop approved of couldn't be too worrisome.

"Well, you'd best be careful, still. My Aaron saw Reuben working with a horse once, years ago when he was buying a cow from an *Englischer*. This Reuben fellow was out in the paddock with a great big horse, one of the biggest Aaron had ever seen. His hoof would be the size of your head, almost. The *Englischer* said the animal was mean and had given a sight of trouble. But there Reuben was, jerking that horse this way and that as if he were nothing more than a stubborn pony. He had no fear, Aaron said, and he bullied that poor animal until—"

"I don't bully horses."

Reuben was standing in the doorway leading to the back porch.

Katie threw Miriam and Naomi a startled glance. "I didn't . . . my husband said—"

Reuben waited, his face impassive, until she floundered to a stop. "If it was me your husband saw, he was mistaken. Some of the things I have to do can look rough if you don't know horses well enough to understand what you're seeing."

"Oh!" Katie's cheeks flushed pink at the dig to Aaron's knowledge of horses, but she offered no argument.

In spite of her sore heart, Miriam found herself fighting a smile. It wasn't everybody who could silence Katie Lapp.

"Naomi," Reuben said, "Joseph was coming in, but he's

got a customer here to pick up a bed frame. He doesn't want you carrying anything heavy out to the buggy. I offered my help." He nodded at the box full of food. "That what needs to go out?"

"Yes." Naomi looked relieved. "That's kind of you, Reuben. Thank you."

Reuben's gaze had lit on little Sarah, who looked up at him with round eyes. His expression softened. "You're welcome," he said.

"Miriam and I could have carried it," Katie pointed out.

Reuben flicked her a quick glance. "You probably shouldn't be carrying anything heavy, either. I don't mind anyhow." He hefted up the box. "I'll set this in your buggy."

"*Denki*," Katie stammered, her cheeks going even pinker at the unexpected reference to her condition.

"And you'd best get your *mann* to look to that gelding of yours," he called over his shoulder. "Unless I miss my guess, he's got a belly full of worms."

With that parting shot, he was out the door.

An uncomfortable silence fell over the kitchen. As usual, Katie was the first to find her tongue.

"Well," she said. "He's sure not long on manners, is he?"

"The dishes are done, Naomi," Miriam said. "I'd best go out and see if Reuben needs any help with Breeze this morning. *Mach's gut*, Katie. It was nice to see you and Sarah."

"You, too. I'll be praying to see you again tomorrow at church."

Miriam walked to the barn, her hands clenched at her sides. Katie was a good, kind neighbor, she reminded herself. Everybody had their little faults, and Katie's just happened to be that she loved to carry tales.

Reuben was in the stall again with Breeze, muttering under his breath and running his hands along the horse's body. Both horse and man looked up as she entered, but Reuben quickly looked away again.

"I didn't think you'd come today."

"Neither did I," she admitted, "but here I am. Do you need my help or not?"

He hesitated. Then he blew out a breath and nodded. "If you're willing, it could be useful. He needs to get used to more folks laying hands on him, and you'll be the easiest one to start with."

"What should I do?"

"Come in the stall and go along his other side. Just like I'm doing, see? Rubbing your hands along his ribs and up and down his neck and legs." Reuben demonstrated. "Do it firm, like, so he feels it. Don't take your hand away from him, even if he tries to move away."

"I understand." Miriam came into the stall and stood on Breeze's opposite side. The horse went suddenly tense. It had made him uneasy, she realized, her coming so close. He'd been calmer with just Reuben.

The change gave her a quick, jealous pang, but she ignored it. "Breeze is learning to trust you."

He glanced at her over the horse's back and quickly away. "That's the point of all this. For him to learn to trust again."

"It's not an easy thing."

"No, it isn't." There was a short silence as they worked their way down the horse's back toward his rump. "It was true, what I told the woman in there."

"Katie?"

"*Ja*, her. I don't bully horses."

"I never thought you did. Likely it wasn't even you Aaron saw anyway."

"It might have been. Her *mann* could have seen me training one who needed to learn who was the boss, maybe. That has to happen if the horse is to be any use to anybody. It does look rough sometimes, but it's necessary. It'll happen with this one, too, sooner rather than later. Getting them to trust you is the sweeter part. Teaching them they're not the boss isn't so gentle."

"I wouldn't think so. Horses probably don't like that any better than people do."

"It's not bullying."

He seemed awful bent on making sure she understood that. "I know you're not a bully, Reuben."

"I wouldn't blame you for thinking I was after yesterday." He was watching her, his face worried. "I shouldn't have flung the news about me working for those film people at you like I did. I knew it would upset you."

And it had. "Why did you, then?"

For a second she wasn't sure he was going to answer her. "You needed to know." His voice sounded rough, and Breeze rolled an uneasy eye in his direction. "Those folks weren't taking care of their animals. The fellow they had watching them acted like he'd never seen a horse in his life. And I really can use the money."

She nodded, keeping her eyes on Breeze's glossy back. She could understand that. Maybe she shouldn't mind so much about him choosing to work for those people.

But she did.

"That's not all of it, though."

She looked up and met his eyes. He looked back with such embarrassed honesty that it reached past her hurt feelings.

"What, then?"

It took him a few seconds to answer. "I had to . . . break away. From this. From you." Just as her heart skipped, he added, "Your family, I mean. I put this life behind me a long time ago." He shook his head. "Spending so much time on this farm . . . I felt like it was pulling me backward."

Having to wear Plain clothing couldn't have helped that feeling any. "And you don't want that to happen."

"No." This time his answer was quick and definite. "I don't. This life isn't for me. It never was." He kept his eyes down, avoiding hers. "But I know the people making that movie have caused a lot of trouble for your family, and I don't want you to think I agree with it. All I'm doing is helping the horses."

"Oh." She remembered what Abram had said about bringing Reuben back into the faith. She should think of something forgiving to say now, something wise.

Instead, all she said was, "How long do we keep this up?"

Her attempt at distraction seemed to work. "Only a little longer. He's almost stopped minding it. We've a day or two more of this at the most, and I'll bring Joseph out to try it, too. Then we'll move on to the next step. That'll be harder. It's the part I was telling you about where Breeze will have to learn he's not the boss. He's been allowed to run things, and it'll be hard for him to accept different."

"I'd imagine so. Poor boy."

Reuben shook his head. "If he doesn't learn that lesson, then you should pity him. A happy horse knows his place, and he's a sight less trouble, too."

"I'll pray that the lessons go well, then," she said. "But I feel sorry for him, just the same. It takes a lot of courage to come under the authority of somebody else. A lot of trusting."

"Like you trust your brother and that bishop. And the Ordnung." There was no mistaking the wry disapproval in his voice.

"Like that, *ja*." She tried a smile. "You're not Plain anymore, but I am. I'm asked to accept the leadership of those *Gott* places over me, so I try to do that." She paused. "We have our differences, you and I, but that's no reason why we can't still help each other."

Reuben looked up. "No," he said. "No, it isn't. Not so long as we both understand how things stand. I'm sorry, Miriam. I should have found a kinder way to tell you about the job."

She smiled. "You're forgiven."

He held her eyes for a second, then nodded. "We're done

here, I think. Praise him and scratch his ears, and we'll give him a treat."

He unclipped the lead and opened the gate to the paddock. Breeze accepted two treats before trotting outside into the thin sunshine.

"Tomorrow maybe you should do this all by yourself, going around both sides," Reuben said. "Then the next day, Joseph. After that we'll be ready to take him out into the pasture."

"I can't help tomorrow. It's Sunday. I'm going to church over at Katie's." She hadn't been sure of that herself until this minute. "Or at least I'm going to try."

"Are you?"

"*Ja.* I've missed being at church, and everyone thinks this will be the easiest way to start back. Katie's house isn't far, but I've not been off the farm at all." Her stomach felt sick at the thought.

"You can do it."

He sounded far more certain than she felt. "I hope so. It won't be easy, though. I'm nervous just thinking about it. Everybody will be . . . looking at me, you know."

"And that will bother you."

Miriam shuddered. "They mean only kindness, but I won't like it. It can't be helped, so I'll just have to do my best to get through it. You could pray for me," she added shyly. "That I won't have one of my attacks or anything, with all the people staring." She couldn't think of anything worse, and she knew it was a strong possibility.

"I'll pray for you." After a second, he asked, "What if the folks weren't staring at you so much? Would that help?"

"They will be, though. They'll be excited to see me, and it'll be something new to talk about." An unpleasant idea occurred to her. Her reappearance at church would remind folks of her parents' deaths as well. They'd be talking about that, too, most likely.

Her heartbeat sped up. She wasn't sure she could manage this after all.

Reuben was watching her. She saw a flicker of sympathy in his eyes—as if he knew just what she was thinking.

He cleared his throat. "Maybe they wouldn't pay so much attention to you if there was somebody else to stare at and talk about."

"There won't be, though."

"There could be." He paused. "Me."

"You?"

"If I came along, nobody'd think so much about you. They'd be too busy gossiping about me." For the first time since she'd come into the barn, his mouth curved up. "Like your friend Katie back in the kitchen. I've lived *Englisch* a long time, but I remember how it was when a stranger came to church. Everybody was curious."

Miriam frowned. "You just told me you took the job in town because you didn't like spending so much time among Plain folks. Now you're saying you want to go to church?"

"I'm not saying I want to. I'm saying I will, if it'll help you." He shrugged. "You've been nice about what happened yesterday. Nicer than I deserved, and I owe you a kindness. I can suffer through one church service, if it will make a hard day easier for you."

Well, this was unexpected. But he was right. People wouldn't be staring at her if Reuben was there. They'd be far too busy staring at him, just like he said.

The bishop would be pleased, certain sure. And who knew? Maybe if Reuben went to church among some kindhearted Plain folks, his heart would shift. He might change his mind and want to stay in spite of himself.

The possibility made her own heart shift a little.

"We'll be leaving at eight," she said. "Naomi wants to get there early in case Katie needs any last-minute help."

He nodded. "I'll be ready. But, mind, I'm only going this once. After tomorrow, you'll have to manage without me."

"I understand. *Denki-shay*, Reuben." She smiled at him.

At first she didn't think he was going to smile back. Then those little crinkles around his eyes deepened.

"*Du bisht welcome*," he responded in *Deutsch*.

CHAPTER SIXTEEN

❧

THE NEXT MORNING REUBEN SAT STIFFLY BESIDE JO-
seph as he drove the short distance toward the Lapps'
home. Naomi and Miriam were huddled in the back, but
nobody was talking. The only sounds were the squeaks of
the wheels and the clop of hooves as Joseph's horse, Titus,
pulled the family buggy over the damp pavement.

It was a raw, overcast day, and the wind chilled Reuben's
freshly shaven cheeks. The too-small coat he was wearing
cut into him every time he shifted position, but the tension
in the buggy made him far more uncomfortable. It hung as
heavy as the gray clouds overhead.

He'd ridden along on countless trips to church just like
this, and he'd sure never figured on doing it again. This felt
unpleasant—and way too familiar—and he was already re-
gretting the whole idea. But none of that mattered right now.

Miriam was struggling.

They'd expected to leave much earlier, but it had taken
Miriam a long while to muster enough courage to climb
into the buggy. Naomi and Joseph had been ready to give

up before she'd finally managed it, and they were both plainly worried about what would happen when it was time to get out again. They'd find out soon because Joseph was turning into the Lapps' driveway. He pulled to a stop and set the brake.

For a few seconds nobody spoke. Then Naomi cleared her throat.

"Come, Mirry. Things will be starting before long. It's time to go in."

There was no answer. Miriam was pressed against the back of the buggy, her face pale beneath her black bonnet. She'd not budged an inch the whole ride over. Reuben knew because he'd sneaked more than one glance behind himself, checking on her.

Miriam was the reason he'd ridden over with the Hochstedlers. He'd intended to drive himself. Since his plan was to draw attention away from Miriam, arriving in a truck would have certainly done it—and it would have allowed for a quick getaway later.

He'd also planned to wear a pair of good jeans and one of his nicer *Englisch* shirts. He didn't have much choice, since the only Plain clothes he had were the ones Miriam had made for him. He'd been wearing those every day for his barn work, and they wouldn't do for church.

The *Englisch* clothes would serve his purpose better anyway, and they'd allow the folks in Johns Mill no illusions about where he stood.

He'd had it all settled in his mind. But early this morning, Joseph had come into the workshop with another folded stack of clothes—this time a white shirt, black pants, and a black vest and coat.

"The coat won't fit too good," Joseph had warned. "It's one of Caleb's old ones and will bind across your shoulders, likely. There was nothing Miriam could do about that on such short notice. The rest of these things should be all right."

He hadn't looked too pleased, Miriam's *bruder*, about

the time and energy his sister had spent fussing over Reuben's church clothes. But in Miriam's mind, he knew, this was a gesture of kindness. Knowing he'd nothing Plain to wear, she'd fixed him up an appropriate outfit, as best she could. She must have worked hard to get these ready so fast, and he hadn't wanted to seem ungrateful by not wearing them.

So here he was, dressed like the rest of them, driving up to church service in a buggy. It was as if the last several years of his life hadn't happened at all.

He didn't like the feeling, not one bit. But after the way he'd hurt Miriam, it served him right. This was his penance.

It was one thing to let a woman know there was no hope of a relationship moving forward. He'd had to do that more than once, with *Englisch* girls. It had been plenty awkward, but he'd never been unkind. Only firm.

He should have done the same with Miriam instead of treating her so roughly. He'd felt like a rat ever since.

"Miriam?" Naomi tried again, shooting a worried glance at her husband.

Still no answer.

Reuben wasn't surprised—he'd expected this. Leaving the farm was a big step for Miriam. She'd been jumpy even at breakfast—a light one so nobody would be tempted to doze off during the lengthy second sermon. She'd barely touched her food, and she'd startled when anybody spoke to her.

By trial and error, Reuben had learned the best antidote to such nerves—at least with horses—was to act as normal as possible. Keep their focus on the routine, everyday things they were familiar with.

So he'd acted matter-of-fact that morning, as if nothing were out of the ordinary. He'd talked about the homemade bread and asked Naomi about the pear preserves he was spreading on it. He'd talked about the next steps coming up with Breeze.

Normally he wasn't much for small talk, especially at the table. His *daed* had never had much patience with it. But today the conversation had served its purpose—it had helped get Miriam into this buggy.

Now he just needed to get her out again. Because if she couldn't manage this, if she had to return home defeated, it was going to set her back badly.

"Miriam?" Naomi was starting to sound desperate.

"You see to your *fraw*," Reuben said to Joseph, who'd just finished tying off Titus. "I'll see to your sister."

Joseph frowned over Titus's back. Plainly the other man didn't like this suggestion—or possibly this whole situation—but he had the sense not to waste time arguing about it. He moved to Naomi's side of the buggy and held out his hand.

"Careful," he murmured to his wife.

Reuben stepped close to the other side and offered Miriam his hand. As he did, he caught her gaze with his—and held it.

It was another trick he'd often used in training. Control a horse's gaze, and the world shrank down to just you two. He'd used it once on Connie, when she'd had a fishhook caught in her thumb. *Look at me*, he'd said calmly. When she had, he'd held her gaze—and jerked the hook out so fast, she hadn't time to pull away.

"Come along, now," he said, looking deep into the brown, green-flecked depths of Miriam's eyes. She stared back, her face tight with fear.

"*'Sis zu hatt*," she whispered with difficulty. It's too hard.

Joseph started to speak, but Reuben made a quick negative gesture, down by his side where Miriam couldn't see it. Joseph had been primed to turn the buggy around ever since they'd started. Seeing his sister so frightened obviously troubled him, something Reuben set to the man's credit. But taking her home would be the worst thing they could do.

"It is hard, *ja*." Reuben kept his voice low and calm.

"Most things worth doing are. But it is not too hard. You are ready. You can do this." He paused. "And when you do it, things will begin to change. You've waited for this chance a long time, ain't so? Here it is, right in front of you, with all of us standing by to help you take hold of it."

For a second, she didn't look as if she'd heard him. But as he watched, the rapid rise and fall of her bosom slowed. She blinked, and the worst of the panic cleared out of her eyes.

She started to take his hand but stopped herself, glancing at the men standing in a half circle in front of the Lapps' barn.

"I can get down by myself," she murmured. "*Denkishay*." She slid to the opposite side of the buggy and climbed out.

That was smart of her. Given his situation, Miriam was wise not to accept his help in front of everybody. It might stir up talk.

Still, it bothered him.

Naomi looked relieved when Miriam was safely beside her. "Here." She tucked an arm around her sister-in-law's waist. "Let's walk together so you can steady me. If you don't, Joseph will insist on coming in the house with the women, and there's no need for that."

Miriam managed a nod, and the two women started across the yard.

Reuben watched them until Joseph cleared his throat. "Best come with me." He nodded toward the group of men. "I'll introduce you around."

Reuben sighed and squared his shoulders. Might as well get this part over with.

As it turned out, introductions weren't necessary. They hadn't made it halfway across the yard before one of the men tiptoed to speak into Sam Christner's ear. The tall man leaned over, frowning, then squinted in Reuben's direction and smiled.

"Reuben!" he said when they'd reached the circle. He offered a beefy hand, gripping down hard to emphasize his welcome. "It's wonderful *gut* to have you visiting here. I met Reuben up in Indiana," he explained to the men nearby. "He's got a fine hand with horses, and he's helping Joseph with my Breeze, as a kindness."

The men murmured short greetings, each offering a handshake in turn. Reuben politely made the circuit, ending up with an elderly fellow, who introduced himself as David Miller.

"Where in Indiana are you from?" the old man asked.

"Not too far from LaGrange," he answered vaguely. Not too far, but not too close, either. His old community was actually located in Candler, a fair distance from the friendlier tourist districts.

"Who's your father?" David persisted. When Reuben didn't answer immediately, he persisted. "What's your family name?"

"Brenneman."

The man's faded eyes narrowed. "You'll be related to Ivan Brenneman then."

"He's my father."

"Well, that's a family what knows horses, by all accounts. How's your *daed* doing?"

"Time to get ourselves inside," Sam interrupted. "Reuben, help me along to the house and we'll sit together, if it suits."

"Suits me fine." Reuben stuck out his elbow, and Sam took it. Reuben waited until they'd walked out of earshot before adding, "We both know you don't need my help going anywhere, but I thank you for rescuing me."

Sam grinned. "David means well, but he's never happy unless he can trace everybody's family back to somebody he knows. It's partly your own fault. If you'd been wearing your *Englisch* clothes, he'd likely have left you alone."

There was a question hidden in the observation, but Reuben ignored it.

Once inside, Sam stuck to Reuben like glue. His old friend might not be able to see as well as he used to, but he was as kindhearted and loyal as ever.

So when the time came for the service to start, Reuben settled on the bench without near as much dread as he'd expected. It wasn't that he hated church services—he didn't. In a way he'd even missed them. He'd tried going to *Englisch* ones now and again. The churches had been pretty and the people nice enough, but he hadn't felt at home among them.

He'd lost his faith in the Plain church and its leaders, but somehow during his childhood, this had imprinted itself in his brain as what worship was supposed to be like. Something about these traditions, the never-changing, solemn ways of the service, spoke to his heart in a way nothing else did.

Maybe because church Sundays had been a welcome spot of safety during his growing-up years. Ivan put up a facade in front of others—mostly. As long as Reuben kept himself and his sisters out of his *daed*'s sight, church time was peaceful. And the food was always better and more plentiful than anything they got at home.

He shifted on the bench. He felt conspicuous, sitting here as an outsider, but it wasn't so bad, and he'd expected nothing different. He was relieved to discover he still remembered all the ins and outs of church. The songs, the prayers, the sermons, it all came back.

He wondered how Miriam was doing. He couldn't see her for himself. She was sitting with her sister and sister-in-law on the opposite side of the room, behind him someplace. He couldn't very well turn to check on her, so instead he examined his surroundings.

The Lapps had knocked a wall out between what had most likely been a living room and a dining room back when this was an *Englisch* home. The result had been a large open area, handy for use when it was their turn to host church services. This sort of space had been common in his old community, too. The benches were more crowded than he remembered, but that might be because Sam took up a lot of room.

Well, he hadn't come here expecting to be comfortable. But he had to admit, sitting here next to a friend, taking part in a church service he actually understood for the first time in years . . . it wasn't as bad as he'd thought.

He pondered that while he sat through the lengthy sermons. Maybe, he decided, Miriam wasn't the only one who'd needed to come here today. Maybe this was a step forward for him, too, a way to find some measure of peace with the church he'd left behind—and break off the angry barb of resentment that had been sticking under his skin.

In any case, he was glad he'd done it—even if he wasn't planning on doing it again.

Afterward, seated at the lunchtime meal—again beside Sam—he felt the people's eyes on him, quick, curious glances. That didn't bother him. Their plan had worked, and Miriam was doing better than he'd expected.

He caught glimpses of her now and again. She was helping to serve the lunch, stepping in and out of the room, no sign of panic in her eyes. The hardest step for her was done. She'd be able to manage church from here on out. Maybe soon, she'd venture farther. He hoped so.

He slathered peanut butter spread on a soft piece of homemade bread and took a bite, as Miriam worked her way up the table in tandem with the other women, filling glasses. He chewed as he watched her. They must make their spread different here than they had at home, he thought absently. It seemed sweeter.

"How's Breeze coming along?" Sam asked, a forkful of ham hovering in front of his mouth.

"Good," Reuben said as soon as he could speak. "Slow."

"I hear Miriam's been helping you."

"She has. It's gone a lot smoother because of it."

"Joseph's worried over it, but it's been good for her, Emma thinks," Sam said. He took a drink of his coffee. "Having something she can do. It's given her some confidence back. Today's the proof. She's here—first church service she's been at since her parents died. We've you to thank, Emma says, and she's real grateful. Don't be surprised if she slips you an extra piece of pie."

"It's not me. Miriam made up her own mind that she wanted to come, and she did. She was scared, but she pushed past it. She's got more spirit in her than people think."

"*Ja*, I've always thought that myself," Sam said slowly. "Miriam seems a shy, skittish little thing—always did, even before. But deep down she has plenty of grit."

"She just doesn't put all her goods in the shop window," Reuben said shortly. "Nothing wrong with that."

"I didn't say there was." Sam squinted, as if trying to get a better look at Reuben's expression. "Anyhow, having her here, seeing her so improved, it's made my Emma happy, and it wasn't part of our bargain. So it seems now I'm the one owing you a favor."

"You owe me nothing." Reuben checked to make sure nobody close by was listening. All the men seated nearby seemed involved in their own conversations, but he kept his voice low. "What you did—slipping me that money when nobody else would give me a dime and sending me to your *Englisch* friend who needed help with his horses—it was a risky thing. If my father—or the bishop—had found out . . ."

"I wasn't worried about them." Sam shook his head. "It would have been riskier to leave you there. It's not often I'd say it's better for a fellow to jump the fence, but with you as things were then, it was the wisest choice." He shook his head ruefully. "I doubt the church would say the same, but that's the way I saw it." He paused. "Your *daed*'s still living?"

"He is."

"You ever planning to go back to see him?"

"No. I meant what I told you that night, Sam. I'm done with that life."

Sam lifted an eyebrow. "You're done with your father maybe, but you're not looking so done with the life just now, Reuben."

"This, you mean?" Reuben gestured at his outfit. "This is nothing but a suit of clothes."

"That," Sam said dryly, "wasn't what I was talking about. I may not see so good anymore, but I see well enough to notice you sitting up straighter whenever our Mirry passes by. And I can tell how your head turns to follow her when she goes."

Reuben clenched his fingers around his fork so hard, he wondered the thing didn't snap in his hand. "We're friends. That's the whole of it."

Sam chuckled. "Emma and I were friends, too, back at the start. You could do worse, you know, if you weren't so set on living apart. Miriam's got a real sweet heart as well as a face that's easy to look at. Now that she's back amongst us, it won't surprise me if some smart fellow snaps her up right quick."

"Some smart *Amish* fellow." Reuben didn't much like the idea, but Sam was right.

"*Ja*, of course." His friend leaned over close to add, "So if I were you, I'd get myself straight with the church in a hurry."

"That's not going to happen."

To his relief, Sam shrugged philosophically. "Too bad. I wouldn't have minded having you for a brother-in-law." He pushed away from the table and headed to where his wife was slicing pies into generous wedges. Miriam was helping her, and as Reuben's gaze trailed Sam, their eyes met.

She smiled at him before returning her attention to the pies, her cheeks a happy pink. As he watched, a young, beardless man walked up and asked for a slice. He stood much closer than necessary, but Miriam didn't seem to mind. In fact, she smiled at the boy when she handed him the pie, and he lingered there, grinning back foolishly.

A lump settled into Reuben's stomach.

Sam was right. Men were already taking notice of Miriam. Soon—likely real soon going by her smile and the interested gleam in that fellow's eye—she'd be some man's wife.

He pushed back roughly from the table, earning a startled look from the elderly man on his right.

"You've not had your dessert yet," the man said. "Best sit back down."

"I'm not hungry anymore." Without looking in Miriam's direction, Reuben headed for the door. It was only a short walk back to the Hochstedlers, and this jacket was cutting into his shoulders something fierce.

He'd done what he'd come for. Miriam was all right, and there was no reason for him to stay. He didn't belong among these people. He never had, and he never would.

CHAPTER SEVENTEEN

❧

THE NEXT MORNING AT HALF PAST TEN, MIRIAM left the square she was piecing on the kitchen table and went to the sink. She turned on the faucet, sneaking a guilty peek out the window.

Reuben was out in the pasture. He had Breeze on a short lead, and the horse was fighting him for everything he was worth. This was the next phase of the training, the part where Breeze had to learn to obey, and it didn't look like it was going too well. Frowning, Miriam tiptoed to get a better look.

Reuben had said he didn't need her—that today's work would be between just him and the horse. Still, she couldn't help thinking it might be going better if she were out there with him.

She sure wished there was something she could do, especially after how he'd helped her yesterday. She was still floating on the success of making it to the service.

It had been wonderful to be there again, among all her friends, some of whom she hadn't seen for over a year. It

hadn't been easy, though. When she'd felt the buggy bump
out of the gravel drive onto the flat surface of the highway,
she'd nearly panicked. Fear had hovered close, ready to
pounce.

Just when she was about to fall apart, Reuben had
glanced over his shoulder at her. Only a glance, and it hadn't
made the fear disappear. But somehow, it had steadied her
enough to keep going.

After that, she'd kept her eyes fixed on his broad shoulders, straining the narrow cut of Caleb's old coat. She'd
planned out how she'd make a coat for Reuben, so it would
be ready if he ever changed his mind and wanted to go to
church again. She'd mentally measured and sewed, and that
had gotten her through the drive.

Then, when they'd stopped in Katie's yard, and she'd felt
she couldn't possibly find the courage to step down from
the buggy, he'd looked up at her, and he'd held out his hand—

"Did you prick yourself again?"

Miriam jumped. "What?"

Naomi lifted an eyebrow, resting the shirt she was mend-
ing on her round stomach. "You're just standing there with
the water running," her sister-in-law pointed out patiently.
"Is your finger bleeding bad?"

Miriam flushed and reached for a glass. A pricked finger
had been her last excuse to get up and look out the window.
"*Nee*, I just wanted a drink of water, and I got distracted.
It's such a pretty day."

"It is. Spring finally seems to have taken hold." Naomi
massaged the back of her neck with her fingers. "I'd like hot
tea better than water, I think. I have some herbal tea that
would hit the spot. Then I'm going to rest awhile. I didn't
sleep so well." She set the half-finished shirt on the table
and began levering herself out of the chair.

"Don't get up," Miriam protested hastily. "I'll make
the tea."

Naomi sighed. "*Denki*. That's kind, but I won't know

what kind I want until I see the boxes. Yesterday I was all set for some peppermint tea to settle my stomach before bed, but when I went to the cupboard, I saw the orange spice tea, and nothing would do but that."

Miriam smiled. "Maybe the baby will like oranges."

"Maybe so." Naomi went to the tea cupboard and rummaged through the boxes. "Lemon sounds good to me today. What do you think?"

Miriam was sneaking another glance out the window. Reuben was right in Breeze's face now, backing him up. He was saying something to the horse, it looked like, not that Miriam was close enough to hear.

"Lemon is fine," she said absently.

"Or I could make lard tea, if that sounds nicer."

"Whatever you want." Breeze tried to bolt, and Reuben caught him up short with the lead. Miriam held her breath as he brought the horse back into line. Even from here, she could see the muscles moving under Reuben's sleeves. Thank goodness she'd made him a bigger shirt. Joseph's would have ripped under the strain, as tight as it had been across his shoulders and upper arms.

Something bumped into Miriam. She turned to find Naomi beside her, smiling. "I've half a mind to serve you lard tea just to teach you a lesson about agreeing to things without listening," she teased. She brandished a small yellow box. "But I think we'll stick to the lemon. Why don't you fill up the kettle, and—oh!"

Naomi had caught sight of Reuben. She glanced between him and Miriam, the happiness fading from her face.

"Oh, Miriam," she murmured.

"I'm interested in what he's doing with Breeze," Miriam explained, flushing. "I've been helping all this time, but this part he wants to handle by himself. I'm curious."

"Whatever he's doing, he's nearly finished. He told Joseph this begins the last part of the retraining. He'll be leaving soon." Her sister-in-law's voice was carefully gentle.

Miriam's stomach flipped over. "I'll be sorry."

"How sorry?"

She understood what Naomi was asking. "Sorry to see a friend go," she said. "That's all. He's been a great help, not only to Breeze but to me. He went to church yesterday just so folks would have somebody else to pick over and they'd leave me alone. It must have been hard on him since he left early and walked home. And you saw how quiet he was at breakfast, and how little he ate. He's a kind man, Naomi, and I don't think Plain folks have treated him well in the past."

"*Ja*, he does seem kind, although I don't think much of his decision to work with those movie people. And there's no doubt he's a treat with the horses." Naomi's expression softened as she angled to get a better look out the window. "I don't suppose it would be easy going to church amongst folks you don't know, especially for someone in his position, but his plan certainly worked. People were much too busy talking about him to pay attention to you. Except," she added with a smile, "for Leben Miller. He wasn't able to pay attention to anybody else."

Miriam flapped a hand. "He just wanted a second helping of pie."

"I never knew him to be so fond of pie before." The memory of Leben seemed to have cheered Naomi up. "Why don't you go ask Reuben if he'd like some tea or some coffee? There are a few molasses cookies, too, if he'd like a snack."

"All right." Miriam suspected she knew exactly why Leben's sudden affection for pie had eased Naomi's mind enough to offer Reuben cookies, but at the moment she didn't care. She was happy for any excuse to go out to the pasture. Snatching up her shawl, she hurried for the door.

It was still chilly, but the sunlight felt stronger than it had in months. Naomi was right—spring might not be fully here yet, but it was finally on its way.

She walked toward where Reuben was working. He had his back to her, but she wasn't surprised when he spoke.

"Thought you were planning to stay inside and catch up on your quilting."

"That's what I've been doing. Naomi sent me to see if you'd like some coffee and cookies."

"No, thanks. Come on, boy." He clucked his tongue and started across the pasture, leading Breeze. The horse lunged ahead, but Reuben held the lead rope firm and pulled the animal up short. "Not so fast." They started off again. Breeze snorted and shook his head, but this time he didn't bolt. "There you go," Reuben muttered. "That's a good fellow."

They made a short circle. Reuben stopped, stepping close to Breeze's head. He seemed to be having a conversation with the horse, so low that Miriam couldn't hear. Then he unclipped the lead and gave Breeze a light slap on the rump. "Go on with you," he said. "We'll have another try tomorrow."

He cut a sideways look at Miriam as he walked toward the fence. "All done," he said. "Nothing more to see."

"How's he doing?"

"Well enough."

"Good. That looked like hard work."

"It is." As Reuben ducked through the fence, the barbed wire snagged on his shirt.

"Stay still. I'll get it." Miriam stepped forward.

Swiftly Reuben pulled himself free. "It's fine."

She made an exasperated noise. "Not so fine for me." She pointed out a tiny rip. "This'll have to be mended now." When she touched the hole on his shoulder, Reuben jumped as if he'd been stung.

"Don't trouble yourself. I'll likely not be wearing this shirt much longer anyhow."

She supposed that was true. The thought—and this whole one-sided conversation—had her feeling deflated.

Talking with Reuben today felt like trying to play a game of fetch with an untrained puppy. You threw the stick over and over again, but the puppy never brought it back.

"Thank Naomi for the offer of tea, but I don't have time. I'm going into town."

"All right." She hesitated, but she had to ask. "Are you angry with me?"

He'd started to walk away, but he stopped and turned to face her. "No."

She waited, but that was all he said.

"Well, you've been acting strange ever since church. Did somebody say something unkind? People do sometimes. I'm sorry if that happened."

"You've nothing to be sorry for. And nobody said anything unkind."

"Then what's wrong?"

He stood silently for a minute. He seemed to be fighting some kind of war inside himself—as if he wanted to say something, and then again, he didn't. Though there was no reason for it—no reason at all—her breath quickened as she waited to see what he'd decide.

Their eyes met, and he flinched, like he had when she'd touched his shirt. He looked toward the pasture, where Breeze was galloping, head high and tail streaming behind him. As he watched the horse, Reuben's face relaxed.

"He has a lot of energy today," Miriam observed softly.

"He's getting his mad out." Reuben kept his gaze fixed on the horse. "He didn't like what I was doing back there—bringing him up short and making him go where he didn't want to go."

Miriam laughed. "I wouldn't like that, either."

"It has a purpose. He has to trust me enough to push past the limits he's set in his fear, and he's got to be stopped from setting new ones. Otherwise, he'll be . . . hindered all his life. He'll be less than he could have been." Reuben spared her a glance. "That would be a shame."

His eyes were such a sharp blue, not so different from the spring sky arching overhead. "You won't let that happen."

"Not if I can help it, but I don't have much time left, and this is slow work. When you're fighting fear, trust is a precious thing and hard to give. But without it"—he shrugged—"not much good can happen."

She suspected he wasn't only talking about Breeze. Her heart was thumping so hard, she felt jittery. He was close enough that she could smell his scent—a familiar mixture of clean barn, horse, hay, and grain.

"That's true. After what happened, trusting was hard for all four of us. Sometimes we struggled to trust God, even. Joseph and Emma came through all right, but Caleb still has trouble trusting the church." *Like you*, she could have added, but didn't. "And I—"

"You don't trust people like me. *Englischers*."

"You're not an *Englischer*."

"Yes." His gaze stayed level and steady. "I am. In every way that counts."

She didn't like hearing that, and deep down, she didn't entirely believe it, but she wasn't going to argue. "Well, anyhow, I trust you. *Englischer* or not."

He lifted an eyebrow. "Enough to ride into town with me?"

She blinked. "What?"

"It'll be a short trip. We'd be there and back in no time."

She tried a nervous laugh. "I barely managed church yesterday. I need to catch my breath before I try anything else."

He shook his head. "Waiting would be a mistake."

"Why?"

"It's not really any of my business. If you want to stay home, stay home." He started toward his truck.

"Why would it be a mistake, Reuben?"

He turned, a heat in his face that she'd never seen before. "Because," he said. "When you're making progress, you never stop where it's comfortable. It's too easy to settle there. You got your courage up and you made it to church. That's good. And you'll make it to church again, but there's more to the world than that. There's the quilt shop—and other shops like it. Bigger ones, outside of Johns Mill. There's even quilt museums. Did you know that?"

She stared at him, stunned.

He went on. "Think of the colors and patterns you'd see—thousands of them. And there's other places you'd like to see, too." He leaned forward, holding her gaze. "There's nothing wrong in that. Even the church allows for it, for travel to see the wonders God's put on this earth." He straightened. "But if somebody doesn't push you—and soon—you'll miss all that. You'll catch the eye of some fellow who'll be happy with a wife too nervous to set foot outside her own yard. He'll hem you in and keep your life small and safe and . . . colorless. I'd hate to see that happen."

Her mind whirled, a familiar panicky feeling starting in her chest. "Even if you're right, I don't see why me going to town with you right this minute matters so much."

"Does it scare you? The idea of getting in my truck and riding to town? Even though you say you trust me, and you know I'd never let anybody hurt you?"

She didn't answer, but apparently she didn't need to. He gave a quick, short nod.

"It does. And once I leave—and I will, soon—is anybody else likely to push you past these walls you've put up? Or are they going to leave you to shrivel up inside them?"

Again she stayed silent—and again, he didn't seem to need her answer. He nodded slowly, his face grim. "That's why it matters, Miriam."

They stood there in silence facing each other.

"So?" Reuben asked.

"What's going on?" Joseph had stopped halfway between the house and his workshop, and he studied them, frowning. "Something wrong?"

"No." Miriam swallowed hard. "Nothing's wrong. I'm . . . going into town with Reuben."

"*Vass?*" Joseph's astonishment had him spluttering. "*You're* going to town? Now?"

She nodded. Reuben remained silent, but she felt his approval washing over her like a warm wave.

Joseph's eyes flicked from one of them to the other. "I'm not sure about this, Mirry. At the least, I should come with you, but—" He looked over his shoulder at the house. "Naomi's feeling extra tired and said she wanted to lie down. I don't like the idea of leaving her here alone."

"No, you shouldn't do that. I'll go with Reuben. It'll be all right, Joseph. I think . . . I need to do this."

Joseph studied her, his brows drawn together over his nose, his eyes worried. He glanced at Reuben. "This will be your doing, I'm thinking."

Reuben didn't flinch. "That's right."

"It was his idea, maybe, but it's up to me, ain't so? And I want to go." Miriam straightened her shoulders.

Joseph pursed his lips and considered her. "You know what you feel ready for, Miriam. I'll not make such a decision for you. But are you sure you want to try this today? Without me or Naomi along to support you?"

"*Nee*, I'm not sure. Maybe I won't get halfway down the road before we have to turn around and come back. But I'd like to try."

Her brother surrendered with a shake of his head. "Suit yourself, then. But don't be too long. Naomi will be worried. And you." He directed his gaze to Reuben. "Look after her."

"I will."

"You'd better." Joseph shook his head again. Then he turned and disappeared into the house.

"All right." Miriam drew in a long breath. "If we're going to do this, we'd best get on with it before I get too *naerfich*."

Reuben smiled—a real smile this time, one that made it all the way into his eyes. "I'll get my keys."

CHAPTER EIGHTEEN

❧

REUBEN STOLE A GLANCE AT MIRIAM. SHE SAT BOLT upright in the seat of his truck, her Amish dress and black bonnet looking very out of place, her hands clenched in her lap. She was nervous, that was plain to see, but she was holding herself together.

So far, anyway.

He tightened his fingers on the steering wheel. He shouldn't have pushed her so hard. He didn't know why he'd done that. He pushed horses sometimes, sure. Like with Breeze this morning, that was part of the process. But he didn't make a habit of pushing people, not anymore.

He'd tried it, with his *mamm* and his sisters, trying to talk them into leaving home. He'd come up with all sorts of options, but he'd only ended up upsetting them. They couldn't envision any life other than the one they lived, no matter how uncomfortable that life might be.

At least his sisters had married and left home, one by one, except for Connie. He'd no doubt Connie would marry, too, if she got the chance. Hopefully, like her older sisters, she'd have the sense to pick a man as different from her father as she could find.

But not somebody like the young man who'd made a point of talking to Miriam at the pie table yesterday. Something about him had set Reuben's teeth on edge.

"The Beilers are selling their place after all." Miriam craned her head to look at a farm they were passing. "Naomi said they were thinking of it, and there's the sign in the yard. Such a shame. That's the prettiest farm in Johns Mill. When I was a little girl, I told *Daed* I was going to marry Eli Beiler so I could live there."

"If that's still your plan, you'd best hurry up."

"It wasn't a very good plan. Eli was fifteen years older than me. He's been married for years, and he's got half a dozen children." After the farm slipped behind them, she straightened in her seat, offering Reuben a shaky smile. "It's been so long since I've been out and about. It's real interesting to see everything again."

That was the first smile he'd seen since she'd gotten in the truck. Her hands weren't clenched quite so tightly, either. He'd keep her talking.

"You like living in Johns Mill." He made it a statement, not a question, because there wasn't much doubt in his mind.

"I do, *ja*. It's got its troubles." A shadow flitted across her face. "But mostly it's nice people here." She seemed to be reminding herself of that. "Anyway," she added with a shrug, "it's home."

"So you expect to stay here? For good?"

Her eyebrows went up as if she was surprised by the question. "That depends on *Gott*'s will for me. But it wouldn't make me unhappy to live here, if that's what you're asking."

"You don't wonder about other places?"

"Well, sure. There's lots of places I'd like to see, if I got the chance. Like that quilt museum you were talking about."

A dreamy expression came into her eyes. "Now, that would be something. I bet I could stay in such a place for hours and hours, just looking. Getting ideas, maybe, of quilts I'd like to make myself. It would be a real treat." She glanced at him. "If I can manage this trip, and if I keep trying hard, maybe one day I can go places like that. But of course, I'll always be happy to come home." He kept his eyes carefully on the road, but he could feel her studying him. "Where's your home, Reuben? You've never said."

"I don't know that I have one. I move around a lot. Right now I rent a house in Kentucky, but I've only been there about six months." And he sure didn't think of it as home—more a stopping-off place between jobs.

"Home isn't so much a place anyhow, is it?" She spoke kindly, a gentle sympathy in her voice. "It's more about the people. When you have friends and family around you, anyplace can be a home." She wrinkled her nose. "Back when things were really hard here, Joseph nearly moved us up to Ohio. None of us liked the idea, but we knew as long as we were together, it could be home for us."

Reuben kept silent. Judging a home by how many family or friends you had there changed nothing on his end. He knew plenty of people—folks he was friendly enough with to share a meal or go to an auction, something like that. But he'd not had a close friend for years.

Come to think of it, he'd spent more time with Miriam than he had with anybody in a long while. And enjoyed it more, too.

When they passed the city limits sign, she started to tense up again.

"Easy, now," he murmured. "You're doing fine."

"I know, it's silly of me." She was trying to laugh at herself, he could tell, but her voice sounded tight and too high.

"You're not silly," he argued shortly.

"I just meant—"

"I know what you meant." He pulled into a parking lot.

"You went through a terrible thing, Miriam, and it scared you. It's something you have to work through, but there's nothing silly about it." He parked the truck and killed the engine.

She looked at him, her face too pale and her eyes too wide. "You didn't know me before. I've always been . . ." Her throat flexed as she swallowed. "Nervous-like," she finished. "Maybe if I'd been a stronger person—"

"You're plenty strong." He leaned back in the seat. "Sure, you're high-strung, a little sensitive maybe." He smiled. "Most Thoroughbreds are, too, and that's what makes them special. One Thoroughbred's worth ten plough horses any day."

As he'd hoped, amusement broke through the fear in her eyes. "Do you think I'm a horse, Reuben?"

"Obviously not." He nodded to a sign in front of them. "Wouldn't do me much good to bring a horse to a fabric store, Thoroughbred or not."

"Yoder's!" She gasped and clapped her hands. "We're going to Yoder's? For real?"

His plan had worked. She was so excited that she'd forgotten about being frightened. Such a big smile spread across Reuben's face that his cheeks ached with the size of it.

This hadn't been such a bad idea, after all.

"I thought you'd like that."

"Like it?" She scrabbled at the handle, trying to figure out how to open the door. "What a treat! I can't wait to— this won't open!" Her expression was such a funny mix of joy and frustration that he chuckled.

"It sticks. I've been meaning to get it fixed. Hang on." He leaned across to tug on the lever. As he did, she curved her fingers around his forearm.

"Thank you, Reuben," she said earnestly. "This is such a kindness."

"*Du bisht welcome*, Mirry." The *Deutsch* came as easily

as the pet name. It suited her. It was short and sweet and different—just the sort of name that should belong to a girl with forest-pool eyes and a cute, pointed chin.

She really smiled then, and his heart swelled, crowding his lungs.

He was too close. There was barely six inches between their faces, and he already had the door unlatched. He should pull away.

He didn't want to. He wanted to stay right where he was, close enough to smell the fresh, clean scent that clung to her like a perfume, feeling her touch on his arm, light and trusting. He looked into her sweet face, the sides of her black bonnet shutting out the rest of the world so that it was only the two of them.

He wished it were only the two of them. No bishops or brothers—and definitely no towheaded, churchgoing fellows who flirted with girls over pie tables. He wished—

He reined in his thoughts and drew back so fast that Miriam looked startled.

"It's open now." He pressed down on his own door handle, suddenly anxious to escape into the fresh, cool air.

He waited for her, trying his best to collect his wits. Miriam hurried around the truck with her face alight with happy expectation. She didn't seem uneasy at all, and he counted that a big win, especially for her first time in town.

"You know, I saw you giving Breeze a treat after you finished the session today." Her head came just to his shoulder, and she'd tilted it back to look at him.

"*Ja*, I always do when the training's tough like that. It helps end things on a good note."

"Is that why you brought me here?" She nodded toward the Yoder's sign as they passed it. "Is this my treat for coming to town?"

He chuckled. "Didn't you just remind me you aren't a horse?"

She smiled. "I'm not. But I do like treats, and this is a fine one."

He smiled back as he reached to open the door to the shop.

The handle didn't budge.

He tugged again before noticing the store was suspiciously dark. He leaned back and looked around—sure enough. The sign in the big window read **CLOSED**.

Miriam saw the sign, too, and her face fell. "Oh, no! I'd forgotten. I heard at church yesterday that Mary's daughter Ella had a new baby on Saturday. Mary's gone to visit for a few days. So naturally the shop would be closed."

"I'm sorry." He was, and he braced himself for her disappointment. "It's too bad."

She only sighed and shrugged. "Well, it can't be helped." She patted his arm briskly. "Thanks to you, I made it all the way to town today with no trouble, so I can make it another day, just as well. That's something to be thankful for."

Something to be thankful for. His *mamm* used to say that, sifting through the mess of her life, looking for anything that sparkled. Maybe there was no money for groceries, but the hens were laying. That was something to be thankful for. Maybe Ivan had gone on one of his rampages, but nothing important had been broken this time. That, too, was something to be thankful for.

He'd grown mighty tired of that saying, but now, hearing it on Mirry's lips, he realized he'd missed it. There was something strong and fine about finding a reason for gratitude in the midst of disappointment. You didn't see enough of that in the world.

At least, not in the world he'd been living in.

He cleared his throat. "True enough. You'll be back here before you know it. But I'm afraid this spoils your treat."

"There are other treats." She tilted a shy smile at him, making his heart roll in his chest. "You could buy me an ice cream over at Miller's." She suddenly seemed shocked by her own daring, and her cheeks brightened. "If you want to, I mean."

If he wanted to. *Ja*, he wanted to. When she looked at him like that, he wanted to buy her an ice cream truck. "Miller's?"

"Miller's Café. It's right there." She nodded down the sidewalk, where a chalkboard was set out on the sidewalk, scribbled over with specials. "They have the best ice cream cones around, and I haven't had one since—in a long while."

No, she wouldn't have had an ice cream cone since her last trip to town, whenever that had been. A treat like that would melt before it could be brought home in a horse and buggy. "Sounds like a good idea to me," he said and was rewarded with another smile.

His heart rolled again, but he didn't care. She was the prettiest thing. He'd thought so the first minute he'd seen her, that day she'd collapsed in the barn. Even then, when her face had been pinched and sad, she'd been sweet to look at. Now, with the shy bloom of hope and triumph on her face, that sweetness was enough to take a man's breath away.

He wasn't the only one who thought so. They passed an Amish fellow on their way into the café. The young man's eyes skimmed Miriam's face, then he glanced at Reuben. Disappointment flickered over his face, and he looked quickly away.

He thinks we're sweethearts, Reuben realized. He mulled that over as he bought a strawberry cone for Miriam and a chocolate one for himself.

They weren't sweethearts, and they never could be. So there was no reason for the idea to make him feel . . . unsettled.

But it did.

He'd felt this way working horses, watching the animal,

trying to figure if he was going to break left or right. It was important then to stay loose on your feet, so you'd be able to shift with the horse once he'd chosen his direction. You couldn't know ahead of time. You had to wait and see which way you'd need to go.

Oddly, *ja*, that's what this felt like. As if he were waiting to see what direction he should jump in. His heart was hammering, and his senses were on high alert.

He glanced at Miriam, who was licking her top-heavy pink cone. She seemed all right—a little nervous, maybe, but more comfortable than he'd have expected. She caught him looking, and her eyes twinkled.

"This is very good. Thank you. You should have gotten the strawberry, too. It's the best."

"Not for me. I'm allergic to strawberries," he said. "I break out in hives."

"Oh." Miriam shook her head and took another lick of her cone. "Now that's a shame. I was going to offer to share."

A ridiculous rush of possessiveness rose in him. He wished they *were* sweethearts. More than anything else right now, he wished that—

"Brenneman?"

He turned, reflexively tucking Miriam behind him. Then he relaxed. Mr. Sykes, the fellow in charge of the film crew's horses—and likely a lot of other things—pushed back from his table, a half-eaten sandwich on the plate in front of him.

"*Ja.* Good to see you," Reuben said. Sykes's gaze shifted to Miriam. She stood frozen beside him, her cone beginning to drip, her eyes large and startled.

"It's all right," he murmured in *Deutsch.* "I know him." Reuben almost introduced her, then thought better of it.

"Ma'am," the Englischer said politely before turning his attention back at Reuben. "Brenneman, I'm glad to see you. Jerry wasn't sure you were coming in today, and we've got a horse limping. I'd like you to look him over, see if it's something we need the vet in for. I tried calling you, but I got your voice mail."

"Sorry." He'd left his phone on his bed back at the Hochstedlers'. He hadn't even thought about it, and the thing probably needed charging, too. "I . . . forgot my phone." How had he done that? "I'll take my friend home, and then I'll come back and check on that horse for you."

"Why not do it now? It won't take five minutes. Jerry will show you which horse is having the issue. Your lady friend can go with you." He offered Miriam a kind smile. "Unfortunately, they're not filming right now, so you won't see any of the actors."

"She needs to get back," Reuben said shortly. Miriam was trembling, and he was anxious to end this conversation. "But I'll be quick. Tell Jerry to expect me in about an hour."

Sykes didn't look pleased, but he didn't argue. "I suppose that'll have to do." He sat back down at the table. "Food's good here, I'll say that much. I was planning on having a piece of pie for dessert, but that ice cream's changed my mind. Yours is about to get away from you there, ma'am."

"Oh!" Miriam looked down at her dripping cone.

"I'll be in touch about that horse," Reuben called over his shoulder. He opened the door and shepherded Miriam out of the café.

He gave her a quick look-over once they were safely outside, trying to gauge how upset she was. She was shaking, and her face was pale, but she didn't seem panicked. He breathed a sigh of relief.

"Sorry to cut our trip short, but I'd better drive you back."

She looked up at him, her brows furrowed. Her eyes were wide and worried, and there was tiny splatter of strawberry ice cream on her nose.

"I'm the one who should be sorry. That'll make extra

trouble for you, ain't so? Having to haul me home and come back again. It'll cost you extra gas money, too."

"It's no trouble."

He felt uncomfortable talking about this with her. He wished they hadn't bumped into Sykes.

In fact, he wished he'd never gotten mixed up with these people. The movie and all the commotion associated with it had hurt Miriam and her family, and he hated ending this outing on such a sour note. If she had a bad experience today, no telling how long it'd be before she found the courage to come to town again.

She took another careful lick of her drippy cone. "I don't want you to have to make a special trip. The man said it would only take a minute, and that I could go with you. Why don't we just do that?"

He stopped on the sidewalk. An *Englischer* huffed irritably as he skirted around them, but Reuben paid no attention.

"Go down to where the movie's filming? Both of us?"

She swallowed, but whether it was nerves or just ice cream, he couldn't tell. "He said nobody was there, right? Just the horses. I'm not afraid of horses."

"I don't know, Miriam. I don't want you upset. You sure about this?"

"I won't be if you keep questioning me." She attempted a smile. "What was it you told me? Never stop where you're comfortable. I've been more comfortable on this trip than I ever expected to be, so maybe this is something I should try."

He hesitated. She'd already taken a big step today. Challenging yourself was good, but sometimes it was important to know when to call it a day.

She shivered. "I'm only going to get more scared standing here thinking about it. Let's just go so you can look at the poor horse. Then you can take me home."

"We can try it, I guess. But if it feels like too much, you tell me, and we'll leave. All right?"

She nodded.

"You're a brave woman, Miriam Hochstedler." He grinned as she spluttered a disbelieving laugh. "And a sticky one. You'll have ice cream all down your arm if you don't hurry and eat it."

Their walk was a short one. At Reuben's suggestion, the film company had set up a circus-like tent in an empty lot at the end of Main Street. The horses spent their off time there, in makeshift stalls. In the evenings, they were moved to a nearby pasture, leased from an *Englischer*.

The arrangement wasn't perfect. The billowing tent canvas made the horses jumpy, and Jerry wasn't great at following instructions. But the animals were better off than they had been, and anyway, from what he heard, the movie wouldn't be filming on location much longer. So this would do well enough.

Jerry was nowhere in sight. No doubt Sykes had called and told the handler to expect Reuben in an hour—so the lazy fellow had hightailed it. It didn't much matter. Apart from pointing out the ailing horse, he'd have been no help anyhow.

Reuben scanned the three horses, zeroed in on one.

"Which horse has the trouble?" Miriam asked.

"The chestnut here." Reuben approached the gelding and lifted his left foreleg, feeling it over with gentle fingers. "Looks like a soft tissue injury—like a sprain. He might have stepped in a hole or something." He dropped the hoof and straightened, thinking. "Normally, I'd wrap it, and we'd see how he did. But it might be better to go on and give the vet a call. These horses are leased from their owners, and it's best to take extra care in situations like that." He reached for his phone, then remembered he didn't have it. "We can go. I'll call Sykes once we get back and tell him what to do."

He glanced at Miriam, but she wasn't paying any attention to him. She was staring at the opening of the tent.

Framed between long sheets of flapping white canvas—which he'd told Jerry twice to tie down—stood a pretty young woman. She wore strategically ripped jeans and a button-up shirt that dipped low in front and was tied in a knot, exposing her flat belly. But oddly, her hair—brown like Miriam's—was pulled back under a demure prayer *kapp*.

She walked toward Miriam, her face alight with interest.

"I know who you are! There were pictures in the police reports they made us read. You're Miriam Hochstedler. I'm Allison Cantrell." She held out her hand. "I'm playing you in the movie."

CHAPTER NINETEEN

✤

"SORRY, MISS. WE HAVE TO GO NOW."

Miriam heard the words, spoken urgently in Reuben's deep voice. She felt his hand in the small of her back, strong and reassuring, nudging her to the side, to step around the girl.

Miriam heard and felt everything, but her mind stayed blank. She couldn't think, she couldn't breathe, and she couldn't get her feet to move.

The girl flicked an apprehensive glance at Reuben, but she kept her hand out, waiting for Miriam to take it. So—slowly, Miriam did.

The girl's fingers closed around hers with enthusiastic warmth.

"It's an honor to meet you. What you went through . . ." She made a sympathetic face. "It was such a tragedy. When I read the script, I just bawled. I want to say, I'm really sorry about what happened to your family."

"I—thank you," Miriam whispered. She looked at Reuben. He was watching her closely, his eyes worried. His hand was still at her back, and she could feel how tense he was. He was poised to step between her and this woman at any second, to whisk her out of this tent if she started to fall apart.

For some reason, knowing that lent her strength. She'd felt the same when she'd been small and *Daed* had lifted her to pet their Jersey bull. She'd been scared before that, but with *Daed*'s arms around her, the animal hadn't seemed nearly so frightening.

The other woman—Allison?—finally let go of her hand and touched Miriam's sleeve with a tentative smile. "These clothes take some getting used to. You really wear this kind of thing all the time? I couldn't stand it another minute, so I changed. They don't kick up too much of a fuss as long as I leave the *kapp* on. It takes a long time to get that fixed right. My hair is super curly, and it never wants to lay flat like it's supposed to."

"Mine doesn't, either," Miriam managed.

The girl smiled bigger, flashing super-white teeth. "It's pretty, though—your hair, I mean." She leaned around, trying to get a look at the back of Miriam's head. "How do you keep it pinned up?" When the girl touched the edge of her *kapp*, Miriam flinched.

"We have to go," Reuben repeated firmly. "You done with that cone, Miriam?"

"*Ja*, I guess so." The last of the ice cream had melted over her hand. Reuben tossed it in an oversized garbage can just outside the tent and snatched a wad of paper towels from a roll sitting in a bucket with some other supplies. He dipped it in a water trough and handed it to her.

"You can wipe off with that," he murmured in *Deutsch*. "Come on."

"It was so nice to meet you!" the girl called after them.

Miriam was too numb to answer. They were halfway to the truck before she found her wits again—or some of them anyway.

"I should have said, 'You, too.'"

He frowned down at her. "*Vass?*"

He was speaking *Deutsch* more and more these days. "To the girl back there. She said it was nice to meet me, and I should have said, 'You, too.' I didn't, and that was rude."

"I wouldn't worry about it." He was walking so fast, she had to scurry to keep up with him. They reached the truck in no time, and he helped her in, slamming the door shut behind her.

He was acting odd—almost as if he were angry, but she knew he wasn't. He was worried about her, worried that she'd have one of her attacks. And no wonder. A month ago, this would have brought one on, certain sure.

But strangely enough, not today.

Miriam settled into the seat and prodded at her feelings, the way she'd cautiously poked a dead snake with a stick yesterday in the henhouse.

Meeting that girl—the one who was supposed to be her—had caught her off guard. Her heart felt stirred up and sore, but there was none of the frantic blankness that came with the fear.

Allison hadn't been so frightening. She'd been very polite, although she'd certainly looked strange. A prayer *kapp* along with those raggedy jeans and an almost-not-there-at-all shirt . . . it was a mismatch for sure.

Reuben climbed into the truck and immediately started the engine. "I shouldn't have taken you there," he muttered.

"It was my idea." Her mind lingered on the actress, trying to remember details. "She's pretty," she said. "That Allison. Don't you think?"

"I didn't notice." He backed out of the parking spot and turned toward the exit from the lot. "I was too busy looking at you."

His words made something sweet and shy bloom in her breast.

She studied his profile as he scanned the highway for

oncoming cars. He didn't look happy. There was a deep crease along his forehead, and his mouth was a straight, hard line.

He blamed himself for this.

"It's all right," she offered softly. Then, in a stronger voice, "I'm all right."

"Thank goodness for that."

"She doesn't look much like me," Miriam went on, her mind still on the girl. "Except maybe for her hair. I wonder why they picked her."

Reuben shrugged tensely. "Because she's the kind of girl *Englischers* like to look at, I guess." He pulled out into the road and turned toward home.

"Is she the kind of girl you like to look at?" The question slipped out, surprising her.

Maybe it surprised him, too. He glanced at her, his eyes skimming over her face so intently that it felt like a touch. "No."

"What kind do you like, then?"

He turned his attention back to the road, veering carefully around a buggy going in the same direction. "The kind with strawberry ice cream on her nose."

That sweet bloom in her breast warmed and grew. She raised her hand to her nose and—sure enough—found a sticky spot right on the tip of it. She wiped it off with a laugh.

"You're allergic to strawberries," she pointed out.

He'd come to a stop sign, but he didn't look at her. "You asked me what I liked, not what I could have."

The warmth in her heart chilled. "Oh."

He tapped the steering wheel as he waited his turn at the sign. "Breeze is coming along." He was changing the subject, reminding her that the horse was all they really needed to talk about.

She swallowed and nodded. "He's getting better faster and faster now."

"That's the way it usually goes when you're close to the end of things."

The end of things.

She clasped her hands tightly in her lap and struggled to keep her voice even. "So you're almost finished with him?"

"I think so. If he behaves himself in the pasture tomorrow, he'll be ready for me to take on the road. That'll be the final test. Once he gets that down, I'll have done all I can."

"I want to come with you. On the road, when you take Breeze out for the first time."

He shook his head. "I don't think—"

"It's been our journey together, in a way, Breeze's and mine. I'd like to be there at the finish of it."

A muscle jumped in his jaw, but he appeared to be thinking it over. "Your *bruder* won't like the idea much."

No, Joseph wouldn't. He would worry. "Maybe not. But I will make this decision for myself. Will you take me with you when it's time?"

He took his time before he answered. "I will." He threw her a look. "It'll be another two–three days at the most. In the meantime, it's best you steer clear when I'm working with Breeze. It doesn't do to baby the horse at this stage. He's got some hard lessons to learn before he's ready for the road."

"All right."

Miriam tried to enjoy the ride home, but an uneasy mood had fallen over them both. Neither of them said much, and when he pulled up in front of the barn, he didn't lean across her to help with the handle like before. He jumped out and came around instead, and when he pulled the door open, he left plenty of space between them.

"I'll let you know when it's time," he said. "Tell Naomi not to worry about suppers for me from now on."

She frowned. "What? Why?"

His gaze skimmed her face, then flicked away over the pasture, where Breeze was grazing the stubby new grass.

"I'll eat in town. Looks like I'd best keep a closer eye on those horses, so I'll run up there soon as I'm done here every day."

"Maybe I could go with you again sometime."

She knew what the answer was going to be before he spoke. "That probably wouldn't be a good idea, since I'll be working." His mouth curved up for the first time since they'd started home. "But you did real good today, Miriam."

"*Denki*. And thank you for the ice cream, too."

"You earned it."

She watched him walk away, toward the workshop. Two–three days, he'd said. She sighed. That seemed like an eternity—and no time at all.

Reuben was right. Joseph didn't like the idea of Miriam riding along on Breeze's first buggy pull, but he didn't argue as much as she'd expected. However, on the day Reuben had set for the trip, she was startled to see Emma driving into the yard—alone. She was surprised again when Naomi, instead of settling down at the kitchen table for a morning of happy mother-to-be talk, excused herself and went upstairs.

Emma smiled. "Why don't you make us some tea, Mirry, and we'll visit?"

"All right." Miriam shot her older sister a narrow look as she went to fill the kettle with water. "Although you're not really here to drink tea, are you?"

Emma lifted an eyebrow. "Do I need a reason to visit my sister?"

"On a busy weekday morning?" Miriam set the kettle on the stove to heat. Taking down a teapot, she chose four bags of Emma's favorite herbal tea. "*Ja*, I think maybe you do."

She plunked two teacups on the table, then sat, resting her elbows on the kitchen table. "Is this about me going along in the buggy when Reuben takes Breeze out this afternoon? Because I want to go."

"I know you do." Emma hesitated, her face serious.

"Joseph was worried about that, and I was, too, to start with. But Sam thinks Reuben will handle Breeze fine, and that there's little danger in it. He told Joseph so, and I think it eased his mind."

Miriam had been braced for an argument, and Emma's unexpected agreement deflated her. "Well, good," she said finally. "You've all been worried about me not leaving the farm. You should be happy that I want to go places now."

"We are." Emma toyed with her spoon. "We're so thankful you're doing better, Mirry. Never doubt that for a minute. But . . ." Her sister looked up, her blue eyes concerned. "We're also worried about you."

Miriam sighed. "If this is about Reuben—"

"It is, *ja*." Emma looked as tense and careful as if she were stepping out onto a half-frozen pond. "All these changes in you—they seem to have come along with Reuben, ain't so?"

"If they're good changes, what difference does that make?"

"I asked the same question, at the start." Emma's face was serious. "Joseph says you're getting stubborn—feisty, he called it." Her sister's somber expression lifted, and her eyes twinkled. "He said you were reminding him of me."

"That's not a bad thing."

"It depends on where it leads, I think. Please don't be angry, Miriam, or hurt. Joseph says he bumbled things when he tried to speak to you about this before, and he still blames himself for Caleb leaving. He thought maybe we should talk this over together, you and I."

The kettle purred. Miriam rose and poured the boiling water into the waiting teapot. Her temper was nearly boiling, too, and it was taking all her self-control to stay calm.

Her brother and sister meant well. She knew that. But she was tired of this, and she didn't like them teaming up to tell her what she knew perfectly well already—Reuben was off-limits.

She carried the teapot to the table. She set it between them and took her seat—along with a deep breath. "Fine. Say whatever it is you've come to say and let's get it over with."

Emma looked hurt, but she held her ground. "All right, I will. Reuben's not the man for you, *schwesdre*. He's not a member of the church."

"I know that."

"Your head knows it, maybe. We're worried about your heart." Emma's face was serious and sad. "It's natural for you to be interested in someone. It's time. Your friends have all married and are starting families. And Reuben's a nice-enough-looking fellow."

Nice enough looking

Miriam's mind brought up a picture of Reuben, working with Breeze in the dim dustiness of the barn. Fighting with all his strength to save a frightened horse, his jaw set, muscles straining against an ill-fitting shirt that he wore out of kindness to a woman he hardly knew.

"Reuben Brenneman is a lot more than nice enough looking."

"Miriam . . ." Emma shook her head.

"Breeze wouldn't be going out on the road today if it wasn't for Reuben. And he hasn't only helped the horse, which is all we asked of him. He's helped me, too, more than all those doctors and pills we paid good money for. Instead of criticizing him, maybe my family should be grateful."

"We are!" Emma's agreement came swiftly, and it sounded sincere. "Of course we are. It's just that he's not—"

"Not a member of the church," Miriam snapped. "Don't you think I know that?"

Emma stared at her, shocked.

Miriam flushed with guilty embarrassment. She'd raised her voice. She'd not meant to, but she had.

"I'm sorry," she said. "I shouldn't have spoken to you like that."

"You're forgiven," Emma murmured. She still looked taken aback. "And Joseph is wrong. It's not me you're sounding like. It's Caleb." She leaned earnestly across the table. "So you can see, can't you? Why he'd be worried? Miriam, we've already lost so much. We can't lose you, too."

"You're not going to lose me." She sloshed tea into her cup and spooned too much sugar into it, watching it dissolve. "Reuben doesn't think about me like that."

"That's not what it looked like over at Katie's."

Miriam glanced up sharply.

"I'd not been too worried about it until then. I know how Joseph frets, and I didn't take it seriously. But I wasn't the only one who noticed how his eyes followed you, Miriam. Sam noticed, too. He thought maybe it was a good thing, that maybe if Reuben . . . cared . . . about you, he'd decide to stay here and join the church. But that reminded me of Caleb and Rhoda, and I wasn't so sure." Emma waited, and when Miriam didn't answer, she went on. "A woman can shipwreck her life if she marries the wrong man. Look at poor Rhoda—at the fix she and the children have been left in because she married a man too proud to yield to the church."

"That's not the same thing. The church hurt Reuben, Emma. I don't know exactly how, but it did. Caleb was angry at the church because they wanted him to forgive instead of going after Trevor Abbot. But Reuben—" She broke off, unable to explain exactly what she meant. "It's not the same as Caleb," she repeated. "It's more like Sam losing his sight, I think. Only Reuben's hurt is hidden away, so people don't see it, and don't make allowances like they do for Sam. But he's just as hurt, in a different way."

Emma sat there for a minute or two, her face pained. When she spoke, her voice was careful and measured. "That may be true, Mirry. And if it is, I'm sorry for him. But—" Emma swallowed hard. "There are hurts our love can't fix. Like Sam's eyes. I love my *mann* with all my heart, but I can't make him see again like he did before. And so in marrying him, I take on that hurt as my own, to bear for the rest of my life."

"But you're happy with Sam."

"I am very happy. But I'm here with my family and my faith to support me. This pain you say Reuben carries—it's worse than Sam's eye problems because it separates him from the things meant to help him. If you bind your heart to his. . . . Don't do it, Miriam. Don't put yourself or this family through that. We've suffered enough already, all of us."

The pain in her sister's voice brought hot tears prickling into Miriam's eyes. Oh, she hated this—she hated causing worry and trouble to the people she loved best in the world.

"It doesn't matter, Emma," she said, working hard to force the words around the tears clogging her throat. "Truly it doesn't. Reuben's leaving soon, and he's no intention of asking me to go with him."

Emma looked at her, and Miriam saw answering tears sparkling in her sister's pretty blue eyes.

"I hope he doesn't," she said quietly. "I pray he doesn't. Because if he does, I think we may lose you, too, whether you go with him or not."

CHAPTER TWENTY

❧

"YOU READY?" REUBEN HALTED BREEZE AT THE END of the driveway and looked at Miriam seated beside him in the buggy. She offered a tight smile and a nod, but he still hesitated.

Something wasn't right. She wasn't acting like herself. Or rather, she was acting more like she had when he'd first come. She was pale and jumpy. Her hands were clenched in her lap, and her brows were drawn together over her eyes.

Seeing her this way again bothered him, and worry put an edge to his voice. "You sure you want to come along? I've not much doubt I can handle Breeze, but things could get interesting if he gets startled. There's no reason why you can't go out on a later run just as well, when he's more adjusted."

"No. I'd like to go now." When he didn't snap the reins, she frowned. "I'm fine, Reuben."

"*Nee*, you're not. Is this to do with your sister stopping by this morning?" He'd seen the old Percheron that Sam's wife drove, waiting in the barn. It had seemed an odd time for a visit, and he'd wondered about it. "Did she come because of what happened in town? Because I took you over to where the movie was being filmed, and we ran into that actress?"

He wouldn't blame any of them for being upset about that. He was still upset about it himself.

She shifted on the seat. "I didn't mention that to anybody. There didn't seem much point in worrying them since nothing bad happened. And you didn't take me. Going there was my idea."

Maybe that was true, but still, if there was any fuss over it, he'd rather they took it out on him. Miriam seemed more upset now than she had been at the time.

Of course, he didn't really know how she'd been feeling over the last couple of days. He'd not seen much of her since their trip to town. He'd been keeping his distance.

These feelings growing inside him—they worried him. He figured the best way to deal with them was to choke them off—and spend as much time away from Miriam as possible. It hadn't been easy. Every day he'd had to fight the urge to go into the house on some excuse or other just to lay eyes on her.

He hadn't gone, not once. But he'd sure wanted to.

"Reuben." She nodded toward the road. "Let's go."

"All right." He flicked the reins and brought his attention back to where it was supposed to be, on the horse. Breeze was uneasy, too. Reuben could tell from the way the horse held his head, but he'd learned his lessons well. When Reuben said to go, Breeze went, whether he liked the idea or not.

The road, though, was a new challenge. The memories lurking in Breeze's brain made him nervous. Roads meant pain, and although he trotted along obediently, he was none too happy about it.

"He's doing real *gut*," Miriam said softly. "Ain't so?"

She was smiling, and some of her gloom seemed to have lifted.

"So far." A car topped the hill ahead of them, and Breeze pulled against the reins, trying to edge off the road. Reuben held him firm. "Here we go," he muttered. "Best hang on, Miriam. *Sell is awreit*, Breeze," he reassured the uneasy horse.

He could sense her holding her breath as the car rushed by. Breeze danced sideways slightly, showing the whites of his eyes, but Reuben wouldn't give him an inch. When the car had passed, Breeze's ears were turned back. The horse was plainly upset, but he clopped sulkily onward.

"He doesn't like being on the road, but it's the cars that really worry him," he explained. "He needs to get used to them again. Once a good many have passed and he's not been hurt again, he'll likely calm down."

Hopefully.

"Like me," Miriam said. When Reuben looked at her, she smiled at him again. It was a real smile this time, and it made the bottom drop right out of his stomach. He looked away fast, trying to focus his attention on Breeze.

"I've calmed down, too," Miriam explained. "It's been gradual-like, but when I think back to when you first came—how scared I was of you . . . Of everything, really." She shook her head. "It's like I was a different person. Like—" She gestured with her hands. "Like I was a chick stuck in its shell trying my best to break out of it. But I just couldn't."

"You managed it in the end."

Another car was coming, this time from behind them. Reuben kept a firm hand on the reins as it blew past them, and Breeze's struggle was shorter this time.

The ears stayed stubbornly back, though. Breeze wasn't enjoying this trip.

Reuben didn't blame him, but he didn't share the horse's opinion. He was enjoying this drive—more than he should.

He'd missed spending time with Miriam. It felt wonderful *gut* to be driving along in this buggy with her beside him, a sweet spring wind cooling his cheeks, and Breeze doing even better than expected.

"I wouldn't have managed if it hadn't been for you," Miriam was saying. "And for Breeze." She drew in a breath and looked forward over the horse's back. "Him needing me—that kept me going. And you, believing I could help, and showing me what to do, being so kind. That's one reason I wanted to come along today. Like you said the other day, we're coming to the end of things, and I want to be along to celebrate with him. And with you."

He felt her gaze on his face, but he kept his own eyes straight ahead. One more of those smiles, and he'd lose his head. He couldn't afford to do that.

"You'd have fought your way out of that shell sooner or later on your own, I expect." Another car came toward them, and this time the horse veered only slightly. "That's better, Breeze," Reuben said. "You're all right."

An ear flicked irritably, the horse's only reaction. Miriam laughed.

"He's doing lots better, but he's mad at you."

"I don't blame him. This is no fun for him."

"It was no fun for me at first, either, working with the man in the *Englischer* clothes. You scared me to death. But now, look at me, riding along here with you. Do you know," she said, "I've been watching for spring all this time, moping because winter was taking so long leaving, and when it came, I barely noticed. Now everything's green and the buttercups are blooming. And here I am, on this real pretty day, going to town just like anybody else. Isn't it funny? I prayed and prayed you'd be able to help Breeze, but I never dreamed you'd be able to help me, too."

"I didn't do so much." The unsettled feeling in his belly was getting worse. He wanted badly to look at her, but he didn't dare.

She was not for him, he reminded himself. It had taken him years of scheming and working to get away from a life like hers—a life of buggies and church services and nit-picky rules that hindered more than they helped. He'd be a fool to jump back into it just because this girl with her slow smile and her pretty eyes had worked her way into his daydreams.

"*Ja*, you did, too."

She had a sweet voice, Miriam did, even when she argued. Soft and gentle, but there was a melody in it. Like a happy bird singing in a tree.

Simply good, just like her.

He snapped the reins on Breeze's back lightly, speeding him up. Another car whooshed past them, but this time the horse didn't react at all.

Which, Reuben reflected, was a very good thing. He was having trouble keeping his thoughts on his work. He didn't need any surprises.

"Where are we going?" Miriam asked.

"Nowhere in particular," he said. "The main thing right now is to get him back on the road, show him it's nothing to be afraid of."

"I wondered if maybe you'd take him back to where the accident happened. It's a bit of a drive, though."

"I might, before I leave. Probably not a good idea for the first time out, though. Anyhow, he might not react to the place at all. It's the cars, mostly, that bother him. That, and the fact he has to bend his will to mine to pull the buggy. Trusting me doesn't feel safe. Once he gets past that, it shouldn't matter where he's driven. He'll do all right anyplace."

Miriam shuddered. "I'm not sorry we aren't going there. I didn't see the accident, of course. I only heard stories, but I could imagine it in my mind. Poor Sam and little Janie. It gave me nightmares for weeks."

"Janie—she's Sam's little niece, the one who was hurt?"

"That's right."

"How's she doing now?"

"Lots better. She has some pretty bad scars, but that's the worst of it. I've seen her once, when Sam's sister brought her by for a visit. But other than the scars, she is all right."

"She's not troubled by what happened? Not frightened-like?"

Miriam shook her head. "*Nee*, she doesn't seem to be. When she came to our house, she seemed like a very happy little girl."

"That's good, then. Scars on the outside, they're never the problem. It's the ones that go deep that cause the trouble."

"Like Breeze's."

"*Ja.*"

"And yours. Ain't so?"

He turned to her, then, surprised. She looked at him steadily. "You've got scars on your arms. Some look like burns."

"Some of them are."

"How did you get them?"

"Farrier work takes heat. I wear an apron and gloves, but sparks find their way around those."

"What about the one on your face? It's not a burn, is it?"

No. It had been a bottle. Unfortunately, drink didn't hinder *Daed*'s aim all that much.

He wasn't going to tell her that. "My scars are my business." He kept his voice gentle but firm.

"Not if they still hurt you," she answered matter-of-factly. "Then they're the business of anybody who cares about you."

He didn't want to have this conversation. Especially not now, in this close buggy. They were practically elbow to elbow. He should have hitched up the roomier family buggy instead of this two-seater.

He shouldn't have agreed for her to come along in the first place, but he didn't have to think very long to know why he had.

"Reuben?"

"I don't talk about the past, Miriam. I've put it behind me, and that's where I want it to stay."

He heard a noise and looked behind them. A red pickup had crested the hill they'd just gone down, and it was coming up on them fast. He nudged Breeze very slightly to the side to give the driver more room to pass.

"But if it troubles you . . ." She put one hand on his arm lightly, and his pulse jumped like a colt turned out to pasture for the first time. "If you talked about it with a friend, maybe—"

The truck pulled out beside them to pass, and Reuben glanced to the side. He caught a glimpse of three laughing *Englisch* teenagers. Just as the pickup drew even with them, the driver looked in his direction, grinned, and laid down on the horn.

Everything happened so fast, Reuben barely had time to react. Breeze reared and lurched onto the shoulder of the road, dragging the buggy with him. Reuben heard Miriam cry out as they bumped over the rough ground, and he braced himself, flipping the reins around his wrists and pulling back. "Whoa!"

The truck zoomed past, horn still blaring, spitting black exhaust as Reuben fought to get Breeze under control.

He'd have to get away from the traffic to settle the horse down. There was a smaller road forking off to the right, and he struggled to veer the terrified animal toward it.

Fortunately, Breeze was as anxious to get off the highway as Reuben was, and in a few minutes, he was able to slow the horse to a stop. Breeze stood trembling, his ribs heaving in and out, his eyes wide with fear. Reuben set the brake and turned to Miriam.

"Are you all right?"

She didn't answer right away. She was holding one hand to the side of her face, a trickle of blood seeping under her fingers. His heart startled, and his worry heated into anger.

"You're hurt. Let me see." His hand shook as he reached for hers, and for some reason that made him madder. *Dumm* kids. What kind of parent gave such a reckless boy the keys to a vehicle?

He tugged her hand away from the wound. "It's not bad," he said with relief. "It's only a scrape."

"I banged against the side of the buggy. It was my fault. I wasn't holding on tight enough."

"It was not your fault." He rummaged in the buggy, looking for something to wipe her face. He found a rag that looked clean, and he dabbed at the spot.

She winced, and he made a soft, soothing sound. "It's all right. You'll have a bruise, but that'll be the worst of it, I think." He was thankful for that. If she'd been hurt—really hurt . . .

And she could've been so easily.

"Is Breeze all right?"

"*Ja, ja.* He is fine." He folded the rag and blotted the blood again. "Don't worry over him."

"Mister? Excuse me?"

Reuben leaned out to look behind the buggy. The pickup was parked several lengths behind them, its engine still running. The trio of *Englisch* boys had gotten out. The teenagers weren't grinning anymore, and one edged a few steps closer.

"What do they want?" Miriam's face went a shade paler, her breaths coming too short and too fast.

She hadn't had one of her attacks in so long, but she was on the brink of having one now. If that boy came another step forward, she'd fall apart.

He wasn't going to let it happen.

"Wait there," he called.

He turned back to Miriam. Cupping her chin in his palm, he looked into her eyes. "It will be all right," he murmured fiercely in *Deutsch.* "I am here, and no harm will come to you. Do you hear me?" She didn't answer, and he tweaked her chin very, very gently. "Do you?"

She nodded, her gaze fixed on his. "*Ja*. I hear."

"*Gut*. You wait here while I have a word with these boys."

She stared deep into his eyes, so close her breath puffed against his lips. She nodded again, and he saw the worst of the fear starting to ebb away.

He waited another few seconds, making sure. Then, after double-checking the brake, he leapt down and strode toward the sheepish-looking boy.

"Are you all right, mister? We saw your horse spook, so we came back to make sure. We're sorry—we were just—"

"Being foolish." Reuben bit the words out. "Which of you is the driver?"

None of them spoke, but he caught the quick looks the other boys threw in the tallest one's direction. The teenager's eyes widened in alarm as Reuben brushed past the other boys, heading in his direction.

"Hey—" The boy held up his hands. "Cool off. It was a joke, okay?"

"There's a woman in that buggy bleeding because of your joke."

"Look, we came back to apologize. We don't want any trouble," the first boy said nervously.

Reuben didn't spare him a glance. He kept his eyes on the driver. "Then you shouldn't have been causing trouble by blowing your horn at buggies, should you?"

The third boy snickered. "Look out, Chase. This guy might stab you with a pitchfork or something."

"Shut up, Mark." Narrowing his eyes at Reuben, the driver puffed out his skinny chest and leaned against the hood of the truck. "It's not my fault you can't control your stupid horse."

Life with his father had taught Reuben to move fast. In two seconds flat he had the boy by the scruff of the neck. "Maybe you'd better be the one shutting up." He gave the boy a little shake. "Or thanking God, maybe, that I *can* control a horse."

"Hey, whoa. Calm down." The first boy had rushed close and was jabbering at Reuben's elbow. "We're sorry, we really are. That's why we stopped to make sure you were okay. We didn't mean for anybody to get hurt. Please, let my brother go." Reuben still didn't glance in his direction, keeping his eyes on the smart-mouthed fellow in front of him.

"I haven't heard this one say he was sorry."

"Chase, apologize," the brother—younger by the sound of his half-changed voice—pleaded. "Don't be an idiot. This guy's got muscles like a freaking bodybuilder. We don't want any trouble with him."

The boy in Reuben's grip looked startled, but he wasn't done showing off yet. "He can't do anything. The Amish aren't allowed to fight."

"That's true." Reuben leaned forward until his nose was an inch away from the teenager's face. "But I," he said, biting each word off distinctly, "am not Amish."

He had the satisfaction of seeing the boy's face pale. "Fine. Okay. I'm sorry, all right?"

Reuben gripped the boy's neck for one more second, before releasing him. Despite his bravado, his knees must have been wobbly. He flopped against the hood of his truck like a rag doll. "I hope you are sorry. And I wouldn't go blowing my horn at any more buggies if I were you."

"We won't. We promise. Come on, guys." The younger brother was herding the others toward the pickup. "Sorry, mister. It won't happen again."

"You're smarter than he is," Reuben said grimly. "If there are any grown-ups in your family with good sense, you'd best tell them what happened today. Otherwise, he'll do it again likely, or something just as stupid, until he ends up really hurting somebody."

The younger boy met Reuben's eyes, and gave a slight,

almost-imperceptible nod. Then he got into the truck, wedging himself into the front seat beside the other two. He barely had the door closed before the driver took off, spinning loose rocks as they turned toward the highway.

Reuben half jogged back to Miriam. She gazed at him from the buggy, her eyes wide.

"I thought . . . I thought for a minute you were going to hit that boy."

"I thought for a minute I was, too." He swung up into the seat. "It might do him some good if somebody did."

Then he flinched. He couldn't believe those words had come out of his mouth. The angry heat in his blood chilled, and the world suddenly came back into focus.

He looked at Miriam. The bleeding had mostly stopped, but fear lingered in her eyes. He'd only frightened her more, he realized, squaring off with that teenager.

"I'm sorry," he said. "My temper—it got the better of me." The words came automatically—and no surprise there. How many times had he heard his own father make the same excuse?

His stomach rolled sickly. He released the brake and flipped the reins. "I'd better take you home."

"But you shouldn't do that, should you? Didn't you say something a few minutes ago about ending things on a good note? This isn't a good note."

"But your head . . . you'll need to wash up and clean that cut."

"I'll be all right for a while longer. We shouldn't undo all your hard work with Breeze."

He wasn't sure what to do. He didn't care about the horse right now, but he didn't want to upset her more than he already had. "All right. We'll go to the end of this road and turn around. But then I'm taking you home." Breeze had lost most of his fight for the moment anyhow, so likely it would be all right. He snapped the reins, and they started off.

"It was the horn, wasn't it?" she asked after a minute.

"*Ja*," he answered grimly. "I'll have to work on that. We'll practice, like, blowing the horn at him until he doesn't startle anymore. I'd have done it before if I'd known it was a trigger for him."

"That's our fault. One of us should have told you. We all knew that's why Breeze bolted the first time—when the accident happened. Because somebody blew a horn, and it frightened him."

Yeah, that would have been important information to have. Reuben tamped down his frustration. "I'm sorry you were hurt, Miriam. I told you I could handle the horse and look what happened."

"It's all right, Reuben. Besides, you did handle the horse. And that boy, too."

"I lost my temper." That bothered him. But seeing that blood on Miriam's face—and worse than that . . . the fear in her eyes. It had set him off.

"Seems to me you held on to it pretty well, all things considered."

He glanced at her and was surprised to see a twinkle in her eye. Her face was still pale, and her forehead was reddening. It would be a fine bruise by tomorrow.

He should know; he'd seen more than his share of them.

The little road had narrowed into an overgrown dirt path that looked like it led nowhere. Trees—pines and still-bare oaks—arched overhead, giving the sense that they were the only two people in the world.

Time to turn around.

He pulled Breeze to a stop. The horse obeyed with no trouble, proof that he was worn out, too.

"This wasn't your fault, Reuben," Miriam insisted quietly. "You didn't know about Breeze and the horn. It's like that day when I ran out of the barn, when you told me not to move. You didn't know—"

He frowned when she stopped short. "What didn't I know?"

She struggled a second or two before she went on. "That it was what he said to me. Trevor, that day in the store. *Don't move.*"

"What?" Reuben stared at her, horrified. No wonder she'd run away.

He fumbled for something to say, some way to apologize. "Miriam," he began, but that was as far as he got. How could a man apologize for something like that? He had no idea.

"It's all right. We can't help what we don't know about. You're too hard on yourself." To his astonishment, she reached out and laid a hand on his cheek. "You're a *gut* man, Reuben." She smiled, and the sweetness of it turned his insides to jelly the way it always did.

Only this time, with her hand resting so gentle and warm against his cheek, he didn't have the strength to resist it. He used the last remaining scrap of his wits to set the brake.

Then he gave in to the foolishness he'd been fighting for days, leaned forward, and kissed her.

CHAPTER TWENTY-ONE

❧

REUBEN'S KISS WAS LIKE REUBEN HIMSELF, STRONG and sure—and unexpectedly sweet. It was over in a few short seconds, but that was long enough for Miriam to feel the thrill of it all the way to her toes.

When he lifted his mouth from hers, she opened her eyes, stunned.

She'd not expected that. Yet, in another way, she'd been expecting it for a long time, dreaming about it in the most secret part of her mind—despite what she'd been telling Emma and Joseph.

Despite what she'd been telling herself.

At first Reuben looked as surprised as she felt herself, but the astonishment on his face faded quickly into something else.

"I shouldn't have done that."

She wasn't sure what she was supposed to say. "I didn't

mind," she managed after a minute. "It was a very nice kiss."

For a second, the worry in his eyes lightened. "Have many to compare it to, do you?"

"No," she answered honestly. "That was my first."

She didn't know anything about post-kissing etiquette, but that must have been the wrong thing to say. The amusement faded from his eyes.

"I knew it," he muttered. "I had no business doing that."

"You mean because you don't . . . like me that way?" She held her breath as she waited for his answer, her insides as tight as a coiled spring.

He blew out a breath. "No, that's not what I mean. Don't smile. It's not good news, not for either of us, if you feel the same way." He waited a beat before asking, "Do you?"

"*Ja.*" She couldn't help smiling at him, whether he wanted her to or not. "I think I do."

Once again the unhappiness in his eyes lifted—for an instant. Then he looked away, over Breeze's back, toward where the road played out ahead of them, turning into a narrow, overgrown track.

"I wish you didn't because those feelings are like this road here. They can't lead us anyplace worth going."

Maybe she shouldn't ask. But she had to. "Are you certain sure of that, Reuben?"

"I meant what I said to that boy back there. I'm not Plain, not anymore, and I never will be. And you—" He ran a hand roughly through his hair. "You're the most Amish girl I've ever met in my life."

"And to you that's a bad thing?"

His face softened. "*Nee*, Mirry. Not bad. You're sincere in what you believe, and I respect that. You're forgiving, and you're unselfish and kind. You've got all the virtues the church preaches about." He blew out a long breath. "And— I know it's not something you're used to hearing, but you're also just about the prettiest girl I've ever seen. The truth is, if somebody was trying to figure out the best way to tempt me to change my mind, it'd be you."

Just when her heart soared upward—such sweet things for him to say—he went on. "But I'm not going to change my mind, Miriam."

That was her answer. He could hardly have spoken any plainer, but she couldn't resist pressing a little. "So there's no chance—no chance at all? I mean, you've never wondered in all these years if maybe you made a mistake? If maybe you ought to come back to the church?"

She held her breath as she watched him think it over. She knew whatever he said next would be the truth, whether she wanted to hear it or not.

He studied his hands, clenched in his lap. "I've always been certain I did right, going *Englisch*. There's never been a doubt in my mind. But since I came here . . . since I met you . . . *ja*, I'll admit, I've wondered some."

Since I met you. Reuben's confession sent a hot burst of joy and hope through her heart. "Well, wondering always comes before knowing, ain't so? You should pray about it and see where *Gott* leads you." An idea occurred to her. "You could talk to the bishop maybe. Abram King. You saw him at church."

"That man whose wife kept taking cookies away from him?"

Not a very dignified description, but she couldn't argue with it. "*Ja*, that's him. Maybe he could help you think things through."

She made herself sound calm and reasonable, but she trembled as she waited for his answer.

He waited so long before speaking that she wasn't sure he'd even heard her suggestion. His eyes moved over her face, lingering on the hurt spot near her temple.

He touched it lightly. "You've stopped bleeding. Is it hurting still?"

"Not so much, not now." She'd nearly forgotten about

her bump on the head. Reuben's kiss had put it right out of her mind.

"I don't like seeing you hurt, Miriam. And I certain sure never want to be the cause of it."

Something about the way he spoke made the back of her neck prickle uneasily.

"But Reuben—" she started.

Before she could finish, he flicked the reins against Breeze's back. He turned the buggy in a series of back-and-forth motions, until they were pointed back down the road they'd come on, heading toward home.

He didn't speak again, and by the time they pulled into the driveway, Miriam almost felt as if the kiss had never even happened.

Almost. But there was a new expression in his eyes as he watched her getting out of the buggy. Something had shifted between them, and she wasn't sure whether to feel hopeful— or worried.

"Come to supper tonight," she said. "Please?"

She thought he was going to refuse, but after a brief hesitation, he nodded. "I will, then, if you want me to."

His eyes lingered on hers for a second longer, then he clucked to Breeze and drove the exhausted horse toward the barn for unhitching.

Miriam watched him go, her mind spinning. So much had happened in the last little while. Naomi would be expecting her to help with the meal, but it might be best if she collected her wits before going inside. So instead of heading into the house, she walked to the chicken coop.

The minute she closed the door behind herself, the chickens hurried over, expecting a treat. When she didn't offer anything, they clucked their displeasure, then went back to scratching in the wood shavings Joseph had brought from his workshop.

She looked around the tiny building, remembering when

even this familiar place had been beyond her reach. Those first awful weeks, she'd not been able to set foot out of the house. Going to the coop had been out of the question because she had to cross the yard to reach it. And the yard ended at the road where *Englischers* stopped and gawked, trying to get photographs of the poor Amish family who'd been all over the news.

Even now the memory made her shudder, and she pushed her mind to happier things.

Like the first time she'd made it back out here. That had been a happy day. Naomi had needed to walk with her, steadying her arm and whispering encouragements the whole time. Miriam had been scared half out of her mind, shaking like a leaf and expecting her knees to buckle at any minute. But with Naomi's help she'd made it—and it had felt like a huge triumph.

Emma had left to help Sam's *aent* by then, but Miriam, Naomi, and Joseph had celebrated together. They'd had scrambled eggs and bacon and pancakes for supper, she remembered, and Naomi had made a lemon pie with a meringue on it. Such a sweet treat—and a fair amount of trouble at the last minute—all for such a tiny victory.

But Naomi had said that they needed to celebrate the happy things together, that it was part of being a family.

They hadn't done much celebrating lately, although her new victories had been much bigger—first going to church, and then to town. It wasn't hard to understand why her family wasn't in a celebrating mood these days.

They were worried. And—in spite of all her protests— they had good reason to be. That kiss . . . and the way she felt about Reuben now . . . it was exactly what they'd been fearing.

She faced that fact while staring at one little hen she'd named after Lydia Zook. The plump bird was always clucking and too interested in whatever the other chickens were eating or doing. She was sweet, though, not like that skinny one there, who was always pecking the others on their heads.

That one she'd named after Sam's grouchy *aent* Ruth.

All the chickens were named after folks she knew. People she'd laughed at and with. People she'd loved all her life. Her family had found it funny, although her mother had finally asked her not to name any more roosters after their previous bishop. Levonia hadn't thought it was respectful, and, she'd said, she didn't want word to get out that she'd throttled Isaac Lambert and stewed him with dumplings.

Miriam smiled at the memory, but her smile faded as her mind went back to the last time she'd seen her mother—on that most awful day.

Her heartbeat started to stutter, and she looked out the window, where Reuben was leading Breeze out to pasture.

Her heartbeat calmed as she watched him. He closed the gate behind the horse. Then he turned and looked at the house for a long, thoughtful moment before vanishing into the barn.

She'd just climbed out of the buggy a few minutes ago, but she wanted to go to the barn and talk with him again. She wanted to see if that special, different look was still in his eyes. She wanted to find some way to convince him to follow her suggestion and talk to the bishop.

Because if he didn't change his mind . . .

She worried her lower lip as Katie Lapp, the hen, tugged at her shoelace.

She'd never once—never in her whole life—imagined leaving Johns Mill. The most she'd dreamed of was getting married and settling someplace close by. A nice little farm, like the Beilers' place down the road, where she could see her brothers and sisters on visiting Sundays. Where they'd all still be in the same church district and could watch each other's children grow, and help each other as long as they lived.

That was the most she'd ever wanted. She still wanted those things, and for the first time her dreams stood a decent chance of coming true. The trouble was, she wasn't sure those dreams would be enough anymore.

Not without Reuben.

CHAPTER TWENTY-TWO

❧

"CALM DOWN." REUBEN GROUND OUT THE WORDS between his teeth. Breeze rolled his eyes and fought the lead rope, trying to bolt across the small pasture. Reuben dug in his heels and held his ground. "It's not going to hurt you. It's just a horn."

It took only a few minutes to get the horse settled, less time than it had before. And already Breeze was acting less terrified and more annoyed.

Things were looking up.

He'd made this training a top priority since their scare on the buggy ride yesterday. Desensitizing the horse to the sound of the horn was step one to making him a safe driving horse. Given how stubborn Breeze could be, Reuben had known it wouldn't be easy.

"Again?" Joseph called from his spot near the fence. Reuben nodded, and Joseph signaled to Miriam, who was stationed in the driver's seat of Reuben's truck.

The horn blared again, long and loud. Even in the middle

of coping with Breeze's reaction to the sound, Reuben found himself fighting a smile.

Miriam might be enjoying her job a little too much.

He soothed the horse until he was standing still, gave him a cookie, told him what a fine animal he was. Then nodded toward Joseph.

Again.

It took three more rounds before Breeze barely spooked at the hated noise. He still trembled and showed the whites of his eyes, though, so there was more work ahead. Reuben fished one last treat out of his pocket for the exhausted horse and called to Joseph.

"That's it for today."

Joseph nodded and walked toward the pickup to tell his sister. Reuben unclipped the lead and let Breeze go. The horse ran off a few paces, then, tired as he was, kicked both his back legs out like a sulky colt. Having made his opinion known, he raced toward the far fence, tail up and streaming.

Reuben watched him go with a weary grin, looping the rope over his arm for easy carrying. Breeze had plenty of spirit. Frustrating as it was just now, that determination would be helpful once it was bent in the right direction. The horse moved well, too, which was no small thing, given what he'd been through. Whoever the vet had been, he'd done a bang-up job on the surgeries.

As Reuben turned toward the barn, his gaze snagged on Miriam—as it always did when she was within his sight. She stood in the yard, talking with her brother. A warm spring breeze rippled her dark green dress, and she put one hand to her hair, steadying the *kapp* against her head. She smiled at something Joseph said, her face lighting up.

Reuben's heart plopped like a rock in a water trough, sending ripples through his chest. She really was the prettiest thing. His stomach twisted into a throbbing knot, the way it did every time he thought about that kiss.

He'd been thinking about it a lot.

She glanced over her brother's shoulder and caught him looking. Her smile brightened, and she lifted her hand in a little wave. He raised his in response, but then Joseph said something, and Miriam's attention refocused on him. She nodded quickly and hurried toward the house.

Just as she'd reached the steps, she turned, her eyes searching for Reuben. She didn't wave again; she only looked at him in a way that tugged at his heart as hard as Breeze had pulled on the lead.

Then she slipped through the back door and vanished.

Reuben shook his head to clear it. He hadn't been this swimmy-headed around a girl in a long time. It was getting ridiculous.

He looked up to find Joseph studying him, his expression unsmiling. The other man turned away and stalked into the barn.

Reuben sighed. He'd prefer to stay in the pasture and give Joseph his space, but he needed to put the lead up and empty his pockets of leftover treats. Anyhow, it might do him good to face up to Miriam's brother. Reuben was overdue for a reminder of how far out of line he was stepping, and Joseph was just the fellow to give him one.

Reuben squared his shoulders and walked into the barn. Joseph was hitching Titus to the family buggy, and he didn't glance up from the task.

"Going someplace?" Reuben asked.

"*Nee.*" Joseph straightened, giving Titus a quick slap. "Not me. I've too much work waiting. Naomi and Miriam are going to town. Naomi wants things from Zook's, and Miriam's hoping to stop by the quilt store."

"Yoder's is open again?" And she was going without him. That was a disappointment. He'd been planning on taking her there himself.

"*Ja*, Mary's back home again now." Joseph busied himself on the other side of the horse now, checking straps. "At least until another grandbaby comes along. So what are you thinking about how things went today? Looked to me like you had him well settled by the end of it."

"It was a good start. Tomorrow, we'll try again. Then it'll be time to take him back on the road. A quiet road someplace where there's not much traffic. You can hitch him to the two-seater, and I'll follow behind in my truck."

Joseph's lips twitched. "Blowing the horn, I'm guessing."

"That's right. And we'll see how he does."

Joseph ran a thoughtful hand over his short beard. "I think he will do all right. He is much better than he was."

"I think so, too."

"He's not the only one." Joseph drew in a breath and shot him a glance over Titus's back. "I've been meaning to have a word with you about Miriam. I've waited for it, and I shouldn't have done. It's well overdue."

Reuben had suspected this was coming, although he doubted Miriam had told her brother about the kiss. But when she'd come home with a cut and a bruise, Joseph must have had questions—questions he had every right to ask.

Reuben raised his chin. "Say what you need to say."

Joseph finished hitching and walked around the horse, giving Titus an absent-minded stroke on the nose. He stood in front of Reuben and looked him squarely in the eye. "What I need to say is thank you."

Reuben stared at him, unsure how to react. He'd been prepared for hard words, not this. So he stayed silent and waited.

"You know I had some concerns about you spending time with my sister. I hope you can understand why. My brother left us and his own family to live among the *Englisch*, and it's a grief we still feel. I know it's different with you. You never joined the church to start with, so you broke no vows by leaving. Even so, I worried Miriam might become . . . unsettled in her faith if she got too *freindlich* with you."

Guilt rose in Reuben's chest, but he pushed it down. That hadn't happened, he reminded himself. If anybody was growing unsettled, it was him, not Miriam.

Joseph scratched at his beard, something Reuben remembered seeing his new brothers-in-law doing as they adjusted to their status as married men. "Miriam was in a bad way after my parents were killed, and I fell into the habit of looking after her. But she's better now, thanks to you."

"I've not done so much."

"You have, though." Despite the words, a certain reserve remained in the other man's eyes. Reuben got the feeling Joseph still worried about how *friendlich* his sister was with this outsider, but he seemed sincere in his gratitude. "None of us could bring her out of her fears, although we all tried. Somehow you did, and you've given her life back to her. I am grateful."

"If I've been any help, I'm glad of it. She's a . . . real nice girl, your sister."

"*Ja*, she is. A sweet girl, with a kind and faithful heart. She deserves a chance at happiness and a family of her own, if *Gott* wills it. Already the fellows are taking notice, going by what I saw at Katie's, so I've *gut* hopes for her future."

Reuben kept his face neutral. He turned aside without commenting, digging in his pockets for the leftover treats. He dropped them in the half-empty bag he'd left by the door, one by one, and changed the subject. "What's your plan for Breeze?"

"Breeze is Sam's horse. I've been happy to bear this small burden for him, but I won't be deciding what's to be done. I'd guess he'll want to sell the animal, once he's safe to drive."

"Miriam might not be so happy about that."

"*Nee*, she might not, and these days my sister has a mind of her own, so I'll not try a guess on how this will all work out. That'll be between her and Sam." Joseph climbed into the buggy to drive it out of the barn.

Reuben stepped back out of the way, but Joseph waited a minute, looking down at him. "I was wrong, I think," he said. "To judge you as I did at the first. There are many reasons why a man might choose not to join the church, and it's not my place to have opinions about such things. My *bruder* knew he wasn't cut out for this life, but he joined the church anyhow. If he'd been a wiser man, he'd have made the same choice you made, maybe, and many folks would be the better for it."

"Don't be too hard on him. There's a lot of pressure to join. Family and friends don't want to see you go, and that makes the decision tougher."

Joseph shook his head. "It wasn't that. Caleb never cared what other folks thought. It was a girl that held him. He didn't have the strength to leave her behind. My parents believed this was a good thing, that a marriage would steady his faith. Maybe Caleb thought so, too. It didn't." He studied Reuben, his expression unreadable. "She could only hold him for so long. You can't change the shape you're made in, I reckon, no matter how much you might want to. It would be best if more people understood that." He tilted his head and looked out the door. "Naomi's waving. They're ready to go, so I'd best get the buggy to them."

Joseph drove out where the two women were waiting. Reuben stayed in the shadows of the barn, watching as the other man helped his wife and sister into the buggy. As Naomi flipped the reins against Titus's back, Miriam cast one last look toward the barn. Then she turned and faced forward, smiling.

After the women had gone, Joseph disappeared into his workshop. The stillness of the farm settled around Reuben, quiet except for the cluck of Miriam's hens, the muffled sounds of Joseph's tools, the low of the milk cow out in the pasture.

It was all perfectly peaceful, but he felt restless. His mind kept circling back to what Joseph had said about his brother.

It was a girl that held him. But she could only hold him for so long.

Reuben rubbed a hand over his face and tried to focus. The stalls needed mucking out. He'd pick up a pitchfork and get to it. Maybe such a job would remind him there was more to this Plain life than a sweet girl with a pretty face. There was backbreaking work and a church that nitpicked you about silly things but went silent when your family's troubles embarrassed them.

He'd barely worked up a sweat when he heard a buggy rolling into the yard. He lifted his head, frowning. Miriam and Naomi shouldn't have been back so quick. Had there been some kind of trouble? Had Miriam's fears gotten the best of her maybe? He leaned the pitchfork in a corner and walked out of the barn to see.

But it wasn't the Hochstedler buggy in the yard. A well-tended horse stood hitched to a two-seater. As Reuben watched, a short, chubby man clambered down from the driver's seat with difficulty and walked around to tie him off. He caught Reuben's eye and smiled.

"Reuben! *Guder mariye.*"

Recognition dawned. That was Abram King, the new bishop of the Hochstedlers' church district—the one Miriam had suggested he talk to.

He nodded briefly—and answered in English, "Good morning to you. If you're looking for Joseph, he's in his workshop."

"*Nee.*" The older man finished with his horse and walked toward the barn. "It's you I've come to see." He peered inside the door with interest. "I've interrupted your work. Find me a pitchfork, and I'll help you while we talk."

Reuben lifted an eyebrow. The bishop of his previous community hadn't visited often, but when he had, he'd never offered to help with any job—especially not a dirty one like this.

"That's all right," he said. "I can take a break for a few minutes. What is it you want to talk about?"

Waving aside the refusal with a smile, Abram walked inside the barn and grabbed the pitchfork. Without waiting for instruction or invitation, he went to Titus's stall and began pitching the soiled straw out into the half-filled wagon Reuben had pulled into position.

"Better to work and talk," he said breathlessly, "than just talk. I'm a farmer myself. Daylight lingers for no man, and there's few among us who've time to stand idle in the middle of a busy day. It's come to my ears that you tangled with some *Englisch* boys on the road yesterday. Is that so?"

Ah. So that's what this was about, not anything to do with Miriam or his own past, two subjects he'd just as soon not discuss. "That's so. They blew the horn beside us when we were driving Breeze—the bay outside there. He's still easy to startle, and horns are a trigger for him."

"*Ja*, I recall what happened with the horse, and I know why you're here, of course. I hear you're making good progress with him."

"Some. Not enough yet to keep him from bolting when those fellows decided to play their little joke."

Abram grunted as he heaved up a particularly large forkful. "These boys made you mad."

"They did, *ja*." Reuben suddenly realized he'd slipped into *Deutsch*. When had that happened? "They were being foolish, and someone could have gotten badly hurt."

"There's no shortage of foolishness in the world, and it sure can get under a man's skin. Well do I know it." The stout man heaved another load of dirty straw into the wagon.

Reuben was no admirer of Amish bishops, but at least this one wasn't a slacker when it came to work. Past time for Reuben to stop staring and start doing his part. He collected a second pitchfork, went into Breeze's stall, and settled to his task.

"Such misbehavior would try any man's patience. But," Abram went on, sounding for all the world as if he were having a casual conversation with a friend, "the problem is, the boys—or one of them in particular—is telling everybody you laid hands on him. And so, I have come to ask. Is he telling the truth?"

"He is."

"I see. I thought I'd best check." The bishop paused to wipe his brow and then went for another forkful of soiled straw. "Sometimes they're a bit loose with the truth, these *youngies*." Then he chuckled wryly. "Well. Older folks can be, too, when it suits their purposes." He drew in a breath, studying Reuben. "But you tell me this young man's story is true. And that's where we come to our problem, you and I."

"I don't see that we have a problem," Reuben replied shortly. "I'm not a member of the church, so the rules you follow don't apply to me."

"No, no." Abram held up a protesting hand. "I was not saying otherwise. I understand this. The trouble is that you appeared to be one of us. You were wearing Plain clothes, driving a buggy. So naturally, the boys assumed—"

"They assumed wrong."

"We know that, you and I, *ja*. I understand why you have chosen to wear such clothes—showing mercy to a girl who was struggling with fears. I think this was a kind thing to do. But it is harder to explain to outsiders. They see our clothes and our buggies, and they believe these outer things make us who we are. It is wrong, but it is also understandable."

Reuben shrugged impatiently. "I'm sorry if it caused you a problem, but that boy was being careless and thought it funny to put a couple driving a buggy in danger. I told him I wasn't Amish when the question came up. But if I managed to scare him into thinking twice about doing the same thing again, could be I've done your community a favor."

Abram dabbed his forehead. "This may also be true. I also believe this young *Englischer* was trying to move attention from his own misbehavior by pointing to yours." He smiled. "I have five sons myself, and I have seen this trick more than once." He forked the last bit of manure and straw into the wagon and leaned the pitchfork against the side of the clean stall. "I accept your apology," he said. "It's kind of you to offer it. As you say, you are not bound by our guidelines, so you are free to do as you choose."

Reuben cut him a wry glance. "I hear a 'but' coming."

To his astonishment, Abram laughed—a hearty belly laugh. "You've got sharp ears. No point playing games with you, so I'll tell you straight out. In future, it would be helpful if you could make it easier for folks to recognize you for who you are—and who you are not. Particularly if you don't plan on reining in your temper."

"Oh, I reined it in. And that boy's lucky I did. You can trust me on that."

"I see." Abram nodded slowly. "Well, we all have our struggles. The boy's is foolishness. Yours seems to be temper. My own"—he rubbed his ample stomach with a wry smile—"is easy to guess. We must help one another with these things when we can. Like my wife, who keeps trying to feed me salads and who hides the cookies in a new place every week." He paused. "Forgive an older man for meddling, but you lived among us once. You will not have forgotten what the Bible teaches on self-control, and I would argue it is true even for those living outside the church. Strength spurred on by temper is rarely used wisely, and without some self-control . . ." The other man shook his head. "Unfortunate things can happen."

That was true. Reuben had learned firsthand that physical strength and anger were dangerous companions—and when you added in a lack of self-control, things got bad fast.

He'd always promised himself that he would never be like his *daed*—and yet here he was, defending an outburst of temper. He wasn't sure what to say next. He had been ready to debate this man, but Abram's well-chosen words had brought Reuben's argument to a full stop, like a pair of skillful hands on the reins of a raw horse. That made him uneasy, and he suddenly wanted this conversation over with.

"You've made your point," he admitted irritably. "From now on, I'll be sure to either act Plain or dress *Englisch*. Will that suit?"

The chubby man cocked his head. "That will solve the problem for me. But will it solve anything for you? We are not meant to be split into pieces—dressing one way and believing another. Sooner or later a decision must be made."

"I made my decision a long time ago."

"Maybe so. But sometimes, since *Gott* is very merciful, we are given another chance, and then we must decide again. Perhaps you will choose the same as before. Perhaps not. Either way, as I told Miriam, I am here if you would like to talk. When a man is torn in two directions, sometimes it is helpful to have a friend come alongside and help sort things out."

"I'm not torn." He wasn't. His decision to put his Plain life behind him hadn't been made in a hurry. Coming here had reminded him of some of the good things this way of life offered, but that didn't mean he'd forgotten the bad. And the foolish daydreams he'd been having about Miriam and a buggy full of children were just that—foolish. And he certain sure should never have kissed her; there was no excuse for—

Suddenly, something Abram had said registered. *As I told Miriam.* Reuben frowned. "Did Miriam send you here, to talk to me about this?"

Abram didn't seem surprised by the question, but he shook his head. "She did not. I spoke to her about you just before you came to church—which I hope you will soon do again. I figured out for myself she was the other half of the couple you mentioned in the buggy you were driving." Abram smiled and tapped the side of his nose. "Five sons, remember. You learn a few things with so many young fellows underfoot."

Reuben refused to be distracted. "Why would you talk to Miriam about me at all?"

"That bothers you?" Abram's smile sagged. "Maybe I shouldn't have, then. It wouldn't be the first misstep I've made. I'm used to being more of a plough horse than the head of the team, and I've always liked to jump in and help where I can. When I heard about this Plain man turned *Englischer* staying among us, I could not resist talking to Miriam, since she seemed to be the one who had your ear. You did the same thing, didn't you? With the horse? You looked for the one closest to him, the one he liked best."

"My job has nothing to do with this."

"I am only pointing out that your job and mine are not so different. You've made a business out of taming horses nobody else can reach, ain't so? Me, I like the difficult cases, too, but my work is with people. It's an interesting challenge, helping tangled-up horses—or people—find their way through their problems. But you know this already. Everybody's talking about how you've helped our Miriam." The twinkle in the other man's eye brightened. "Johns Mill is a small town. Word gets around. It is a blessing to see her doing better, and we are all rejoicing over it. Naturally, this makes us want to get to know you more, to help you in some way if we can."

"There's not much to know and nothing I need. But thanks."

"Oh," the other man said cheerfully. "There's always something. You have had some sort of rift with your family, I'm hearing. That is regrettable. Family is a very important thing, and there's no reason to keep yourself separated from them, since you left before joining the church."

"The choice to remain separated is theirs as much as my own. More," Reuben added, thinking of the many times he'd tried to convince his *mamm* and his sister to leave his father and come live with him.

"I understand. Parents are often deeply hurt when a son or daughter makes such a choice. I have a stepson who left the faith many years ago, and it is a sorrow my wife bears every day. It would make me very happy to hear he'd visited a church service as you have done. If someone—like me, maybe—wrote to your father—"

Reuben frowned, alarmed. "That would do no good, and I'd rather you stayed out of it. My family troubles are no business of the church, seeing as how I'm not a member— and not planning to become one."

Abram's bushy eyebrows flicked upward like startled swallows, but he nodded. "Your parents are, but of course, when it comes to you, yourself, you are right. If I have over-stepped, I hope you will forgive me. I want only to help."

Reuben didn't answer. If he opened his mouth, he hon-estly wasn't sure what he would say. He had no reason to care what this man thought of him, but he didn't want to cause trouble for Miriam's family.

Abram waited a few seconds then sighed. "Well," he said finally, "I will go on my way and leave you in peace. But I meant what I said, Reuben. If you would ever like to talk, to ask questions, my door is open to you, always. *Mach's gut.*"

Reuben nodded shortly without returning the greeting,

but the chubby bishop didn't seem perturbed by the rudeness. He only smiled, walked outside, heaving himself into his buggy with some difficulty. Five minutes later, he was clopping down the road toward town.

Reuben watched him go, feeling agitated.

The man wasn't like any bishop he'd ever met before. He wondered what Abram King would say if Reuben took him up on that offer of a talk, if he told him what it had really been like, growing up under Ivan Brenneman's thumb. He'd like to hear this bishop's explanation of why the church had only said pious words, and then turned away and left Ivan's family in their predicament.

That would likely be pointless, though. After all, he'd described his father's drinking and abuse to more than one church leader in the past. It had done no good. He'd even been told his father's behavior was his own fault for not joining the church as he should have—that if he did, things would get better. That he should honor his parents and be willing to forgive.

Reuben realized his fists were clenched. He opened his hands and took a deep breath.

Abram was right. Sometimes a decision you thought you'd put behind you had to be made a second time. Only this time it wasn't his father and the failures of the church pushing him to leave.

It was Miriam, tempting him to stay.

Whether she meant to or not, she had him nearly ready to throw aside the hardest lessons he'd ever learned in his life and return to the faith and the lifestyle that had almost destroyed him.

That would be a stupid thing to do, and the cautionary tale Joseph had told earlier about his brother had only made that clearer. Reuben wouldn't make the same mistake Caleb Hochstedler had made.

He was starting to tilt in that direction, though, every

time he looked into Miriam's eyes. Or at least he had been until he found out she'd been talking about him to the bishop. That was news he could have done without.

Reuben hurled the pitchfork into the corner of the barn, where it clattered and fell. Then he strode outside into the fragile spring sunlight.

CHAPTER TWENTY-THREE

❧

THAT EVENING MIRIAM HAD NEARLY FINISHED SET-
ting the supper table before Joseph walked in the door. She
looked up and smiled, glancing expectantly over his shoulder.

But Reuben wasn't with him.

"It's just us for supper." Joseph went to the sink to wash
his hands. "Reuben's not coming in."

"What?" Miriam crumpled the napkin in her hand, staring at her brother's back. "Why not?"

"He didn't say, and I didn't ask." Joseph dried his hands
on a towel and came to the table to take his seat. "I figured
it was his own business. He's missing a good meal, though.
This looks wonderful *gut*, Naomi."

Naomi smiled, pressing one hand lightly on her husband's shoulder before sitting down herself. Joseph bowed
his head, and Miriam belatedly followed suit, but she had a
hard time focusing her mind to pray.

She'd had an extra special day today. Going to town and
getting to visit Yoder's had been such a treat, and she'd

looked forward to telling Reuben about it. There was something cozy about sharing news with him at the supper table along with Naomi and Joseph, all of them together. It felt . . . right . . . and hopeful—as if someday Reuben might truly belong here among them.

Now he wasn't even coming in. With no explanation.

"Should I fix him a tray?" Naomi helped herself to a spoonful of steaming mashed potatoes. "He's not been anyplace today, has he? So he'll not have eaten since lunchtime. He must be hungry—unless you think he's sick?"

Joseph shook his head. "He's not sick, and a tray might be a kindness. I'm not sure what happened, but I do know Abram came by while you were in town. I think that might have something to do with this."

"What?" Miriam's knife clattered to her plate, the lump of butter intended for her slice of bread sliding off to melt into her green beans. "The bishop came by? Why?"

Her brother shrugged. "I've no idea. I was busy in the workshop. To start with, I thought he must have come about the table I'm making for his wife. But he never came to the shop at all. He went into the barn and talked with Reuben instead."

"Oh, dear." Naomi's gentle face crinkled with worry. "Do you think Abram said something to upset him?"

"I'd guess so, judging by the look on his face just now."

"What would the bishop be talking to him about?" Naomi asked.

"Who knows? Joining the church maybe? Or something else. You never know with Abram. He means well, but he's not got his feet under him yet, and he wants to meddle in everybody's business." Joseph shook his head. "He wrote a letter to Aaron Lapp's uncle—that one who sold Aaron the bull who dropped dead two days later? Abram suggested the money be refunded or the bull replaced. Aaron was plenty irritated about it. He knows his uncle's a bit of a skinflint, and he'd no wish to stir up trouble in the family, so he was going to let it go."

"That might have been the wiser thing," Naomi agreed.

"Abram thought he was helping. Since he's a farmer himself, he understood what a loss it was, and he assumed the uncle would want to square things up. It didn't work out that way, and now Aaron has both a dead bull and an annoyed *onkel* on his hands. Abram would do better to stick to church matters."

"Well, new brooms sweep clean, they say," Naomi observed with a wry smile. "And as far as being a bishop goes, Abram's a new broom for sure. But to my mind, brooms always get the corners better once you've broken them in a little. Abram's good heart will be a blessing to all of us, I think, once he settles in."

"Likely so," Joseph agreed. "But you might have a hard time convincing Aaron just at the moment."

Miriam was only half listening to their conversation. What, she wondered, could Abram have said to upset Reuben?

"I'll take the tray to him," she offered. "Right after supper."

"I can do that," Joseph said quickly. His wife shot him a warning look.

"Miriam can manage it," Naomi said lightly. Joseph didn't look pleased, but he nodded and forked up another bite of potatoes.

Miriam finished her supper fast and fixed Reuben a generous plate. She covered it with a napkin and set it on a tray, feeling her brother's worried gaze on her the whole time.

"I'm not sure—" Joseph began uncomfortably, but Naomi cleared her throat.

"Let it be," she suggested softly. "Tell Reuben we missed him at table, Miriam, and that we hope he will join us for breakfast."

"I will." Miriam and Naomi shared a look. She read

worry and resignation in her sister-in-law's eyes, but Naomi said nothing else. She only rose and opened the kitchen door. Then she followed Miriam onto the back porch, pushing that door open as well, so it swung wide over the back steps.

"*Denki*," Miriam murmured. "For the help with the doors—and for stepping in back there with Joseph."

"He is concerned about you. I am, too. But I think this has moved past the point where our interference can do much good. Ain't so?"

Miriam wasn't sure how best to answer, so she kept silent.

Her sister-in-law sighed. "I thought so. You're much stronger, and you must make decisions for yourself. Our job now is to pray that you will allow *Gott* to guide you." Naomi smiled sadly before stepping back inside and closing the door.

Miriam picked her way down the path leading to the old dairy barn, careful not to jostle the tray too much. She'd forgotten her shawl, but she didn't really need one. The air was cool, but not cold. Spring was definitely here— although she knew from experience that there were likely some chilly spells yet ahead. This time of year was always unpredictable.

Managing the door was difficult, but she made it inside without spilling anything. Setting the tray on one of her brother's scrupulously clean worktables, she called.

"Reuben?"

There was no immediate answer, but she heard a stirring behind the closed door. A second later, it opened, and Reuben stood framed in the doorway.

He was wearing his jeans and a dark red *Englisch* shirt, the first time she'd seen him in his old clothes in a long time. Her heart jumped, and she laid one hand against her breast, pressing hard, willing it to slow down. She couldn't afford to get flustered now, not if she wanted to find out what was going on.

"I've brought you some supper," she said.

"You shouldn't have bothered. I'm not hungry." He didn't sound like himself—or rather, he sounded as he had when he'd first come. As if he barely knew her.

Her heart twisted with worry. "Reuben, what's wrong? Joseph said Abram stopped by and talked to you. Is that what's troubling you? You shouldn't take whatever he said to heart. He's a well-meaning man, everybody says so, but he's not been bishop very long. He's making more than his share of mistakes right now."

"That's no surprise to me. He made one while he was here. He let it slip that the two of you'd been talking about me—that he told you he'd like to meet with me to talk over my situation."

"Oh." A blush stung her cheeks, and she was thankful the light wasn't any brighter than it was.

"And as I recall, after our . . . buggy ride, you made a point of saying I should do that very thing."

"*Ja*, but not because Abram asked me to!" He didn't look as if he believed her, so she hurried on. "Because, like I said, I thought he might help you think things through. I had nothing to do with him coming by today."

"I'm glad to hear it." He studied her, his face cold and set. "I was starting to wonder if that was all this . . . friendship . . . of ours amounted to? A chance for you to win points with the bishop by bringing a prodigal back into the church."

"Of course not!" Tears of angry hurt threatened, but she crossed her arms over her chest and frowned at him. "I do want you to think about coming back to the church, but that has nothing to do with Abram. Like I told you after—in the buggy, I . . . I like you, Reuben." She couldn't help it. Her voice choked a little on the words. "I like you very much."

Their eyes connected. For a second, she thought she saw . . . something. But it was gone so fast, she couldn't be sure exactly what it was.

"And like I told you, how we feel about each other doesn't matter. *'S hot kenn vayk.*"

There's no way. Miriam's heart fell. Had he made his decision already? "How can you be sure there's no way, though?" she whispered. "If you won't even think—"

"I can be sure because I know myself." He made a frustrated noise. "Or I thought I did. You know . . ." He frowned at her, his face like a thundercloud. "Before I came here, I hadn't said a *Deutsch* word in years, except when I was working with horses. Now I don't even realize I'm speaking it half the time. And I'm not only talking in *Deutsch* again. I'm driving a buggy . . . wearing pants without zippers. No wonder Abram thinks he's got me cornered."

"Nobody's trying to corner you," Miriam protested. "It's true Abram spoke to me about you. He tends to meddle, and you being outside the church . . . that was hard for him to resist. But nobody wants to make you do anything you don't want to do. We couldn't anyway."

"Abram couldn't, no. You, though . . . you could come close," he muttered. "If it wasn't for you, I'd never have—" He cut himself off and glanced at her.

She was trying her best not to cry, not to fall apart, but she was getting close. Maybe he saw that, because when he spoke again, his voice was gentler.

"I'm sorry. That's not fair. This isn't your fault." He shook his head. "I must've been . . . lonelier than I realized. I've never felt too comfortable with *Englisch* girls, and with you, I just—" He stopped short again. "I guess I miss some parts of the old life more than I knew."

She twisted her hands together tightly to steady herself. "If all that's true, if you miss this life and never felt easy among the *Englisch*, I don't see why you're so angry, why you won't even think about—"

"That's the trouble. I am thinking about it. And I shouldn't be."

"Why not?"

"I have my reasons."

She paused, then pressed gently. "Won't you explain them to me, Reuben? I've shared a lot of my past with you. And," she went on softly, "it might help me understand better."

For a second, she didn't think he was going to answer. Then he sighed.

"My *daed*," he said. "He was the reason I left home. He always had a temper, blowing up over nothing, throwing things sometimes. It wasn't so bad when I was little, but as his farrier business grew, he worked with a lot of *Englischers*. His customers would hang around the barn while he worked. A lot of them were drinkers, and my *daed* started drinking with them."

Miriam's heart sank. Alcohol wasn't allowed in the Johns Mill community, but she knew it was allowed in moderation elsewhere—and that it could cause terrible troubles sometimes. "And things got worse?"

"Things got bad, *ja*. Drink made him mean, and he's a strong man, my father. Muscles come with the kind of work we do. Most of the scars I've got came from him."

"Oh." Miriam thought back to her own kindhearted *daed* and tried to imagine what that must have been like for Reuben.

Horrible. It must have been horrible.

"I have four sisters. Three older than me. One younger. He wasn't . . . so bad with them. Bad enough, but it was mostly me and my *mamm* who got the worst of it. But I knew—I could tell—if I wasn't around, it would be harder for the rest of them. It's like there was something in him that needed to be mean to somebody, and when he was drinking, it came out. So I waited awhile to leave, though I knew I'd never join the church, not when they'd stood by and done nothing. My older sisters married off, and then it was just Connie, *Mamm*, and me. By then *Daed*'s drinking was so bad, he'd started bumbling at his job. The shorter the money got, the shorter his temper got. And that just made him drink more."

"But . . . the church—the deacons or the bishop. Couldn't they help?" Miriam's heart was pounding hard, for once not in fear, but in indignation and disbelief.

"My *mamm* tried going to them once, and they spoke to him. It didn't do any good, so I went to see them myself. I was about fifteen, I guess. They talked to my father longer that time, and he cried, made a big show. Promised he'd change. Got on his knees before the church, and all that. And then the first time he got drunk after, it was worse than ever because I'd brought such trouble on him. *Mamm* and I learned better than to tell. Didn't matter anyhow. They knew what was going on—they had to know. But it was easier to ignore it." He snorted. "Of course when my sister wore a dress to town that wasn't one of their approved colors, then we got a visit."

"Our folks here would have done something," Miriam said. "Our ministers, our deacon, they'd never let such a thing go on. They'd have found some way to make your father listen."

He shook his head. "I believed that about ours, too, Miriam, at first. You don't really know how any church—or any person—will react until they're put to the test. Not that I can cast stones. You know the main reason Abram came out here to talk to me?"

She shook her head.

"Because of what happened with those boys. Because I lost my temper and put hands on the one who was driving. Maybe I don't have my *daed*'s drinking problem, but there's something of him in me. Back at home, there were times when I'd be struggling with him, trying to keep him from hurting *Mamm* or breaking stuff we couldn't afford to replace." A muscle twitched in Reuben's jaw. "I wanted to hurt him. I was big enough to hold my own in a fight with him by then. I could have put him down and kept him down—I knew it. And I wanted to."

"But you didn't," she pointed out. "Stop being so hard on yourself."

"Life is hard, Miriam. The world is hard."

"You don't have to tell me that," she said sharply.

For a moment he was silent. Then his expression softened.

"No," he said. "I don't. I'm sorry. I forget, sometimes, what all you've been through, Mirry. You're still so . . . sweet. It wonders me that such sweetness could survive everything that happened to you."

"Don't apologize. I think that's one reason I like you so much," she said softly. "Because you forget. When you look at me, you don't see what happened—or all my troubles. You see what I can be—what I can do. You're the first person in a long time to see me like that, and you've helped me so much." She took a step toward him, struggling to put what she wanted to say into words. "I'd like to help you, too."

He lifted an eyebrow. "By talking me into staying here and joining the church?"

She lifted her chin. "I will miss you if you go, so *ja.* That is a hope of mine. But I wouldn't want you to stay if you're happier as you are, if you're really where *Gott* means you to be. Are you, Reuben? Are you truly happy out among the *Englisch*?"

He shrugged. "I thought I was happy. Happy enough anyway. I could be all right there, I think." He paused, and something in his eyes made her breath come quicker. "Could you, do you think? Could you ever be happy someplace else?"

"Someplace other than Johns Mill, you mean?"

He nodded, watching her.

"I think I could. I would miss my family very much, but—" *If I were married, and starting a new family of my own . . . ja, I could be happy.*

She was too shy to speak that part aloud.

"But," she went on, because she knew she'd better say this now—and clearly—for both their sakes. "Wherever I went, I could never leave the church."

Disappointment flickered in his eyes. "There are *Englisch* churches, Miriam."

"I know. But this is where I belong." She chewed the inside of her bottom lip. "You were right, Reuben, about what you said. The world is a hard place, and you and I have both learned that lesson. But I learned another lesson with it. When you have your faith and *gut* friends and a loving family around you, that lightens whatever load life gives you to carry. Maybe . . . maybe if you stayed here among us, you'd find that out for yourself. Won't you at least think about it?"

For a long minute he didn't answer. Then he said, "Would you really be so glad if I stayed, Mirry?"

There was something about the way he said her nickname, the pet name her family had used for years, that made her stomach do funny things.

"I would be, *ja.*" She paused, swallowed, and added bravely, "Very glad."

He stood there looking at her, and she watched one feeling after another play across his face. A fierce joy that faded into doubt. Worry, mingled with hope.

She waited, holding her breath, to see what he would say. But when he finally spoke, all he said was, "Thanks for bringing out my supper, Miriam. You can tell Naomi I'll be in for breakfast."

She blinked. "All right."

She was almost at the door before he spoke again.

"I will think about it, Mirry."

Her heart leapt upward in her chest. Looking back, she caught his eye and offered her very best smile.

"*Gut*," she whispered.

Anxious to leave well enough alone, she slipped outside. She walked toward the house, her heart beating far too fast. It was a familiar and once much dreaded feeling, but now, she realized, it didn't worry her so much.

Nowadays, it wasn't usually fear that set her heart racing. It was almost always Reuben.

CHAPTER TWENTY-FOUR

❧

"DIDN'T YOU JUST MISS A TURN?" SAM ASKED.

Reuben shifted in the buggy to glance over his friend's broad shoulder. Sure enough, he'd gone right past the road leading to the intersection. "I did. Hang on, and I'll get us turned around."

Sam chuckled. "It's a sad day when I'm the one giving the directions, being as how I can barely see beyond the side of this buggy. Mind what you're doing, please. I'm plenty *naerfich* about taking this horse back where the accident happened without having a featherheaded driver added into the bargain."

His tone made it clear he was joking—mostly. But Sam, usually an easygoing fellow, was sitting stiffly, his big hands clenched into fists on his knees.

No wonder, Reuben thought. There'd be all sorts of feelings connected with returning to a place where your life had taken such an unexpected turn.

Reuben guided Breeze onto the wide shoulder of the country road, waiting for a few cars to pass. "You didn't have to ride along, you know. I could have managed by myself."

"*Ja*, sure, you could've. But I needed to come. Do you know, I've not driven by that intersection since? Emma goes out of her way to avoid it. She says it's for her own nerves' sake, but I think it's more for mine. She fears being there will upset me."

Reuben flicked the reins, urging Breeze onto the highway. "Will it?"

Sam lifted one shoulder. "I guess we'll find out. About me and about Breeze, too. You expecting much trouble from him?"

Reuben considered the question as the horse jogged back toward the missed turn. "Not really, but you never can tell. He may recall the place—the smells and the feel of it—and react badly. Sometimes they do. Sometimes they don't. After the slip-up with the horn, I figured it was best to make sure before I turn him over to another driver."

Since he wasn't positive how Breeze would react, he hadn't wanted Miriam on this trip. Seeing her with blood on her face once had been one time too many. She'd wanted to come, so he'd been relieved when Sam had asked to ride along. Miriam had understood why, and she'd quickly offered to stay home.

Joseph and Naomi had an errand to run, and that meant Miriam would be alone at the house for a few hours, a first for her. She'd hardly seemed nervous about it at all.

She'd come a long way.

"*Ja*, probably smart," Sam was saying now. "It's not everybody who has the hand with horses you do, and I know myself how this one can surprise you. Better safe than sorry." He shifted in the buggy seat, which creaked a protest.

Before the accident, Sam had used his big build and his muscles to make a name for himself in construction work. Reuben had privately wondered how his friend had felt about putting on a storekeeper's apron, but apparently the arrangement was working out well. So well, Miriam had told him, that Sam and Emma were in the process of buying the business outright.

"Emma doesn't mind tending the store by herself today while you and I go off joyriding?"

"Joyriding." Sam repeated the unfamiliar *Englisch* term and shook his head. "I'm not feeling so much joy on this trip, but it'll be a relief to have put this behind me. *Nee*, I had Emma close up the store for the afternoon. I don't want her working alone there while the movie folks are in town. They've been drawing a good bit of attention these last few days. Lots of people crowding around, trying to catch sight of the actors and all that sort of nonsense. And of course, they always want to come in the store. Good for business, but not so good for my patience. Some people have mighty poor manners. Yesterday one of them asked Emma to show him where her parents were standing when they were shot."

"*Vass?*" Reuben's hands tightened on the reins. He called that worse than poor manners. Disgusting, more like.

"That one won't ask such a question again," Sam said grimly. "I was right short with him. But there are new ones every day, so you have to teach the same lessons over again. You'd think grown folks would have better sense."

"Well, the good news is I hear they're about to finish up. Sykes told me the other day that he wouldn't be needing my help much longer. Just another week or so and they'll be done here."

"I'll be glad to see them go. For all the business they bring us, they're more trouble than they're worth." He made an exasperated noise. "Do you know, the director came up and asked if they could lease the store building? They didn't want to film in there, said there were problems with that—'lo-gis-ti-cal problems,' I think the man said." Sam sounded out the word carefully. "But they wanted to get some photographs, and the actors wanted to spend some time in the room to get the 'feel' of where it all happened.

He offered me a tidy amount of money for a full day's time."

"What did you say?"

Sam shot him a look. "What do you think? I packed them off quick. I'll have no truck with the likes of them. Emma talked to that screenwriter, you know, back last summer when she was helping with my *aent*. The Ian Mc-Millan fellow. But he wrote her a note and said the producer didn't much like his ending for the movie. Said it was too . . . I forget the word he used exactly. But anyhow, not good enough. And I'm hearing some talk about what the new ending's going to be like. I don't think it has much to do with the truth of things."

"I'm surprised. Not," Reuben explained, "that the movie won't be truthful. That's to be expected. But that you've heard anything about the story they're telling. I thought all that was supposed to be kept a secret." One of the actors had been chatting about the script in the barn the other day, and an official-looking fellow had hushed him up, shooting a wary look in Reuben's direction.

Of course, that might have been partly because Reuben had been wearing the Plain clothes Miriam had fixed for him. He'd been wearing those a good bit lately, even when he went to town.

He'd not thought too much about why—that was a subject he was skirting around carefully, even in his own mind. But lately he reached first for these clothes rather than his *Englisch* ones.

"I don't think they are supposed to talk about it," Sam was saying, "but people do, especially when they think nobody can hear. One of the things about not having such good eyesight anymore—I have ears like a rabbit. Emma says I can hear her thinking about making popcorn before she even gets the bowl out. So, working at the store, I've heard a few things here and there. Enough to know this movie's only going to cause us more trouble. I'm praying

Ian was at least able to keep them from making Trevor out to be some sort of hero, but from the sound of his letter, there's no certainty of that."

"Trevor's still on the loose, I guess." Reuben shook his head. "He's been a slippery fish to catch."

"He has, more's the pity. I sure wish I could have held on to him when he surprised Emma in my *aent*'s barn." Sam gazed out over the passing scenery even though Reuben knew he couldn't see it clearly. "Although maybe the one I should have held on to was Caleb. Emma's breaking her heart over that hardheaded twin of hers." His tone made it clear what he thought of the pain his wife's brother had caused.

"No word?"

"None." Sam flexed his jaw a few times before going on. "It's rough, that. Coming on top of everything else, especially. It's hit them all harder than they let on. I think that's why they've been so worried over Miriam."

Reuben had been thinking about Caleb—he knew Miriam was grieved about her brother, too—and he'd been watching Breeze for any sign he recognized this road. Reuben had driven his pickup out this way yesterday to make sure of the route, and they weren't far from the site of the accident.

But when he heard Miriam's name, his attention snapped back to Sam.

"Worried about Miriam. Because of me, you mean."

Sam had never been a man who shied away from the truth. "*Ja*. They worry you'll talk her into going with you when you go back to the *Englisch* and ruin her life. Don't splutter," he commanded calmly. "It's not like that. Nobody thinks you'd do anything other than marry her if you could get her to leave. Even I can see you're as moony over her as she is over you."

"Moony?" Now Reuben was the one shifting in his seat. "Sam—"

"That bothers you?" Sam's eyes twinkled. "I figured you'd lived *Englisch* long enough that you'd like talking about your feelings."

"I'm not that *Englisch* yet."

"You don't hardly look *Englisch* at all nowadays. Besides." Sam settled back in his seat, crossing his arms over his chest. "Like I told you before, Mirry has more gumption than folks think. I'm not sure you could talk her into running off with you, moony or not. She'd be separated from her folks, shunned by the church. No man could make up for the loss of all that, not to a girl like her. No matter how bad he wanted to."

Reuben agreed with that. He did. But still, Sam's confidence stung. Irritated, he flicked the reins against Breeze's back. "Well, you can all rest easy. I've no plans of talking Miriam into anything."

"Maybe not, but you've thought about it. And now you're thinking about something else. If Mirry won't leave Johns Mill, the only way you can be with her is to come back. To the church and to this." Sam gestured at the buggy and horse. "Unless I miss my guess, you're considering it. Am I right?"

Reuben cut him an irritated glance. "You're like a cat after a mouse today, Sam. Let it go."

Sam only chuckled. "I have to say, Reuben, you've surprised me. I've seen more than one boy jump the fence over the years, but I've never seen a fellow more determined than you were the night you came and asked me for help. Your mind was made up firm. I got the feeling it had been made up for years." He shook his head. "It wonders me you're thinking of doubling back, all for our shy Mirry." The big man lifted an eyebrow and smiled. "But then I remember how I felt about Emma at first. How I still feel about her now—more with every day that passes. And then it wonders me a lot less that you're leaning this way."

"I'm not leaning any which way," Reuben argued shortly.

"Well," Sam said, "you'd better start picking one side or

the other. This isn't a fence you want to straddle. Have you taken it to *Gott*, this decision?"

That was another thing about Plain folks, Reuben thought. They talked about *Gott* constantly, holding every decision, big and small, up against His word and His character. After living outside, that took some getting used to.

"I've done some praying over it," he admitted cautiously. "But I've not heard any clear answers."

"Well, *Gott* takes His own sweet time. Then again, sometimes we're slow to hear because we don't much like what He's telling us," Sam responded. "Trust me, I know something about that."

"Intersection's coming up," Reuben announced.

His attempt at distraction worked. Sam turned his attention to the road and to the horse clopping along in front of them. He leaned forward in the buggy, squinting, straining to see, best he could.

"I can't tell much," he said. "But it feels like he's still jogging along all right."

"He is. I don't think this is bothering him."

"That makes one of us." Sam gave a half-hearted chuckle.

"It's all right." Reuben reined Breeze to a stop at the end of the road, waiting their turn. "He's not going to bolt. I don't think he recognizes this place."

"I do." Sam shook his head. "Even though I can't see it so good, I can feel it, like. I'll never forget what happened here. It made too much of a mark on me for forgetting. In a split second, my life—and Janie's life—changed for good."

It was their turn to go. Reuben clucked to Breeze and flipped the reins against the bay's back. Breeze walked calmly forward, turning obediently onto the wide shoulder lane on the highway, made to accommodate buggies.

"You can rest easy, Sam. It's behind us," Reuben said. And so it was, just that quick. They were past the place where the accident had happened. From what he'd heard, Breeze had never made it this far that terrible day.

And of course, neither had Sam.

His friend breathed a sigh of relief. "He did *gut*."

"He did, *ja*." Reuben freed one hand to clap the other man on the back. "You didn't do so bad yourself."

"I'll do better if you keep both hands on the reins. At least till we're off the highway," Sam said.

"You've nothing to worry about." Two cars passed them, one after the other, but Breeze showed little interest. "See? He's minding me and paying no attention to the traffic. He's come a long way, this one."

"Thanks to you," Sam agreed. "Miriam, too, of course. She's come a long way herself. And so have you."

"I'm not so sure," Reuben muttered. "I feel like I'm going backward."

"*Ja*, it can feel so when you're still in the middle of it. After the accident, I was a terror for a while. It wasn't only that I felt guilty and worried about Janie. Emma and I had just started to take notice of each other. Well," Sam added with a smile. "Truth is, I'd taken notice of her a while before that. But she'd finally started taking notice of me, and the whole world was opening up. I was just getting things worked out in my mind. How our life would be, and all that. Then I lost my sight and everything fell apart."

"Seems like you've patched it together all right."

Sam smiled. "*Gott* does *gut* work—although He had His own ideas about how to go about it. I never saw myself as a storekeeper. No more than you saw yourself wearing clothes like those again, I guess." He nodded at Reuben's outfit.

"No, I never saw this coming. I'm not so sure I like it, either."

Sam slapped him on the back with a laugh. "I understand. I fought this harness like a mule at first."

Reuben was interested in spite of himself. "What changed?"

"Nothing. Only me, I guess. The way I looked at things. Funny, ain't so?" Sam wrinkled his brow thoughtfully.

"That when my eyes quit working, that's when I started seeing things clearer? *Gott* has a sense of humor. *Nee*, this isn't a life I'd ever have picked out for myself—except for marrying Emma. Yet here I am, happier than I'd ever have been if I'd followed my own path."

"I'm glad for you."

"*Denki*." Sam scratched at his chin. "One thing about working in a store, you do a lot of talking with folks, and I've fallen into a bad habit of giving advice. I'd like to give you some."

"You might as well. I've been getting plenty lately."

"Talk to our bishop. Abram's still working to find his feet, but I've known him for years. He's got a good head on his shoulders and a kind heart. He'll help you sort through this, if you let him."

Reuben sighed. First Miriam, now Sam. Although the truth was, he hadn't disliked Abram near as much as he'd expected.

"Maybe I will," he conceded cautiously.

"We go right past his farm on the way home," Sam pointed out with a grin. "What say we stop there, you and me, and you two set up a time to talk?"

When Reuben only grunted, Sam seemed to sense he'd said enough. They rode along in silence for several minutes.

When Sam finally spoke again, he nodded toward the right. "There's Abram's farm. I've got no place to be in a hurry. If you wanted to make a stop, that is."

Reuben wasn't sure how to answer—until he found himself pulling in the driveway. From the satisfied look on Sam's face, that must have been answer enough.

Abram poked his head out of the barn, squinting to see who'd come visiting. He hurried in their direction, wiping his hands on a rag.

He greeted Sam, before turning to Reuben, his chubby face worried.

"This is *Gott*'s mercy for sure. I was about to walk down

to the phone shack to leave a message for you. I'm afraid I have caused some trouble—not meaning to, of course."

Reuben and Sam exchanged puzzled glances.

"What kind of trouble?" Reuben asked.

Abram kept wiping his fingers, looking distressed. "I wrote a letter to your father," he confessed. "Mentioning how happy we were to have you here in our community, attending church and all. And he's . . . well, he's come to town looking for you."

"He's *what*?" Reuben's hands clenched down on the reins. "*Daed*'s here?"

"Well, yes. The driver he hired sent me a message just a while ago. He was . . . concerned. Your *daed* is . . . in a state."

"Drunk, you mean." Reuben gritted his teeth. This was trouble all right. He stiffened suddenly. "Wait—in that letter, did you tell him where I was working? Exactly where?"

Abram nodded miserably. "I mentioned it, *ja*."

Reuben turned to Sam. "Get out."

"Reuben—"

"Miriam's home alone, Sam, and the lighter this buggy is, the faster Breeze can pull it. Get *out*."

Before Sam's feet hit the ground, Reuben slapped the reins on Breeze's back and was off.

CHAPTER TWENTY-FIVE

❧

UPSTAIRS IN HER ROOM, MIRIAM PLACED THREE lengths of material—rose, navy, and gray—on her bed and studied them. Then she removed the rose, substituting one in a pale gold.

Then she put the first one back again.

She made a frustrated noise and gathered the material up roughly, bundling it into the trunk where she stored her treasured fabric. She might as well give up on planning out this new quilt today.

She'd thought this would be a perfect way to busy her mind while she waited for Reuben and Sam to get back. She'd been looking forward to this task ever since she'd picked the material out at Yoder's. Matching fabrics and mixing colors into a design she loved—that was her favorite part of quilting. Right now, though, she couldn't think of anything but Reuben.

She wished she could have gone with them, but she'd understood why Sam had asked to make this particular trip, and she hadn't liked to intrude. Still, she felt restless and disappointed, as if she'd been shut out of something important.

She'd go outside and check the eggs. It wasn't time quite yet, but that was all right. Being in the henhouse soothed her, and she needed to put more straw in the nesting boxes anyhow. She could tend to that, since she didn't seem able to do anything else useful.

She stepped into the hall, pulling her bedroom door behind her. The hall—the whole house—was silent, and she stood with her hand on the knob, listening to the quiet.

Everybody was gone. For the first time in . . . well, longer than she could remember, she was home alone.

Joseph had needed to make some deliveries, one at the home of a friend who had a month-old baby. Miriam had caught the flash of longing in Naomi's eyes when her husband had outlined his afternoon schedule, and impulsively, she'd suggested Naomi ride along.

They'd both looked astonished by the idea, but after asking Miriam half a dozen times if she was certain sure it was all right, they'd agreed to the plan. They'd driven off about an hour ago and wouldn't be back until close to suppertime, likely.

"I'm not afraid." She said it out loud, her voice echoing in the empty hallway. She repeated it louder. "I'm here all by myself, but I'm not afraid."

Nobody answered, of course, but Miriam smiled as she went down the steps into the kitchen. Her smile widened when, egg basket in hand, she stepped outside into the warm, spring sunshine.

Not so long ago, she'd looked out the kitchen window, wondering if she'd ever find the courage to set foot off the farm. She'd listened to her sister and sister-in-law chatting about babies, certain she'd never have a *boppli* of her very own.

Back then she'd never have been able to handle being left on the farm alone. And now look at her. *Gott* had been so kind. Not only had she been to church service and to town, but here she was, all by herself and not in the least bothered. Her heartbeat hadn't skipped once.

Well, except when she thought about Reuben.

From deep in her chest, optimism bobbed up, the way ice floated in lemonade in the summertime. The long, stubborn winter was behind them now, and better, more beautiful days lay ahead.

Miriam's lips curved up in a smile as she remembered Reuben's promise.

I'll think about it.

While he was thinking, she was praying—as hard as she'd ever prayed about anything. And if *Gott* was willing, maybe—just maybe—her life, which had already become so much happier, would soon be happier still.

Meanwhile, she had a beautiful afternoon to enjoy. Miriam paused to trail her fingers across a bobbing row of daffodils. She'd pick a big handful, she decided, on her way back. There were plenty to spare, and they'd look cheerful sitting on the kitchen table. Yellow was such a happy color.

Her mind drifted to the material she'd been considering. She'd use that pale gold, she decided. It would brighten the drabber navy and gray, and she'd sprinkle a bit of rose in there, too, to add some sweetness.

The design bloomed in her head as she gathered the few eggs the hens had already laid and raked old straw out of the nest boxes for the birds to scratch in. By the time she'd made a trip to the barn to gather fresh straw in an old feed bag and had restuffed the boxes, the design was complete in her head. She was itching to get started on it.

Although it wasn't feeding time, she scattered some scratch from the bin in the corner. The hens would have fun scrabbling in the straw, and Miriam was too happy not to be generous.

She opened the door to the coop, stepped outside, and stopped short.

There was a car in the drive—one she didn't recognize—and a tall man dressed in *Englisch* clothing was walking around the side of the house. As Miriam shrank back, fumbling for the door latch behind her, the man looked in her direction.

"Hey, ma'am!" He hurried toward her. "Hey, there!"

Miriam's heart was pounding so hard, she couldn't breathe. She finally found the latch and lifted it, ducking inside. Dropping the egg basket on the ground, she slammed the door shut. The startled hens squawked and flapped, setting up a chorus of agitated clucking.

It was a *dumm* thing to do, she realized, hiding in here. There was only one way in or out of this coop. She was well and truly trapped. Her breathing grew shallow and loud, ugly gasps she couldn't muffle even with one hand pressed hard over her mouth.

"Ma'am?" The man was right outside the door now. "My name's Ray Donaldson. I do a lot of driving for Amish folks back up in Indiana. I'm sorry to bother you, but . . . uh . . . could we talk? It's kind of important."

He's a driver. Miriam told herself that over and over as she fought for breath. Just a driver who'd accidentally come to the wrong house. Nobody to be scared of, even if she was here all alone.

Her brain understood that—sort of. But her heart wouldn't stop racing long enough to catch up.

"Ma'am? I knocked on the door, but nobody else seems to be home."

It took Miriam three attempts to speak, but she managed it finally. "You're in the wrong place."

"This is the Hochstedler farm, isn't it?"

"Yes." She got that word out more quickly. "But nobody here needs a driver today."

"I know. I didn't come for that. I came to . . ." The man's

voice trailed off. "I don't know how to explain it. Warn you, I guess. You see, I drove this fellow down from Indiana. Ivan Brenneman. Do you know him?"

Ivan Brenneman. Reuben's father.

Before she realized what she was doing, Miriam cracked open the door and peered through. "Ivan is here?"

"No. I mean, yes." The man, an older *Englischer* with wire-rimmed glasses and salt-and-pepper hair, seemed flustered. "I drove him to Johns Mill, but I drew the line at bringing him out here. He was intoxicated, and he seemed intent on causing trouble. Kept going on and on about his son. I'll tell you, ma'am, I've been driving Plain folks for years, and I've never seen anything like this."

"But what did you do with him?"

"I let him out in town. He was spitting mad, but by then I'd had more than enough. He was bent on coming here, but I'm glad I didn't bring him, you being all by yourself, ma'am. He's an unpleasant man, and I don't mind telling you he made me nervous. I won't be driving him anyplace else, but he'll probably find another way to get here. I just thought—"

He was interrupted by the sounds of clattering hooves and spitting gravel. Reuben was barreling into the drive, the buggy tilting sideways in his hurry. Breeze looked as though he'd been driven hard—there was lather on him, and froth around the bit.

Reuben leapt down and raced toward Miriam, nearly knocking the *Englischer* over in his haste.

"Are you all right?"

"*Ja!* I'm fine. Reuben, your father. He's—"

"I know." He spoke in *Deutsch.* "He's here. Abram told me. He'd sent a letter, the meddling—" Reuben stopped himself short of using whatever word he'd chosen to describe Abram. He turned to the stranger, his eyes narrowing. "Who are you?" he asked in English.

"I'm the one drove your father in. Sorry," the man added.

"I wasn't trying to eavesdrop, but I've been driving Amish around for years, and I've picked up some of the language."

"He came to let us know. He wouldn't bring your father because he was very . . ." It was Miriam's turn to search for a word. "Upset," she said finally.

"Drunk?" Reuben asked the driver.

"As a skunk. He must have started sneaking drinks at some point during the trip. I didn't notice at first. He had a flask under his coat. I'm sorry. I wasn't sure how to handle it."

"You did all right. Where is he now?"

"Like I was telling the lady, I put him out in town. He wasn't happy, and it was no easy thing to get him out of my car. He's a strong fellow, your dad, and not somebody I'd like to be in a tussle with."

Miriam saw Reuben skim the other man's skinny frame. "No," he agreed shortly. "Best you not try that."

"Fortunately, he saw that movie commotion going on down the street. I guess it caught his interest because he hopped out of the car and headed in that direction. I wouldn't count on him not coming here, though, as soon as he can find a ride. He was dead set on it."

Reuben nodded, his face grim. "Thanks for the warning, and for not bringing him like he asked. It was the right thing to do."

The *Englischer* studied Reuben for a minute. "You look a lot like your father, you know. Same muscles, same jaw. But seems like you're cut from a better cloth. I hope you get this worked out all right. My apologies for startling you, ma'am."

They watched silently as the stranger returned to his car and drove away. Then Reuben looked down at her.

His face was set and hard, and the hurt in his eyes reached straight into her heart and set it aching in sympathy.

"Are you all right now? Because I need to go deal with this."

"I'm fine, Reuben, but—"

He'd already started for his truck. She hurried after him. "If you're going to town, I'm coming, too."

"No." Reuben turned so swiftly that she took a step backward. "Go inside the house and lock the doors. Here." He fumbled in his pocket and made a frustrated face. "My phone's in my room out in the workshop. I keep forgetting the thing. You know how to use one, don't you?"

"*Ja*, I think so, but—"

"Take it in the house with you. If my father shows up, call 911." He moved toward his truck.

"Reuben, wait!"

"Miriam, I understand you want to help, but you don't know my *daed*. Him drunk and angry in town is a problem. If I don't get there quick, somebody's liable to get hurt." He lingered for a second, his eyes on hers. "I'm only thankful it won't be you. This," he added in a low voice, "this is why I can't be Amish. Abram started this trouble in the name of the church, writing to my father, thinking there could never be a good reason for a break between a parent and a son. He's about to learn different, but he won't be the one fixing the mess he's made. I've got to deal with it. I've always had to deal with it."

"But if you'd let us help you . . . surely there's something the rest of us could do." She looked over Reuben's shoulder to see Joseph turning in the driveway. Naomi was in the back and Sam rode beside him, his broad face set in stern lines. "See? Joseph and Sam are here now. Let them go with you."

"There's nothing they could do. They can't fight back, and my father doesn't respond to words. If you want to keep the people you care about from getting hurt, keep them here." He turned away.

"I care about you, too," Miriam whispered.

He halted where he was. His shoulders tensed, and for a second she thought he was going to turn around again—to say something to her—but he didn't. He started toward the truck, and seconds later, he was roaring off down the highway.

Miriam hurried to the buggy, where her brother was helping Naomi down. Joseph listened to her breathless account of what had happened. When Miriam described the strange *Englischer* coming to the house, Naomi reached out to catch her sister-in-law's wrist in a comforting grasp, but she kept silent, listening.

Sam was the first to speak. "It's a shame, that's what it is. We stopped there at Abram's. Reuben was going to fix up a time to talk to him about maybe joining the church, but—"

Miriam drew in a quick breath, and Sam's eyes drifted in her direction.

"*Maybe*, I said," he repeated gently. "There wasn't anything set about it—not yet, but I was hopeful. Then Abram came out with this business about writing to Reuben's *daed*, and it all went downhill fast. He near pushed me out of the buggy, he was that worried his father would get here before he did. Abram's son Menno gave me a ride to town, and we crossed paths with Joseph and Naomi there. I told 'em what was going on, and we came here quick as we could." Sam shook his head. "I knew Ivan Brenneman was a piece of work. You hear things. But for Reuben to move like that, to have such a look on his face at the thought of his *daed* being here with you . . . it's worse than I thought. Got to be."

A chill tickled up Miriam's spine. She turned to her brother. "Joseph, we have to help him."

"*Ja*, I think so, too." He turned to his wife. "I'll drive to the phone shack and call around, best I can. Then I'll go back into town and see who I can gather up there. Sam, would you mind staying awhile, just in case Ivan makes it out here? I'll rest easier in my mind if you do."

"I'll stay." The lines of Sam's face hardened.

A few minutes later, when Joseph was driving Titus back onto the road, Sam turned to Miriam and Naomi.

"Let's go sit ourselves down in the kitchen and have a cup of tea. It'll calm our nerves and do us all good."

"I'm not staying here drinking tea," Miriam stated firmly. "I'm going to town."

"Miriam," Naomi started.

"I'm going. All his life, Reuben's been left alone to deal with his troubles. I'm not leaving him alone with this one."

The two women's eyes met, and Naomi's expression shifted from concern into understanding. And then to a worried resignation.

"Joseph took Titus. Can you manage Breeze, do you think?"

Miriam straightened her shoulders. "I can. He's tired out anyhow. He'll not likely give any trouble."

"The horse ain't the trouble you should be worrying about," Sam said, his face alarmed. "Joseph said—"

"Sam can go with you," Naomi interrupted. "You'll be safe with him."

"Now, wait a minute, both of you," Sam protested. "Not that I wouldn't just as soon be there in the thick of things myself, but Joseph made it clear I was to look after you. Naomi shouldn't go to town, and I'll not leave her here by herself."

"You won't have to," Naomi said. "You can drop me off at Katie Lapp's on your way, and I'll stay there until this is all over with. Come on, now, the both of you." She moved toward where Breeze stood, still hitched to the buggy. "The longer you wait, the more chance you give trouble to grow. And sounds to me like this trouble's plenty big enough already!"

CHAPTER TWENTY-SIX

❧

REUBEN'S PICKUP BUMPED OVER THE COUNTRY highway, the fields and farms rolling past. His hands were clenched around the steering wheel, and he was struggling to keep his boot from pressing too far down on the gas. His heart hadn't stopped hammering since Abram had dropped the news that Ivan had shown up in town—and that he knew Reuben was working at the Hochstedlers'.

He hadn't seen his *daed* in a long while, but from what he'd gathered from Connie's hurried conversations, things had gotten worse. He hadn't been sure what Ivan might do there alone with Miriam if he was in one of his rages.

All the way from Abram's, he'd driven Breeze harder than he should have, braced for a showdown with his father. When instead he'd found Miriam facing off with some *Englischer*, he hadn't known what to think.

All he'd known was that he needed to keep Miriam safe. He'd stepped between his father and the women in his family plenty of times, but he'd never experienced the level of desperation he'd felt racing across that yard.

Miriam was all right, thanks to that driver's good sense. Reuben had been reminding himself of that over and over, hoping it would sink in. He needed his heart to settle and the thinking part of his brain to kick back into gear.

Actually, Miriam had been better than all right. She'd been startled, but she'd stood her ground. She'd changed a lot since the day Reuben had scared her into a faint in the barn.

The memory flashed into his head. For a moment he saw her again as he had that first day, limp in his arms as he walked outside, as the last of the winter sunlight touched her face.

He pushed the image aside. He couldn't think about Miriam right now. He needed to gather his wits. He'd never had much success facing off with Ivan, but that was about to change.

It had to.

Reuben slowed the truck when he reached Johns Mill's main street. As he scanned the scene, his apprehension grew. Something was going on, all right.

A crowd was gathering just beyond Hochstedler's General Store, where the orange cones and wooden barricades had been set up for the day's filming. There were always people hanging around that area, starstruck *Englischers* mostly. But today black bonnets were sprinkled like pepper throughout the sea of onlookers, and Reuben's heart sank.

He could guess why these Plain women had interrupted their shopping to linger there. He knew, even before he saw his father in the middle of the road, facing off with a pair of the film company's security guards.

He pulled into the first parking spot he saw, jumped out, and jogged toward the crowd. As he pushed through the people, he heard his *daed's* angry voice.

"I want my son. They told me he works here sometimes. Go get him!" He was speaking in *Deutsch*, but his words were so slurred and sloppy that Reuben doubted they'd have understood him even if he'd had the sense to speak in English.

The security guards held up their hands. "Sir, you need to calm down. We don't know what you're saying."

"My son!" Ivan yelled louder, the effort at volume making him stagger. "Get him!"

Reuben's gut tightened. If *Daed* didn't have enough of his wits left to realize the *Englischers* couldn't understand him . . . *ja*, he was worse than he'd been. A lot worse, since he was making a spectacle of himself on the street like this. In the past, Ivan had at least had the strength to hide his drinking problem—or to attempt to.

"I thought the Amish didn't drink alcohol." A middle-aged woman in a blue pantsuit spoke to the man standing beside her, her tone tart with disapproval.

The man chuckled. "Well, that one's three sheets to the wind, all right. Just goes to show, all that religious stuff doesn't go too deep."

Two Plain women standing close enough to overhear glanced at each other, their mouths tight. Reuben felt a too-familiar flush of shame.

Wherever *Daed* went, he brought trouble. Most of it fell on his family, but plenty was left over to splash on other folks.

Ivan staggered again, and one of the security guards stepped closer. "Sir—" he started.

Before he could finish whatever he was going to say, Ivan lunged forward and pushed him, saying something so garbled that even Reuben couldn't decipher it. Ivan wasn't steady on his feet, but he had enough muscle to knock the guard onto the pavement.

The crowd gasped, and one of the Amish women next to Reuben pressed her fingers against her mouth.

"That's it." Sykes had been standing off to the side, watching. Now he pulled out his phone. "I didn't want to do this," he muttered. "We've already made too many people mad around here, but enough's enough. I'm calling the cops. You hear me?" He raised his voice. "I'm calling the police. If this man belongs to anybody here, you'd better come claim him before he gets hauled off for being drunk and disorderly."

"I don't know who he is, but he's asking for his son," a woman's voice called from the side of the crowd. Heads swiveled to consider an older Amish woman, standing with her hands folded in front of her apron. Her face, like that of all the Plain women in the group, was troubled.

"Thank you, ma'am. Would you happen to know where his son is?" When the woman shook her head, Sykes lifted his voice. "Anybody?"

"Right here." Reuben shouldered his way through the people clustered around the barricade. Sykes raised his eyebrows.

"This man's your father, Brenneman?"

Reuben nodded, watching his *daed* warily. Ivan was squinting in his direction. His father's face contorted as recognition dawned, and Reuben quickly moved clear of the crowd. If—no, when—his father came barreling toward him, he'd better not be standing close to anybody. Ivan would mow down whoever was in his path and never notice.

His father was far too drunk to think straight. It was obvious in the way he wobbled on his feet, and in the bleary, bloodshot eyes fixed on Reuben's face.

No telling how much alcohol was in his system. If this had been any other man, he'd have passed out by now, but Ivan had developed a high tolerance over the years. He was also strong as an ox, and when he was drinking, what little sense of right and wrong he possessed vanished.

"They're about to call the police, *Daed*." Reuben tried to pitch his voice low enough that the Plain folks in the crowd wouldn't hear. "Best calm down, and come with me. You don't want trouble with the law."

"Trouble." Ivan spit the word out. "You're the trouble.

This is your fault—all this." He gestured widely at the group of people, almost toppling over with the effort. "If you'd stayed home, like a good son should, I wouldn't have had to come after you. You were never a good son." His voice cracked. "You broke the family. Your mother—she's not thinking straight. All this trouble with her and with Connie, too. It's because of you." His father pointed a shaking forefinger at Reuben.

All this trouble. Reuben's pulse skipped. "What trouble? Has something happened to *Mamm* and Connie?"

"Your fault," his father repeated, blurring his words. "You put ideas in their heads."

"Brenneman?" Sykes called from behind him. "I'm sorry, but if you can't get this under control, I'll have to call the authorities."

"Come on, *Daed*." If the police got involved, it might be hours before he could get the truth out of his father. "Let's go before this gets worse."

"Worse." His father hunched over, his beard straggling over his stomach, his wide shoulders shaking. "It can't get any worse," he muttered.

"What do you mean?" Reuben walked closer, trying to read his father's face. "What's happened?"

"They left!" His father raised his head and roared the answer, moving toward Reuben, both his hands raised.

Reuben braced himself, but before his father made contact, somebody stepped between them. He found himself staring at a wall of sky-blue fabric, stretched over a man's broad back.

Ivan bounced off Sam Christner's chest as if he'd run into the side of a mountain. He backed up, looking confused.

"Settle down." Sam's voice was quiet and firm.

Reuben stepped around the other man. "Sam, I thank you, but this is my problem."

"It is a problem, *ja*." Sam squinted down at Ivan, who

seemed unsure of how to deal with the giant standing in front of him. "That's for certain sure. But it's not yours to handle alone. Come on." Sam fished keys out of his pocket. "We'll take him into the store and get this sorted out."

Ivan stuck out his chin. "This has nothing to do with you. This trouble is between my son and me. This is family business."

"You are both right and wrong." Abram King made his way through the crowd, followed by several other men. The bishop's round face was solemn. "It is family business, but since we are all members of the same family, it has everything to do with us." He gestured toward the store. "We should go talk in private."

As he spoke, seven other men fanned out around Ivan, forming a close circle. Ivan looked around, his expression shifting from anger to uncertainty. "I don't know these people. Who are they?"

"Friends," Abram assured him quietly. "People who care that you are sick and unhappy and wish to help you climb out of the pit you've fallen into. Come." The bishop put a hand behind Ivan's back. "Enough of this. Let's go."

Ivan's eyes darted from one face to another, and the men met his gaze impassively. "All right," he said after a second. He took a shaky step forward, and Abram's arm flexed as he kept the unsteady man from stumbling.

"Mind yourself." Abram held out his free hand for the keys, and Sam dropped them in his palm. "We will go inside this store here. Your son will follow, and we will get everything sorted out."

Reuben watched with disbelief as the group edged past him. He felt a light touch on his arm and turned.

"Miriam." For a second, his addled brain couldn't quite take it in. "What—how did you get here?"

"Sam and I drove Breeze in," she said. "Are you all right?"

His head was slowly clearing. He glanced at the men, who now were helping Ivan navigate the curb.

"I'm not sure what's going on. He said something about *Mamm* and my sister leaving. Connie hasn't called, so I've no idea what's happened."

"You'd better go find out. Tell Sam I'll wait at Yoder's until he's ready to leave."

"You can't." Joseph came up behind them, his face grim. "Mary's closed up and gone home, and half a dozen reporters are headed this way. Some are the same ones who ate with us at the wedding, but there are others I don't recognize."

"What?" Reuben's overloaded brain struggled to grasp what Joseph was saying. Reporters at an Amish wedding—and his father being dealt with by a bishop.

Nothing made sense today.

Joseph cut him a glance. "It's a long story. But at least some of these folks know me, and I'll talk reason to them, and it'll likely be all right. But you, Mirry, you should get out of sight. No sense stirring this pot. I saw our buggy parked close to Yoder's. Tell Sam to walk you back there, and you two can go home. It would have been wiser if you'd stayed there in the first place." He scanned the crowd and made a face. "Here they come. You'd best go in the store yourself, Reuben, before they make an even bigger story out of this. Miriam, you drive back with Sam, *ja?*" Without waiting for an answer, Joseph edged through the crowd toward a group of people carrying cameras.

"Come with me," Reuben said to Miriam. "I'll take you to Sam."

She nodded, but she didn't speak. Her face was taut, and she kept her eyes on him, pointedly not looking at the people standing around her.

The crowd was making her nervous, he realized. All the more reason to get her back to Sam and on her way home as quick as he could. He took her arm and led her toward Hochstedler's. Sam was holding the door open for the bishop and the other men. His eyes widened when Miriam and Reuben drew close.

"Miriam—" Sam began.

"She shouldn't be here, Sam," Reuben interrupted. "Take her home."

"No." Sam's face had gone white and was twisted with sympathy. "She shouldn't. I'm sorry, Mirry. I wasn't thinking. I—"

Miriam shook her head. "It's all right. And I'm not going anyplace, not until this is over with." She gripped Reuben's arm tightly, her eyes fixed on his face. "I can't be much help, maybe," she murmured fiercely. "But I can stay close, and I can pray, and that's what I'm going to do. You're not alone, Reuben."

"Mirry—"

"Go on," she said. "Deal with your father. I'll be all right. And, Reuben," she added softly, "I'll be praying *hard*."

"*Denki*." In the dim light of the store, the sweetness of her face shone like a lamp.

Sam cleared his throat. "I think the bishop's waiting on you, Reuben."

He pulled his eyes from Miriam with difficulty. Then he squared his shoulders and went to face down his father.

He'd never been inside Hochstedler's before. The store building was old and high-ceilinged, with wide plank floors. It was full of the sort of attractive homestyle goods likely to appeal to *Englisch* shoppers—aprons, food items, wooden toys. And unless Reuben missed his guess, the beautiful, bright quilt hanging on the wall behind the counter was one of Miriam's creations.

Reuben's eye skimmed over all that, noting the location of the doors and windows out of habit. Whenever he found himself in a room with his father, he always made sure he knew where the exits were.

Ivan had stepped apart from the other men. He leaned heavily against a wooden hutch showcasing a display of jams, looking unsteady and confused.

Reuben's gut tightened. Cornering *Daed* was always risky, and as drunk as he was now, there was no telling how this would go.

"There you are, Reuben," Abram said calmly. "Now that we are all together, we'll talk this problem over and see what is to be done."

Ivan focused his bleary eyes on the bishop. "My only son left to live in sin among the *Englisch*. He has never come back to see his mother or me, nor his sisters. I'm not a well man—you can see this for yourself—and he should be helping with the family business. But he doesn't care because his heart is rotten with selfishness. That's the problem."

Reuben felt his face go ruddy. Outside Ivan had talked as if he'd had a mouthful of marbles, but of course his complaints about his son came out clear as a bell. The other men studied his father, their faces solemn. For a few seconds, nobody spoke.

Reuben straightened his shoulders and set his jaw. What these people thought of him and his choices didn't matter. They didn't know the whole story. Nobody did because nobody had ever cared enough to listen to it.

Abram cleared his throat, and Reuben braced himself. Here it came—the lecture.

"*Ja*, you are not well. That is easy to see, and I am sorry for it. But, my friend, your son is not the problem," he said. "You are."

Both Reuben and Ivan turned to stare at the bishop. The man's chubby face was perspiring, but when Ivan started to sputter, Abram stood his ground.

"It is so," he said simply. "Whether you like to hear it or not. You have been drinking. We all see that, and we smell it, too. And I am guessing this is no new problem for you, and that it is one of the reasons your son left home."

"You—" Ivan lifted a shaking finger and pointed at the bishop. "You don't know anything about me and my son!"

"Maybe I don't know everything, not yet, but I know what I told you in my letter. Your son has done skilled work here and done it well. I have talked with him and found him to be a smart and reasonable man, capable of heeding instruction." Abram shook his head and went on in a gentle voice. "It does no good to blame your boy for your own problems. It's only when we admit our faults that we can begin to fix them."

Reuben tensed. He could see Ivan's fury building. *Daed* never liked to be crossed. He had a loose grip on his self-control on a good day.

And this wasn't a good day.

"You don't know *anything*," Ivan repeated, spittle flying from his mouth. "If you did, you wouldn't say such things. He's talked his *mamm* and his sister into leaving home. He sent them money so they could do that, leaving me alone. And you stand here defending him?"

Abram looked at Reuben, lifting an eyebrow.

"I know nothing of that," Reuben said. "I sent them money because they said they needed it. I've done that before, many times. I didn't know they'd left." He turned back to his father. "But I'm glad they finally did, and I hope they never come back."

His father's eyes widened, then narrowed with rage. "See! You see, all of you!"

Abram blew out a long, weary breath. "That," he murmured, "was not a helpful remark, Reuben." The bishop turned back to Ivan. "Your son never joined the church. He is allowed to send money to his family if he chooses. He is not to blame for what they do with it."

"He is to blame! They'd never have gone otherwise! You're wrong!" Fumbling behind himself, his father picked up a jar of jam.

Reuben knew what was coming and got ready to dodge.

But to his astonishment, Ivan didn't aim the jar in his direction. He hurled it straight at the bishop.

For such a heavy man, Abram was nimble on his feet. He stepped deftly to the side, and the jar sailed past him, slamming into Miriam's quilt.

Ivan might be almost too drunk to stand, but he'd not lost much strength. Even the padding of the material couldn't keep the glass from cracking against the wall. The broken jar clattered to the floor, leaving a red smear across the pretty fabric.

Abram surveyed the mess with distaste, and turned to Ivan, his face hard. "*Shemm dich!* Your temper shames you."

Even in his inebriated state, Ivan registered that he'd crossed a dangerous line. His expression drooped into pitiful lines. His shoulders sagged, and he staggered feebly. The remaining jars of jam clattered as he bumped against the hutch. Burying his face in his hands, he began to cry, loud, racking sobs.

The men looked at each other uneasily, but Reuben kept his eyes rigidly ahead, unmoved. He'd seen this before, more than once. *Daed*'s tears never meant anything—except maybe that he'd gotten himself in more of a fix than usual.

Abram looked tired but resolute. "All right, all right. We will go to my house, you and I and the other elders of the church. You will drink *kaffe*, and we will wait for your sense to return. When it does, we will pray together and speak of what must be done to make things right."

Ivan only sobbed on, nearly bent double.

"Reuben," Abram went on. "We are leaving now and taking your father with us."

Reuben met his gaze. "I'd take a bucket, too, if I were you. He's likely to need one before you make it home."

Abram didn't flinch. "You are probably right. Speaking of buckets, I would like you to stay here, if you would be so kind, and do what you can to clean things up." He shook his head. "I'm afraid all too often children are left to clean up the messes their parents leave behind. When you're done, maybe you will drive to my home? You should be a part of this talk, I think."

"I've had this talk with my father and a bishop before, more than once. It's never served much purpose."

Abram studied him. "Perhaps you will find it in your heart to try again. If so, I will pray *Gott* will give me the wisdom to help." He walked over and put his arm around Ivan's waist. "Come now." As they walked slowly across the floor, the bishop glanced up at the stained quilt and *tsk*ed his tongue. "What a terrible waste."

"The quilt may wash clean," one of the other men said.

"*Nee*." Abram shook his head sadly. "I was talking about the jam."

As soon as Sam shut the door behind the men, Miriam walked over to examine the stained quilt. Sam squinted after her, and although Reuben knew he couldn't see clearly, there was no mistaking the concern in the other man's expression.

Sam cleared his throat. "There's cleaning stuff in the storeroom. I'd stay and help you, but I'd like to see Mirry home." He sent Reuben a desperate look. "She shouldn't be here."

At first Reuben didn't understand—then a horrified realization dawned. The store. Miriam hadn't been inside this store since the day her parents had been killed.

"Yes," Reuben said quickly. "Take her home, Sam."

"No." Miriam stood in front of the counter, her hands clasped in front of her dress, her eyes fixed on the quilt. "I will stay and help you clean."

"Miriam—" Reuben's voice was hoarse. He could only guess at the awful memories she was battling, at the pain and grief she'd faced while he'd been distracted by his father's drama.

She looked at him then, and the expression on her face

cut at his heart. "I need to stay," she said. Her voice shook, but it was firm.

An uncertain silence fell. Reuben was the first one to break it.

"Sam, would you mind stepping outside? I have to talk to Miriam alone."

CHAPTER TWENTY-SEVEN

✧

"I'LL BE RIGHT OUTSIDE, MIRRY."

Sam's reassuring words barely registered, but she nodded.

At first, in all the excitement, she hadn't really thought about where she was. She'd been too worried about Reuben to think of herself. It wasn't until Abram and the other men had walked outside with Reuben's *daed*, when Sam had shut the door behind them, and the room had fallen silent. Then it had hit her.

It was like the nightmares she'd had over and over again after that day. Right in the middle of an ordinary dream, she'd suddenly find herself back in the place she feared most—the place where the worst had happened, where everything in her life had changed.

Strangely, the dreams had seemed more real than this. Maybe because the store didn't look the same at all. Emma and Sam had been busy.

Her mind wasn't working well enough to pick out all the little changes, but the big room felt very different now.

When her parents had opened the store, it had the feel of a big warehouse, half-empty and echoing, and a little musty.

Now it was brighter and warmer, and it smelled of fresh wood and cinnamon. It seemed smaller, too—probably because it was crammed so full of pretty things. Red jams with blue-and-white labels. Crocheted potholders and a rainbow of women's aprons, hung in a row. Glossy wooden toys and children's books, all neatly displayed.

She didn't remember there being so many colors before.

Some things, though, were still the same. She touched the old wooden counter with a trembling hand—the one her father had polished to a glossy shine. He'd been standing behind it that day, with *Mamm* beside him like always. And Miriam herself had been just there, over to the side, right below where the quilt hung on the wall, globs of red jam still dripping from it onto the floor.

She swallowed hard and tried to focus on the quilt. It was one of the first ones she'd made . . . after. She and Naomi had pieced it together that winter. For Naomi, the work had been a kindness. She'd no love of sewing. But for Miriam, each stitch had been a tiny step out of the darkness, the first ones of a long, long journey.

She'd offered it to Emma after the store had reopened, when her sister had been struggling to find good pieces to stock the shelves in a hurry. The quilt was hard to part with, but it was the only thing Miriam had worth giving. Emma had accepted it with thanks and a suspicious sparkle in her eyes, but she'd never sold it.

I like the way it looks on the wall, her sister had insisted. *It's got all the colors of springtime. Besides, it'll make the store lots more money hanging there because it's such a good advertisement for your work.*

"Miriam." Reuben spoke gently behind her, sounding worried. He'd been through so much today with his father, but she knew the pain in his voice wasn't about that.

No, now he was hurting for her.

She drew in a ragged breath and faced him. "Would you get the cleaning things out of the storeroom? I'd like to get started."

"Go on home with Sam, sweetheart. I can handle this."

She lifted her chin and looked him in the eye. "So can I."

He studied her, a muscle jumping in his jaw. She braced herself, thinking he was going to argue, to insist she leave this job to him. Joseph would have done that. Emma, too.

Instead, Reuben nodded shortly and went to do as she'd asked. Miriam released the breath she'd been holding. He understood.

Of course he did. He always did.

Miriam walked toward the counter. When she'd reached the swinging gate separating the narrow workspace from the rest of the room, she hesitated. She rested her hand on its well-worn top, remembering the last time she'd pushed through this little door.

She'd been so *naerfich* that day, her stomach full of butterflies, dreading the prospect of facing customers. She'd felt resentful, too. She hadn't understood why *Mamm* and *Daed* had made her come, knowing how uncomfortable she was working at the store. She hadn't questioned her parents, of course, but it hadn't made sense. Emma enjoyed storekeeping, and she was so good at talking with the *Englisch*. Miriam wasn't.

No, she hadn't understood.

She pushed, and the door swung easily open. She stepped behind the counter, her eye skimming the low shelves. They were full of neatly stacked sacks and other odds and ends that were useful to keep handy.

Like that little feather duster still where *Mamm* had kept it, ready to whisk over the displays first thing in the morning before the customers started coming in.

Tears welled up in Miriam's eyes. Such a silly thing, but it brought a vivid picture of *Mamm* scurrying over the store with that energy she'd always had, feathering the dirt away.

She'd only just put it back in its place that last morning when Trevor Abbott had walked in, asking where Emma was, why she wasn't in the store like usual.

Miriam's heart jolted hard, and she pushed the memory aside. Reaching for one of the wooden stools behind the counter, she dragged it under the quilt, and climbed onto it.

"What are you doing?"

Reuben set a bucket of cleaners on the end of the counter and leaned the broom against it. He approached her slowly and steadily, reminding her how he'd acted with Breeze at the start.

He was trying not to startle her. She almost laughed because he needn't have bothered. She was beyond startling right now. Her nerves had gone numb.

"Getting this quilt down," she said. "It'll need washing."

"Let me get it for you."

"I can manage." Emma had doubled the border over a thick dowel that hung from a nail by a rope, pinning it in place. Miriam unfastened it, carefully sticking the pins through her sleeve for safekeeping. She worked quickly and methodically, and the quilt began to sag. She supported its weight with one arm, removing the remaining pins with her free hand.

Reuben had walked over to stand beneath her. "Hand it down to me," he said.

She pulled out the last pin and lowered the quilt into his arms as the dowel rattled against the wall, empty.

"Mind the dirty side," she said. "You'll get jam on your shirt if you're not careful."

He draped it carefully over the counter, stained side up. Then he offered her a hand to help her down.

She took it, his hard, calloused fingers closing firmly over her own, steadying her. A warm rush of comfort hit her at his touch, making her knees go weak. Maybe he sensed that because even when she had both feet safely on the floor, he didn't let go of her hand.

"I'm sorry, Miriam."

"The quilt will probably come clean."

"That's not what I meant."

"If you're talking about your father . . ." She tightened her fingers over his. "I pity him. He's driven his family away, and my *daed* always said a wife and children were a man's greatest treasure."

"I stopped apologizing for my father years ago. And don't waste your sympathy on him. Whatever troubles he has, he's brought on himself."

"He's in plenty of trouble now, for certain sure," she said. "Abram's good-hearted, but you don't go flinging jam at a bishop without some sort of reckoning."

"It won't matter." Reuben's face was grim and tired. "He's been talked to by a bishop before, back when he wasn't near as far gone as he is now. It didn't help. He'll sober up, and he'll pretend to listen. He'll make whatever promises it takes to get the church off his back, but he won't mean a word. He'll start drinking again the minute they stop watching him. Nothing ever changes, and nobody ever cares."

"That's not so. I care. Abram will care, especially once he understands the situation. You can explain it all to him when you go to his house—"

Reuben shook his head. "I'm not going. At least . . . I'm going, but not to Abram's."

She stared at him, the encouraging words she'd planned to speak dying on her lips. "What do you mean?"

He met her eyes. "I'm leaving."

"Leaving." Her heart skipped a beat and then sped into a painful, uneven rhythm. "But you said—"

His eyes stayed on hers, sad but unflinching. "I said I'd think about staying. And I have. When I stopped at Abram's this afternoon, I was planning to talk to him about it. I was going to see if he could help me . . . sort things out and decide if there was enough faith left in me to join the church."

"Oh, Reuben—"

He cut in before she could go farther. "That's when he told me my father was here in town. And that he'd written to him—without so much as talking to me about it first. Because, of course, if there's a problem between a father and son, between a member of the church and someone outside it, it was obvious to him where the fault must be."

Miriam didn't know what to say. Abram, with his well-meaning, bumbling tendency to meddle. She felt like throwing a jar of jam at him herself.

Of course, she'd never do such a thing, not in a million years. But Reuben had come so close to changing his mind. So very close. Knowing that broke her heart more than if he'd never wavered at all.

Still, a tiny, stubborn hope flickered, refusing to go out. Because maybe, if he'd thought that way only a few hours ago, he could think that way again.

"It's not a good idea to make decisions when your feelings are stirred up." She tried to speak reasonably, but the words came out shaky and desperate. "You should think this over some more, Reuben. And pray about it, and—" That was as far as she got before her throat closed.

"My feelings are stirred up," he muttered. "You're right about that. But that's not likely to change, not so long as I'm here with you. I've been mixed up inside since the minute I laid eyes on you. I wanted so bad for things to be different here. I wanted to be different myself because I couldn't stand the idea of leaving you behind."

"Then don't." She put her whole heart into those two words.

"Miriam . . ."

"I know the church isn't perfect. But nothing in this world is, Reuben."

"No." His eyes traced her face. "But some things come pretty close." He shook his head and looked away. "It's no use, though. To belong here—to really belong—I have to be willing to follow the church leaders and their rules blindly. And I just—I can't do that, Miriam. I can't pretend for the rest of my life this all works when I know it doesn't."

"It hasn't worked with your father's situation, maybe, but it does work a lot of the time. Not all the time because people are . . . people, and they make mistakes." Miriam struggled to express what she meant. "The world is a broken place, Reuben, in Plain communities same as everyplace else. But if we trust *Gott*, and . . ." She faltered. "And we do our best to . . . love . . . each other . . ."

At the word *love*, Reuben looked at her sharply. Something flickered in his eyes—something that made her breath catch in her throat.

Then it ebbed away, and the lines around his mouth tightened. "Love's not enough. My *mamm*'s proof of that. So's your brother Caleb, from what I'm told. I wish that wasn't so. I think, deep down, I've been wishing it ever since I carried you out of the barn. I've been tangled up in knots, trying to figure some way it could work out for us. But it can't. Because I can't stay, and you . . ."

"And I can't go," she whispered. "I'm sorry, Reuben. But no. I can't."

"I'd never ask you to."

"I know that. Joseph and Naomi and Emma . . . they all worried about that. That you'd ask, and I'd go."

"Then they must not know you as well as they ought to." As if he couldn't help himself, he reached out and rested his finger on the point of her chin.

"Maybe they don't know you too well, either," Miriam said. "Because you never asked."

"They know me better than you think. I wanted to. I want to yet, because I hate the thought of you marrying some . . ." He made a frustrated noise. "Some blockhead without enough sense to know he's hitching a Thorough-bred to a plough. Who might not see to it that you have everything you truly need—not just food and clothes, but . . ." He trailed off.

"What?"

"Colors," he finished softly. "All the colors in the world, Miriam, not just the ones in your backyard. The best and the brightest colors, heaped up in your arms, so you'd never have to make beauty out of leftover scraps again. That's what I'd have given you, if I could've. I'm sorry I wasn't able to."

He sounded so sad—and so certain. So very, very final. Her heart cracked.

She wanted to plead with him. She wanted to cry, to beg him to stay, to talk to Abram, to do anything but leave. But that would only make these last few precious moments ugly and sad.

She didn't want that. So she lifted her chin and looked him in the eye.

"Don't be sorry. You've given me so much, Reuben, so many beautiful gifts." She gestured around them at the silent store. "Just look at where I am. I never thought I could find the courage to stand in this store again, but here I am."

His mouth curved a little, but the crinkles around his eyes didn't change. "Not such a nice gift to end things with, bringing you back here."

"You're wrong about that. This is the best gift of them all. It's like Breeze, isn't it? And Sam, too. Going back to that intersection where the accident happened. I needed to stand here again before I'd be able to stand anywhere else. And thanks to you, I've done it. Now I'll be able to have a good, full life. A useful life."

She'd seen many expressions on Reuben's face over the last few weeks, but she'd never seen his mouth tremble. But it was trembling now, and it took him a second to answer her.

"*Ja.* A nice, Plain life with quilts and chickens and a pie-eating blockhead." He was trying to joke, she knew, but his smile still didn't reach his eyes.

"I don't know about that last part," she said. "I'm not so good at pies. I do better with cinnamon rolls."

Something sparked in his gaze. He leaned closer, and for one heart-stopping second she thought he was going to kiss her.

Then his expression changed, and he stepped back.

And waited.

She knew what he was waiting for. It broke her heart, and she didn't want to say it. But there was really nothing else left to say.

Because he was right. Love wasn't enough.

"I'll finish the cleaning up," she whispered. "Sam will help. You've . . . other places to be and other work to do." She cleared her throat. "*Mach's gut*, Reuben."

He studied her, his face set and pale, as if he was trying to memorize her features.

"You be happy, Miriam. Promise me that."

She managed a shaky smile, but she didn't answer. She couldn't.

Happiness—without him—wasn't something she could imagine.

They looked at each other in silence for one long, last moment. He took a deep breath and squeezed her hands tightly.

Then he let her go.

He walked away without looking back, the big door closing behind him with a heavy thud.

Chapter Twenty-Eight

❧

SAM WAS LEANING AGAINST A POST OUTSIDE THE store. He straightened up quickly when Reuben walked outside.

"She all right?"

Reuben nodded shortly. "She will be." He believed that—he had to.

Whether or not he'd be all right was iffier.

Sam looked relieved. "I never even thought about it," he confessed. "This store . . . for me and Emma it's normal now. Most days I don't even think about what happened here, and I don't think Emma does, either. At first it felt strange, but working here together as man and wife . . . it's cleaned the place for us, if you get my meaning."

"I do." Reuben looked over the street. The crowd had dispersed, and it looked as if the movie crew was packing up, too.

"For Miriam, though . . ." Sam went on. "It's much worse, of course. And she'd not been here since it happened. I should have thought . . ."

"Don't blame yourself. She's handled it well. She's cleaning up that jam now. She said you'd help her."

"Of course I will." Sam shook his head admiringly. "She's had her struggles, but deep down, she's a real brave girl, Mirry is."

"She is that." The ache in Reuben's heart ramped up a notch.

"Since the jam ain't the only mess that wants mopping up, I reckon you'll be heading out to Abram's now."

Reuben made a noncommittal noise. He wouldn't tell Sam he'd no intention of heading out to Abram's, that instead he was driving to the Hochstedler farm to collect his belongings. It would only start an argument he was in no mood for.

Sam waited, one hand on the door handle, frowning, as if he sensed something wasn't quite right.

"*Mach's gut*, Sam," Reuben said firmly. "Best you go and help Miriam now."

Sam nodded slowly, his broad brow furrowed. "*Mach's gut*, Reuben."

Reuben's stomach felt heavy as he walked back to where he'd left his truck. He fished out his keys and started the engine, which roared obligingly to life. He drove out to the Hochstedlers', but his mind—and his heart—were still back in the store with Miriam.

Back at the quiet farm, he changed into his jeans and a musty-smelling *Englisch* shirt. He looked at the discarded Plain shirt and trousers crumpled on the bed, wondering if he should take them or leave them behind. In the end he stuffed the shirt into his duffel bag, ignoring the ache in his belly. She'd made that special, just for him. He'd keep it.

When his bag was packed, his gaze lingered on the bright quilt spread across the bed. Another thing created by a woman he knew he'd never forget. He reached down and traced a crisp triangle with one finger.

Endings were funny things. There was often a window

of time when you could change your mind, back up a couple steps, and switch directions. For a little while, two lives were laid out in front of you, yours to choose between.

Like the night he'd left home. His family hadn't known he was gone, and wouldn't, not until morning when he didn't show up for chores. At any time before the dawn, he could have retraced his steps, climbed into his bed, and given up the idea of leaving.

That option had lurked in the back of his mind the whole, dark night. It had been a relief when the sun had come up and there'd been no choice left to make.

Somehow he doubted he'd feel the same way about this decision—about leaving Miriam behind. But he had to do it.

She'll be all right, he told himself as he threw the duffel in the bed of the truck and climbed into the cab. Joseph would look after her, and Sam, too. If—when—she married, they'd see she wasn't mistreated like *Mamm* had been.

Besides, he didn't believe Miriam would stand for such mistreatment anyhow, not now. The way she'd acted in the store was proof of that.

Miriam was right in what she'd said back there. It was an important part of every hard journey to circle around to where the trouble had started. Standing in the same place didn't scare you so much once you were sure of your own strength. And that was the kind of thing you could only know for certain if you were brave enough to go there again—to the intersection or the store building.

Or to talk over a problem with an Amish bishop maybe.

It seemed Miriam had more courage than he did.

He reached a stop sign and put on his left blinker, ready to take the turn leading out of Johns Mill and back toward Kentucky. He kept his boot on the brake even after it was safe to go, listening to the turn signal clicking off the seconds, his heart torn between the two very different directions in front of him.

He reached down suddenly and flipped up the bar, moving the signal to the right. Toward Abram's house.

"*Schtupid*," he muttered under his breath.

But he kept driving.

It seemed no time had passed before he was pulling up in the bishop's driveway—because, he realized, he'd grown reaccustomed to going places in the slower-moving buggies. He very nearly threw the truck in reverse and left right then. Before he could, Abram stepped onto the porch and beckoned.

"Your father's asleep," Abram told him as soon as he'd mounted the steps. "He was past any kind of discussion, so we thought that best, to let him sleep. Maybe afterward he'll be in his right senses again, and we'll be able to talk with him."

Reuben stayed silent. Ivan would talk, all right, and saying exactly what he thought the bishop wanted to hear. But of course, it wouldn't mean a thing.

He shouldn't have come. This was a waste of time.

"Sit." Abram gestured toward a wooden rocking chair. "I'd like to have a word with you in private before we go inside."

Here it came. Reuben gritted his teeth as he dropped into the chair.

"This man is your father," Abram said quietly. His hands were folded over his ample belly, and his eyes were down. "So this will be a hard thing for me to say, and a hard thing for you to hear."

"I've heard pretty much everything where my father is concerned. Go ahead."

"As sympathetic as I feel for you, this can't be overlooked. No—" Abram lifted a hand when Reuben started to speak. "I have to take action. I understand how you, as a son, might feel about this. And I know people say I meddle where I shouldn't, so I talked it over with the ministers and the deacon. They all agree that something must be done. Your father's drinking has pushed him outside of *Gott*'s will, we believe. This is a serious matter, and it must be dealt with seriously." Abram darted a look at him. "I am sorry, but truly I can see no other way forward."

Reuben realized he was frowning. He shook his head to clear it and studied Abram as he would a horse.

"What are you planning to do?" he asked carefully.

"I will take him back to Indiana myself," Abram said. "I have talked to a driver, and we've started making arrangements. I feel I must discuss this with the bishop of his district in person, to make sure he fully understands what happened here. I am sure he will agree there must be very serious action taken." Abram shook his head sadly. "It is all going to be unpleasant for your family, I'm afraid, but your father must be brought before the church. I am very sorry."

Reuben tried to make sense of what he was hearing. "Brought before the church. You mean excommunicated?"

"Hopefully not. But that will depend on your father. Has his drinking caused problems before?"

Reuben couldn't help it. He laughed.

"You could say that."

"Ah." Abram drummed his fingers on his belly. "I see. Why don't you tell me about this? When I speak to the church leaders there, I can present them with all the facts."

"They've been presented with all the facts more than once. They never did much with them. But all right."

As Reuben described his father's drinking and abuse, the concerned lines on Abram's forehead deepened.

"This . . . trouble with your *daed* and the church's lack of action. That's why you left home?" The older man blew out a long breath. "I wish you had told me this."

"I had no reason to think you'd listen."

"I am listening now. And I will not be the only one." For such an amiable fellow, Abram looked surprisingly fierce.

Then his face relaxed into its usual friendly lines. "At least we can be thankful this has been brought to a head so it can be dealt with. All will come right yet."

"I wish I believed that."

"You should. Don't be discouraged, Reuben. *Gott* can use our shortcomings and mistakes in amazing ways—even grievous ones like your father's. After all, if you'd not left home, you might never have come to Johns Mill." A twinkle sparked in the bishop's eye. "And perhaps you are not so sorry you did. Perhaps you have met a particular young woman who seems well worth the trouble that brought you here."

Reuben shot him a startled look, and the other man chuckled and tapped the side of his nose.

"Five sons," he said sagely. "You learn a lot when you have five sons. But," he went on, "since you aren't a member of the church, there's no way you and this girl can move forward. Unless maybe you've decided to take hold of this second chance that *Gott* is offering you?"

"I've been . . . thinking about it," Reuben admitted uncomfortably. "When I stopped by earlier . . . I was going to ask about that. About how one goes about it."

"The how . . . that's the simpler part. Not easy," he warned. "And not quick. But not so difficult for a fellow like you who started off Plain. The why . . . now that's what we'll have to talk over, you and I. Because it can't only be because of Miriam, you know."

"I know. But I won't lie to you, I'd never have considered this if I hadn't met her."

Abram gave a philosophical shrug. "Well, so she was the start of it. That's not such a problem. All roads must begin somewhere. One person drove you from among us, and another person has drawn you back. But people—" Abram waved a hand. "They are here for us to love and to look after and to enjoy. But if we put our faith in them, we're sure to be disappointed. We have to look much higher than that. That, too, is something we'll talk over. If, that is, you're willing?"

Reuben let the bishop's question hang in the air for a few seconds.

Then he nodded.

"I'm willing. And Miriam might have drawn me here," he added, "but if you'd been a different sort of person, we'd never be sitting here having this conversation. Maybe you're new as a bishop, but you're doing a better job than most."

A smile broke across Abram's face. "That," he said, "is a relief to hear. Especially since I have made so many mistakes, even in this matter. But as I said, *Gott* is merciful. He delights in using such mistakes for His purposes. And," he added, leaning in closer, "with me serving as bishop, He'll never run short of material!" He laughed and slapped Reuben's arm affectionately.

"Now." Abram rose from his seat. "We have a great deal to talk about, you and I. Many plans to make. We will make our start while we wait for your father to wake up. And hopefully," he went on with a wink, "even my *gut fraw* will understand that such talking is very hungry work."

Reuben fought a smile as he got to his feet. "Cookies, you think?"

"*Ja*," the bishop agreed happily. "Definitely cookies."

CHAPTER TWENTY-NINE

❧

THE SUN WAS SLANTING LOW BEFORE SAM AND MIR-
iam started home, but when they'd locked up the store,
there'd been no trace left of what had happened. Except, of
course, for the smears of jam on the quilt. That was folded
in the box strapped behind the buggy, and Miriam planned
to set it to soak as soon as they got home.

With care, the stains likely would wash out. If they
didn't, she'd sew another quilt for Emma to hang on the
wall and keep this one for herself. Even ruined, it would
make a warm bed cover or a nice, soft padding for baby
nephews and nieces to nap on. And they could spread it out
for family picnics down by the creek on pretty summer
days. It would be a good reminder that broken things—
quilts or hearts—could still serve a purpose.

A truck passed them in a whoosh of air. For a second,
Miriam's heart lifted—but it wasn't Reuben. The driver, an
older *Englisch* man, lifted two fingers from his steering
wheel in a greeting as he went by. Miriam nodded politely
before turning her eyes back on the road.

"You'd never know he's the same horse," Sam observed with grim admiration. "When that truck passed, Breeze didn't even flinch. And," he added, "I notice, neither did you."

No, she hadn't, although just now she couldn't manage to feel too happy about that. She couldn't feel much of anything except an aching emptiness. She cleared her throat.

"Reuben was a great help to us both." Her voice cracked on his name. She'd have to get used to saying it, knowing he was gone. She didn't want to forget him, ever. He'd changed her life, and at the very least, she owed him the memories.

"He was a help in some ways." Sam agreed uncomfortably. "But, Mirry, I'm real sorry—"

"Let's not talk about that." She couldn't stand to, not yet. Not even with kindhearted Sam.

To her relief, he nodded. "All right."

She drew in a breath and sat up straighter on the seat. "But there's something else I'd like to talk to you about. What are you going to do with Breeze?"

"Well." Sam scratched at his beard, apparently relieved to be on a safer subject. "I'm not sure. He's safe enough, I think, for anybody to drive now."

"He is." Miriam swallowed hard. "I'd like to have him. I'll pay you," she hurried on. "Whatever you think he's worth. I've got some quilt money saved, and I'll be getting more soon. I'll have . . . lots more time for sewing now. And I've been thinking, maybe I could talk to Mary Yoder about working in her store sometimes. With so many grandchildren coming along, she's having to close up a lot. She might be pleased to have some help."

"If you want Breeze, he's yours, and you'll not give me a cent. If you hadn't stepped in, he'd have been sold for slaughter."

"*Denki*, but I'd rather pay for him." When her brother-in-law began to protest, she shook her head. "It's important to me, Sam. He's scarred up maybe, and he has his troubles, but he deserves more than to be given away as if he wasn't worth anything. I want to have . . . earned him."

"You've earned him already, the way I see it," Sam said. "But if it matters to you, I'll not argue. I'll take only what he'd have brought from Stoltzfus, though. Not a penny more."

That seemed fair. "Fine."

When they drove into the driveway, she couldn't help glancing at the empty spot where Reuben's pickup had been parked for weeks. She hadn't thought her heart could possibly sink any lower, but it did.

She slowed the buggy to a stop. "Go on inside, Sam, I'll unhitch."

"I can handle that."

"I want to do it," Miriam said firmly. "Breeze is to be my horse now, and I'll take care of him myself."

Sam didn't look happy, but he climbed out of the buggy. Once he was safely down, Miriam drove into the barn.

The unhitching took her much longer than it would have taken Sam, but Breeze stood calmly and cooperatively. When she turned him into his stall, she noticed the near-empty sack of horse cookies, still where Reuben had left them.

She took a couple from the bag. Breeze accepted them from her hand happily, and she stroked his nose.

"There aren't many of these left, but don't worry. I'll get more when this bag is empty," she promised. "I'll find out how, even if I have to get somebody in town to order them special. You're mine now, and I'm going to look after you best I can."

Breeze bumped his nose into her palm and shook his head playfully. She smiled, and leaning forward, she pressed her forehead against his.

He went still, and she stayed there, her eyes closed, feeling the bony warmth of the horse's head against her face.

"We'll miss him," she murmured. "You and I. We won't

ever forget him because he left us better than he found us. And that's a thing we should be always grateful for, ain't so?"

The barn door creaked open behind her, and her heart stopped. Slowly, afraid to hope, she straightened and turned.

Naomi came in slowly, her shawl wrapped around her rounded figure, her face full of a kind sympathy.

"Oh!" Miriam said. "I didn't know you were home."

"Katie dropped me off a while ago. You've been out here a long time, and Sam was fretting. He wanted to come out and make sure you were managing all right, but I thought . . ." Naomi paused. "I thought maybe I should do it. So I distracted him with a plate of fresh-baked ginger cookies and some tea." She walked closer. "*Are* you managing all right, Mirry?"

Miriam opened her mouth, but instead of words, a sob came out. That was all the invitation Naomi needed. In seconds, her arms were wrapped tightly around Miriam.

"I understand," Naomi murmured in her ear. "Sam has told me what happened in town, but I knew already that Reuben was gone. He came while you were away and gathered his things. I watched from the window, but he didn't come inside to say goodbye. When I saw the look on his face, I understood why he was keeping his distance. It was real hard for him to go, I think."

"Then why did he?"

She felt Naomi's bosom heave with a sigh. "People must make their own choices, Mirry."

"This—isn't the choice I hoped he'd make."

"I know," Naomi whispered, and Miriam realized her sweet-hearted sister-in-law was crying with her. "I prayed for a different choice, too. But we must trust *Gott* always, even when things don't turn out as we hope."

Miriam dabbed at her eyes with her sleeve. "Do you really believe it's *Gott*'s will for Reuben to go back to the *Englisch*?"

"I don't know. My heart says no, but our hearts don't always lead us wisely. Reuben's heart may not be leading him well, either, but that's for him and *Gott* to straighten out." Naomi's hands still rested on Miriam's shoulders, and she squeezed gently. "Meanwhile, we must trust *Gott* and give Him our thanks, even in this."

"I don't feel very thankful just now."

"Of course not," Naomi said softly. "It's what we all feared—this pain. We saw it coming. Hurt for you if he left, or hurt for us if you went with him. But now I think we were wrong to worry. This sorrow is just the other side of caring, a sign your heart has woken up again and is ready to love." She smiled. "When Joseph proposed, he asked if I liked to take risks. At the time, I thought it was a funny way to ask such a question, but I came to see the sense of it. I try to remember that now when your *bruder* pesters me to be careful, to rest when I'm not tired, to eat when I'm not hungry, to hold his arm when I go up the steps. The great love he feels for me and our *boppli*, it's a risk for him. That's why he fusses so, and it's the only thing keeping me from thumping him on the head with my rolling pin some days."

Miriam snuffled a sad laugh.

Naomi laughed, too. "One day you will have a worry-wart husband of your own, and you'll find out for yourself how frustrating they can be." When Miriam sighed, Naomi squeezed her arms again. "You will, *schwesdre*, now you've come back to life again. Let's go inside and have some tea and cookies. Joseph can finish up whatever needs doing out here when he puts Titus in his stall for the night."

"I'll come in," Miriam promised. "In just a minute. I want to take the quilt out to the wash shed and put it to soak. I don't want the stains to set in too deep."

For a second she feared Naomi would offer to help, but her sister-in-law nodded. "All right. Take your time." She gathered Miriam close for one more hug before walking out of the barn.

Miriam had just unbuckled the straps of the carrying box when Joseph's buggy rolled into the yard. Her heart fell. She didn't want to face her brother just now, not while her heart was still so raw. She bundled the heavy quilt into her arms, listening. He might go inside first to check on Naomi. He did that sometimes—part of the pestering Naomi had grown so tired of. If he did, she could slip to the wash shed in peace.

She heard the back door of the house opening and Naomi's muffled welcome, and she relaxed, breathing a sigh of relief.

Then the barn door opened, and Reuben stepped inside.

She gasped, the quilt falling in a puddle on the barn's dirt floor. The noise gave her away, and he turned quickly in her direction.

"*Sell is awreit*, Mirry," he said. "It's only me."

For a second she couldn't do anything but stare. Then she ran toward him, tripping over the quilt so that she stumbled into his arms. They closed around her with a warm, reassuring strength, and the throbbing knot she'd been carrying in her chest ever since he'd left her in town dissolved.

"*Ja.*" She choked against his chest. "It's only you, Reuben. Only ever you."

She felt his breath hitch in his chest, and release—as if he were letting go of a heavy burden. His chin came down to rest on her *kapp*.

"This is the second time I've had you in my arms in this barn," he murmured. "I like this time better than the first, I think."

She sputtered a wet laugh. "Me, too." She drew back to look up at his face. "I thought you'd left," she whispered.

His lips tightened. "I meant to. I was going to. But I couldn't."

Her heart was beating so hard, she could feel it pulsing in her ears. "Why not?"

"Because I had no place to go to. At least no place that

mattered. Turns out I have no home in the world, Mirry, except where you are."

She tilted her face up to his for a kiss, but he made a low, pained sound and moved her back. "We have to talk," he said doggedly. "Abram's gone inside, and he told me I could have a few minutes with you, but nothing more."

"Abram?"

"He drove me over in his buggy. I went to his place after I got my things from here. And we talked—a long time. About my *daed*, and about you. And about *Gott* and the church. We agreed I'm to make a start."

"A start? To join the church?"

"*Ja.*"

"Oh, Reuben! Do you mean it?"

He smiled at her. "Abram has the keys to my pickup, if that tells you anything. I'll not be needing them anymore."

Again she moved toward him, but he kept her at arms' length.

"It's going to take a while, Mirry. Abram was real clear about that. He was clear about a lot of things." Reuben shook his head. "He's a funny little fellow maybe, but there's something true about him. And he sure doesn't mince his words." Reuben's smile faded. "He doesn't think it would be a good idea for us to spend much time together, not at first."

"Oh!" In spite of her joy, she couldn't keep the disappointment out of her voice.

"It'll be hard, *ja*. For me, too. But I think we'd best trust his judgment on this. What I'm . . . hoping for . . . it has to be built on the firmest foundation. It can't only be built on how I feel about you. It has to be built on what I believe. About *Gott* and the church . . . about everything that matters, deep down." He shook his head. "I'm not saying it right."

"You're saying it right," she argued softly. "I just don't much like hearing it."

"I didn't, either. But I'll do as he says because it's not

just my heart on the line here. It's yours, too. At least . . ." He paused. "I hope that's so. Is it, Mirry?"

At first she couldn't find the words to answer, so she nodded. As soon as she could manage, she said, "That's so, Reuben. It surely is."

She felt the strength coming back into him, saw him stand straighter. "Then it's worth it, no matter how long a road Abram sets in front of me. I'll take every care, Miriam." He spoke with such fierceness, she had to believe him. "Every care to make sure your heart is safe with me. Abram said I wasn't to ask you for any promises yet, so I won't. But he didn't say anything about *me* making promises, so I'm going to make you one. As soon as I know for sure . . . as soon as Abram gives me the go-ahead, I'm going to come straight here, back to you. I can't ask you to wait for me—"

"I will be waiting. No, I understand what Abram said." She smiled up at him. "And that's all right. You don't have to ask for my promises, Reuben. I'll give them without being asked. You take as long as you need to build this foundation you're talking about. And when you're done with that—if you still want to—you come back, and we'll talk again."

He nodded, the crinkles around his eyes deepening. "And then, just as soon as Abram says we can, we'll make plenty of promises to each other. Lasting ones."

She nodded because her heart was too full to speak. This time when she moved to come back into his arms, he let her, holding her so tightly, she could barely breathe.

She didn't care. She didn't need to breathe. She only needed Reuben.

"We'd best get ourselves inside," he murmured. "Abram will be waiting, and I don't want to start off on the wrong foot with him. I'd prefer this whole thing to go smooth—and quick."

He couldn't see her answering smile because her face

was buried against his chest, so she whispered, "Me, too, but we can stay a minute longer. Naomi just took a batch of cookies out of the oven. Abram won't be thinking of us for a *gut* while yet."

His answering laugh rumbled under her cheek. She smiled, soaking in his steadying warmth and the familiar scent of this man she loved. And even though her eyes were closed, and so many promises were still unspoken, she saw their future sparkling ahead, almost within reach, bright and warm and achingly sweet.

EPILOGUE

❧

ON THE FIRST VISITING SUNDAY IN AUGUST, MIRIAM stood at the kitchen counter, slicing lemons. Emma sat at the table, her chair pulled back to make room for her swollen middle. Her face was flushed, and she was fanning herself with a folded newspaper.

"I'll have your lemonade ready in a minute," Miriam promised, reaching for the glass juicer. As she did, she sneaked a glance out the kitchen window.

Still nothing. It was nearly two o'clock in the afternoon. Reuben had told her last Sunday at church that he'd be driving over after lunch today, but so far there was no sign of him.

Emma gave her a tired smile. "Thanks. I hope you're making plenty. I could drink a gallon of it. And please put in a lot of ice. It's not even so hot today, according to the thermometer, but it sure feels hot to me."

"You'll feel better once the baby's here," Naomi said as she came down the steps. "It's hardest in the summertime."

"Especially when you're a week overdue." Emma shifted

uncomfortably in her chair. "But enough of my complaining. Is the baby asleep?"

"Yes." Naomi smiled, as she always did whenever her little daughter was mentioned. "She went right down."

"Elizabeth is such a good sleeper," Emma said. "You'll have to give me tips when this *boppli* finally gets here."

"She didn't sleep so well at first," Naomi admitted. "I mentioned it in a letter to Rhoda, and she told me swaddling the twins helped. I tried it, and it worked real well."

"I've been thinking about Rhoda a lot lately." Emma shook her head. "It must have been so hard on her, going through the pregnancy alone. And now she has two babies to raise without Caleb's help."

"*Ja*, she's been through a hard time, but her letters sound happier. I think she's finding her feet again. Our prayers for her are being answered."

"Not all of them." Emma sighed and shifted again in her chair. "I'm glad she's doing so well, but it makes me sad, too. I feel as if Caleb's being . . . shut out of her life. I'm worried there won't be any room for him when he comes back."

Miriam and Naomi exchanged glances but said nothing. Emma always spoke of her twin's return as if it was a certainty. Miriam tried to believe that, too, but as months rolled by, it was harder and harder.

"As you know so well, Emma, the waiting is the hardest part," Naomi said gently. "And the part when we must trust *Gott* the most. Now, while Miriam mixes the lemonade, I'll get a wet washcloth to put on the back of your neck. That'll make you feel cooler."

Miriam glanced out of the kitchen window again as she twisted the lemon halves against the pointed juicer, but the yard was still empty.

She sighed. Naomi was right. Waiting was hard.

Today was the first time Abram had agreed to let Reuben drive out. It had been long months since she'd seen him, except at church, and she was so excited—and nervous—she could hardly stand it.

Emma was on her second glass of lemonade before Miriam heard the noise of a buggy pulling into the yard. She bounced to the window so fast that the other women laughed.

"Reuben's here," Miriam announced happily. "Although I don't know whose buggy he's borrowed, nor whose horse. Those aren't Abram's." She snatched her bonnet from the peg. "I'll be outside."

She reached the bottom of the steps just as Reuben jumped from the buggy. They faced each other, and she felt suddenly shy.

It had been such a long time since they'd been alone together. Their conversations at church had been brief, and usually in the hearing of family—or Abram. The bishop seemed to consider Reuben his special project and tended to hover.

Reuben looked *gut*. And, she noticed with some satisfaction, very Plain. His hair was longer and in the simple cut all the men in their community wore. He wore a blue shirt and black trousers, and a straw hat waited on the front seat of the buggy.

He looked at her hungrily, as if he couldn't look enough. When she caught his eye, he smiled, and she felt her cheeks go pink.

"Feel like going for a ride with me?" he asked.

"*Ja!*" Joy bloomed in her heart like a summer rose. Naomi was framed in the kitchen window, watching. Miriam pointed to the buggy and mouthed the words *Going for a ride*.

When Naomi nodded and smiled, Miriam's joy overflowed. Was there anything, she wondered, nicer than going for a ride with the fellow you liked best in the world, and having your family happy about it?

Reuben helped her into the buggy and circled around to

take his own seat beside her. As he released the brake and
flicked the reins, she looked around with interest.

"This is a nice, roomy buggy. That's a new horse up
front, too, ain't so? She's a pretty thing. Are you training
her for somebody?"

Reuben had been training horses at Abram's over the
past few months. He had plenty of customers already, some
coming from several counties over, and Sam had told her
there was already a waiting list.

"*Nee.*" He glanced at her and smiled. "This horse and
buggy belong to me."

"You?" Miriam sat bolt upright, her eyes wide.

"None other. I bought the horse a week ago, and Abram
and I picked up the buggy last Thursday. It's used, but I
figured it would do well enough. What do you think?"

"I think they're beautiful!" She did. The trim mare was
a lovely, glossy black, and the buggy looked to have been
well kept—but the thing she liked best was what such a
purchase meant.

"If you're buying buggies, then I'm guessing you're
planning on joining the church soon?"

He nodded. "That's the plan. Come springtime, I'll be
baptized."

So many feelings flooded into Miriam's heart at once
that she couldn't choose which words to say. She'd hoped
this was coming. She'd prayed for it and expected it. But
still, it was such a joy and a relief to hear Reuben say it out
loud.

"I'm glad," she said. Then she laughed because it was
such a simple, silly thing to say.

He glanced at her, and the creases beside his eyes crinkled in the way she loved. "I am, too," he said. "I feel . . .
right about it. And although it's been hard to stay away
from you for these months, I'm thankful now Abram
wouldn't give in. It helped me to figure things out, to settle

my mind." He shot her a teasing look. "I don't always think so clear when you're around."

Miriam fought a smile, her heart trilling so happily, she couldn't help bouncing a little on the buggy seat. "I'm thankful as well, then, although it's been hard for me, too. The truth is, I've been tempted to name one of our new roosters after Abram just so I could pop him in a stew."

Reuben laughed. "Abram's not perfect, and sometimes I've chafed at following his instructions, but he's been a real blessing to me and to my family."

"How is your *daed* doing?" Miriam held her breath. She'd not asked before, and Reuben hadn't offered any information.

A shadow crossed Reuben's face. "He's tried all his usual tricks, and he's still drinking. But Abram's kept in touch with the bishop up there, and from what Connie says, it's kept *Daed* in line a bit better. Enough that she and *Mamm* have been able to stay at home anyhow. Still, I'm relieved Connie's getting married in November. I remember the boy, and I think he'll be good to her. It won't be easy for *Mamm* when Connie leaves, though." A spasm of pain crossed his face. "But I'm hoping once I'm baptized, she can come to visit."

"We'll keep praying for your parents," Miriam promised. "*Gott* has done so many wonderful things already. He will work this problem out, too, in His good time."

"Enough about my family. How are things going with you, Mirry? I've seen you working at Yoder's." He smiled. "Through the window. I found plenty of reasons to pass by whenever we were in town. I thought I was being sneaky, but Abram knew what I was up to." Reuben tapped the side of his nose and went on in the bishop's deep voice, "'Five sons, Reuben. I know what's afoot when a young fellow starts hanging around a quilt store.'"

Miriam laughed. "*Ja*, I've helped Mary some. I was a

little *naerfich* to start because *Englisch* folks shop there, too, but now I'm all right. It helps that it's mostly women customers we have. They don't bother me so much." She darted a glance at him. "That girl—that Allison, from the movie? She stopped by once."

Reuben twisted in his seat to look at her. "What? Why?"

"Oh, she didn't know I was there. She ducked in to get away from some reporters." Miriam shook her head. "She says that happens all the time. Mary let her wait in the storeroom until they were gone, and I brought her a cup of tea to steady her nerves. She was very upset. Seems we have more in common than our curly hair. And this time I remembered to tell her it was nice to meet her."

Reuben smiled. "I'm sure that was a load off your mind."

"It was. Before she left, she ordered a special-made quilt. That's another good thing about working at Yoder's. Mary gives me a nice discount on the material so now I make a better profit. It helps to buy Breeze's feed and hay. Joseph said I didn't have to pay for that, but he's mine, and I want to tend to him. And of course, I'm putting money aside for—"

She broke off abruptly. She was also saving for the future she was hoping they'd share, but since Reuben hadn't brought that up, maybe she'd best not talk about it, either.

A tiny flutter of worry flickered, but she ignored it. This was their first buggy ride in months, too soon to discuss such things. Besides, probably Abram had instructed Reuben not to rush ahead with anything before he was baptized.

"I'm glad you're saving money," Reuben was saying. "As it happens, I'm not doing so well with that myself."

"Oh?" Miriam's heart dipped. "I heard your business was going well."

"I've plenty of customers, but there's a limit to what I can do since I can't easily travel long distances. Folks have to come to me, and there's not the space at Abram's to board more than a couple horses at a time."

That didn't sound too bad. Miriam smiled. "Well, maybe soon you'll find a bigger place for your business."

He smiled back, but there was a serious look in his eyes. "That's the thing, Miriam. I think I have already. I've been working out how to manage it, but—I need to talk to you before I go further. From something you said before, I've hoped you'd be willing . . . but I want to be sure."

Miriam's heart pounded. He'd found a place, and he needed to talk with her about it. He was planning a future that included her. That was good—so good that she could barely contain her happiness.

But that seriousness in his eyes, the way he was looking at her—maybe he wasn't sure she'd like this place he'd found. Suddenly she remembered what she'd said when he'd asked if she'd be willing to leave Johns Mill.

She'd said she would—as long as she could remain faithful to the church.

At the thought of moving to an unfamiliar place away from her family, her heart sank. She'd not know anyone, and of course, there'd be *Englisch* men coming by wanting Reuben to train their horses. For a second, fear surged, crowding back her joy. But then she swallowed hard and lifted her chin.

"If you've found a place that will work for your business, you should buy it. You don't need to ask me."

She'd meant to reassure him, but to her surprise, he shot her an alarmed look and turned the horse into a handy driveway.

"Mirry, maybe I wasn't clear. I'm hoping . . ." He cleared his throat. "I'd planned on doing this different, but . . ." He set the brake and reached for her hands. "I want you to marry me. Of course, that can't happen until I'm baptized, but Abram's agreed it can happen real soon after. I'm thinking next May. I know it's not the usual month, but I'd rather not wait until fall. But if you do—"

"No!" She was vibrating with such joy that her hands trembled in his. "I don't want to wait, either, Reuben, and people get married at all times of the year now. May will be . . . just fine."

His face relaxed into a smile. "Then we'd best be planning out our future together, ain't so? We'll start with a wedding in May, and maybe a trip after that to see that quilt museum I told you about."

"Oh!" She couldn't decide whether she felt more nervous or happy about that prospect.

"Afterward we'll settle down on this place I've found, if you like it well enough. If you don't, I want you to tell me straight out. I mean for you to feel safe and happy with me always."

She tightened her fingers around his. "I'll be happy with you, Reuben, for as long as *Gott* spares us to each other. As for safe—" She shook her head. "When you love another person as much as I love you, there's no safety in it. But of all the risks in the world, it's the one most worth taking. I trust you, Reuben, to know what place is best for your business, and I'll do my best to make a home for us wherever that may be."

He leaned forward and kissed her gently, lightly.

It was over far too soon, and she opened her eyes and smiled. "You'd best be careful. If Abram hears we're kissing on the side of the road, we're likely not to get another buggy ride until after you're baptized. Now tell me about this place you've found." She swallowed. "Is it very far away?"

"Not so very." His eyes twinkled. "Take a look in front of you, Mirry."

She looked. The Beilers' farmhouse sat in front of them, its big red barn behind, acres of green pasture rolling beyond it.

It took a minute for her to understand. "This? This is the place you're buying?"

He laughed. "Going by that look on your face, I'd say so, *ja*."

She glanced around, and when she saw no cars or buggies on the road, she leaned across the seat and kissed him quickly. "I can't wait for spring," she whispered.

"Me, either." Reuben slipped an arm around her, pulling her close and resting his chin on the top of her head. "This will be a long winter."

It sure would. Miriam sighed, thinking of the long months ahead. But as she looked at the snug farm that would be theirs, her heart lifted. Together she and Reuben would brighten this home—and their lives—with all the colors of love and laughter and faith.

She smiled. And—*Gott* willing—lots of babies to grow up alongside plenty of little *kossins*.

Her broken family was growing strong again. *Gott* was answering their prayers one by one, healing heart by heart. And He wasn't done yet, because she suddenly believed that Emma was right.

One day Caleb would find his way home, too.

Winters could be awful cold and dark, and some lasted longer than others. But sooner or later, in *Gott*'s good time, spring and all its sweetness would bloom again.

It always did.

ACKNOWLEDGMENTS

As always, I owe a huge debt of appreciation to Anna Mast for her insights into the Amish lifestyle—and for her patience with my many questions.

For this particular story, I offer a special and extra-devout thank-you to Jami Delacruz, a skilled third-generation farrier, who patiently explained the ins and outs of her fascinating profession. Without her detailed descriptions of the behavior and treatment of traumatized horses, Reuben Brenneman's character could never have come to life.

Another big thank-you goes out to Dr. Jennifer Wilson, DVM, who graciously double-checked my depiction of horse injuries and treatments.

I deeply appreciate the willingness of these people to share their areas of expertise with me as I wrote this story. Any errors are completely my own.

Big thank-you hugs to my critique partner, friend, and fellow author Amy Grochowski; my eagle-eyed proof-reader (and bookstore buddy), Amanda Boyt; my amazing agent, Jessica Alvarez; and my wonderful editor, Anne Sowards. Your brilliance made this story shine.

And finally, as always, I offer this story back to God—the author of all things good in my life—with humble gratitude.

Ready to find
your next great read?

Let us help.

Visit prh.com/nextread

Penguin
Random
House